THE CHARMER

"With its rich historical texture, steamy love scenes, and indelible protagonists, this book embodies the best of the genre."
—*Publishers Weekly* (starred review)

THE SAINT

"[An] assuming, witty, and intriguing account of how love helps, not hinders, the achievment of dreams."
—*Booklist*

THE SEDUCER

"Lush in detail and thrumming with sensuality, this offering will thrill those looking for a tale as rich and satisfying as a multicourse gourmet meal."
—*Publishers Weekly*

ALSO BY MADELINE HUNTER

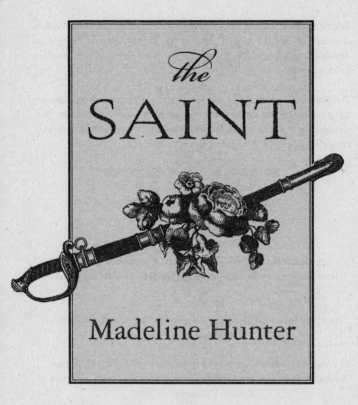

the
SAINT

Madeline Hunter

BANTAM BOOKS

The Saint is a work of fiction. Names, characters, places, and incidents are the products of the author's imagination or are used fictitiously. Any resemblance to actual events, locales, or persons, living or dead, is entirely coincidental.

2009 Bantam Books Mass Market Edition

Copyright © 2004 by Madeline Hunter

Published in the United States by Bantam Books, an imprint of The Random House Publishing Group, a division of Random House, Inc., New York

BANTAM BOOKS and the rooster colophon are registered trademarks of Random House, Inc.

Originally published in mass market in the United States by Bantam Books, an imprint of The Random House Publishing Group, a division of Random House, Inc., in 2003.

ISBN 978-0-553-59273-3

Cover art: Alan Ayers

Printed in the United States of America

www.bantamdell.com

9 8 7 6 5 4 3 2 1

For my sister Julie
the "sergeant" with a heart
as big as the sky

chapter I

~1823

Vergil's grudging appreciation of Jane Ormond's aria did not salve his anger one bit. He resented like hell that he couldn't have her thrown into Newgate Prison where she belonged.

She had costumed herself like a French queen from the previous century, but she appeared uncomfortable with the illusion. She held herself stiffly whenever she moved, as if she expected the high white wig to topple off or the padded, hooped gown to tip her over. The confidence of her voice contrasted with her physical awkwardness. Poses of professional self-possession contrasted with short strolls of vulnerability.

He was not fooled by her calculated charm. With her wide eyes and full lips and intimations of frailty, she affected the most dangerous type of innocence. It was the kind that prompted a man to want to lay down his life to protect it, but which provoked another, darker part to imagine stripping off her clothes and destroying it.

She moved in his direction, raising her head for the high notes of a vocal display. Her gaze met his. A flicker of curiosity passed, as if she perceived that he would not be here if duty did not demand it.

He knew that nothing in his appearance told her that. This gaming establishment had added staged shows to cater to men of his class. They took breaks from their gambling to eat in this salon and enjoy a concert of opera, or, later, entertainment of a much baser sort.

She looked longer than she ought, boldly meeting his inspection with one of her own. He suppressed the alarming combination of protective and erotic inclinations that those wide eyes summoned, by concentrating on all of the trouble that she had caused him the last two weeks.

Morton slid into the other chair at his table. Morton did look out of place with his bearish form and unfashionable beard.

"The girl is here," he said. "In a room in back. Miss Ormond brings her every night, to wait there while she sings. I spoke with the man at the door and he saw them come in together tonight."

Vergil rose. "Miss Ormond sings an art song after this aria. Let us do it now. We will have the girl out before she finishes." The unsuspecting Miss Ormond warbled on. "If she is smart, she will run for the coast when she learns her plans were foiled. As for the girl, we will bring her to the country to recover, and no one will be the wiser."

He was assuming, of course, that Miss Jane Ormond

had not already sold the girl to the highest bidder. He narrowed his attention on the deceptively ingenuous face beneath the towering white wig. There was something intelligent in those eyes. No, she wouldn't have risked all of this for so small a prize as a virgin's price. Perhaps she had planned to ask for a ransom, but most likely her intentions were to sell the girl in marriage. Since she had served as the girl's maid and they had traveled from America together, she undoubtedly knew about the inheritance.

This all might have been avoided if Dante had been more alert. His own fault that, sending his brother to meet their ship, but whoever expected this chit of a maid to dare such a thing.

The seedy back corridor contrasted with the opulence of the dining salon. Morton gestured to a door tucked beneath a stairway. Vergil turned the handle.

He had visited singers' preparation rooms before and they were normally disasters of confusion. This tiny space had been carefully organized. A brace of candles sat on a small table that also held a mirror and containers of paint. Costumes and day clothes hung from a row of hooks on the wall. A chair crowded the shadows to the right of the table, and a young woman sat mending there with her needle and cloth held close to the flames.

"Miss Bianca Kenwood?"

She looked up in surprise and he immediately began calculating how much he would have to increase the bribe to Dante. She could well be a sweet girl, but Dante judged females by appearance, not character, and hers was not impressive. The brown wisps of hair escaping her cap looked more frizzy than curly. Her nose turned up at the end, which might have been charming if the nose had been less broad.

"Miss Kenwood, I am Laclere."

"Oh!"

"This is Morton, my valet. I have a coach behind the building and we will take you there at once. Your ordeal is over, and I assure you that no one will ever know about this unfortunate interlude."

"Oh! Oh, my . . ."

"If you will come at once, please. I will deal with Miss Ormond later. Right now it is best if we remove you from here."

"Oh, I don't think . . . that is . . ." She cowered back, making gestures of resistance and confusion. He bent toward her and smiled reassuringly. He noticed that her gown was of the most common sort, a gray simple broadcloth. Evidently she had no sense for fashion, either.

"Come, my dear. It would be best if we left before—"

"Who are you?" The voice asking the indignant question was feminine, melodious, and young.

Vergil pivoted to see Marie Antoinette standing in the doorway, hands akimbo on her little waist, the broad-hipped gown flaring out to span the threshold. "Well? Who are you, sir, and what are you doing here?"

Miss Kenwood leapt up and darted over to Miss Ormond, who embraced her protectively. So that was how it was. Of course she had befriended the girl. It wouldn't have worked otherwise.

"Your concert is finished?" he asked.

"The *lieder* are brief works. Now, if you would leave please. My sister and I—"

"Miss Ormond, this young woman is not your sister. She is no relation to you whatsoever. You may have convinced her to come with you, but your behavior has been nothing less than abduction and will be seen as such by the magistrate."

Miss Ormond eased the girl away, then pressed her gown so that she could squish into the room. The breadth of the ridiculous skirt forced Morton against the wall.

She crossed her arms over her chest. The gesture brought Vergil's attention to the upper swells of firm breasts crushed under the top of her stiff bodice.

"Which one are you?"

"Vergilius Duclairc, the Viscount Laclere. Miss Kenwood is my ward, but then you know that."

Her gaze drifted down, then up. "I know nothing of the sort."

Her poise, despite being caught at this crime, annoyed him to no end. "Do not think to play a game of wits with me, young woman. Your betrayal of the trust that made you her companion on the crossing is abominable. The danger and potential scandal to which you have subjected her these last weeks is inexcusable. I will not stand for any interference now. If you act quickly, you can be on your way back to America before daybreak, but I only make this concession for Miss Kenwood's sake."

She didn't even blink. She stepped forward until her flounces brushed his leg, and looked up in a considering, curious way. "Ah. You are one of those."

He stared her down. If she were a man, a good thrashing would be in order.

She glanced at the distraught girl, cowering against the doorframe. "It appears that it is over, doesn't it? Too bad, I really thought that I might pull it off." She gestured, and Miss Kenwood joined her while she began removing the garments from their hooks and folding them.

He stepped between them, took a gown from his ward's hands, and cast it aside. "We will leave now. If Miss Kenwood has belongings here or at your lodgings, I will send for them."

Miss Ormond smiled in a damned insolent manner. "Oh, you are most definitely one of those. Very sure of yourself. A man who sets his course and always knows it is the right one. I was warned that this country has a lot of men like you, men who are positive that they never make mistakes."

He felt his face flush at this soiled dove's presumption. Enough. He took a gray broadcloth arm in his hand.

Miss Ormond shifted and blocked his retreat with the eternal span of her gown. Her warm, soft hand covered his and gently pried his fingers loose. The gray broadcloth slipped away.

Blue eyes looked up with mocking delight. "Well, this time you *have* made a mistake, Vergilius Duclairc, Viscount Laclere. In fact, you have got it all backward. She is not Bianca Kenwood. *I am.*"

He had a moment of incomprehension before the meaning of her words struck. Intimations of trouble flurried through his mind, a light snow of foreboding that suggested fairly simple arrangements had just become dangerously complicated. He glanced to the timid gray wren kneading her hands together, and then at the self-confident, painted bird of paradise, and wondered how Dante would react to this shocking development.

Thwap. Thwap, thwap.

The riding whip slapped against the high boot of the Viscount Laclere while he paced in front of the fireplace.

Bianca embraced Jane on the chaise longue, patting her shoulder. Across the drawing room, the Countess of Glasbury, the viscount's sister, blinked with drowsy dismay in her Oriental-style green dressing gown.

Bianca thought it had been very rude of Vergil Duclairc to rouse the countess from her sleep when he dragged Jane and Bianca here to the countess's town home. If he would stop brooding and pacing she could clear this up in a snap and they could be gone.

Thwap. Thwap.

"You don't plan to use that do you?" Bianca asked. Her voice cracked the tense silence that had ensued with the end of his explanation to the countess about where he had found his missing ward after two weeks of searching.

He pivoted in midpace and glared at her. He was a tall, lean, well-framed man in his middle twenties, with startling blue eyes and wavy dark hair dishevelled in the current fashion. Attractive, actually. Perhaps even handsome when he wasn't scowling, but then she wouldn't know.

"The whip," she said. "You don't plan to use it? I should

tell you that I am twenty years old and Jane is twenty-two, which makes us far past the age for such things. Although my aunt has a maid who was courted by an Englishman who told her that there are quite a few men who whip grown women here in England, which I found very peculiar, and others, it turns out, who actually want women to whip them, which I don't think makes any sense at all."

The countess gasped. She appeared fully awake suddenly.

Vergil turned to his sister with strained forbearance. He threw out his arm toward the chaise longue in a gesture that said, *"See?"*

"Really, Miss Kenwood," the countess said with a wavering smile. "Of course my brother has no intention of...of..."

Vergil's lids lowered as if there were no "of course" to it. He clasped his hands behind his back and studied her severely. "My brother came to meet your ship in Liverpool. How did you miss him?"

Bianca considered whether to use the elaborate history of misadventures that she had concocted in the event things ever went this wrong. It suddenly struck her as very thin.

She examined the blue eyes piercing her. Aunt Edith had said that the English aristocrats were an overbred, indolent people, and a bit stupid, and Bianca had counted on that being accurate. Unfortunately, this one appeared the exception, at least with regards to the last descriptive. He didn't seem likely to be bought off with confused tales of hapless innocence.

"There was a sailor on board who helped us remove our

trunks and find a hired coach before anyone came and called for us."

"You befriended a sailor?" The countess glanced askance at her brother, who briefly shut his eyes.

"Miss Kenwood, perhaps there has been a misunderstanding. Your grandfather's solicitor contacted a Baltimore attorney, a Mr. Williams, to handle this matter. He did come to speak with you, did he not? I was not misinformed, was I?"

"He most certainly came. He is a very nice man. In fact, he secured our passage on the ship."

"As he wrote to me that he would. Did he explain to you that a member of our family would meet you in Liverpool?"

"He explained it very clearly. My aunt would never have permitted me to come if she were not reassured that I would be met."

"So you admit that you disembarked on your own without waiting for an escort, that it was no accident that my brother missed you?"

"It was no accident. It was very deliberate."

For some reason her frankness left him speechless. He looked at her as if she were incomprehensible.

"I think it would be best if you sat, Vergil, so you do not fluster her by hovering like that," the countess said. "Then maybe we could discuss this calmly. I'm sure that Miss Kenwood has an explanation for everything."

Vergil sat on a small bench, but he still managed to hover in her direction all the same. "Do you have an explanation?"

"Of course." Jane had fallen asleep on her shoulder and the dead weight distracted her. Their embrace had unsettled the wig and she could feel it tilting askew. These old gowns were not designed for sitting, and the pads formed a platform all around her. The stays under her costume dug into her waist and side.

She felt a little ridiculous and very uncomfortable, and annoyed that this high-and-mighty viscount had not given her time to change or wash before hauling her into his coach.

"The explanation, Miss Kenwood. I should like to hear it."

"Actually, Mr. Duclairc, I really do not think that you would."

His eyes narrowed. "Let us try, anyway."

She tucked one leg up under her rump, to prop herself up more. The countess's lashes fluttered. The viscount cocked an eyebrow censoriously. Realizing that her dangling leg was uncovered to midcalf, Bianca smiled apologetically and pushed the skirt hem down.

"Mr. Duclairc, I was aware of the plans arranged for my visit here. I simply decided to make a few alterations. If Mr. Williams communicated with you about me, you may know that I lived with my great-aunt Edith more as her companion than her ward. I traveled extensively when my mother was alive, and learned to take care of myself. I am regarded as very mature for my years."

"He only wrote that your aunt is a bulwark of Baltimore society and that you are a well-bred young woman." His tone implied that Mr. Williams had some explaining to do.

"I know that my grandfather named you as my guardian in his will. It was a charming and quaint gesture. He probably wanted to cover the eventuality that I actually needed a guardian, which I obviously do not. Besides, I am American, so I do not see how an English will can establish that kind of authority over me."

"I will be happy to explain that later."

She already knew the explanation. She just did not accept it. "At Mr. Williams's urging, I agreed to come here to see matters regarding my inheritance settled in person. I never actually agreed, however, to stay with your family." She omitted the minor point that she had never disagreed, either, and had boarded that ship with both nice Mr. Williams and old Aunt Edith assuming that was exactly what she would do.

"With whom did you intend to visit, dear?" the countess asked. "See, Vergil, I told you there was an explanation. She expected other friends to meet her and they didn't show."

A peculiar wariness entered his expression. "Is that so, Miss Kenwood?"

"No," she admitted. Oddly enough, he looked relieved. "It is my intention to live by myself, with Jane as my companion. The offer of accommodations at your country home . . . well, I would feel like an intruder and besides, I prefer city life. And, of course, I did not want to have to delay my lessons."

"Lessons?"

"Singing lessons. That is why I have come. To procure professional training for the opera. My instructors in

Baltimore have told me that they have taken me as far as they can, that I need better teachers. My plan is to arrange for that in London until the inheritance is settled, and then use the income to go to Milan."

The viscount sighed, rose, and paced to the fireplace again. The countess leaned her dark-haired head forward confidentially. "I think it is wonderful that you are devoted to your music. How accomplished! When we come up to London for the season, I'm sure that we can find a voice master. I know quite a few people in the art and music circles."

"Thank you for the kind offer, but I do not want to wait for the season, whenever that is. This really was my purpose in coming, and I intend to start right away."

Vergil rubbed at shallow creases between his eyebrows. "Miss Kenwood, I do not want to embarrass you, but I need to know how you came to be singing in that establishment."

"Vergil . . ."

"No, Penelope, it is best to have it out now and learn exactly what we face. Miss Kenwood?"

"Well, hiring that coach all the way to London was very expensive. It cost most of what I had with me. When we arrived in London I found employment singing, to support us until I could obtain money from my grandfather's estate."

"How very clever and capable of you," Penelope said.

Vergil looked as though "clever" and "capable" were virtues he neither admired nor expected. "Are you aware of the reputation of that place? Do you know what occurs on that stage after your arias?"

"We never stayed afterward. It seemed a common music salon to me."

"Very common. We can only hope that your costumes obscured your identity and that no one who meets you in the future recognizes you from this last week. It is scandalous for a woman to sing on a stage of any sort, but one like that, painted and frilled as you are..." He made a gesture toward her gown, her face, her wig.

"My mother sang onstage, Mr. Duclairc, and these are her costumes."

"I'm sure that she was a lovely singer," Penelope inserted quickly.

"Stop humoring her, Pen. That may be acceptable in the United States, but not in England, Miss Kenwood."

"Since I am not English, that doesn't bother me. I think it would be best if we avoided any social connection so that you are not embarrassed by my performances, don't you?" She forced a smile, to encourage him to accept the undeniable logic of it. "Since you have executed your duty by assuring that I am safe, please return Jane and me to our lodgings now."

"You will remain here tonight. Your belongings will be sent for, and I will have the proprietor of the gaming rooms informed that your performances have ended."

"I must decline your offer, Mr. Duclairc. I will not impose on your sister, and I intend to continue my employment. As a singer, I need experience with audiences and—"

An autocratic slice of his hand cut her off. "No.

Absolutely not. You will not live independently of mature chaperons, nor will you parade yourself on a stage. While you are here you are my responsibility, and you will conform to the behavior expected of a young lady."

Bianca glared back at the intractable, towering viscount. That an old miser, whom she had never met, could complicate her life with a few scratches of a pen struck her as intolerable. She hadn't expected the viscount to find her so quickly. She hadn't planned to have this conversation until she was ready for him.

Vergil crossed his arms over his chest. The pose made him look very tall and powerful. It was the sort of stance a king might take when he ordered someone's head chopped off.

"Tomorrow my sister will accompany you and your maid to the country," he intoned, stating the lord's will. "You will not speak of this experience, not even to the other members of my family. As far as the world is concerned, you were met at the ship and have been in our protection from the start."

"If you take me out of London, you do so against my will. As you noted earlier, that is abduction. I, too, can complain to the Justice of the Peace."

He faced her coolly. "It is legally impossible for me to abduct you, Miss Kenwood. I am your guardian. Until you turn twenty-one or marry, you are under my complete authority. Pen, have the housekeeper show Miss Kenwood and Miss Ormond to their chambers."

Dismissed like a naughty schoolgirl, Bianca found herself and a drowsy Jane handed over to a woman in the corridor. Vexed that her plan had failed, and confused by this stranger's determination to take up a responsibility he surely could not want, she followed the woman up the stairs.

Something about the end of their confrontation troubled her. It wasn't until she reached the top landing that she found the vital omission. *Until you turn twenty-one or marry, you are under my complete authority.*

Or until she left England, of course. Right?

"Don't you think that you were a little too firm with her?" Penelope asked.

"Not at all." Vergil watched Bianca Kenwood tottering up the stairs on her dainty silk mules. The snow shower of foreboding had turned into a blizzard.

What a disaster.

"She is a stranger here, Vergil. Ignorant of our proprieties. No doubt, behavior is less formal in America."

"Don't believe it, Pen. She knew precisely what she was about." Which was doing exactly what she wanted, and guessing that the doing of it would induce him to wash his hands of her, so she could go on doing it.

He turned away, thinking that a glass of port was in order before he left. He needed to plan how to prepare his brother, and how to curb Miss Kenwood so that even a rake wouldn't be shocked by her.

Penelope touched his arm, stopping him. "It was kind of you not to say anything about how she addressed you, to understand it was only her naivete. All of those Mr.

Duclaircs. She was embarrassed enough as it was, and you were quite generous. I'll explain it to her tomorrow."

Is that what Pen had seen in those big blue eyes? Naivete? Embarrassment? Normally his older sister was more astute than that, despite her good-natured optimism.

"Explanations won't be necessary, Pen. I will wager one thousand pounds that Miss Kenwood knows full well the proper way to address a viscount."

Vergil threw his soaked hat to his valet and tore at the knot of his cravat. "Whisky for both of us, Morton. After that journey, we need it. Then show Hampton up when he arrives."

Within ten minutes Morton had not only produced the spirits but also some cold fowl and cheese, built a low fire in the library, and gotten Vergil dry and presentable. Not that there was anyone to present himself to. Only a few rooms in the expansive London house were open anymore and, in addition to Morton, there were only two servants.

Nor did he have to be presentable for Julian Hampton. The family solicitor had seen him most unpresentable before. Still, the life he lived here in London demanded that appearances be maintained.

He sat by the fire, sipping his whisky with two ledgers on his lap. He already knew what these documents would show and what Hampton would say. The Duclairc family finances were not healthy. Only Vergil's careful steward-ship this last year had prevented a total fall.

Recently, however, he had not had as much time to de-vote himself to such things. Other matters, more pressing and also more interesting, demanded his attention. Mat-ters such as the one he had just attended to up north.

And now, of course, he needed to deal with the new matter of Bianca Kenwood. The potential complications that she presented made him close his eyes.

Her image flashed behind his lids, as it had too often the last two weeks. He saw her sitting in Pen's drawing room in that absurd costume, with one slender leg dan-gling down the front of the chaise longue and the silk mule arching her little foot just so. She had been most *un-presentable.* Also irredeemable and impertinent and sly and fascinating . . .

Fascinating? What a peculiar thought. Wherever did it come from?

"Mr. Hampton," Morton announced.

Julian Hampton entered, wearing his solicitor's face. He always did that when they met for business reasons. Since he was an old friend it was probably necessary, espe-cially when it came time to discuss bad news. Vergil had seen that expression a lot in the last year.

"Have you studied them?" Hampton asked, gesturing to the ledgers as he took a chair and accepted a glass from Morton.

"I expect that little has changed."

"A bit. Solvency beckons. If your sister would live at Laclere Park—"

"I cannot ask her to be that dependent."

"Or if Dante would live within his allowance—"

"He never has, so there is no hope there."

"You could consolidate the farms and lease the land."

"This is an old litany, Hampton, and you know my answers. My father and brother did not displace those families, and I will not, either."

"Well, at least you no longer live on the brink."

They were closer to the brink than even Hampton knew, in ways these ledgers would never reveal. However, Vergil had a plan to deal with that. Unfortunately, an essential part of the plan might cause trouble. The part named Bianca Kenwood.

Hampton smiled. That was never a good sign, especially when he had on his solicitor's face. "You might improve things the easy way. The traditional way."

"Yes, I expect that Fleur's father would be very generous. I should be grateful that my value has risen so much with my brother's death. With time, I expect that I will agree to marry. Right now, however, other entanglements make that impossible."

Hampton was not an expressive man, so the light of curiosity and concern that flickered in his eyes let Vergil know that he had said too much. "Can I be of assistance? I have some experience in negotiating my clients out of entanglements." He stressed the last word in a way that alluded to problems of a romantic nature.

The entanglement that Vergil found himself in would take more than Hampton's skill to unravel. "You are unsurpassed at that, and I would hand mine to you if I thought it would help. I can only imagine how you convinced the earl to release my sister."

"All men have secrets that they want to hide. The Earl of Glasbury simply had more than most. How is the countess faring?"

"She is happy enough, and has come to prefer those social circles that accept her."

"Her fall would have been far worse if not for you."

Vergil knew that. Through ostentatious correctness he had managed to blunt the impact of Pen's separation from the earl, and of Dante's various sins, and even partly rectified the age-old reputation of the Duclaircs for unconventional behavior and ideas. Instead of his family pulling him down, he had managed to keep them afloat. Barely.

"Are we done?" Vergil asked, lifting the ledgers.

"It appears that you are."

He dropped them on the floor. "You can explain the sad details another day. Tell me what you have been up to, besides advising fools like myself."

"If all my clients were so foolish as you, I would starve."

Hampton's expression dropped its seriousness and he became the friend whom Vergil valued.

It turned out that he had been up to very little. Hampton did not seek out society much, and participated on the periphery when he did. Women thought him brooding and mysterious, and men considered him proud and dull. With his dark hair and sharp, perfect features, Hampton looked like a figure drawn in pen and ink by an illustrator. The problem for most people was that no captions came with him.

"St. John has come up to London," Hampton said. "Burchard and I are meeting him at Corbet's tomorrow. Witherby and the others will probably come too. Since you are back from wherever it was you went, why not join us? The Dueling Society will be whole again."

He was referring to the group of young men who had been meeting in Hampstead at the Chevalier Corbet's fencing academy for five years now. Vergil had not partaken of that sport or company in months.

His absence was all the odder because he had been the hub that had brought all those spokes together. He had known Hampton since boyhood, and become friends with Cornell Witherby while at university. Adrian Burchard, an earl's son, had been found in the circle of the peerage. Even Daniel St. John, the shipper, had been appended to the Dueling Society through Vergil because of St. John's friendship with Penelope.

"I wish that I could, but I must find Dante and bring him to Laclere Park. There are matters to attend there."

"Burchard will be disappointed. He has been looking for you, to discuss something that he will not divulge. I assume that means it is political."

If Adrian Burchard was looking for someone, he would soon find the man. Adrian was the last person Vergil wanted curious about his activities. "I will write and invite him down to visit. I expect to be there for several days."

"Why not invite Witherby as well? The prolonged absence of the countess from London has turned him melancholy."

"Perhaps it will inspire him to write another ode.

Witherby will have to bide his time. Miss Kenwood has arrived in England, and Penelope has taken her to the country for a long visit."

"Any trouble there?"

It wasn't clear whether Hampton referred to Bianca Kenwood or the way Cornell Witherby had been dancing attendance on Penelope. Although the former promised nothing but trouble, Vergil could also do without the latter. Having a good friend develop a passion for your older sister, especially when that sister was estranged from her husband and lonely and vulnerable—it was the kind of situation that could ruin a friendship.

"No trouble at all. Miss Kenwood is a delight. I look forward to your meeting her."

That was how entangled his entanglements had become. He was lying to a man he had known half his life.

Hampton turned the conversation to politics. As they talked of Whigs and Tories, of violent demonstrations and of the adjustments still occurring after the death of the last Foreign Minister, Vergil's mind dwelled on the private matters waiting in the country.

Over and over there appeared in his head the image of a young woman dressed like a French queen, challenging him with too much self-possession, and of a pretty leg dangling below a hem that had been hiked improperly high.

"I still don't understand your impatience," Dante said. He flicked cigar ash out the coach window. "No reason to drag me back from Scotland. She doesn't come of age for almost a year."

That was an eternity by the way Dante calculated his calendar with women. Normally he would court, seduce, bed, and discard two mistresses in that time. Vergil studied his younger brother's beautiful face and limpid eyes and dark brown hair. Dante's history with females had almost been inevitable with features like that. Vergil had seen ladies of the highest breeding lose their breath when Dante approached.

"The season starts well before her birthday, and with Charlotte coming out, we can hardly leave Miss Kenwood here while we all pack off for town. You need to be married before then, not just engaged."

"Why? Do you think some fortune hunter will cut me out?" Dante's tone implied the notion was preposterous.

No, I think that if she is married we can prevent her from going up to London at all, if necessary, Vergil thought. The very notion of Bianca Kenwood in polite society, calling dukes and earls "Mister," and announcing that she intends to study performance opera, was enough to ruin his spirits on this late August day.

But Dante's question also pricked at the foreboding that had continued plaguing him since he had left Penelope's house that night. It might be best for Dante to get this over while the field was clear.

Dante looked him squarely in the eyes. "We are almost there. Don't you think that you should tell me now?"

"Tell you?"

"You haven't said much about this Miss Kenwood,

whom I am expected to marry. I find that suspicious. After all, you have met her. We both know that I have no choice except to agree to this, but if warnings are in order, you are running out of time."

"If I have not described her in detail it is because it would be indelicate to do so. This is not one of your racehorses."

"You have not described her at all."

"Very well. She is of middling height and slender, with blue eyes."

"What color hair?"

Damned if he knew. What color hair had been hidden by that ridiculous wig?

"Just how bad is she?"

Vergil had fully intended to warn Dante, but had failed to come up with the right approach. A tinge of guilt colored his reflections while he debated the appropriate one now. After all, he had practically forced his brother into this. Not that Dante had resisted much once he learned that over five thousand a year came with her.

"It is not her appearance. Her manner, however . . ."

"Is that all? Just like you to get stuffy about a few *faux pas*. What did you expect? She is an American. Pen will shape her up in no time."

A few *faux pas* did not do Bianca Kenwood justice, but he let it pass. "Of course. However, even so, she is . . . distinctive."

"Distinctive?"

"One might even say unusual."

"Unusual?"

"And perhaps a bit...unfinished. Which can be reme-died, of course. Pen has her in hand even as we speak."

Dante peevishly looked out the coach window at the passing Sussex countryside. Vergil hesitated continuing, but they *were* almost there and he *was* running out of time. "She may need a strong hand. She is a bit indepen-dent, from what I could tell."

His brother's gaze slid back to him. "Independent, now."

"She has certain notions. It is her youth, and they will pass."

"It would help immensely if you would balance some of this by adding how beautiful she is."

No doubt. The problem was, he didn't know if she was beautiful. He only remembered big eyes, interesting be-cause of that intelligent and spirited spark in them.

What else could he offer? All that stage paint had been obscuring. The possibility of a lovely complexion, but who could be sure until he saw her washed? A nice form, but that may have been the costume. The suggestion of an underlying sensual quality...not something one noted about a brother's future bride.

"Damn it, if she is vulgar I won't go through with it, Vergil. Nor should you want me to. Aside from the fact that she would reflect on me and this family, I could hardly avoid her completely once married, even living in town and leaving her out here, which is how I plan to arrange things. And until you marry Fleur, which you are taking your damn sweet time doing, and set up your nursery, I am your heir and this American could end up the Viscountess Laclere."

Vergil did not need his younger brother to list the pitfalls dotting this path. Pits much deeper and more numerous than Dante imagined. A honeycomb of them. If he could think of an alternative, he would use it, but two weeks of debating options always led him back to the same conclusion. Bianca Kenwood needed to be bound to this family with unbreakable chains.

Dante bit his lower lip and again looked out the window from beneath heavy lashes. "The income from her funds will be mine? As trustee, you will not interfere? And my allowance continues until the wedding, enhanced as we agreed?"

"Of course. I also promise to continue management of the financial investments, as you requested. The income from the funds is secure, but the others require occasional oversight, and I know that you hate such things."

Dante gestured dismissively. "Sordid and nettlesome things. I doubt they are worth the trouble. Sell them out or hold them, as you judge best. After how you scraped us through when Milton died, I would be a fool to question you."

They rode in silence through the oak and ash forest filling the back of Laclere Park. Vergil much preferred this approach to the broad sweep of landscape facing the front, and always instructed his coachman to take it. Normally it served as a transition space for him, a few miles in which to prepare himself for the role of the Viscount Laclere and the responsibilities that it entailed.

He had first come this way when summoned by news of Milton's death, choosing the longer route in order to delay that arrival, churning with conflicting emotions and spiking resentments at the changes in his life suddenly decreed by his older brother's demise.

It was in this forest that he had finally accepted the new reality and its attendant restrictions. Little had he guessed how complicated his brother's death would make his life. Along with restrictions, mysteries and deceptions had waited for him at journey's end.

Dante suddenly leaned toward the window. He squinted. "What the..."

"Is something wrong?" He pushed Dante's head a bit and stuck his own to the opening.

"There, over in the lake. Wait, some trees are in the way. Now. Isn't that Charlotte?"

The trees thinned while they began to pass the lake. Two women bathed in the water, laughing and splashing. *Naked,* for all intents and purposes, since their chemises had gone transparent from the water. Hell, yes, it was their younger sister, Charlotte, with that maid, Jane Ormond.

The water broke and a third feminine body rose up. A soaked chemise adhered to her skin and obscured little. Pretty shoulders...tapered back...nipped waist... graceful hips...finally the tops of enticing rounded buttocks slid into view. Long blond hair fanned in the eddies and then sealed to her body in a thick drop from a well-formed head.

Her slender arms began skimming the water's surface, creating waves in the direction of her playmates. The other two squealed and started a massive counteroffensive of splashes, sending sprays of water all around her until she appeared like a vision emerging out of a misty dream.

A shriek of joyful protest reached them. Laughing, she turned to run from the assault.

Vergil could not be sure that those large blue eyes actually saw the passing coach with its two stunned occupants. But she paused, and one arm slid across her breasts and the other hand drifted to the shadowed triangle just above her thighs. For the briefest instant before she turned and knelt, she assumed the pose of a Botticelli Venus, a goddess lovely of face and luscious in form, dripping wet, still virginal and modest, but ripe and waiting. The combination of protective instincts and erotic suggestions that he had experienced in the gaming hall surged with force.

He and Dante found their sense at the same instant. They straightened and sank back into their seats.

His brother eyed him with suspicion. "Who was that?"

"I cannot be certain, but I think it was Miss Kenwood."

Dante closed his eyes and rested his head against the seat's back. "Let me make sure that I understand my position, Vergil. I am required to marry *that*? I am to be sacrificed on the altar of the god of financial stability and be forced to take as my lifelong partner *that* female we just saw? A girl so *distinctive, unusual,* and *independent* that she bathes almost naked in full view of a road, in broad daylight, and influences our sister to do the same thing? You intend to coerce me, if necessary, by threatening my allowance? *She* is the bride whom you have chosen for me?"

"Yes." There really was nothing else to say.

Dante held his pensive pose a moment longer. His eyes opened. Their limpid warmth glowed. A very male smile slowly broke. "Thank you."

"Very good, Pen. *Very* good."

Penelope flushed an even deeper pink than the hue her skin had assumed while he told his tale. "Do not blame *me.* I certainly did not countenance such a thing. She has been the most gracious guest. Her behavior has not been untoward. Well, to my knowledge, at least."

She added the last with a little grimace. Penelope was smart enough to recognize that today's lark indicated that she might not know the full extent of Miss Kenwood's activities. Vergil imagined a whole string of scandalous episodes played out under the unsuspecting Penelope's nose.

"Our time here has gone swimmingly well."

"Under the circumstances, *swimmingly* is not the best choice of words, Pen."

She hung her head, embarrassed at failing at her charge. He patted her shoulder reassuringly. She simply did not have it in her to see the worst, and was always too understanding.

Bianca Kenwood probably had seen immediately what she had in Penelope, and had taken advantage of it.

What was needed for Miss Kenwood was an old harpy of an aunt whose force of will would brook no defiance, whose steely gaze would make young women tremble, whose strict admonishments would summon immediate submission.

Unfortunately, no such aunt existed.

"Perhaps bathing thus is common in America."

"*Please,* Pen."

"I will speak with her, and give Charlotte a good scolding."

"You will do no such thing."

"You intend to instead? Oh, Vergil, I wish that you would not. She gets a peculiar look on her face whenever your name is mentioned. I suspect that she sees you as a gaoler, and if, on meeting you again, the first thing you do is lecture on behavior..."

"I won't say a word about it. No one will. Not to Charlotte, either. To mention it would be to admit Dante and I had witnessed it." He didn't even want to contemplate *that* confrontation. To mutually acknowledge what had occurred would create an impossible awkwardness and a difficult... intimacy. "We are left with no choice but to ignore it. I will speak with Charlotte in more general terms about not permitting herself to be influenced."

Dante joined them, looking happy and refreshed in a change of clothes, perfectly pressed and exquisitely tailored. His expression glowed expectantly beneath carefully mussed hair, slightly long in the romantic fashion.

"It was kind of you to join us for a few days," Penelope said, rising to give him a kiss.

"One misses the family sometimes, Pen. In fact, I shall probably stay, oh, about a week. Yes, a week should do it."

He cast Vergil a wink that made Penelope frown curiously.

Vergil returned a reproachful glance. Penelope did not know about their plans for Miss Kenwood. Also, for some reason, his brother's self-confidence rankled him.

"A whole week? That is wonderful, Dante, and very kind. I know how you hate the country unless there is good sport."

"Well, Pen, there is sport and then there is sport. I'm told Verg has bought a new horse that needs breaking and I felt obliged to help him, since I have such a hand with the animals and it is a gift to me besides."

"A new horse? Vergil, you didn't tell me."

"It arrives in a few days," he muttered. Clever Dante. Enjoying his metaphor and getting a horse in the bargain. Not such a bad metaphor. Miss Kenwood did not really strike one as unfinished so much as unbroken. Just like Dante to size a woman up in a few seconds from seventy yards, and delight in the challenge awaiting him. No wonder he looked so insufferably content.

The filly in question joined them shortly, arriving with Charlotte in a faint rustle of petticoats. Charlotte looked charming as usual, her willow-thin elegance still softened by childish innocence. Beside Charl's dark hair and white skin and pale pink dress, Bianca Kenwood appeared a bit of a country miss.

Her blue dress was a little dated and plain. Her skin bore a light, unfashionable tan, but his sense of its flawless beauty had been correct. Her golden blond hair was coiled into a simple knot that emphasized the feminine but firm jaw outlining the bottom of her heart-shaped face. She hardly fit the definition of a fashionable beauty, but she possessed a singular prettiness and exuded health and carried herself with mature grace.

Dante studied her with calculating eyes during the few moments before Penelope called him over for an introduction. That examination made Vergil uncomfortable. Suddenly he felt soiled by this business. Ridiculous. Such things were arranged all of the time, and usually with less subtlety.

Dante advanced on his prey. His success with women resided less in pursuit than in magnetism. A lady had once blurted out to Vergil that when Dante looked in a woman's eyes, she felt as if he could see her soul, and his attention absorbed the breath out of her body.

If so, Miss Bianca Kenwood's soul was not easily observed. She took Dante's greeting with ease and didn't appear the least bit breathless. Vergil could not help but admire her poise, even though the plan had been for her to fall in love at the first sight of Dante.

"And you remember Vergil," Penelope added quickly, gesturing in his direction.

"I could hardly forget Mr. Duclairc. I am delighted to see you again. Perhaps before you leave we might have some conversation."

"Of course, if you wish it."

Oh, she wished it. She had been saving speech after speech for two weeks now. She had hardly buried her resentment of the imperious interference that had sent her here.

She realized that she was glaring at him, and that everyone else was watching her do so.

"You are finding your stay pleasant?" Dante asked, guiding her toward the settee.

"Very pleasant, thank you."

He sat beside her, giving her his full attention. He was a handsome man, but a little fine in form and face, as if God, in sculpting the bones of his older brother, had used up the best materials and then had to make do. Beautiful brown eyes regarded her from beneath thick lashes. A spark of inappropriate familiarity glowed in them.

Yes, they had seen. She had argued with Charlotte that no one had looked out the carriage that passed. In truth, she thought that she *had* seen faces peering at her for a moment, but when nothing was said during the hours since their return, she just assumed . . .

"So you are named after the Italian poet," she said, very discomforted that Vergil Duclairc had gazed upon her practically naked body. Oddly enough, the fact that his brother had also done so didn't bother her much at all.

"It was my father's unfortunate idea. He fancied himself an epic poet and named his sons after the great ones. Our eldest brother was Milton."

"It might have been worse. He could have chosen your names from among the heroes and not the authors."

Charlotte giggled. "That would have been horrible. Ulysses and Aeneas and such."

"Or he could have moved into his fascination with the Arthurian tales sooner than he did," Dante agreed. "Lancelot, Gawain, and Galahad."

They played with that awhile, Penelope joining in. The man at the window did not, but Bianca sensed him following the banter with more interest than his occasional look indicated.

She could see her adversary clearly from her position. He cut a fine figure, tall and lean, but with shoulders and legs that suggested more strength than obviously visible. He did not scowl now and, yes, he was quite handsome in a strong-boned, harshly chiseled way. The blue eyes still startled, piercing out from beneath dark eyebrows.

They pierced now, catching her looking at him. She turned her attention to Dante, managing, she hoped, not to flush. She had the uncomfortable sensation that in that glance the viscount was remembering what he had seen by the lake.

Dante had been saying something to her. She responded with a question of her own, falling back in her ill ease to the sort of small talk typical at home. "And what do you do?"

Total silence faced her.

"Do?" Dante repeated after a ten count.

"Your brother sits in Parliament, as I understand it. What is your occupation?"

Charlotte giggled. Vergil's jaw looked more set than usual, but a glint appeared in his eyes while he turned his full attention on his brother.

Dante smiled. "I am a gentleman."

"I would never suggest otherwise, but how do you employ yourself?"

"When my brother says that he is a gentleman, he does not beg your question, Miss Kenwood. He answers it," Vergil said.

In other words, being a gentleman meant that one had no gainful employment. The refined young man beside her suddenly appeared as foreign as the Indians she had seen on occasion when her mother toured the towns near the frontier. This was another example of what Aunt Edith had meant when she had warned that Bianca would find this country familiar in some ways, but very odd in others.

"Surely you have gentlemen in the United States," Penelope said.

"We have men of great wealth and position. There are estates as large as this. But a man who does not work . . . well, it is considered almost sinful."

She immediately wished that she hadn't put it quite that way, even though such indolence was evidence of a serious fault in character. She had no desire to insult these people, three of whom she had no argument with.

The one with whom she did have an argument broke the awkward silence. "How quaint. But then your country is young still."

Coming from any of the others, she would have let it pass.

"Old England is learning that there is strength in youth."

"You refer to our last war. A minor skirmish. It would have ended differently if Bonaparte did not occupy us as well."

Somehow, barely, she kept a civil tone. "My father died in that skirmish, Mr. Duclairc."

Another thick silence fell. Penelope smiled weakly and rose. "Why don't we go in to dinner?"

Dante demanded Bianca's attention during the meal. The viscount did not speak much. She looked over several times to find him scrutinizing her, as if he wondered what he had. Nothing but trouble, she wanted to warn him. You really should send me packing at once.

She had every intention of cornering him after dinner in order to make that clear, but Vergil excused himself as soon as they returned to the drawing room. Dante stayed, however, and joined them for cards.

He complimented her play far more than her skill deserved. With familiarity and the passing hours, his smiles assumed an unsettling warmth. She began to get suspicious that Vergil was avoiding her, and using Dante as a distraction.

"Where is the viscount?" she finally asked Charlotte. "Perhaps he would like to take my place here."

"He is in the library, I expect. Or his study."

She rose. "Excuse me. I will invite him to join us."

She did not wait for permission, but walked from the drawing room and aimed down the corridor for the library.

He was there, sitting at the desk and poring over some papers in a folio. He glanced up at her entrance and rose.

"You appear startled to see me. Have I done this wrong? Am I supposed to apply for an audience?" she asked.

"Of course not. I assumed that my brother and sisters would keep you entertained this evening, that is all."

"Cards do not amuse me long if the hands are thrown to me. If we were playing for money, I would have already won your brother's entire fortune. I decided to give his pride and generosity a rest."

"He is only trying to make you feel welcome. However, I am glad that you sought me out. I want to apologize for my careless comment in the drawing room. I should have been more sympathetic to the possibility that you suffered in the war. I did not intend to demean your father's sacrifice."

The sincerity of his expression disarmed her. He did not appear nearly as stern as was normal for him.

"Perhaps now you understand why I do not welcome a long visit in this country, Mr. Duclairc, and why I do not want to partake of the society for which your sister tries to prepare me. I want to return to London so that I can tend to my affairs there as quickly as possible."

"The war is long over, Miss Kenwood. Our countries are friends again. As to your affairs, I am tending to them for you." He said it with a firm smile that indicated he considered that particular direction of conversation ill-advised.

"You are convincing me that I made a mistake in coming to England. I should have followed my first inclination and told Mr. Williams to have the investments that I inherited sold out."

"That cannot be done. Most of it is in trust. Short of petitioning the Chancery Court, a very lengthy process that would take years, it is impossible to break the terms."

"So he explained. My second inclination was to have him arrange to send the income to me in Baltimore."

"Then why didn't you? Especially if you blame us for your loss?"

"As I explained in London, I had reasons for coming."

"Yes. Your opera lessons." His tone managed to convey relief that those plans were now dead.

It would take more than this man's disapproval to kill them. They were very much alive, and she was desperately impatient to progress with them.

"Whatever my reasons, I am in England for only a short spell and I have interests that cannot be satisfied while I am in this house. I do not accept your interference. I do not need a guardian."

"Considering how I met you, I think it is obvious that you do. Today has done nothing to change my belief in that."

He was referring to the lake. Nothing in his expression really changed, but a provocative ripple eddied from him to her. It entered her body and shivered down her limbs. Yes, he had seen her in that soaked chemise. Despite his dispassionate demeanor, he was seeing her in it again right now.

For an instant, lights entered his eyes that said he

knew that she knew. That acknowledgment added a dangerous nuance to his masculinity. She suddenly felt at a disadvantage and had to struggle to regain her indignation.

"I fail to understand why you are so determined to take on the trouble of me."

"Your grandfather's will gave the responsibility to the Viscount Laclere. He had intended it to be my brother, but since he did not change the will after Milton's death, it falls to me. I do not shirk my duties, no matter how troublesome they may be."

"I relieve you of the duty. Now, I demand that you allow me to leave for London in the morning."

"No."

She waited for more, but nothing else came. That one word was his entire response. No.

She glared at him, searching for a way to win this stupid battle. He gazed back like a general who knew he had the superior army.

She turned on her heel. In a few days she expected her reinforcements to arrive. She looked forward to throwing them at him.

"Miss Kenwood, if you are returning to the drawing room, please tell Charlotte that I would like her to join me here before she retires."

Bianca mounted the steps and strolled her way through the huge Gothic-style house, to her room. It was the largest and most luxurious bedchamber that she had ever used, with a gilt-framed mirror and heavily carved furniture.

Jane moved toward her, to begin unfastening her gown, chattering away with gossip about the servants and tenants. That lower world sounded a lot more fun and interesting than the high one in which Bianca lived out her days.

The last two weeks had felt like two months. They took walks. They arranged flowers. They exchanged visits with neighbors she didn't know. They talked about fashions and who was who in society. All the while Pen instructed the American savage on the proper address and acceptable behavior here in England.

Bianca had gotten to where she envied the servants who polished the silver. Finally she had arranged a few ways to break the monotony for herself.

Charlotte arrived just as Bianca drew on her batiste dressing gown. It had been a short meeting with her brother.

"He didn't say one word about the lake." She scooted onto the bed while Jane began brushing Bianca's hair. "Actually, he wanted to talk about you."

"Me?"

"Asked what you had been up to. He did not put it that way, of course. He inquired if you were content and occupying yourself."

Why, the intruding . . .

"I think that he knows about the lake and blames you, and wanted to know if you had done anything else scandalous."

The arrogant, self-righteous . . .

"Then he gave me a lecture. How you were raised differently and permitted more freedoms than is proper, and how I am not to be influenced by you to do things that aren't proper. I counted at least ten propers before he had finished. I had to promise him to behave very correctly while you were here." Charlotte giggled. "I think that you have my saint of a brother very concerned."

Bianca didn't know what to say. She *had* been raised differently, and permitted more freedoms than Charlotte would ever know, but there had been nothing improper in any of it, just unconventional, even by America's standards. She also planned a life fated to be unconventional but not at all improper, although Vergil Duclairc would probably assume that it was.

Charlotte laid back on the big bed. "I am glad Dante came to visit. He doesn't much. He prefers London." She looked over slyly. "I am not supposed to know this, but I think that he has a mistress there. I have surmised this last year that my brother may be a rake. What do you think? Would Dante make a good rake?"

"I wouldn't know," Bianca said, but she guessed that Dante would make a magnificent rake. It also occurred to her that this rake had seen her almost naked and had spent the evening giving her intent looks and warm smiles.

"I always thought Vergil would make a good rake, too, so long as one never actually met him. He looks like he might be one, but of course he is *so* proper. He has been courting Fleur for over a year and I have never seen him do more than touch her hand."

Bianca had heard all about the perfect, ethereal, very wealthy Fleur, who was Vergil's presumed intended. They expected a visit from her and her mother soon.

She did not intend to be here when they came. "Charlotte, is this the only property that your family holds?"

"There are several others here in Sussex, but no one visits them except Vergil. They are not in the best repair. Father let some things go, what with his writing and then rebuilding this house. Vergil also has a manor up north. It was his portion from our mother."

"Do any relatives live at these other places?"

"There are none there, or any with whom we are close. Father was reclusive and we lost contact with them while he was alive. Milton was a bit odd too. Vergil isn't the least eccentric, but he has not revived the connections."

No close relatives. No aunts or female cousins on whom to foist an errant ward.

"I think that my brother likes you," Charlotte said.

Which brother? Bianca caught the impulsive question before it left her throat, shocked by the jolt of excitement that had accompanied it. "I am sure that he just felt obliged to entertain me."

"Dante rarely feels obliged to do anything. He let you win at cards and he kept smiling at you."

"You are mistaken, but if you are not and he is a rake, I am hardly flattered."

"Oh, you do not need to worry about *that*. He knows that you are Vergil's ward and our guest." She slipped off the bed. "I had better get some sleep. Dante is going to take us for a carriage ride tomorrow. It should be fun. He is a crack whip, and always drives fast."

"Will the viscount accompany us too?"

"You don't need to worry about him spoiling the fun. By the time we rise, he will have lived a whole day. He rides at dawn, and then tends to the estate affairs."

When she was gone, Bianca sat on the bed and embraced her knees.

So, Vergil Duclairc worried that Miss Kenwood might badly influence his sister. He had warned Charlotte to be on her guard. What would the saint do if he became convinced that Miss Kenwood was not just a little different, but quite unconventional, and a bit wild?

No other relatives to send her to. Too dangerous to keep around. No remedy but to sever all social ties and let her go her own way. It would be the only responsible decision for a very responsible brother.

She would have to make sure that this viscount concluded that her presence and influence were totally unacceptable.

"Jane, I want you to borrow a few garments from the servants for me. The male servants."

chapter 3

Vergil took the polished boots from Morton and pulled them on. He accepted the starched white linen and adroitly tied his cravat in a conservative knot. Morton held out a black riding coat.

These morning preparations were a routine at Laclere Park or in London, and Vergil performed them instinctively while his mind organized plans and duties. It still amazed him that he had no trouble abandoning certain details of these habits when circumstances demanded it.

Light had barely broken when he let himself out a side door and walked through the dew to the stables. He much preferred these silent, solitary rides at daybreak to the official circuits that he made with his estate agent later. It was one of the few habits continued from those free years as the second son. He could sometimes recapture that youthful belief in unfettered opportunity permitted by his insignificance back then. He could simply *be,* not the lord surveying his domain, but merely a man riding through the countryside, admiring its beauty and dreaming in time to its rhythms of life.

Sounds came from the stable. George, a lanky red-haired young groom, was laughing while a younger boy in breeches and a straw hat mumbled something. Together they were fitting the bridle on a chestnut mare.

George heard Vergil's bootstep and jumped back with a flushed face.

The younger boy merely stiffened. Vergil noted a familiar something in that slender back, and took in the peculiar way the breeches stretched over curving buttocks. He had seen this form before, rising all but naked out of water.

"Miss Kenwood, I see that you rise early too."

She turned with nonchalance, as if no one should be surprised to find her like this because she donned breeches every day. Maybe she did. Who would know? Pen, Charlotte, and Dante probably would not emerge from their rooms until noon.

"I thought that a morning ride would be pleasant." She fit the bit like she knew what she was doing.

"George offered to escort you? How chivalrous of him."

"I planned to ride alone."

"Well, we cannot have that at such an early hour. You can ride with me, however." He examined the mare. "You have made an error, George. If that is Miss Kenwood's animal, it will need a sidesaddle. Then you can prepare my horse. We will wait outside."

Bianca paced into the yard with him. He stepped back

in the silver light and raked five and a half feet of trouble with his gaze.

Her cotton shirt bagged around her body, but managed to drape revealingly over the swells of her breasts. The breeches hung loosely from her thighs to the boots into which they were stuffed, but were loose nowhere else. The straw hat crushed low over her brow emphasized her eyes.

She looked thoroughly disreputable and provocative as hell.

He walked away and slapped his whip against his leg. The slight sting distracted him from the flaring impulse to . . . not something to contemplate and certainly not to name. "It will take George some time with the horses. Go back to your room and change your clothes."

Her lids lowered at his order. He expected her to refuse. What the devil would he do then? No one under his authority ever defied him, least of all a woman. Fortunately, she turned on her heel and strode off in the direction of the house.

He went back into the stable.

"Does Miss Kenwood ride alone often?" he asked George.

George shrugged. "Just the last few mornings, m'lord. Heard some noise in here last week, and found her saddling up that mare, so I helped, didn't I?"

"And the garments?"

"Showed up in them this morning. Makes sense, since she always rides astride. She be a good sort, just a little free-minded for these parts. They's different, them

Americans. Talk like they know you right off." He bent to check a hoof.

"Yes, they are different. Do not let me suspect that you misinterpret that familiarity."

George shot him a glance of horror, as if the insinuation were too shocking to contemplate. Vergil took the mare's reins and led her out to the yard.

Miss Kenwood emerged from the house just as George brought Vergil's gelding out. She had dressed in a violet riding habit of severe cut and little decoration. A tidy high-crowned hat perched on her sedate hairstyle, its brim skimming her eyebrows.

"Where were you planning to ride?" he asked after they had mounted.

"Oh, I just wander about."

He led the way into the park. She kept fussing with her position on her saddle, scooching this way and that while she frowned down at her legs.

"You are not accustomed to it?"

"I did not live on the edge of civilization. The dreadful, dangerous things are given to women in Baltimore too."

"Did you ride astride there?"

"Yes." She glanced a challenge at him, then grinned. "Aunt Edith forbade me to use a sidesaddle unless I just poked along, and I was not inclined to do that. She knew too many women who had fallen from one when doing serious riding."

"And what was the reaction when you rode astride through the city, with breeches and boots?"

"If I had been anyone but Edith's great-niece, some

might have been scandalized. Her position is unassailable. As a young woman she was active in our war of independence. She knows all the great men from that time. If presidents pay calls on a woman, no one else is inclined to criticize her much."

"She sounds very interesting. It is a pity she did not accompany you on this journey."

"If she were not so old, she would have. She would be back there now, lecturing George on how he is your equal and should not grovel."

"England hardly needs to import radicals. We are growing plenty of our own. Nor did George grovel. He retreated because he knows it is suspect for a man to be alone in such a familiar demeanor with a young lady, especially at such an hour."

"I see. However, you are a man and now I am alone with you, aren't I? Is that suspect?"

The insinuation took him aback. Her mocking smile hinted that Miss Kenwood was not some naive schoolgirl who remained ignorant of what might occur between a man and woman alone together for hours.

"I am your guardian. Like a parent."

She broke into low peals of laughter, melodic like her voice. "Heaven spare me, Mr. Duclairc. With a father like you, I would have grown up to be the dullest of women."

"Are you implying that dull fathers make for dull daughters?" *Are you insinuating that I am a dull man, you vexing piece of baggage?* An inclination to show her just how undull he could be had been trying to poke into his awareness since he saw her in the stable.

"No, sir. I am thinking that strict fathers make for very narrow daughters."

"Your less orthodox upbringing did not leave you narrow, I assume."

She turned those big blue eyes on him for a long, knowing look, as if she could see inside him and identify the veiled, improper images creeping around the edges of his mind and alluded to by his impulsive, indelicate question. The impact of that naked gaze was so staggering that she might have caressed his thigh.

"I have had experience in the world, Mr. Duclairc, and that is why I am not narrow. When my father died, my mother needed to support herself and me, so she returned to singing. I was eleven at the time, and for the next six years we lived a peripatetic life, traveling part of the year."

Experience in the world. Bianca would have been seventeen before her mother died, a pretty girl traveling in the wake of a mother whose profession was sure to attract men.

"I would have thought that she would leave you with your aunt, and not drag you to strange cities and towns."

"*You* would, wouldn't you?" She implied he was so predictable as to offer no surprises whatsoever. "I wouldn't have it, not after just losing Father, and Mother needed someone to look after her. She was not a very practical woman. It was left to me to make sure that she got from one place to the other."

"An odd role to give to a child, surely."

"Not a child so long, and it wasn't planned. I found myself taking care of it because she was so bad at it."

Not a child so long. "Life must have become very dull when you went to live with your aunt."

"I was ready. Mother's death knocked the life out of me, and I needed time to sit in one place and sort things out. Only when Aunt Edith employed a music tutor for me did I begin to feel normal again."

Vergil pictured them, the precocious child and flighty mother, arranging subscription concerts in the churches and halls of rough towns, roles reversed while the little blonde girl negotiated for transport and managed their funds. Exciting perhaps, and obviously maturing.

Not a normal childhood, however. No hours of carefree play, and probably no friends. No protection or security except what she created for herself. He felt a little sorry for her and admired her strength, inconvenient though it promised to be.

Their wanderings took them to the southern edge of the lake and he began the route around it. Miss Kenwood appeared annoyingly indifferent at finding herself at the location of yesterday's indiscretion.

"Our family has lived here since Norman times," he explained, deciding he should impress her with the family history and prime her for Dante's attentions. "Both our name and the estate's derive from this water. Clear lake. Duclairc is a corruption of *du clair lac,* as is Laclere."

"Norman times. Back then, the ancestors of the Kenwoods probably lived in hovels."

"Well, money has a way of leveling such differences."

"What a democratic notion, Mr. Duclairc. Almost American."

He pulled onto a path leading to the farms. "You can stop that now. You have made your point."

"Stop what?"

"Mr. Duclairc."

"It is not intended to offend you. Aunt Edith made me promise to bow to no aristocrat, not even your king."

"Your diplomats conform when they are here, as do most visitors."

"I am not a diplomat. And Aunt Edith—"

"Yes, yes, the Revolution and all. If addressing me as Lord Laclere will bring the ghost of Washington down on you, you may simply call me Laclere."

"How generous of you. Then perhaps you should call me Bianca."

He would rather not. Really. Even vague familiarity with this young woman was breeding uncomfortable feelings in him. She was his ward and would soon be his brother's wife and he found her exasperating, to say the least. All the same, an alluring, disconcerting simmer flowed in him. Boiling bubbles broke to the surface on occasion, tiny little explosions not at all acceptable under the circumstances. Under any circumstances. To call her Bianca would only make another bubble pop each time he did so.

"I think that would be too familiar."

"Well, then, perhaps Laclere is too familiar as well." She cocked her head. "I know. I will call you Uncle Vergil.

Despite what you say about a guardian being like a father, 'Papa' would be ridiculous."

Uncle Vergil, indeed. He glanced under that brim and caught a fleeting smile. She was deliberately teasing him and he kept rising to the bait.

Worse, her provocative ambiguities and sidelong glances gave her a very worldly air, and made that simmer relentless.

"Uncle Vergil, are we near the border with Wood-leigh?"

"It is just over that hill. You can see the house from its top. Would you like to go up?"

She accepted. It did not miss Vergil's attention that she knew how to find the easiest path without his help.

She reached the crest of the hill that overlooked the fields leading to Woodleigh. In the distance she could see the gargantuan bulk of the classically inspired mansion that Adam Kenwood had built.

"It is very big, isn't it?"

"Yes." He said it quietly, but she heard a criticism. Too big. Too much. Vulgar in its mass, especially for a newly minted baronet. *Nouveau riche* from its foundations to its cornices. He must have been Adam's friend or her grand-father would have never made him guardian, but that did not spare the old financier from the judgment of this aris-tocrat who dated his lineage back to Norman times.

She did not resent that censure. In fact, she welcomed it. Adam Kenwood may have left her a fortune, but she hated him anyway. If he had bequeathed this house to her, she would have burned it to the ground. He had committed one great sin that she knew of, and she did not doubt that others shadowed his entire life.

She cantered down the hill and over the fields. Vergil pulled up alongside her when she stopped in front of the house.

"Help me to dismount, please."

"Miss Kenwood, your cousin inherited this property, and he has not returned from France yet. You should wait until he has taken up residence before you visit. The house has been closed for months, and there are only a few servants tending the property now."

"Actually, my cousin returned a week ago, but has gone up to London for a few days. Either help me down or I will jump and be ungraceful."

He helped her off the horse. "You intend to go in, don't you?"

"My cousin, Nigel, may have gotten the house and lands, but I was left my grandfather's private effects. I want to see what they are. Once you explain who I am and what my rights are, the servants will allow me to do so."

He accepted her plan more quickly than she expected, and talked their way in. He accompanied her to Adam Kenwood's study.

Bianca stood in the chamber's center and breathed in the scent of her grandfather's presence. Wainscoting covered the lower walls, and a huge desk angled off one corner. Some shelves held folios and ledgers, but other records had been heaped into wooden crates that lined one wall and surrounded a small trunk.

She felt Vergil watching her from the threshold.

"Did you know him well?" she asked.

"After he built Woodleigh, he formed a friendship with my older brother, Milton. With Milton's death, I came to know him fairly well."

"You have the advantage on me there. I knew there was the grandfather in England, but my parents never spoke of him. As I grew older I realized that this old man had left my father to live in poverty while he himself amassed this." She swept her arm to indicate the luxurious house.

Vergil strolled into the chamber and peered at the crates. "Your grandfather built a lot of wealth in shipping and other trade. During the early Napoleonic Wars, his ships were of great service to the government, and the king gave him his title of baronet. Like most such men, he planned for his son to be a gentleman and gave him the education for that. I gather that your father had other ideas and went to America."

"I think that his decision to go to America did not create their estrangement, but rather his decision to marry my mother. She was not a suitable wife for the son of a man clawing his way up in your society."

He pulled a folio out of a crate and flipped through it. "As I explained, such a profession carries a certain taint here."

"I suspect that it does everywhere. My mother was less tainted than most, in part because of her relationship to Aunt Edith. She stopped once she married my father. He served as a tutor, and she kept a proper house despite our circumstances. That was not good enough for this old man."

That folio went back, and after further inspection he lifted out another. "Well, he remembered you in the end."

"Unfortunately, the end came a little late."

"You sound bitter."

She did sound bitter. She could hear the resentment in her voice. "A tiny fraction of this inheritance would have spared my mother much grief, and probably saved her life. She died from a fever contracted while we traveled."

He looked up from the folio as if she had said something of singular interest. "I see. So now you will take revenge on Adam for her death by using his fortune to become a performer like the woman he repudiated."

His accusation made a little fury spin in her head. "You trivialize my purpose. I set my sights on an operatic career long before I heard of the inheritance." She surveyed the chamber again. "However, now that you point it out, there is a certain justice in using his money to become what he despised."

"It sounds more like a great joke than it does justice. Before you enjoy it too much, I should explain that one part of your knowledge about your grandfather is wrong."

"What is that?"

"From what he said to me, I am sure that he did not break with your father. Your father broke with him."

"I do not believe that."

"Believe what you choose, but that was Adam's memory of it."

It did ruin the joke, and the justice. It fractured the soul-chilling resentment that had formed in her heart while she watched her mother cough her life away in that rented lodging on the edge of the world.

"He only told you that so you would not think him cold and heartless."

"My opinion was not of great concern to him."

"Then he lied to himself, so he could die without guilt."

"Perhaps."

She looked at the records in the chamber. The truth was probably in them somewhere. She might find letters from her father. There could even be some from her mother, asking for help when she was widowed.

It should not really matter how it had been, but it did. If she was going to build a life on this man's wealth, she wanted to know whether she should be grateful or laughing while she did so.

"Is there any way to know what in here is mine?"

"His solicitor separated his papers. These crates contain the personal ones, while the estate accounts are on the shelves." He pointed to the small trunk. "I assume that the contents of his desk and anything of value are locked in there."

"I want to read these personal records. I will ask my cousin if I can visit and do so."

"It would be more convenient to move it all to Laclere Park. Then you could peruse the materials at your leisure. I will arrange for that."

"I am sure that my cousin will not mind if I do it here."

"I will mind."

She looked him right in the eyes. "There is no point in moving it twice. I will wait until I can send it all to my private lodgings in London."

He looked straight back. "You have no London lodgings, nor will you for a long time."

She did not expect it to be very long at all, but he hadn't realized that yet. "Fine, as a start, let us bring it to Laclere Park."

As they left the house, she noticed that he still carried a folio. He saw her glance curiously at it.

"There are some letters from my brother in this one. I hope you do not mind if I borrow it so I can read them."

"Not at all." It touched her that he wanted to do that. It was more sentimental than she expected of him. "When did your brother pass away?"

He helped her to mount her horse. "Just under a year ago."

"Perhaps there are other letters. When we get it all to Laclere Park, we can see."

As they paced their horses toward the fields, a fair-haired young man galloped toward them, hailing with his arm. He looked like a figure out of a fashion plate, with his elaborately tied cravat and beaver high hat and fashionable coat.

The young man pulled up his horse and whipped off

his hat. "Miss Kenwood! A happy coincidence to see you again. To think that if I stayed in London another day as I had planned, I would have missed you."

Vergil didn't turn a hair at the *again.* "You must be Nigel Kenwood, my ward's cousin. I am Laclere."

"A pleasure to finally meet you, Lord Laclere."

"I would have called if I knew that you were in residence at Woodleigh. I thought that you were still in France. My apologies."

Nigel smiled at Bianca. They resembled each other a little. His eyes were the same blue and his hair the same gold. A nice-looking man, she had decided, except that his expressions hinted at a tendency toward moodiness.

"I have only been back a week. Just sorting through Woodleigh's affairs has occupied me, but life is settling down now."

"Then you must call at Laclere Park soon. I am sure that the ladies would be grateful. There are so few new faces in the country."

"Thank you. I shall do so."

Nigel smiled appreciatively at her again. Bianca smiled sweetly back. Vergil smiled thinly at the two of them.

She gave Nigel her rapt attention longer than necessary.

Thank goodness Vergil was an intelligent man. She had no intention of lying, just planting enough concern for him to decide not to risk sweet Charlotte to her influence.

They declined Nigel's offer of refreshments and took

their leave. Vergil pulled up beside her. "You have met the new baronet before. You did not mention that."

"Didn't I? Several mornings ago I rode down to take a closer look at Woodleigh and he was out. It seemed only polite to stop and speak since he is my relative."

"Did he show you Woodleigh itself?"

Did you enter the house? Were you alone with him in his domicile? His expression remained so carefully impassive that she wanted to laugh. "Yes, he did. It was my grandfather's property, so of course I am curious." In fact she had only surveyed the gardens, but she felt rather smug at leaving another ambiguity for the viscount to chew on.

"It was your intention all along to visit Woodleigh and investigate Adam's study this morning, I think. I am happy that I could accommodate you."

She did not think he was happy at all. He appeared to be contemplating the implications of her visiting Woodleigh in breeches and shirt on a day when perhaps she knew Nigel was not in London after all.

On the whole, she decided that this had been a very successful morning ride.

They took a more direct route back. Feeling more secure on the sidesaddle now, she galloped through the park and did not slow when they entered the woods. Rosy sunlight dappled through the branches, creating marvelous blurred blotches while she sped along. The visual effect distracted her and she was unprepared when suddenly, inexplicably, her horse violently reared.

A different blur now, of trees and ground swirling while she struggled to control the animal. It acted berserk, and twisted on its hind legs. The sidesaddle could not hold her. She landed on her stomach with an impact that dazed her senses.

More shocking was the weight immediately pressing her back, and the forearms bracing the ground on either side of her head. Vergil was on top of her, covering her back and head with his body. She struggled against him with indignation and opened her mouth to protest.

A crack split the morning quiet. Vergil pressed firmly between her shoulders and pushed her back down into the dirt.

"Watch your fire," he shouted angrily in the direction of the sound. His right hand grasped the ends of reins and both horses whinnied and pranced.

She suddenly did not care that they must look ridiculous, sprawled together like this. "Who would be shooting?"

"Poachers, most likely after fowl. Very bold of them to use guns instead of traps. They would only dare it in early morning. We are several miles from the house and they expect the family to still be abed."

Another crack rang. This time she heard a little *thump* as the ball landed in a tree to their left. The horses reared and almost broke loose. Vergil cursed and shouted again.

He still pressed against her, his weight all along her back. His breath tickled her nape. The cloth of his sleeves flanked her cheeks, brushing them softly.

She did not feel in danger at all, but secure and

protected in the warmest way. The intimate proximity kindled a glowing response in her. She inhaled his scent of soap and leather, and a strange little flutter scurried from her heart to her stomach.

"Now you see why you should not ride at this hour. It is dangerous," he said.

"*You* were going to ride."

"That is different." The words were spoken near her ear, as if he had moved his head closer. He had her hugging the ground, her chin crushed in the leaves and soil. The warm breeze of his breath caressed her temple, making that flutter beat its wings furiously.

He rose up but he did not move away completely. He still hovered. Something she could not name poured out of him and into her. It frightened her. The flutter rose and filled her chest.

She rolled onto her back and looked up at him, right into his eyes. No one in her life had ever looked at her so...specifically. At least not from this close. That gaze seemed to penetrate right into her mind and explore at will.

She did not feel protected and secure anymore. Rather the opposite. The flutters multiplied and beat a frantic, humming rhythm, taking over her body and limbs. Wings of warning. And excitement.

His tight expression made him astonishingly handsome. He pushed away from the ground and knelt to offer his hand, to help her to a sitting position. "Did the fall hurt you?"

She moved her limbs gingerly. "It just knocked the

breath out of me. I was not really thrown, but I will be a little sore in the morning." She scrambled to rise. "As guardians go, you are superior, Uncle Vergil. Not many men would throw their bodies between a musket ball and a woman whom they barely know."

"All honorable Englishmen would do so, Miss Kenwood."

They walked the horses for a while to get them calm, then rode the last miles back to the house. His silent company unsettled her and that strange excitement still hummed. At the stables, he swung down and walked over to help her dismount. She paused when his arms reached up to guide her.

He noticed her hesitation. His blue eyes met hers in a most startling manner. She became breathless and incapable of looking away.

Strong fingers closed around her waist and lifted her down. It seemed to take a long time for him to release her, a stretched moment when he held her mere inches from himself. The subtle pressure of his hands and the closeness of his tall body shook her.

"Thank you. I enjoyed the ride very much." She collected her composure and turned away.

"I am glad that you did, especially since it will be your last one."

She whirled around to face him. "Are you saying I can never ride while I am here?"

"Of course you can, with company and later in the day. However, I will inform the grooms that you are not to be given a horse this early again, nor any time when you plan to go alone." He acted as imperious and calm as ever, but a tense power surged across the ground at her. "Nor are you to arrange any more morning assignations with your cousin Nigel. You may see him when he calls here, or if Penelope decides to call on him."

Assignations? His imagination had explored those ambiguities more thoroughly than she had intended.

She walked away without correcting him.

Let him think the worst.

Vergil pulled a chair next to the bed, sat in it, and raised his boot to give his brother's hip a good nudge.

Dante groaned and threw an arm over his eyes. He peered out below it, saw Vergil, and groaned again in resignation. With an irritated sigh, he pushed himself up against the headboard. "Morning, Vergil."

Vergil took in his brother's naked chest and noted the two glasses and empty wine bottle on a nearby table. "Up most the night with Marian, I gather. I have told you to leave the servants alone, Dante. I will not have them molested."

"A man does not molest Marian; he fights for his life. But then, you wouldn't know, even though she fancies you. Not discreet enough."

"Not discreet enough for you, either. Your intended is in the house."

Dante rested his head against the board and smiled. "Ah, yes, the fair Bianca. Your description did her a disservice. She is really a sweet young thing, just a bit naive is all. It is charming to watch her grapple with our ways."

A bit naive? "I just took a long ride with your sweet young thing."

"From the condition of your coat, it looks more as if you took a crawl with her."

"Some poachers were shooting and we ended up unhorsed." Not exactly how it had happened, but there was no point in inviting detailed queries about it. "I am glad to hear that Miss Kenwood suits you. However, I should warn you that you have competition."

"Nothing serious," Dante said as he yawned.

"You haven't even heard who it is yet."

"Not you, I trust."

Vergil shot him a scathing look that hid an uncomfortable spike of guilt.

"Just joking, Verg." Dante laughed. "It is so clear that you two don't rub well together, that she all but despises you, that I could not resist."

Unless he had misread things entirely there on the ground, they rubbed together disturbingly well. "Not me, but a title."

That checked his brother's mirth. Dante may have supreme confidence in his ability to attract women, but as a younger son, that did not translate into the ability to marry anyone he chose.

"Which title?"

"Her cousin, Nigel Kenwood."

"The second baronet of Woodleigh? All but newly patented, and very minor a title at that."

"She does not care about the finer points of birth and rank, and they are related, which gives them a natural bond. I thought him safely in France, running through whatever old Adam left him, but I fear he ran through it faster than I calculated. He has returned and taken residence as our neighbor. I suspect he did so hoping to find her with us. She got most of what wasn't left to charity, after all. To his mind he is practically entitled to her, I would guess."

Dante didn't exactly look concerned, but Vergil had his attention. "What do you know about this cousin?"

"He is the grandson of Adam's brother. They had started in business together, but the brother got into some financial scrape and Adam bought out his share. Nigel's father would not touch the trade, although Adam offered to take him in. Nigel fancies himself an artist and has lived in Paris since he attained his majority."

"A dabbler? Be serious, Vergil, I don't think—"

"Not a painter. A musician. Adam groused on occasion about the boy and his pianoforte."

"Oh, well, a musician. Now *there* is cause for alarm."

"Miss Kenwood is a musician, too, so there may be reason for concern, if not cause for alarm."

Dante raised his eyebrows at this new tidbit.

"A singer," Vergil explained. "She prefers opera. So you see Nigel's potential attraction. Similar interests and common blood."

"You make too much of both. We are talking marriage here, not a lover's liaison. Did mother and father have similar interests? Do you and Fleur have similar interests?"

He and Fleur had the most basic of similar interests, but that was beside the point. Vergil pushed himself to his feet. "Well, you had better move fast. I will try to discourage frequent visits from Nigel, but I can hardly bar him from the house."

He walked to the door. Dante's voice followed. "Well, now, big brother, just how fast do you want me to go?"

Vergil looked back at Dante. Pictures of those naked arms and chest embracing a barely clothed Bianca burst into his mind, inciting an ugly reaction. He did not respond for a moment, while he suppressed both the images and the anger. That embrace would be inevitable. And necessary.

"Do not even consider dishonoring her," he said. "And keep your hands off Marian while you are in this house. I will not have the ladies scandalized."

chapter 4

Penelope visited Vergil's study that afternoon, to inform him that she had received a letter in the day's post saying that Fleur and her mother would visit in ten days.

"I will be gone for the week prior, but I promise to return by then," he reassured her.

"I think that I will invite a few friends down from London too," Penelope said. "It will give Bianca a chance to try her wings."

"Not too many, Pen. And choose carefully."

"There is something else, Vergil. I suspect that Dante is developing a *tendre* for her."

He tried to focus on what Pen was saying, but his mind's eye was seeing Miss Kenwood lying on the ground and looking up at him with a startled blush that produced a charge through his veins. His hands felt her feminine waist once again and his body warmed from the closeness when he brought her down from her horse. The shadowy scent of lavender filled his head.

"Do not concern yourself, Pen. Dante will not get himself entangled inadvertently."

"I am not concerned about Dante. Bianca, however, strikes one as so guileless."

Guileless?

"And Dante . . . Vergil, I do not know if you are aware of this, as I am sure that no one speaks to *you* about it, seeing as how you are such a . . . but it is said that he is a merciless rake."

He wondered what Pen thought men talked about when they got together after dinner with their port and cigars. He had spent years being goaded about his brother's conquests, and on more than one occasion had been forced to stare down an irate husband.

"Even Dante respects the basic rules. If he has an interest in her, it is an honorable one, I am sure."

She blinked stunned eyes at him. "You will permit that?"

"Why shouldn't I?"

"She is very ignorant of the ways of the world and will be very disillusioned when she learns the truth about him."

"I would not interfere, Pen. Let things develop as they might. If he wins her, they will work things out the way couples always do with such things."

"If you say so, but I always resented that no one warned me about Anthony."

He had wanted to, but as a mere youth it had not been

his place, especially with their mother alive and managing things. A boy did not go to his older sister and inform her that her wonderful earl had a reputation as a libertine, and that shadowy allusions suggested his sins were not typical ones.

Someone should have, however, and he remembered well his sister's unhappiness. Pen's formal separation from the earl these last five years had brought her some peace, but at the cost of her social standing and a perpetual loneliness. The reminder that a bad marriage could be hell made him ill at ease about Bianca, and he wished Pen had not brought up her own loveless, childless union.

She gave him a look of female skepticism. "I will hold my tongue and see how things develop, but if I suspect that he toys with her, I will scold him severely, Vergil. That is something I will not tolerate."

"Do as you think best, Pen."

She left, and he lifted the letter that he had been reading when she entered.

He scanned its contents again. The biggest problem with a secret was that it always demanded your attention at the most inconvenient times. He had planned to stay here as long as Dante did, but that would not be possible now.

He left the study and went to his chambers to tell Morton to expect a journey the day after next.

The next afternoon Bianca sat in the drawing room, tapping her foot impatiently. She expected a visitor sometime soon. Unfortunately, the one whose card the butler delivered to Pen was not the one she anticipated.

Nigel breezed in, looking very romantic in his nip-waisted Parisian frock coat and dark muffler and tousled shoulder-length hair. He bestowed a warm smile of familiarity on Bianca while Pen greeted him.

"You are recently returned from Paris," Charlotte said. "You will have to tell us all about it."

Nigel obligingly entertained them with some descriptions of the latest fashions. Bianca barely heard, even though her cousin directed most of his attention to her. She listened for sounds of another arrival.

The doors opened, but it was only Vergil and Dante.

"I hope that you plan to make Woodleigh your home, at least through the autumn," Penelope said.

"It is my intention to do so."

"I will be hosting a house party here soon, and I will count on your riding over to join us whenever you can."

"That is most kind of you. I rarely visited my great-uncle, so I am all but new to these parts."

"You have not spent much time in England these last years, have you, Kenwood?" Vergil asked.

"I have preferred Paris. I found the culture there to be of surpassing quality. The artistic life is very rich."

"You have an interest in the arts?" Penelope asked. "Then you will enjoy the company of my party. Your cousin is no mean artist herself. She sings like an angel and has graciously entertained Charlotte and me on occasion."

Nigel's expression showed polite interest, but also

carried a patronizing tinge. Bianca guessed that he had met many young women whose friends believed they could sing like angels.

"Let us cajole her to sing now," Charlotte said. "Vergil and Dante have never heard her."

"I would be honored to accompany you," Nigel offered. "I am passably competent on the pianoforte."

Bianca felt a little cornered. She had only entertained Penelope and Charlotte with popular drawing-room songs, and had managed little serious practice over the last two weeks. All the same, the opportunity to sing, even if it couldn't be her best effort, excited her.

They all went to the music room and Nigel took his position at the pianoforte. "My repertoire of popular songs is limited," he warned her in a slightly superior way.

"Perhaps an aria would make more sense, then."

He looked up in delighted surprise. They agreed on one by Mozart, which she had learned just before leaving Baltimore. The prospect of this little performance quickened her heart.

The others positioned themselves on benches and chairs. Nigel played a few measures, to introduce the piece.

Her spirits immediately soared with the notes. No need to restrain her voice like she did in her room while she practiced scales. No cold isolation such as she experienced when she snuck away to sing on the grounds. Her joy in letting her voice vent its strength colored the sounds.

The reactions of her little audience produced a type of

power. Penelope looked stunned, Dante enthralled, Charlotte confused, and Vergil sharply interested. She glanced aside at Nigel and saw surprised approval. His skill at the pianoforte was considerable, and she suspected that he understood that the audience gave the skill meaning.

When she finished, the room was so silent she could hear insects through the open window. She held the swelling euphoria for a priceless heartbeat and then released it.

"That was astonishing, dear cousin," Nigel said quietly. "You have been training in earnest."

"You amaze us all, Bianca," Penelope said. "And your playing was masterful, Sir Nigel. I can see that music is a serious interest for you."

"Not an interest, but a passion." His eyes met Bianca's with a glimmer that said they shared a secret these others could never understand.

"You must promise to play when my guests are here. Perhaps we can induce Bianca to sing as well. It will make for a wonderful evening."

"I would be honored."

He began to take his leave, imploring Penelope to visit Woodleigh soon. The butler entered before Pen called for him, carrying a card.

"A man has arrived, my lady. He requests to see Miss Kenwood."

Penelope examined the card and raised her eyebrows when she handed it to Bianca. Bianca knew the name before she read it.

The visitor she had been expecting had finally arrived.

"It is business, Penelope. Is there someplace where I may meet with him alone?"

"Put him in my study," Vergil instructed the butler. "Miss Kenwood can conduct her business there."

Bianca saw Nigel off and then ran down the corridor to the study, still feeling lighthearted from singing.

She had never visited the study before. It faced north, and the light coming through the pointed Gothic windows offered veiled illumination of the dark wood desk, the wall of books, and the watercolor landscapes.

Her visitor rose from a chair near the window.

"Mr. Peterson, I am delighted that you came."

"I was relieved to receive your summons, Miss Kenwood. When you did not make our last appointment I grew concerned."

"Lord Laclere found me and had other plans for my visit in your country."

She took a place on the padded window seat. A deep sill ran inside the window. It held an assortment of what appeared to be unusual toys. One was a wood-and-chain catapult. Another was a wood-and-leather carriage. A third appeared to be nothing in particular, just a series of grooved ramps leading one to the other, decorated with chains and wheels.

Their construction was somewhat rustic. She guessed that Vergil had made them when he was a boy. The notion that the proper and stern viscount preserved memories of his childhood in his inner sanctum charmed her, even though, for the life of her, she could not imagine such a man as ever being boyish.

Mr. Peterson was a man of middle years, balding and pale, with gray eyes that could look shrewd or deferential depending on the circumstances. When she had first visited him in London, the shrewd side had been quick to understand her explanation that, while she could not pay his fees now, she had expectations that would ultimately settle things quite nicely.

"You have reviewed the will?" she asked.

"I have. I met with your grandfather's solicitor. He seemed surprised that you had engaged me, but cooperated to the extent he was obliged to. No more, however."

"What did you learn? Can Lord Laclere's rule be broken?"

"If you are not cared for, or if there is evidence of fraud, it is possible to have that provision set aside, but the court will not permit you the independence that I think you seek. If the viscount is not your guardian, someone else will be named. With a man of his stature, any abuse of his position would have to be egregious before a court took action."

She fumed with disappointment. The pointless toy caught her attention and she noticed a little lead ball at its base. Debating her next move with Vergil, she absently lifted it and dropped it on the uppermost ramp. It rolled its way down from one to the other, back and forth, setting off little wheels and pulleys when its weight hit different levels.

"Miss Kenwood, it is not a permanent situation—less than a year. You are a wealthy young woman, and it is understandable that your grandfather did not want to leave you the unprotected prey of unscrupulous fortune hunters."

"How wealthy?"

"Excuse me? I assumed that you knew."

"I know in general terms. Exactly how wealthy?"

"The income from the amount invested in the funds should reach at least three thousand pounds this year."

"That is a fortune in itself, and far more than enough for my purposes."

"Your guardian will control it, releasing funds to you as necessary, to cover your expenses. He is required to be reasonable regarding your requests."

She doubted that Vergil would be so reasonable as to hand her several hundred so that she could escape to Milan. If he controlled her income, he controlled her movements. In point of fact, he controlled her life.

"Now, the other part of your inheritance is more complicated," Mr. Peterson said, continuing his report.

"What other part?"

"Your grandfather was a man of business. Toward the end of his life he sold out of most of them. However, he held on to three partnerships. Two were minor holdings in transportation companies, and the third was a majority in a cotton mill in Manchester. You were also bequeathed his interest in those businesses, less ten percent of the mill, which was given to your cousin."

"The viscount is also my trustee, however. He manages those investments."

"These partnerships are not a part of the permanent trust like the funds are, however. If you marry or come of age, he must relinquish control of them. Actually, it surprises me that he has not sold out of those businesses. They represent a threat to your wealth. Should anything go wrong, all owners are fully responsible for debts incurred."

These business did not really interest her much, unless... "Is there income from them as well?"

"The solicitor was not inclined to let me see those records. I think that the mill does pay."

"What will happen with that income?"

"It will go to your trustee, who presumably will invest it in more funds. Or it will be sent to your guardian."

Who was the same person. Trustee. Guardian. Everywhere she turned in this conversation she kept bumping into Vergil Duclairc.

"Mr. Peterson, I would like you present while I speak with Lord Laclere. The situation he has created is intolerable. I am being kept a prisoner here."

She sent the butler to request Vergil's attendance. Mr. Peterson looked very discomforted at the notion of the upcoming interview. By the time Vergil came through the door, deference had replaced shrewdness in those gray eyes, and the balding pate showed tiny beads of sweat.

"Lord Laclere, this is Mr. Peterson. He is my solicitor."

Vergil coolly examined the attorney with bored, aristocratic hauteur. Mr. Peterson dissolved into an obsequious fluster. Bianca fought the urge to scold him to be a man.

Vergil turned critical eyes on her. "I did not know that you had engaged a solicitor, Miss Kenwood."

"It was one of the first things I attended to when I arrived in London."

"Your grandfather's solicitor, or mine, or I myself, would have been happy to explain anything that you needed to know."

"I thought it best to have my own representation and to decide for myself what I needed to know."

"I trust that Mr. Peterson has satisfied your curiosity on all points."

"Almost all. He has explained about the business partnerships that I have inherited, and suggested that you should have sold them out, for safety's sake."

"I did not put it that way, my lord," Mr. Peterson rushed to explain. "I only explained the law regarding a partner's financial responsibilities."

"As you should for your client. I am obtaining information about the value of the partnerships. As trustee, it would be irresponsible for me to give them away. There have been several inquiries regarding purchase that I will pursue when I am in a better position to judge their fairness. These things take time, however. It is difficult to obtain honest information from the managers and other owners."

"Excellent, my lord. Just the sort of careful oversight one would expect. I think it is obvious that all is in perfect order, Miss Kenwood, and that you are fortunate to have Lord Laclere taking care—"

"When do the companies pay out the profits?" she asked.

Steely forbearance set Vergil's jaw and mouth. "If there

are profits, the companies pay out once a year. It will be reinvested in government funds."

"Have the funds themselves paid since my grandfather's death?"

"They have."

"Has that income also been reinvested?"

"Most of it."

Most, but not all. "Mr. Peterson, would you be so kind as to wait for me in the library?"

Mr. Peterson was delighted to do so. He almost stumbled in his hasty retreat.

Bianca took a chair facing Vergil. "I want you to arrange for the income to be at my disposal."

"I have no intention of doing so."

"It is *my* inheritance."

"Even if you were the most sensible of young women, I would fail in my duty if I handed it to you. As it is, you have expressed intentions that would make me a conspirator in your ruin. It is out of the question."

"Mr. Peterson explained that a guardian is expected to be reasonable in releasing those funds."

"A sum is available to meet your needs. Tradesmen need only send their bills to me. Modistes and others who cater to women are accustomed to that. Barring extravagant spending on your part, we need never speak of this again."

"Since there are no modistes in this house, I am in no danger of being accused of extravagance."

His expression cleared a little. "My apologies. Of course you would like to enjoy the fruits of your good fortune. I will arrange for Penelope to take you up to London in a few weeks."

"Thank you. However, I would like some pin money now. I need to purchase a few items of a personal nature."

As she expected, the word personal kept him from probing. He opened a drawer in his desk.

"I expect that twenty pounds should suffice," she said.

"That is a lot of pins, Miss Kenwood."

"I will use some of it to pay Mr. Peterson."

"Mr. Peterson can send his bill to me."

"I prefer he does not. I prefer that he remembers just who has engaged him. Nor do I think it right that I ask him to await my expectations."

Vergil removed several notes from the drawer and placed them on top of the desk. He walked to her chair, no longer hiding his irritation. He towered above her and she barely managed not to cower.

"I am not accustomed to such blunt discussions of money, especially with women. Nor am I accustomed to questions that imply suspicion regarding my honesty and judgment in managing your estate, especially in front of a man with whom I have no acquaintance."

He bent and grasped the arms of her chair. She shrank against its back, away from the sparks flashing in the eyes just inches from her face. "The fact is, Miss Kenwood, right now Uncle Vergil is thinking that his disrespectful ward could use a good spanking."

Her mouth fell open in indignation. He whipped away and strode to the door.

As soon as he departed, she scooped up the notes and

joined Mr. Peterson. She handed him ten pounds. "This is to pay you for your fee and expenses so far. I want you to take what is left and establish an account for me at a bank. Use your own name if necessary."

"Surely Lord Laclere has an account on which drafts can be written."

"I want my own, and I don't want him to know about it. Write to me with the information once it is done. I also want you to find out about these offers to purchase the business partnerships."

"If you insist, I will see what I can learn. Should I write to you here?"

"Yes. I don't think the viscount intends to allow me to go anywhere for a very long while." Probably not until she married or turned twenty-one.

She had no intention of doing the former, and refused to wait for the latter. If Mr. Peterson obtained the names of the parties interested in her partnerships, she might find a way to procure the funds necessary to go to Italy, despite the obstacle of Vergil Duclairc.

Vergil had barely cooled his temper after the surprise meeting with Mr. Peterson when another unexpected visitor arrived late that afternoon. Adrian Burchard, one of Vergil's friends, entered Vergil's study, mercifully distracting him from insistent, erotic images of taming Bianca Kenwood.

"It has been too long, Burchard," Vergil said, welcoming him.

"If you spent more than a few days in London at a time, it would not have been so long. Where have you been keeping yourself?" Adrian's dark, foreign-looking eyes revealed no expectation of an interesting answer.

Nor did he get one. Vergil gestured to the desk. "The family's affairs occupy most of my time, I'm afraid." The statement was true, but not the gesture and its implications. He spent no more time at Laclere Park than he did in London.

Of all his friends, Burchard was the most likely to become aware of the gaps. "I escape north frequently, to my own property there. I do not have to be a viscount then," he added, to cover that eventuality. "It is good of you to ride down and save me from being one this afternoon."

"I regret that this is not a social call. Let us walk outside, and I will explain."

Curious, Vergil accompanied him out the drive. Adrian led him to the spot where another lane broke off to circle the property. There, in the shade of a tree, a carriage waited.

A graying man with a prominent hooked nose sat inside it.

Vergil pulled Adrian aside. "You could have warned me that you brought Wellington with you."

The duke overheard. "I told him to bring you here without announcing my presence, and Burchard fulfills his missions to the letter," he said as he climbed out of the carriage.

"Your Grace honors us with this visit."

"This isn't a visit, which is why I had Burchard bring

you to me here. It is no insult to your sister, Laclere. I merely don't have the time today for drawing room chats." He gestured with his walking stick. "This appears a pleasant, shaded path. Let us take some exercise."

Vergil fell into step, with Adrian alongside. Adrian had become a protégé of Wellington's. The great man's patronage had secured a seat in the House of Commons for the Earl of Dincaster's third son.

The rhythmic fall of their boots beat out a few minutes of time. The duke did not even try to fill it with pleasantries.

"I have come to speak of a delicate matter," he finally said. "There is no good way to broach it, so I will be blunt. I have come to ask you about your brother's death. I am always curious when men accidentally inflict mortal pistol wounds on themselves. I am in a position to know that it is not an easy thing to do. I want to know if, in your brother's case, it was not an accident, but suicide."

Vergil gave Adrian a resentful look, only to have his friend subtly shake his head. The evidence that Adrian had not been disloyal or indiscreet checked the anger.

"Yes. Only the family and a few friends know."

"I appreciate your confidence in my discretion as well, but receiving confirmation of my suspicions is hardly good news. Tell me, did you never think it odd that we had two prominent suicides in the same week? Your brother's and Castlereagh's."

"My brother was prone to fits of deep melancholy. The Foreign Minister was deranged. It was a coincidence."

"Laclere, I am not convinced it was a coincidence. Is

there any chance that your brother was being black-mailed? Did you find any evidence of that? I ask because there is some indication that Castlereagh was."

"I thought that suspicion had been laid to rest. By you."

"Considering his position, I could hardly let it stand. The man was clearly delusional, so I gave it little credence. However, the last time I saw him he did say something to me about receiving a letter. He alluded to fears of exposure."

Exposure. Vergil suspected where this was going and he did not want to tread that path. "As you said, he was delusional."

Wellington paced five steps before he spoke again. "The letter writer claimed to have proof of certain criminal activity."

Vergil stopped, forcing Adrian and Wellington to as well. "And so, after months of mulling it over, that detail led you to see some connection to my brother?"

"Laclere, hear him out," Adrian said.

"I'll be damned if I will."

"I understand your anger, Laclere. I assure you that the only connection I saw was two suicides, one of which may have been the result of blackmail." Wellington's voice got stern. "I ask you again, do you have reason to think that your brother was being blackmailed too? Lest you be tempted to lie to protect his name, let me say that I think that others are being victimized now, that Lord Fairhall's hunting accident in May was not what it seemed, and that we will see more ruin and death if we do not get to the bottom of this."

The fury spun out of Vergil. It was not the Iron Duke's severe tone that caused that. He had been carrying this secret for almost a year, wondering if the pattern and connections that he suspected were his own delusions.

"Yes, I think that Milton was being blackmailed. I think that is why he killed himself."

"He left a letter. I found it in his papers, where he knew I would look after I took up the reins of the estate. It alluded to a betrayal, whether his or another's, I do not know. Mostly it spoke of the family, and how it would be better if he left the stage before we were ruined. I wanted to believe he meant the finances, which were in dire condition by then. However, I have wondered if his hand was forced."

They had sat down on a fallen tree while he told his story. Wellington drew pictures in the dirt with his walking stick as he listened.

"Let us assume that it was blackmail in both cases. Was the goal their deaths?" Adrian asked.

"That is the question, isn't it?" Wellington said.

"For my brother, it may have only been money. There would be no way for someone to know that he could not pay. Our financial condition was not obvious. He spent as if there were no problem."

"Normally, one would assume that a blackmailer only wants to bleed his victim. However, the timing—we have had evidence that there are radicals trying to assassinate members of the government and House of Lords. How much easier, and safer, to affect things this way."

"My brother was not prominent in the government."

"He had an interest in politics."

"A theoretical interest."

"A radical theoretical interest. It may have brought him into contact with men who espouse violence, and who would entangle him, and, through him, others," Wellington said. "He may have innocently communicated or associated with such men, only to have them use the connection against him later."

The comment hung in the air, begging a response. The duke had neatly articulated Vergil's own fears about the reasons for Milton's death.

"Did you find letters to indicate a friendship between your brother and the Foreign Minister?" Wellington asked.

"I did not look for any." It was a lie. A damn lie. He would not allow supposition to become fact so easily, however.

"Perhaps you should."

"I have been pursuing other directions. I do not think there is any direct connection between these deaths, except perhaps the same blackmailer. I am more interested in finding that man than in learning the sins he discovered."

"So that is why you have not been in London much, nor here," Adrian said. "Have you made any progress?"

"A little." Damn little, considering how much of his time and his life he had invested in the search.

"There is nothing that I can do in this, except observe

men's demeanors and wonder if they are worried," Wellington said. "I have reason to think that several are. It is a diabolical notion, that someone is ferreting out secrets and using them to intimidate or extort your friends. Or worse, that men are being pressed so much that they take their own lives to escape."

"And you, Burchard? What is your interest in this, or did you only come today to arrange a private meeting for His Grace?" Vergil asked.

Wellington answered as they all stood to make their way back to the hiding coach. "He is making some discreet enquiries for me regarding Lord Fairhall. Since you know him to be trustworthy, it is my hope that you will share anything that you learn with him so that we can resolve this quickly."

"Of course."

It was another bold lie. Adrian was a friend, and experienced in both enquiries and discretion, but Vergil had no intention of telling anyone what he learned if it would reflect badly on either Milton or the Duclairc family.

He suspected that the truth would, for all of the reasons he had carefully avoided discussing today.

chapter 5

D o you see what I mean?" Charlotte whispered.

She sat with Bianca in the drawing room while the house-party guests arrived.

Vergil stood by the mantel, chatting amiably with Fleur and her mother, Mrs. Monley. They had arrived just after midday, pulling up in a magnificent carriage.

"Nothing," Charlotte muttered, shaking her head. "No . . . well, I do not know what. Vergil may as well be talking to me, and Fleur to her father."

Sitting on Charlotte's other side, Diane St. John, one of the countess's dearest friends, patted Charlotte's hand. Her soulful eyes showed amusement as she glanced to the mantel. "I would not worry for your brother or Miss Monley. Things are not always what they appear to be in such matters. They look perfect together, don't they? A matched pair."

They did look well matched. Fleur was all grace and

elegance, tall and slender, alabaster-skinned and dark of hair. Ringlets falling from a little beribboned topknot framed her oval face, which possessed a rose of a mouth. She had struck Bianca as an intelligent, soft-spoken person whose deep brown eyes did not miss much.

Bianca experienced a vague disappointment that she could not instantly dislike Fleur, as well as an inexplicable pang of melancholy whenever she looked to the group by the hearth.

"I fear that Vergil is sacrificing himself for her fortune," Charlotte said. "He looks happy to see her, but considering that her family left London eight weeks ago and they have been apart all that time . . ."

"You do not know that," Mrs. St. John said. "Perhaps when he is not here or in London, he is visiting her sometimes."

"I think not. He goes to his manor in Lancashire, mostly. He has to tell his agents and Pen and the governess who comes to stay with me where he can be found. If it were anyone but Vergil, one might suspect that he visits a woman up there. Someone he loves but cannot marry."

Bianca snapped her head around and stared at Charlotte's wistful expression. "That is a scandalous thing to suggest."

"Such arrangements are very common, I have gathered. Pen has even suggested to me that I should expect my husband to form other friendships on occasion."

Mrs. St. John lowered her lids. "I think that too many

people have been very indiscreet when speaking around you, Charlotte."

Bianca noted that Mrs. St. John did not say that Charlotte was wrong, or that her ignorance had led her to misinterpret Penelope's instruction.

"It *would* explain a lot. *That,* for one thing." Charlotte nodded her head toward the mantel. "The delay in announcing a formal engagement for another. With her beauty and portion, she does not have to wait for him. The odd thing is that Fleur does not seem to mind how things stand. It is her mother who grows impatient."

Yes, the mother was growing impatient. The eyes of Mrs. Monley were the brightest pair by the fireplace. She followed her daughter's conversation with a lovely smile and a cocked head that set the feather in her silk, corded turban at an inquisitive angle.

"The evening promises to be full. You should retire and rest," a male voice said.

Bianca tore her attention from the mantel to see that Daniel St. John had joined them, and was addressing his wife. A handsome man who could quickly slip from passive coolness to intense attention, he now focused the latter on the subject of his interest.

"Daniel is very protective when I am in the family way," Diane confided to them with a smile. "After two children, you know I am not very frail, my dear."

"All the same, some quiet is in order." He held out his hand to escort her.

Bianca did not miss the look that passed between them. Warmth, humor, and total absorption flowed in that fleeting connection. It was as if years of memories colored how they saw each other, and enriched even this commonplace exchange.

She glanced back to the mantel, and noticed how the demeanor that Vergil and Fleur displayed contrasted with this other couple's. She comprehended Charlotte's comment in new ways. There need be no overt demonstration to show passion and affection. In silent ways that involved no physical contact, a man and a woman could be intimately connected.

Diane St. John accepted her husband's command and rose. "I suppose a short rest would be a good idea." Side by side, saying nothing, but speaking volumes, they strolled from the drawing room.

Activity in the hall heralded another carriage.

"Finally the last." Charlotte rose to her feet. "This must be Mrs. Gaston. She is one of Pen's friends and a great patroness of the arts. She stood by Pen when others forsook her after the separation. I think Pen invited her just for you, because of your singing."

Bianca and Charlotte followed Penelope and Vergil out to meet the new guest.

Mrs. Gaston had come in a large coach. Pen advanced with outstretched hands of welcome. "So good of you to make time for our little party."

Mrs. Gaston was a beautiful woman with a winning smile, high cheekbones, and coppery brown hair. She carried herself with prideful elegance, and wore a dress with an exotic pattern and a bonnet with extravagant feathers. "It is you who are good to give me a chance to escape the city for a few days. I fear, however, that I have committed a *faux pas* and must beg your indulgence for it."

"A *faux pas*? You? Never."

"Alas, yes. You see, I have brought a friend with me."

"I wrote that your friends were welcome."

"So you did. Normally I would have written to alert you all the same. This friend, however, arrived in town unexpectedly."

A footman reached through the open door of the coach. A gloved hand and a sleeve *en gigot* emerged. An elaborately coifed and hatted dark head ducked as the friend in question bent to step down.

"Maria," Pen cried, embracing the statuesque figure swathed in pale blue muslin. "No one said you were coming to visit this year. This is a wonderful surprise for me."

The woman's face was not beautiful, with its prominent features, but her manner possessed solid dignity and confidence. "It was an impetuous decision on my part, *cara mia*. Milan is horrible with heat, my musicians are acting like spoiled children, and the tenor for the next production is an arrogant young idiot who will not take direction. I simply left them all. Let them see how they fare without Catalani."

"Oh, my, what fun," Charlotte whispered to Bianca. "Do you know who that is?"

Bianca knew. For years the preeminent opera singer in England, Maria Catalani had returned to Italy six years ago and now managed an opera company in Milan.

What a wonderful twist of luck. With Mrs. Gaston

and Catalani here, this house party promised to be vastly more interesting than she had expected.

Vergil stepped forward to greet Catalani, and kissed her hand smoothly. She said something quietly that brought a smile to his face.

If the unexpected visit of an opera singer to Laclere Park distressed him, he did not show it. Probably he would take the matter up with Penelope later.

Penelope brought the newcomers toward the house. Bianca's knees wobbled with excitement.

"This must be Charlotte. A young woman now, and so lovely," Catalani said. "Are you out yet?"

"Next year," Pen explained. "Vergil does not approve of the young age some girls come out these days."

Catalani glanced back at the trailing viscount and her lips pursed with humor. "A good ploy, and it will be very effective. Let them wait for such a diamond. You will be the sensation of the season, Charlotte. I predict that your brothers will need four extra footmen just to guard the garden walls."

Pen drew Catalani toward Bianca. "This is Bianca Kenwood, from Baltimore. She is Vergil's ward."

"I have never had the pleasure of visiting your country. We will be sure to talk. I have many questions for you."

"And I for you. I will be visiting Italy very soon."

"You plan a grand tour for your sister and ward, Lord Laclere?" Catalani asked while Pen guided her into the house. "Ten extra footmen, then, if you send such beauties to my country."

Bianca scooted to catch up with Charlotte, ecstatic by

the turn of events. This party promised to be the high-light of her entire stay in England.

"That is all of them for today," Charlotte explained. "Pen said that Mr. Witherby wrote that he would arrive tomorrow morning. Let us go rest before dinner."

Bianca refused to do so unless it became clear that Catalani herself would retire. She waited until the stately Catalani floated up the stairs with Penelope beside her.

She found herself standing alone in the empty entrance hall, knowing it would be impossible to rest now. Looking for some way to relieve her itching excitement, she went into the library, found the volume of Shelley's poems that she had been reading, and tucked herself into the corner of a divan facing a far window.

This was her favorite spot for reading, especially in the afternoons. Shaded light flooded in the window and the breeze was divine. No one could see her here unless they walked around the divan. It had become one of her little nooks of privacy.

Bootsteps entered the room. She stretched and turned to see who had come. Dante spotted her and walked over, carrying his hat and riding whip. He threw himself onto a chair, facing her, and stretched out his booted legs.

"They are all here?" He had disappeared from the house after Fleur's arrival.

"All but Mr. Witherby."

"I am surprised he is delayed. I would expect him to take advantage of every moment with my sister."

"Charlotte?"

"Pen. He has become a special friend to her during the

last year. Or at least he thinks that he has. Don't know Pen's idea of it, although she appears to welcome his company. I'm sure that is why she has invited him, even though he is an old friend of Vergil's as well."

The phrase "special friend" alluded to more than companionship. Dante often lapsed into speaking to her in this familiar manner, as if they shared some secret understanding of the world. His conspiratorial tones implied a type of intimacy.

He lounged casually, looking at her from beneath thick lashes in a way that always made her uncomfortable. They were always alone when he looked at her like that.

"Maria Catalani recently arrived with Mrs. Gaston. It was a surprise for everyone," she said.

That caused his attention to sharpen. "Mrs. Gaston is here? I should have asked Pen who was attending before agreeing to stay myself."

"You do not care for her?"

"Through sheer persistence she has managed to insert herself into many circles. She sees herself as a great patroness of artists, and wants others to know how she advances careers."

"Does she? Advance careers?"

He shrugged. "I wouldn't know. Pen's artistic circles do not interest me much, and that seems to be what we have here. Mrs. Gaston and Catalani, you say. Lord Calne is another patron of the arts. Cornell Witherby will be good company, at least, although with the others here he will probably only talk about his poetry. Hopefully Vergil will distract him from that."

"Do you think that Vergil will allow Catalani to stay?"

"Why wouldn't he?"

"I thought that, perhaps, with Fleur here and Charlotte and..."

Her allusion amused him. "This is Pen's party, and my brother knew what that would mean. Vergil may be a saint, but he is never rude. Besides, fame like Catalani's has a way of obscuring the means by which it is achieved." He rose. "I think that I will go for a walk. I would be honored if you joined me. I will show you the ruins."

Bianca had already found the ruins of Laclere Park's medieval keep, and she did not want to visit them alone with a rake. Especially one who looked down at her with the light currently shining in Dante's eyes.

"Thank you, but I think that I will continue reading my book for a while longer."

A subtle annoyance altered his expression. To her astonishment, he reached out and stroked one finger along her jawline. "You do not have to be afraid of me, Bianca."

She angled away from his touch. "Your brother said that it is not customary to address women in such a familiar way here."

"I am not my brother."

No, he was not. The last week had been full of this young man's attention. She had tried to discourage him. Unsuccessfully, so it appeared.

His hand touched her again, cupping her chin. Her eyes widened in disbelief when he tilted her head up, bent, and kissed her lips. It happened so quickly that shock left her immobile.

He misunderstood. Sliding down beside her, he deepened the kiss and moved to embrace her.

She broke away and made it to the window with a staggering lunge. Furious with embarrassment, she faced him down. "Do not dare do that again."

He rose. "My apologies. I should have asked your permission first."

"You would not have received it."

"I think I would have."

"You misunderstand our friendship."

"I do not think so. You are fearful and confused, and that is appropriate in one so innocent. I will not kiss you again without your permission, but when I ask, you will give it."

She groped for a scathing response. He smiled in an insufferably self-confident way and walked out.

She sank back into the divan, pulled up her legs, and huddled in its corner. What had given this rake the idea that she would welcome such a thing? Had he learned about her performances in London? For all she knew, he had attended one.

Just her luck that the wrong brother had concluded that she was a little wild, and careless about proprieties.

"Hiding from the duties of state?" Dante asked as he strolled into the study where Vergil read his correspondence.

"Resting my face before I must smile so long my lips crack."

"It shouldn't be too bad. She invited Witherby and St. John so you would be diverted."

Vergil was grateful that Pen had invited Daniel and Diane St. John. He had not seen them for months. They were Pen's friends too. She had befriended Diane St. John when the young woman first came to London, and had played a role in the dramatic events that had led to Diane's marriage to the shipping magnate.

As for Witherby, he suspected that Pen had offered that invitation for reasons other than her brother's diversion.

Dante lounged against the window frame and absently dropped the lead ball onto the ramps of its toy. "Fleur is looking lovely as always. Should we expect an announcement some night after dinner?"

"I do not think so."

"It is past time, Verg."

"Of all the people to lecture me, Dante, you are the last. My responsibilities to the living members of this family far outweigh any to those of the future."

"Are you saying that we are so expensive that you cannot afford a wife?"

"I am saying that any woman who marries me will have certain expectations that I cannot fulfill at this time. Which brings us to the matter of your own marriage, which will significantly relieve the financial burden. I turn the question back to you. Should we plan an announcement? I recall a confident young blood saying smugly that a week should do it."

"Damn it, these things take time. Furthermore, she is . . . confusing."

He pulled a chair over to the desk and sat flush along its other side, his arm resting on its edge, propping up his head, his booted legs crossed. It was the pose of Dante settling in for a "man to man."

Since the topic of conversation was Bianca Kenwood, Vergil wished that he could be spared any confidences. Bianca continuously intruded on his thoughts, and last night, after his return to Laclere Park, he had found himself loitering in the drawing room with the ladies until she retired.

"I often think that I have gained some ground, only to find it is an illusion. She appears very warm one morning, but that afternoon I hear her being just as warm with a servant. She turns those big blue eyes on me and I think I should propose then and there, only to have her ignore me for the next hour. Sometimes I think that I am dealing with a girl so ignorant that she does not even notice my interest, and other times . . ."

"Other times?"

"Sometimes I wonder if she is far from ignorant and leading me in a fine dance. Forgive me, but we are speaking frankly here."

"*You* certainly are."

"I wonder if she is being deliberately intriguing. Elusive in a calculating way."

"It sounds more to me that you are failing and looking to blame her for it."

"Perhaps. But there is something about her, indefinable . . . an air, a scent, I don't know. I look at her and see a springlike innocence, and then all of a sudden she will look back and I find myself thinking that she would make a splendid mistress. It is a confusing and compelling combination."

So Dante had finally sensed what Vergil had that first night in the gaming hall, and too often since. "I trust not too compelling."

"Of course not. But it puts one off one's game. There is an art to this, and knowing the woman is essential."

"I am always grateful for your instruction on these matters, Dante, but let us get to the point. If you proposed tomorrow, do you think that she would accept?"

"Damned if I know."

Which meant probably not. "Does she even know that you are interested? She might interpret your attention as mere friendship, a helping hand in a strange country."

"She knows now."

"What is that supposed to mean?"

"I just saw her in the library."

"You declared your intentions?"

Dante looked away and Vergil instantly knew that the interest had been articulated with actions, not words. He almost reached across the desk to strangle him. "Let me rephrase that. Does she know that your intentions are honorable?"

"What else could they be? She is your ward."

Vergil rubbed between his eyebrows. "Well, let us just suppose that she has heard about you—"

"From whom? Pen would hardly go telling tales."

"From anyone else. A servant. Her maid, Jane. Nigel Kenwood."

"She hasn't seen Nigel all week but once, when Pen went to call on him, and they weren't alone, so he could not—"

"From *whomever,* Dante. Suppose someone has told her. If you did not express honorable intentions, she may think that you pursue her for other reasons."

Dante straightened. "If so, I am insulted."

"All the same—"

"I am not a scoundrel."

"I recommend that you clarify things. If she has misunderstood, she will only avoid you now."

Dante rose and paced back to the window. "Of course, you are right. However, if I propose and she turns me down, the game is up. Explaining my intentions, short of a proposal, does the same thing. Girls get these notions, and a man who pursues despite them looks a fool. I sat there in the library and I found myself wondering, what if it isn't contradictory?"

"You are not making much sense."

"What if she is in fact innocent, but has the other inside her? The man who tapped it would be in a very strong position with her. Talk about an inside track, why—"

"No."

"I am not talking about anything really dishonorable, Vergil. Just a mild dalliance that would save a lot of time."

"You will do nothing that even remotely compromises her."

"You are being impractical and too concerned with proprieties. This was your idea, remember? If I did compromise her, marriage would be inevitable."

It was not his much-vaunted sense of propriety that rebelled against Dante's insinuations, but something more visceral, having to do with a relentless simmer and the scent of lavender and a melodic voice that had sung in his memory during a week of travel and duties. Still, being a saint had its uses. He would not abort these arrangements, but he would not allow Dante to trap her.

"Winning a woman's honest affection may seem a long, tedious effort to a man accustomed to exploiting quick passion, Dante, but if you intend to have her, that is how you will have to do it."

"At least someone in this family has some passion, damn it. Between you and Milton . . ."

At their brother's name, Vergil's whole body tightened. "I would think that you would be very careful not to mention Milton and your reckless appetites in the same breath."

Dante's face darkened with resentment. "You still blame me for something I could not foresee."

"You are wrong. I do not blame you. There was no way for you to know what he intended to do. But do not pull him into these discussions. Insult me as cold, if you want, but leave our brother and his memory out of this. All of that has nothing to do with Miss Kenwood and your behavior toward her."

"Ah, yes, the lovely Bianca. You are drawing some fine lines in your concern for her, Verg. Your protection is oddly selective and shortsighted. You will not have your ward compromised, but you would tie her for life to a man whom you despise."

His words found their mark for reasons Dante would never know. "I do not despise you."

"Do you not? You may not blame me, but you have never forgiven me."

Vergil saw pain in the beautiful face that never showed a care. He should have been more perceptive to the guilt that Milton's death must have caused Dante. Odd that the discussion of a girl who had nothing to do with that episode was drawing this out.

"I may criticize how you live your life, but it does not reflect my feelings about the role you inadvertently played in the disaster last year. You do not need forgiveness for that, Dante. Ignorance is not a damnable offense. If I never spoke of this with you before, it was not because of blame, but only because I do not seek reminders of it. Perhaps my reticence on the subject has not been fair to you, however."

Dante's face was a visage of strained composure, but his eyes glowed. "I was here. I dined with him. I should have seen—"

"I am grateful that you were with him during his last hour. I think that he was too."

The air in the room flowed heavily with the raw intimacy born of unanticipated frankness. An invisible barrier had fallen that Vergil had never realized existed. A chasm dug since the crisis of Milton's death had unexpectedly been breached, and all because of the conflicting emotions created by Bianca Kenwood's presence in this household.

He looked at his younger brother with new eyes, and saw a depth carefully obscured by the rake's carefree persona. *She could do worse.*

Dante smiled wryly and sauntered to the door. "I'll do it your way, Verg. Should be interesting, trying to inspire a chaste affection with only intimations of something more later. Unfairly limits me, though. Can't play my best card. After all, I have nothing to offer the girl except pleasure."

An hour ago, Vergil would have agreed.

chapter 6

Vergil was the first to the breakfast room the next morning. He wanted to get a ride in before his guests roused themselves.

He had just settled down to his plate when a movement at the window caught his eye. Green and gold flashed by as a blond head and trim figure disappeared behind some bushes.

Bianca Kenwood had risen with the dawn again.

He turned from the window with annoyance. Dante had said that she had only seen Nigel Kenwood once, but Dante wouldn't know about Bianca's early wanderings. The possibility existed that she and Nigel had been meeting secretly for over a week.

He drew a mental curtain in front of the image forming in his mind. There was no evidence that she contrived assignations with her cousin. All the same, whatever her purpose, she had blithely walked into the park at dawn despite the danger she had faced from poachers that day on her horse. That episode would have kept a normal young woman fearful of venturing forth unless half an army accompanied her.

But then, she was not a normal young woman.

Foregoing his meal, he slipped out into the garden and crossed to the path she had been walking.

"Laclere."

Vergil pivoted at the call. Cornell Witherby strode toward him along the lane that led from the stables.

Down the path, gold and green got swallowed by the forest.

"Don't tell me that you rode through the night, Witherby." Vergil noted that the new arrival was well turned out in brown riding coat and fawn trousers. The boots looked new and the sandy locks visible beneath Witherby's hat appeared newly styled.

Witherby looked very dashing and in damnable good humor.

"I rode down most of the way yesterday afternoon, and stayed over at an inn."

"Eager, were you?"

"The city has gotten raucous the last few days. Demonstrations daily. Lots of arrests. Some country air will do me good. The muse gets petulant if there are such distractions."

"I trust that you will not be distracted here. There is breakfast waiting, but you must feed your muse in isolation. My sister has not risen yet to do the hostess duties."

Witherby smiled vaguely at this reference to Penelope.

He knew that Vergil knew what was up, and Vergil knew he knew, but a man did not discuss another's pursuit of his married sister, even if they were old friends.

"You will be happy to know that the gathering is artistic, as one would expect from Pen," Vergil said.

"The countess's parties are always delightful. I expect this one to surpass all others."

Vergil decided not to speculate on just how much delight Witherby might be anticipating. A big, quiet country house offered all sorts of opportunities for privacy.

He firmly shut contemplation of that out of his mind.

"You are dressed for riding," Witherby observed. "I am keeping you."

"A walk first, then a ride. Go and settle yourself as best you can. St. John is here, by the way, and he normally comes down early, too, so you should not be bored too long."

With a happy, jaunty stride, Witherby aimed for the house. Vergil waited until he was out of sight, then turned and headed after Bianca.

When she came into view, he slowed so that he would trail behind her.

He followed out of concern for her safety, but admitted that he also wanted to determine whether Nigel waited somewhere up ahead.

A mile into the trees she turned onto a western path. He realized that she headed toward the ruins. Not a good sign. The medieval castle provided an ideal spot for couples to meet.

She was nowhere in view when he stepped into the

high grass around the remains of Laclere Park's early fortifications. The keep survived as half a shell, and only one section of the old battlements endured, with the wall down in places and crumbling in others. Large stones scattered the overgrown clearing that had once served as the bailey. Of the whole structure, only a single, square wall tower still stood in reasonably safe condition.

Memories of childhood play tugged nostalgically, reminding him of the easy bond that he had once shared with Dante, and which secrets and neglect had almost destroyed. He scanned for signs of Miss Kenwood.

Suddenly a muffled, sweet sound floated through the morning silence. It rose and lowered like a gentle wave on the breeze, sending eddies out to surround him. He followed it to its source in the square tower and stepped through the stone threshold.

Sound submerged him, pitching off the walls and vaults. Above in the guards' chamber, Miss Kenwood practiced her scales, her voice gaining volume with each recurrent rise. He paused and listened to the repetitious climb of an instrument being tuned and warmed.

She stopped and he heard her speak. To Nigel? The man might use her music to entice her here. If so, she was in no immediate danger. He doubted that she would set aside her primary passion in order to explore other ones right now.

The sound broke again, pouring down the stairs. Not scales now, but a Rossini aria.

The melody washed through him. Precise and disciplined, like a bird's elaborately textured song, it drenched the mind and flooded the heart and churned indefinable sentiments the way the best music always did. The sensual undertones in her voice inundated a hidden reservoir that he had been struggling to keep dammed.

Almost involuntarily, his legs took him up the dark stairway toward the siren who unknowingly lured him toward a forbidden shore.

She stood alone in the chamber, her back to him, framed by the lines of walls tapering up to the stone vaulted ceiling. No Nigel. No one at all. She must have been speaking to herself.

He rested his shoulder against the portal's frame, to watch and listen. He wished that he could see her face, but his memory provided the radiant expression that he had witnessed that day when she performed in the music room.

He did not fight his reactions. He would have been incapable of doing so even if he sought to. Instead he let her notes raise a tide that submerged everything in the world except her pure passion and his own astonished desire.

It felt so good. Transporting. Glorious. Her voice took over her body and dissolved its substance until only the singing existed. The stones enriched the timbre like no other room ever had. She wished that she could bring Catalani here.

It ended too soon, and she regretfully held the last note longer than the score required. It hung above her, dripping like a single bud's nectar into her exposed spirit.

And then it was over, leaving her spent and a little melancholy.

She abruptly sensed that she was not alone. Fearing that Dante had followed her, she turned with misgivings.

The viscount leaned casually against the portal opening, arms crossed over chest, watching her. He looked very handsome there, and somewhat intense despite his nonchalant pose.

"Did you follow me here, Uncle Vergil? To spy on me?"

"I thought of it as protecting you, but yes, I followed."

"Surely I am safe at Laclere Park. Your bold poachers must have moved on or switched to traps. There have been no firearms shot this last week."

"If you know that, you must come here often. Always to sing?"

The chamber had a window, no more than an arrow slit. She moved toward it, away from him. The stones heightened nuances in his tone that made her cautious. His eyes carried a hooded expression that she could not read. His presence struck her as dangerous. A ridiculous reaction to have, but she could not shake it.

She examined the view, avoiding his fixed regard. "I do not accept the situation that makes you think that you have a right to quiz me. Yes, I come here often, usually in the morning like this. I found this tower one day while riding. And yes, I come to sing."

"Alone?"

She looked back over her shoulder. "You thought perhaps I arranged assignations here with Nigel? You followed to protect me from any improper intentions?" The notion made her want to giggle. Such careful protection of her virtue on the grounds, while his own brother accosted her in the library. "You missed your ride to no purpose. The convenience of this tower for such meetings never occurred to me. I shall have to keep it in mind for the future."

"I doubt that you will. You would not have time to practice then. I never noticed before, but this chamber affects sound the way the ancient Norman churches do. Whatever your cousin's potential attraction, these stones hold more."

"Perhaps he will come to listen. As you did."

He pushed away from the wall with a little smile. "If so, you will definitely need protection."

He paced casually toward her. She found herself edging away. Silly, really, but there was something different about him today. A compelling something, but also disconcerting.

"Pen announced that you will sing this evening. Are you practicing for your performance, to be sure that you are in top form for Catalani?"

"Yes."

"You spoke at length with her last night. Quite a *tête-à-tête*. I assume that you informed her of your plans."

"Do not worry that I embarrassed you and Pen. No one else heard me and I think she knows the necessity of discretion with a viscount's guests."

He kept moving, looking around the chamber as if he had not been here in a long time. She felt a continued compulsion to stroll away.

"What did Catalani advise?"

"She agreed with me, that if I want the best training I must go to Italy, or bring one of their premier voice masters here. Until then, she gave me the name of a tutor who might work with me in London. She recommended a Signore Bardi, who serves as *bel canto* master to some of the best singers in London."

"No other advice? I would not have expected Catalani to be so reserved."

"She asked if I understood the life, what it would entail."

"Do you?"

"I know about the hard work. The travel. The need to perform despite exhaustion and illness."

"That is not what she meant."

A flush warmed her face. "I *know* what she meant."

"I do not think that you do. Not really. I doubt that you have any idea of what it means to be someone whom respectable women will not have as a friend. This opera singer may visit houses like this one, but there is only one Catalani. It will not be thus for you. There will be no Aunt Edith in England or Italy to blunt the scorn."

Annoyance made her stand her ground. "I know what so-called decent people think about such women. I saw very decent men indeed approach my mother at times. As I grew older I understood what they wanted. I will deal with them as she did. Am I supposed to forego something important to me, *essential* to me, because of unfounded prejudices?"

He kept walking. Circling, circling. If he were not a

citadel of propriety, if his demeanor were not so casual, she might succumb to the sensation that she was being stalked. His height kept him to the center of the chamber, and the circle seemed a rather small one now that she stood in its center.

"The prejudices are well-founded for most actresses and singers," he said, as if discussing women of ill repute were a perfectly acceptable topic.

"The life is an insecure one, and I expect many performers need to accept the protection offered to them."

"You think that it is desperation that makes such women into mistresses and courtesans, and that your inheritance will spare you? Your judgment is harsher than mine. I assume that it is loneliness. A decent marriage is almost impossible. There are wastrels who will offer, but none whom you will want."

This indelicate conversation had suddenly become personal. "I know that too. Some things are worth sacrifices, however."

"A lifetime of them? You think so now, but in ten years? Fifteen? No marriage, no children, no home. I find it more sad than scandalous that for most of these women the day comes when someone offers the semblance of love and they take it. No matter what their resolve when they start, after a period of virtuous, unnatural isolation, the choice is probably inevitable."

"How dare you presume to predict such a bleak and sordid future for me. You are very cynical to contend that if I pursue my singing my fall is preordained. Not that I can see why it should make any difference to you."

His pacing stopped, leaving him several feet away. "I am responsible for you."

"So you interfere with my life, to protect me from myself. For all of ten months."

"Longer, if I can find the way."

Longer! "Don't you dare try to manipulate further obstacles. I will not tolerate it."

"Your resolve leaves me little choice. You may think that you can live like a nun, but I doubt that you have it in you to do so indefinitely."

"Your implication is insulting and scandalous."

"Not insulting at all. And scandalous only if you end up as some man's mistress instead of some man's wife."

"You have crossed a line, sir. It is improper for you to speak with me like this, even if you are my guardian."

He cocked his head and a wry little smile flickered. "I have crossed a line, haven't I? Rather decidedly. I astonish myself."

He glanced around as if suddenly realizing where they were. "Are you finished, or did you intend to practice further?"

"I want to rehearse the aria once more. I will return to the house shortly."

"I will wait and escort you back."

He settled against the wall again, in a pose of relaxed patience. She experienced a peculiar shyness.

She began to turn away, but he shook his head. "If you cannot practice with one man watching, how can you perform in front of an opera house full of them?"

Because that is different. An irrational response, but it *was* different. The focus of two eyes, *these eyes,* discomforted her more than a sea of faces. The attention of one person, *this person,* unsettled her more than a packed music hall. If even one other body were present, it would dilute the singular connection. After all, he had been present in the music room and she had not reacted this way.

She averted her gaze and tried to erase the awareness of him, but it didn't really work. The aria started weakly, as if her breath dodged an obstruction in its path to her throat. The blockage was her swelled heart pounding nervously. Stupid. *Stupid.* She located some composure within resentment at his intrusion, and hit her stride.

The music took care of the rest. Concentration on technique and expression absorbed her. The exhilaration transported her. It was not like the last time, however. Another spirit joined her on the journey, following, crowding, encompassing. As the song progressed, she could not resist looking at him. He waited with a detached manner, looking down, a man courteously biding his time before moving on to important things.

He sensed her attention. His gaze rose and met hers. She almost faltered into abrupt silence. His eyes were more startling than usual. Their expression glowed deeply warm, subtly savage, and definitely male. Not the least avuncular or aloof, and hardly protective.

Goodness, had her singing done *that*?

Despite her startled dismay, an amazing thrill streaked through her. Instead of stumbling, her voice soared. She could not look away and the aria created a provocative union between them. Spiritual. Sensual. Almost erotic.

Perplexed alarm shook her, even while a heady sensation of power grew. The euphoria transformed into something undeniably physical within their mesmerizing link.

She could not have ended it even if she wanted to. Unknown emotions propelled her voice with new passions. She closed her eyes at the end, as much to contain the sensations as to savor the finale. The stones held the last sounds like a silent echo for a long heartbeat.

She did not want to open her eyes. Something had happened here that she did not want to acknowledge, something wordless and touchless, but more improper than Dante's kiss. He should have known better. She should have stopped it. She did not want to look at him until this terrible breathlessness abated.

A breeze of warmth caused her to open her lids a slit and see polished boots very close to her skirt. His fine, strong hand took hers and raised it to his lips for a fleeting kiss. "Your singing is nothing short of magnificent, Miss Kenwood. Catalani should be suitably impressed this evening."

She had to look then. He gestured formally toward the stairs. His expression had resumed its normal restraint and hauteur, but the other still shadowed it, as if the drape of reserve he had drawn was translucent.

He led the way, handing her down the winding stones, a careful representation of detached, courteous concern. As they strolled along the wall toward the path, he paused and looked up at the battlements.

"It is very picturesque," she said, hoping small talk would vanquish the odd mood throbbing between them.

"My father considered restoring and rebuilding it. Just as well he chose to remodel the house instead. This would have cost three fortunes instead of one, and resulted in a dwelling barely habitable."

"I think that it is nicer as it is, with bits and pieces of history breaking through the brush. It would look a little silly all repaired and newly mortared."

"We used to play here as children. Dante and I were the knights, and we pressed Pen into playing the lady imprisoned by her evil guardian." A broad smile broke as soon as he said it. "You can have that role now."

The little argument that he invited might help diminish how conscious she was of him standing beside her, but she simply could not pick up the cue.

"Didn't your older brother join your play too?"

"When we were very young he did. Then he outgrew us, I suppose." His gaze on the battlements turned reflective. "As he got older he retreated into his own interests, and his own mind. By the time he went to university, he was a stranger."

"Is that why you want to read his letters and such now? To get to know him in ways he did not permit in life?"

His head snapped around and he gave her a very odd look, as if she had surprised him. "I suppose so, in part."

His attention called forth the emotions from the tower again. She forced her own gaze away, up the wall. "I would like to explore the keep one day."

"I do not advise it. It has been unsafe for years. The wall

walk too. Not all of these stones scattering the ground were here when I was a boy."

As if to emphasize his point, a fist-sized stone plummeted to the earth, landing at their feet. Vergil frowned up, his eyes scanning the battlements. Bianca turned to scoot away.

An ominous scraping sounded above. Another stone fell, hitting her shoulder.

Suddenly everything blurred. He grabbed her arm and swung her around, smacking her against the wall. She found herself wedged between unyielding stone and a hard body, her shoulders embraced by covering arms, her face tucked against his neck while his head pressed down on hers. Her sight had barely righted itself when a lethal avalanche of large rocks fell right beside them, one of them bouncing above their heads before grazing along Vergil's back.

She stared aghast at the shower of death and cringed inside her haven. It seemed forever before the scrapes and rumbling stopped.

Vergil raised his head to examine the upper wall. "A whole machicolation came down."

"An apt lesson to give these ruins wide berth in the future. Who would expect peaceful Laclere Park to be so dangerous?"

She spoke nervously into his starched cravat. The blue superfine of his coat caressed her cheek and her fingers rested on the silk embroidered roses of his gray waistcoat. The shock had made her extra alert and a part of her mind absurdly contemplated the varied textures of his garments. And the blissful protection of his arms. And his masculine scent. "Could my singing have done this?"

"It was most likely gravity finishing off what time began. Still, the odds of witnessing such a thing are rare. It is possible that your voice added a push." He angled his head down to see her face. "Were you injured?"

"I do not think so."

One hand slid along her back to gently press her shoulder. "Does that hurt?"

"It is a little sore. I will probably only have a bruise."

He had not released her. One arm still circled her and his other hand rested carefully on her arm below the injured shoulder. The cocoon of his strength felt very reassuring.

"That is much what you said after the horse threw you. You are supposed to swoon when faced with such danger."

She knew that he referred not to rocks and poachers, but to the physical closeness both episodes had fostered.

His warning sounded as clearly as a horn blowing in her ear. She could not heed it. His masculinity made her feel small and helpless in a sinfully delicious way.

She looked up into his deliberating eyes. "I never swoon."

His expression from the stone chamber returned, filling her with wonderful flutters. The hand on her arm slid down to her elbow, then up again. "Do you not? Never?"

The slow caress glided again. Its gentle friction created a rippling sensation. Inside her. All through her. That aria had left her vulnerable, and fear had stripped her of normal restraint. She should say something arch to end this little game, but she only wanted those fingers to glide again.

"Never."

"Every girl should swoon at least once."

That hand caressed up, not down. A slowly trailing touch. Gently over her shoulder, warmly up her neck, softly over her cheek, firmly into her hair.

She almost *did* swoon when his head angled and his lips met hers.

Warm lips. Firm and controlling like everything about him. Deliberate. Restrained but determined. He brushed her mouth with caresses before playing more seductively. Subtle nips made her lower lip pulse and quiver. Devilish tongue flicks sent scattered prickles through her face and neck. A sensitivity awoke in her breasts and she instinctively embraced him, searching for the contact that their heavy tenderness craved.

He pulled her closer and looked down in a tense, appraising way. A sigh escaped her throat with the pressure of his chest. Kissing her with fierce capitulation, he dragged her back through the threshold of the tower, into the mottled light and cool stones.

He leaned back on the wall and pulled her against his length and into a whirlwind. His arms surrounded and dominated, holding her firmly to his body and the ravishments of his mouth. Fevered kisses assaulted her neck and ears, arousing a frenzied, insistent yearning. His lips seduced hers open for an internal probing of shocking intimacy. She held on to him and submitted, dizzy with amazing sensations, soaring helplessly into a blurred euphoria.

It felt so good. Glorious. Transcendent. The exaltation of her singing made physical. The power and potential of that last aria given substance.

Here. Now. Yes. With an inaudible voice her blood pounded demands between her gasps. *Here. Now. Perfect.* Shocking pulses in her body joined the chant. Even her mind, the part that should know better, echoed a litany of scandalous urgings. Her hands shamelessly slid beneath his coat to caress and clutch his sides and back.

Something tensed within him. She felt a dangerous change and knew that her gesture had been an affirmation of some sort. His arms moved in possessive caresses and her arched body stretched in immodest reply. His hands explored for her through the petticoats and stays. His commanding passion and where it ventured should frighten her, but her excitement only allowed resentment that the layers of cloth interfered and separated and inhibited.

Yes. I want . . . I want . . . She did not know what. A crying hunger pulsed through her, with sources and destinations she did not understand. *Closer. More. I want . . .*

As if he heard her silent begging, his hand slid to her waist. Thumb on midriff and fingers on back, he caressed up the sash of her gown. Begging anticipation reduced her breath to a series of sharp inhales. A surprisingly gentle kiss accompanied the rise of his hand to her breast.

Oh . . . Oh. The luscious feelings aroused by his touch stunned her. The sensations streaked and flowed, joining those being stimulated by his inflaming kisses on her neck and his mind-obscuring invasions of her mouth. He gave and took pleasure at will and her limp, overwhelmed body could only accept and submit, too ignorant to offer more than acquiescence to a fervor that both liberated and subjugated.

Fingers playing at nipples grown hard and needful . . . *yes* . . . Searching now at the frill of her neckline . . . *please* . . . Sliding beneath fabric to explore the new wildness of skin on skin . . . *Ah, yes* . . . Arms pulling closer, harder, and a knee pressing between petticoats and skirt, the pressure disgracefully welcome . . . *oh my . . . heavens* . . . Dress loosening and puffed sleeve sliding and her naked breast being cupped up to a dark, lowering head . . . *oh* . . . Gently sucking lips . . . *oh* . . . Wickedly titillating licks . . . *OH* . . . Exquisite streams of pleasure descending, filling, demanding . . . *YES* . . .

. . . a movement, a soft crunching, echoing into the stones.

He straightened abruptly, crushing her exposure into the protection of his chest, shielding her with surrounding arms while he listened. The possible meaning of those sounds crashed through her dazed senses, obliterating the dreamy sensual world and plunking her mercilessly back into reality.

"Is someone . . . ?" she whispered, gritting her teeth against the slow unwinding of her physical excitement. She could still hear something, more of a vibration carried through the wall than an actual sound. It intruded like an invasion between the pounding of their hearts.

He pulled up the band of her chemise and the shoulder of her dress, then set her away from him. "Stay here."

He strode out of the tower. She grappled frantically with her garments, managing somehow to refasten the dress, experiencing the stark guilt of a criminal caught in the act. A pit opened in her heart.

If they had been seen, it would be disastrous.

She could hear him outside, walking around. The pit widened until it became a sick, hollow void. The full impact of her behavior hit her. This had been madness. She had been shameless. They didn't even like each other.

She heard him returning and braced herself.

He appeared in the threshold, a lean dark form surrounded by light. She could not see his face well.

"If someone was here, they are gone. It may have just been an animal."

She prayed so, and hoped if someone had come from the house to explore the keep, that they had not peered inside the tower portal.

He held out his hand in a gesture commanding her forth. Wondering what women were supposed to say and do after such brazen behavior, and feeling almost nauseous with confusion and embarrassment, she emerged into the morning. They started back to the house.

He didn't say a word. It was the longest mile that she had ever walked in her life.

She tried to find consolation in the notion that she had proven she was too dangerous to keep around Charlotte, but the idea of leaving Laclere Park unaccountably increased her dismay.

He stopped in the trees near the stable.

"I find that words fail me, Miss Kenwood. My behavior has been abominable, and an apology is not sufficient. I promise that I am not in the habit of importuning young women like that. I have no explanation except that I am clearly not myself this morning."

Aren't you? What had occurred suddenly did not impress her as entirely surprising from this man. It struck her as a natural extension of his demeanor, something controlled but always there, like a subcurrent beneath the calm, a depth one sensed but never saw and couldn't name. It had produced a tension between them from the start, like a dangerous undertow. She had felt its effects, but until today she had not understood them.

He still looked down the path, not quite facing her. His words blamed himself, but she wondered what he really thought. That he had proven she could not live like a nun? That she had the nature of a courtesan and should be permitted the ruination which she sought? "Importune" did not really describe what had occurred and they both knew it.

"I was not harmed."

"If we were seen, you most definitely were."

"I do not think that we were seen. We would have noticed someone at the portal."

"If you are right, that only avoids the worst of the potential repercussions. It does not negate the fact that my actions were inexcusable and dishonorable, most significantly because I am responsible for you. I have compromised you, whether anyone else knows it or not. If you require it, I will do the right thing by you."

"The right thing? You mean . . . Oh, no, that is an absurd idea."

"It certainly promises to be a complicated one, what with . . . well, complicated. All the same . . ."

"Let us not get carried away by your sense of propriety and duty, please. I do not feel compromised or ruined."

She received a sharp look for that. "Do you not? You are a remarkably composed young woman."

So, there it was. The insinuation of unseemly compliance on her part. Of encouragement, if one wanted to face it frankly. That look and question revealed his mind and she was hard-pressed to blame him, considering all those ambiguities she had deliberately dropped regarding her experience.

"Let us say that I do not feel compromised enough to require such an extreme measure as marriage in order to be redeemed. Perhaps we should merely forget about this."

"Your equanimity impresses me. I should be grateful that you prove so forgiving."

She didn't feel at all forgiving. She felt shattered, devastated . . . disappointed. To descend from such glory to this formal discussion on how to expiate that potent sharing . . . It made her want to hurt him, hit him, strike a blow that would defeat his cool deliberations on how to rectify their imprudence.

"I simply do not choose to complicate things further than necessary, especially in a way that removes my future from my command and requires a sacrifice on both our parts that promises a lifetime of unhappiness. I would not marry you no matter what scandal threatened. However, our further relationship becomes awkward. I think that it would be best if you agreed to my preferences regarding my stay in England. Jane and I will find a house in London and—"

"I will be the one to make myself scarce. I expect my visits to Laclere Park will be infrequent and brief during the next months."

"It is hardly fair to your sisters."

"When you come up to the city for the season, my presence will be unavoidable, but by then, perhaps time will have dulled my insult."

He didn't mean a word of it. He knew there had been no insult, not really. He had hardly forced himself on her.

She turned away, both relieved and saddened that after this house party she would rarely see him again.

chapter 7

Dante had been right. She would make a splendid mistress.

He tried to block the thought while he strode back to the ruins. It kept blurting into his head, the thoroughly dishonorable reaction of a man who had succumbed to dishonorable inclinations.

His behavior had been disgraceful. Reprehensible. *Insane.*

Which did not stop him from reliving it in his mind and experiencing anew her joyful consent. Feeling her soft lips and sweet breast with his mouth. Exploring her throbbing arousal with the pressure of his knee.

If the intruder had not stopped them he would have carried her up to the chamber and made love to her until those stones rang with her cries.

And she would have let him.

He stopped and slammed his palm against a tree,

seeking a tangible reality that might obliterate his resurgent desire.

Confusing, Dante had said. Damn right, she was confusing.

She didn't even like him. They rarely spoke without arguing. He might have loitered in her presence the last two days, but she never sought out his. To then jump that chasm in such an uninhibited way . . .

He paced with determination through the trees, a dangerous mood gripping him. Her calm at the stables had been further unsettling. Infuriating. Barely a blush. Total composure. He had been a mess of conflicting impulses, but her demeanor had been incredibly calm.

I was not harmed.

I almost stripped your clothes off and took you on a stone floor.

I do not feel compromised or ruined.

Well, damn it, I *do.* Men who seduce their wards are disgusting.

I would not marry you no matter what scandal threatened.

He paused at the edge of the castle's clearing as those words echoed again and again.

He *should* have been grateful for her abrupt rejection. Instead he had experienced an irrational anger. In part because her composure left him wondering if it had all been a capricious game to her. Mostly because her resolve left him with the depressing awareness that he would never have her the way he wanted.

Just as well. She would make a splendid mistress, but an impossible wife.

Let Dante deal with her.

That notion incited a primitive, possessive resentment. He suppressed it by forcing his attention to the castle's battlements.

A stairway rose at one end of the wall, so badly ruined that whole steps were missing. He could only mount it by stretching his legs for perilous footholds. A few small sections of rock fell into the grass while he climbed. He paused each time, trying to identify whether they resembled the distant sounds he had heard while he held Bianca in the tower.

The wall walk at the top existed in gaps. Someone had replaced some missing sections with new wood, but others consisted of remnants of rotten planks, themselves no doubt repairs from the last century or so. He picked his way along until he came to the spot of the wall where one whole tooth of the crenellations had just fallen away. Down below he could see the new pile of stones.

Who would expect peaceful Laclere Park to be so dangerous?

A damn good question.

He examined the rough surface from where the machicolation had lately risen, and probed at the mortar of the stones still standing. Decayed binding fell in a little shower, joining a pile of coarse dust at his feet.

Nothing so extensive could be seen near the other partial crenellations. He examined the surface of the stones again, feeling for evidence of a tool. Did he only imagine subtle scrapes created by a metal implement?

Poachers who used firearms and now a falling wall.

Perhaps just a coincidence. No proof of anything else. All the same, he didn't like it.

He climbed down from the wall, looking for evidence that someone else had come this way recently. The sounds picked up by the tower stones haunted his memory. Not the sounds of someone walking on the paths. Still, that intruder may have merely been one of the guests exploring Laclere Park's picturesque castle.

He returned to the house. When he passed the breakfast room he saw Bianca at the table with Cornell Witherby and Daniel St. John.

She smiled and laughed at some joke Witherby made. Incredible composure.

Possibly it *had* just been a capricious game to her, a way to show the saint he was not so pure. *Perhaps we should merely forget about this.*

He strode to his study, resenting like hell the spot of honesty that admitted she might be able to forget it, but he would not.

I never swoon.

For me you did!

He was reacting like some untried boy and that irritated him even more. He sent a footman for Morton, then threw himself into his chair and pulled out some paper.

Morton arrived while he was finishing his writing.

"I want this letter to Adam Kenwood's solicitor to go to London by express delivery," he said while he sealed the missive. "Take it to the town yourself, at once." He handed the paper into Morton's thick fingers. "I may leave you here when I go north again. I do not like the idea of leaving Miss Kenwood at Laclere Park without someone watching over her."

"You think that she is in some other danger?" By *other,* Vergil knew that Morton referred to any lovely woman's danger from Dante.

Possibly she was in danger. He didn't know. However, between poachers and falling walls and assaults by the Viscount Laclere, her danger from a rake might have become the least of her concerns.

After dinner Bianca found herself sitting between Fleur and Mrs. Gaston, chatting with Pen and Cornell Witherby.

"It will be a series of epics," Mrs. Gaston explained. "Sold by subscription, although I will finance the printing. Mr. Witherby's poem will be first."

Cornell Witherby smiled modestly. Penelope bestowed an admiring gaze on him.

Mrs. Gaston held herself like a queen accepting homage and bestowing favors. Her reddish brown hair glowed like copper in the firelight and her contentment in her significance showed on her face. "The printers are at work even as we speak. I expect it to be a sensation, and for many editions to be required. Not that the profit matters, of course. Exposing people of high taste and sensibility to Mr. Witherby's prodigious talent is my goal."

She spoke as if divine guidance dictated her patronage, but Bianca suspected that Mrs. Gaston's own importance as a patron drove her as much as any love of art.

"Who will the other poets be?" Fleur asked.

A discussion ensued on the merits of young poets who might deserve such patronage.

Bianca barely heard what anyone said.

An afternoon of Fleur's gentle company had induced a horrible guilt. Vergil's cool displays of courtesy had instilled a hollow devastation. An internal clock noted the passage of every minute of the very long day with ticks of agony.

She had tried never to look at Vergil or have cause to address him, but she was aware of him at every instant. She felt him when he was nearby. She heard every word he spoke, if even from across the room.

Two Biancas reacted to his every move. The old one, the smart one, cataloged his deficiencies with a scathing anger. A new one prayed for some sign of the lord's favor. This new Bianca demeaned herself with pitiful sighs, but the old Bianca could not make her disappear.

Somehow, *somehow,* she would get through this day.

". . . there will be hell to pay if we repeal the Combination Act," Lord Calne intoned as he and Vergil and Mr. St. John walked toward their little group. "If the lower classes are permitted to mass, order is threatened. Can't have it. Too dangerous. It could end up like France in '93. You'll be regretting it, Laclere."

Little fires appeared in Daniel St. John's eyes. He looked at Lord Calne as if the man was an ass. "It sounds as if you know little of what happened in France. If you did, you would know that the people cannot be kept under a boot forever."

Lord Calne's face turned red.

Vergil spoke appeasingly. "England cannot create policy based upon the excesses of the French people a generation ago, Calne."

"Oh, spare us all. Politics," Cornell Witherby moaned softly to the ladies. "It is good for nothing but satire."

A special warmth sparkled in his eyes as he turned his good humor on Pen when she giggled. It looked as if Dante had been correct about the special friendship.

Feeling in a critical frame of mind where men were concerned, Bianca gave him a thorough scrutiny. He cut a good figure and was of average height, but his posture possessed a very unpoetic strictness, as if a rod of steel had been welded to his backbone. Blond hair fell around his forehead and cheeks. His face was a bit too long, but he was a nice-looking man of about twenty-five years of age.

That he wooed a woman who was officially married counted for nothing in her deliberations of whether he was good enough for Pen. More significant by far was his thoroughly engaged expression right now as he looked at Penelope.

She had never seen Vergil Duclairc look at any woman like that, not even Fleur. When the Viscount Laclere examined a woman, she got the impression that he was assessing her shortcomings.

Unless, of course, he was listening to her music.

Or deciding to kiss her.

Or pulling off her dress.

Or . . .

"Well, at least these political deliberations keep your printer busy," Mrs. Gaston said.

Witherby sighed. "It was only to support the literary arts that I took on the hobby of that press. I would rather tell the men to refuse every commission that was not poetic. However, the tracts subsidize the important work very nicely. As does the patronage of great ladies like yourself."

Mrs. Gaston appeared pleased with the flattery, and with her success in diverting his attention back to her.

"The repeal is a moral necessity. It is unconscionable to prohibit free men free assembly," St. John was saying to the men standing nearby.

"If they are so dissatisfied, let them leave," Mrs. Gaston said, joining the conversation. "Free passage to New South Wales for malcontents. I do not understand why no one proposes such a bill. It makes perfect sense to me."

"Give all men the vote so they can affect their futures, and there will be less discontent," St. John said.

"Should the rabble of Manchester be making laws?" Lord Calne asked. "The Commons is disrupted enough, what with radicals and Irishmen."

Pen gave St. John a beseeching, quelling smile. The shipper bit back whatever disruptive retort he contemplated.

"The people of Manchester are not rabble," Vergil said. "They are helping England become the wealthiest nation in the world. Industrial cities like Manchester cannot remain disenfranchised because of borough rights drawn up centuries ago. Reform of Parliament is inevitable."

Pen rolled her eyes at her brother, reproving him for encouraging this argument.

Lord Calne looked like he would suffer apoplexy. "I'll be damned first. Support that, Laclere, and you betray your blood. Those northern cities are terrible places. Filthy with mills and machines and base men made rich by stinking trade. Worse than London, I hear. No, give me clean country air and a good hunt. We will never let them take that from us."

Pen saw her chance. "And how is the game at your estate this year? Can everyone expect the usual magnificent shoots?"

"Looks good, looks good. A continuous battle with the poachers, though. Had to bring five men up at the Quarter sessions. . . ."

The shift in topic gave Bianca an opportunity for escape from Vergil's close proximity. She excused herself.

The less politically minded men had fanned out in the room. Nigel spoke with Catalani and Mrs. Monley near a window. Her cousin favored her with a warm, inviting smile as she passed.

She joined Diane St. John, Charlotte, and Dante instead.

They were discussing the St. Johns' two children. Dante displayed more interest in the little boys' antics than Bianca would have expected, but he moved to sit beside her and allowed the ladies to carry the conversation soon after she arrived.

"You have been very quiet today," he said softly. "I hope that you are not distraught by my bad behavior."

She had all but forgotten that kiss in the library. "I am

overwhelmed by so many new faces. I have little to talk to them about."

"Well, here comes St. John. He is in shipping, as your grandfather was, so you have a bit in common with him."

Daniel St. John had removed himself from Lord Calne's company and now approached theirs.

"St. John, you knew Adam Kenwood, didn't you?" Dante asked, to make things easy for her.

"I first met him when I was very young. In fact, my first voyage as a boy was on one of his ships. That was long before he moved into finance, of course."

"When did that happen?" Bianca felt obliged to continue the conversation since Dante had started it for her sake.

"Years ago. He sold out his ships, what, ten years back or so."

"Did you sail with him long?"

"No, only that once. I jumped ship in the West Indies and found a berth with another master."

"My grandfather's rule did not appeal to you, I gather."

"Your grandfather was not the master himself. He only owned the ships and arranged for their cargo. I merely decided to sail elsewhere."

He was lying. Bianca just knew that from the overly polite way he spoke.

"Odd that he sold out the whole lot all at once," Dante said. "To own a fleet of ships one day, and then none the next."

"Since I bought two of them, I was glad that he did," St. John said.

"What did his ships carry?" Bianca asked.

"All sorts of things, I imagine, as mine do."

She got the sense that Mr. St. John was humoring them, and not being very forthright. Dante was right, it was odd that her grandfather had sold out all those ships at once, no matter what this other shipper said.

She did not have time to press him for a clearer explanation, because Penelope walked to the center of the room and called for attention. "We are fortunate to have several accomplished musicians among us tonight, and I have imposed upon two of them, Sir Nigel Kenwood and Miss Bianca Kenwood, to perform. Let us regather in the music room and give them our grateful attention."

She led the way out. Dante moved to escort Bianca, but Mr. St. John claimed her attention first. "It appears that Catalani knows when to give way to youth."

"It is kind of you to say that, but I doubt she fears competition from me."

"She has given up performing for a reason. She knows that the instrument is not what it was." He tucked her hand into his arm while they strolled down the corridor. "Nervous?"

"Horribly. I was looking forward to this, and now . . ."

"Then that explains your distraction today. My wife commented on it to me. She is very observant in her quiet way, and worried that you were distressed about something. She will be relieved to learn that it was your fear of blundering tonight's performance. I told her that was so, and perfectly normal."

No it wasn't. Not for her. But this was different. She

had dreaded this moment all day. To sing that aria again, in front of all of these people, with *him* sitting there... Her insides twisted tighter with each step.

Nigel took his place at the pianoforte. The guests sat in chairs arrayed in front of her. Vergil chose to stand near the wall, next to Fleur's place.

She looked at him, hoping for a smile of reassurance. He didn't notice, as he bent to say something to his intended. Her heart filled. He looked so appealing in his dark green frock coat and cream trousers, with waves of hair framing his face and his blue eyes lighting with humor while he smiled at his lady.

She realized with a start that Nigel had begun the introduction. She scrambled to prepare herself.

From across the room, Vergil looked at her.

She blundered it. That first note simply wouldn't come. She turned to Nigel with a desperate, wordless plea.

He improvised until he brought the melody around to the beginning again. She focused on the floor and pulled herself together. When she looked up again she saw a green frock coat slipping out the door.

Thank you.

She hit every note perfectly, but her soul wasn't concerned with precision. Vergil might not be present in the room, but he was in her head, confusing her with that startling look, spiritually intruding with improper memories. This aria wasn't like the last one at the ruins, with its thrilling exaltation. A different emotion dripped through it this time. A strange hollow existed inside her

and the music deepened it and then filled it with pene-
trating, regretful yearning. By the time she finished
she did not know if the performance had been successful
or not.

"Magnificent, cousin," Nigel whispered into the silence that followed.

The effort left her in a melancholy fog. She glanced to
Catalani's pensive expression even as she accepted the
praise of the other guests.

Catalani walked over, took her hands, and pulled her
aside. "I have grown jaded, and confess that I expected a
pretty voice, suitable for drawing rooms and churches. I
was mistaken. You possess great talent, my dear. You are
not ordinary."

On any other day Catalani's judgment would have produced euphoria. Tonight it only added one more big knot
in the tangle of emotions that confused her.

Pen led the way into the library for cards, but Bianca
begged off, saying that she wanted to retire. She followed
the retinue down the corridor, but turned away at the
stairs.

Nigel held back from the others. "I had hoped that we
would find ourselves at the same table, cousin."

"I would have been a poor partner tonight. The excitement of singing with Catalani present . . ."

"Of course. I understand. Still, I would be grateful for
some time with you. We have much in common, cousin. I
would like to know you better."

All the "cousins" in the world, all the formal, proper
address and tones, did not obscure what he meant. His

interest glowed in his expression. She suspected that if they were alone right now in the garden, Nigel would try to kiss her.

Three men in two days. She had no idea that becoming a loose woman was this easy.

Her experience this morning was making her cynical. Maybe Nigel's interest was an honorable one.

"Will you be joining the others on the ride in the morning?" he asked.

Pen had arranged for everyone to tour the estate, ending with a luncheon at the ruins. Going back there so soon would be horrible. "I do not think so. I am not feeling well, and will stay here and rest."

The study door opened down the corridor. The tall figure of the Viscount Laclere emerged, heading to the library. He saw them and paused, standing sentry. Nigel glanced to him and gave her a private smile.

"I should like to speak with you sometime when your guardian does not glare over my shoulder. We are both alone in the world, and relatives can be a source of solace for each other. If you ever need my aid, I hope that you will call on me."

"It is very kind of you to offer. Now, you should join the others and I must seek my privacy."

Vergil did not move, even when Nigel passed with a greeting and entered the library. He just stood there, looking at her. She wanted to flip her head and turn away with haughty indifference. Instead she couldn't move.

"You retire?" he asked.

"Yes. The evening has been a trial."

"I think the evening was a triumph. I listened. You outdid yourself. As for the day, I expect it has been a trial, and I apologize for it."

She did not want to hear any more of his apologies.

"Your grandfather's personal papers arrived this morning," he said. "Most of the boxes are in my study so they will not crowd you, but I had the ones from the years when your father lived with him brought up to your chamber, along with the contents of his desk."

"Thank you." She forced herself to move and turned to the stairs.

"There is something else. I must insist that you do not go about on your own in the early morning in the future."

"Do you worry for my virtue?" It came out before she could stop herself.

He didn't even have the decency to look embarrassed. "I worry for your safety."

"I will go where I wish, and practice when I can."

"Not in the morning, and not alone. If you want to practice in private and you worry that you will disturb others in your chamber, use my study. But do not leave the house."

"You keep shortening the leash, Laclere. Why not just tie me to my bedpost?"

His blue eyes regarded her in a way far removed from the day's bland acknowledgments.

"You have a talent for provoking the most astonishing images, Miss Kenwood." He turned away. "Until tomorrow, then."

Jane was waiting in her chamber. It felt good to be alone with someone who had known her for years.

"The guests have certainly livened this old place up, haven't they?" Jane said. "All those handsome men in their fine clothes."

Jane had viewed this journey from the start as a good opportunity to find Bianca a husband. She had never recognized that the lack of suitors in Baltimore was intentional, and the result of careful discouragements.

"That Mr. Witherby looked promising. A gentleman, it is said, and nice-looking enough."

"I suspect that he has an interest in Penelope."

Jane frowned. "A married woman? Separated or not, that is what she is. Well, the viscount is out, what with being all but engaged to Miss Monley. Just as well. Who would want such a strict, stern man? There is always Charlotte's youngest brother, although it is said—"

"I know what is said."

Jane helped her into a dressing gown. "All these unmarried men, and not even a flirtation? Who would expect England to be so dull."

Anything but dull anymore, and a flirtation didn't begin to describe just how undull it had become. "My cousin Nigel has made his interest known."

"I've never liked the idea of relatives. Not good for the blood."

"He is some ways removed."

"True. Only it is said downstairs that he is much like Dante. Lives in debt. Can't afford all those fine things. Your grandfather left you most of the money. It's said your cousin only got enough money to maintain the estate, tied up proper so he can't get it, only the income every year."

"Where do you learn these things?"

"Servants here know the few servants remaining there. Tenants talk among themselves. It is just like one of our neighborhoods. It all comes in through the kitchen door," Jane said. "If he has expressed that kind of interest, you should know that he may be like Dante in other ways too. Seems your cousin is not always alone in that big house. A woman secretly visited last week. Take my advice. That is one man whose interest I don't think we want."

Bianca didn't want any man's interest. Absolutely not. Nothing but distractions, that was what men were. Potentially permanent distractions, the way the world worked. And, as she was learning the hard way, sources of confusion and hurt.

She yearned for sleep, but knew it would only come with total exhaustion. After Jane left, she moved the candles over to the crates and trunk stacked near the hearth, and sat on the floor to see what they might reveal.

A key poked out of the trunk's lock. Turning it, she lifted the top and examined the contents of Adam's desk at Woodleigh.

She fingered the quills and cheap inkwell. She poked amidst scraps of paper that bore cryptic notes. One had the name of Vergil's brother along with some others, and she guessed it had been among the last that her grandfather made.

A stack of letters, tied together with twine, caught her

interest. She was about to open them when she noticed the salutation on the top one. Written in a man's hand, it addressed Adam as "My dearest friend."

They could not be from her father, with a salutation like that. Probably they were from the previous viscount. She would give them to Vergil.

In a little leather case she found a miniature of a blonde woman. She guessed that it was her grandmother. She saw a resemblance to her father, which called up memories of his love and noble honesty. Her throat burned as an old sorrow joined the new ones.

A dried flower dropped from the depression onto her lap as she lifted the tiny painting from its velvet nest.

The flower did not look very old. It did not crumble when touched, as it would if it had been in this case for years.

She pictured an old man picking a flower as he walked in the garden and later opening this case to the memories of his wife. She imagined Adam leaving this tiny offering to her.

She snapped the case closed. She did not want to become sentimental about him. Probably the flower had been there forever, and put there by her grandmother herself.

The other trunk held portfolios. Adam had been an organized man, and each year's correspondence had its own, with the year written on its front. She searched for the ones from the years before she was born, when her father had left England.

It took her some time to find the right year. She had

not realized that her father had gone to America a full six years before she was born.

It was a thin portfolio with very few letters. Three were from her father. She read them, and learned the reason why Adam Kenwood and his son had become estranged.

It was not because of her mother. It had happened before her parents had even met. Vergil had been correct about how it had happened too. Her father made the break. In a letter refusing Adam's offer of an allowance, he laid out the reasons.

His explanation emptied her heart of its last shreds of joy and confidence. The dream that had sustained her since her mother's death wobbled as if its foundations had been attacked. The inheritance suddenly struck her as an evil joke, a devil's lure to join his sin.

No wonder her father had turned his back on the estate and status Adam had built.

Her grandfather had made his first fortune in the slave trade.

chapter 8

Very early the next morning, Bianca rose and dressed and headed to the viscount's study. He had said she could practice there, which meant that she could enter. She did so, but with no intention of singing.

The rest of the boxes containing Adam's effects were stacked against the window seat. Kneeling, she began to line up the wooden crates so she could examine their contents.

She wanted to know just how much she should hate Adam Kenwood before she made her decision about the inheritance. She ruefully admitted that she hoped to find some evidence of his redemption, so she would not feel obligated to renounce all of it.

Pushing the crates this way and that absorbed her, and she did not hear the bootsteps until they stopped right beside her. Out of the corner of her eye she saw polished boots and doeskin breeches. She trembled with an alert, stupid excitement.

"You were riding again," she said. "At least one of us is allowed to enjoy the mornings."

"You are welcome to join me any morning."

"I do not think that would be wise. Do you?" She fussed with some files, not really seeing what she handled. "If you want me to leave, I will do this later. I am trying to find out if my mother wrote to him after father's death, asking for help."

He walked to the other side of the row of crates and lowered to his knees. "You said it was during the war. Those years seem to be in this crate here."

She scooted over and pawed through it until she found 1814. "He was a slave trader. Did you know that?"

She guessed from his hesitation that he did know.

He poked through another crate. "Many families have that trade in their background. Lord Liverpool's father was a slaver, but he worked for passage of the law that made it illegal."

"Did my grandfather work to pass that law?"

"I do not think so."

"It was why my father broke with him. In America, my father wrote and spoke against it. We almost moved to Philadelphia so that we would not live in a city that had a slave port, but he believed he could do more good in Baltimore." She pulled at the ties binding the two paste-boards of the 1814 portfolio together.

A letter from her mother lay on top of the others. In re-sponse to an offer of financial assistance from Adam, she had refused for the same reasons her husband had never accepted any money.

And so, to get his way, to force his son's family to accept who he was, he had left a huge amount to her, his granddaughter.

She knew what she had to do. It saddened her no matter how right and just and noble it was. Without the dream of her singing, she was not sure that she had anything left.

"My inheritance was built on slavery. You were correct, and using it will be a great joke rather than a great justice. The joke, however, was Adam's."

"He sold out of shipping long ago. Most of his fortune came from other things."

But it had started there. She could not reconcile it, much as she ached to. Her conscience forced a choice that she dreaded. To have a dream within reach and then to voluntarily not grab it—

"I cannot accept it. I want you to sell out anything that you can, and give it to charity. When the funds pay out, give that away too."

"It will be reckless to sell out, even if it is your desire. A court oversees my stewardship, not you. A court made up of men who will not understand or accept that I should agree to your direction, especially since it will leave you impoverished."

"Are you saying that you will force me to accept this tainted fortune?"

"I am saying that the fortune will remain intact while

I control it. When you begin receiving the income, you can give that away if you choose."

"Fine. In the meantime, there is no reason for me to remain in England any longer. I want you to secure passage for Jane and me back to Baltimore."

"I am not inclined to do that either."

"Your inclinations do not interest me."

"I think that you are making this decision too hastily, and perhaps for the wrong reasons. Furthermore, your first reason for coming, to see the estate settled, is still important even if you have decided the tainted money forces you to abandon the other."

"I said nothing about abandoning my plans to train for the opera. I will find a different way to make it happen. One that does not defy my parents' beliefs and sacrifices."

"Now I am even less inclined to purchase your passage back to Baltimore."

"In addition to being abducted, it appears that I am now a hostage. You merely delay the inevitable, to the vexation of us both. When I decide to do something, I find a way to accomplish my goal."

He had gotten that resolute, stern expression again. It was pointless to try and sway him when he was like that, she already knew. Nor did she have the heart to try now. The last day had pummeled her spirit, and she had little heart for arguments.

To feign acquiescence, she gestured to the crates and changed the subject. "Did you find anything else of your brother's?"

"I have not looked. This is your property."

She rose on her knees. "Let us look now. I will help you. When did Adam build Woodleigh, and the friendship start?"

"Six years ago."

"These will be the ones we want, then." She lifted a heavy stack onto the floor.

Vergil's hands quickly closed on the top four. He sat cross-legged and began flipping through their contents. He appeared so interested that it occurred to her that he had lingered with her now in the hopes that she would make this invitation.

She examined the two that were left. "This is odd. There are letters from Adam himself in these as well."

"They are copies of letters he sent. At some point he probably adopted the practice even for private correspondence."

"Most of these concern the building of Woodleigh. From their tone, I do not envy the architect. Have you found any to your brother?"

"Yes, but nothing surprising." His tone suggested otherwise. She looked over to see him scrutinizing a letter with a frown. He appeared very serious and a little sad.

His honest, revealing expression disarmed her. It was easy to forget that he was not only a viscount and trustee, but also a young man who was never supposed to have the title and responsibilities he now bore. She wondered if he had welcomed that unexpected change in his life. Since it had come at the cost of his brother's life, she suspected that guilt shadowed any joy he took in it.

"You can keep it," she said. "Keep anything of his, or about him."

He looked over at her. "Thank you."

His gaze did not return to the letter. It stayed on her and she could not move her own away. The silence of the study pressed on her, but a primal song sounded like a silent melody that went on and on, taking over the space in which they sat too closely and too isolated.

She might have been back at the ruins, being held by him, looking up at a face made stern with passion. She half-expected him to cast aside the letter and reach for her.

Frightened of that impulse, and of the way her heart begged him to do it, she jumped to her feet and backed away to the door.

She awkwardly gestured to the crates. "You have my permission to examine all of it. We will trade. If I find any letters concerning your brother, I will give them to you. If you find any about my parents, you do the same."

Not waiting for his agreement, she fled the room.

"Laclere."

The melodic voice drifted to Vergil that afternoon while he climbed the steps to the terrace. Maria Catalani stood at the open door.

"Maria. You did not ride this morning?"

"I am well past the age when bumping along on some rude animal is amusing, *caro mio,* and when it comes to ruins, well, my country has them in abundance. And you?"

"I have business to attend."

She fell into step when he passed into the drawing room. "You go to your *studio*? I will walk with you."

The house was silent, emptied of its noisy guests. Catalani strolled beside him as if she crossed a stage. Her form had grown matronly in the last few years and the passionate voice had failed her, but she still knew her worth.

"Thank you for the invitation. I was pleased that you extended it, and Mrs. Gaston was kind to allow me to join her so we could make your little surprise for your sister work."

"When I heard that you had arrived in London, I thought that the country might offer some rest after your journey. Also, as I told you yesterday, I had an ulterior motive besides Penelope's surprise. I need a professional opinion, and yours is the best. What did you think of Miss Kenwood's performance?"

"She is very talented, Laclere."

"How talented?"

"You do not need me to tell you. Anyone with an ear can hear it. Anyone with a heart can feel it."

"Some ears are better than others."

"She needs training, of course. It will take some time. She also must learn the languages so the words have specific meaning for her, but she is intelligent and that will be easy. Her range at the upper levels may prove limited. Roles for *mezzo-sopranos* may prove her strength. She can have many years in opera, however. She has the talent and the determination and, most of all, the heart. Quite a find, Laclere. Are you going to ask me to take her back to Milan as my protégée?"

"Absolutely not, and I must ask that you not make such a suggestion to her." Bianca had spoken of renouncing the inheritance and finding another way. He did not want Catalani to be that other way.

She studied his face. "You are not pleased with my assessment, I think."

"I confess to hoping that it would be less positive. It would have simplified things."

They had reached the library door across from the study. Maria considered him with a tilt of her head. "I think that I understand. You do not intend to allow this young woman her way, and my judgment was going to absolve you. If you have listened to her, your heart knew it would not turn out that way."

Yes, his heart knew that, but he had been hoping that lust had been obscuring his judgment.

"She will not permit you to interfere, *caro*. When we spoke, I was very frank about the sacrifices, but she remains undeterred. Was that also to your plan? That she would seek me out and become discouraged by what I described? As I said, she has the determination. It is hopeless to try and stop her."

"Perhaps, but it is my duty to try."

"Your duty? Ah, I see. You must save her. Very charming and very male. I thank God no man saved me." She shook her head and opened the library door. Hand on the latch, she turned and smiled with a warmth that made the years fall away. "What has happened to you, Laclere? Where is the young man of dreams and passion who came to my door with an armful of roses that day?"

The gentle scold provoked more nostalgia than anger. "Life happened, Maria. Duties happened. I grew up."

"Deadening duties, from what I see and hear. I should have kept you as my lover longer than one summer, if you so quickly surrendered to such a fate."

"I counted myself fortunate to have a summer. You had little taste for boys, as I remember."

She closed the door and leaned against the wall. "You were so moved by the music, who could not be charmed? Have you lost that too? Is that why I had to come and tell you what would have been obvious to you years ago? Does it no longer speak to you?"

"Sometimes it speaks as powerfully as ever."

"I am glad, *caro*. We should embrace whatever makes us young dreamers again, even if it is only for a few minutes now and then."

She did not enter the library, after all, but strolled down the corridor toward the stairs.

Bianca huddled low on the divan, not daring to move. Even after the door closed again and the voices became low mumbles, even after silence fell, she stayed in her ball of arms and legs.

She couldn't believe what she had overheard. Catalani and Vergil . . .

Astonishing. Astounding.

The *hypocrite*.

No wonder he assumed all performers became courtesans and mistresses. He probably had a whole string of them in his background, accumulated after that summer with Catalani. He probably had one ensconced in that manor up north, just as Charlotte speculated. It was isolated and discreet and no one would ever know.

Poor Fleur.

The *scoundrel*.

And yesterday morning at the ruins . . . This certainly shed an unpleasant light on that too. For all she knew, he was a predator keeping her nearby for the most dishonorable of reasons. He could be . . . He could be *dangerous*.

Prolonged silence indicated that Vergil and Catalani had left the corridor near the door. She untwisted herself and tried to accommodate this startling development.

She wasn't going to solely blame herself for yesterday anymore. She had begun to do so, in part because of Fleur, in part because it had seemed an inexplicable lapse on his part when thought of any other way. But if he hadn't been a saint when young, he probably had not truly become one later, and, in light of this news, the lapse had not been inexplicable after all.

It would be nice to blame him completely instead, but her memories wouldn't let her. Fine. They both were to blame then.

Or not, depending on how you looked at it.

She didn't feel inclined to blame anyone. That embrace and those kisses had been glorious and exciting. They had produced an intimacy such as she had never known, and a connection that seemed unbreakable. That was why she sensed his presence all the time, and why her heart beat so hard when he moved nearby. She admitted now that she had been hoping for some recognition that he also felt the invisible links forged by that brief passion.

She threw an arm over her eyes and groaned. An experience like that might transport her, but it would hardly turn a man like the Viscount Laclere inside out. He had once had the great Catalani as a lover. A few kisses and gropes with a raw recruit to passion could easily be forgotten.

She would simply have to forget as well. Clearly he expected her to.

She tried to fix on that decision. Her head was willing but her heart would not cooperate. She kept seeing that look in his eyes and experiencing anew the exciting magic of his embrace. Her chest filled with a hopeful joy that urged her to sing, and then emptied with a disappointing sadness that almost moved her to tears.

She sighed and sat up. She didn't recognize the sad, confused person she had become. She needed to find the Bianca she had been before yesterday.

She would simply step backward and pick up the strands. She would renew her plan to make him send her away, only this time to Baltimore. Leaving had become essential now. She couldn't live the next ten months like this, absorbed by a man who obviously regretted their behavior and only wanted to keep his distance from her.

She needed to settle matters quickly. She would have

to do something very shocking, something Vergil could neither ignore or forget.

An obvious solution presented itself. Vergil could rationalize a lapse with himself by blaming himself, but he would hardly miss the implications if she lapsed again with another man soon after. He might have affairs with women like Catalani, but a good brother could not permit a Catalani to live with Charlotte.

Who should the other man be? Not Nigel. Vergil might decide to call him out.

Dante?

She felt more like her old self than she had in twenty-four hours. Planning her next move helped keep her mind off the sadness that nibbled inside her.

Yes, Dante would do very well, and a rake would hardly disappoint her.

The next day the party spread out along the shores of the lake, enjoying a lazy afternoon. They had brought books and sketching pads with them in the carriages, and lots of parasols for the ladies. Dante and Cornell Witherby had stripped off boots and stockings and waded with fishing rods into the low water.

Dante walked out of the lake. She caught his eye while he dried himself. She smiled. After he pulled on his boots he came over.

She had never realized how susceptible men were. If he weren't a rake, she might have felt guilty.

Dante lounged beside her. "You do not sketch?"

"I never learned. My education was not the typical drawing room variety."

She noticed Vergil rising from his spot and meandering into the trees. As if his movement had been a cue, the other members of the party began regrouping. Pen and Catalani carried their parasols over to Fleur.

"Your walk in the lake must have been refreshing on this warm day," she said. "I envy you."

His lids lowered and he regarded her with that private look. She knew he was remembering her own dip in this lake the day he first arrived. It reminded her that she played a dangerous game here. She had better choose her moment with the greatest care.

"I tire of sitting. I think that I will take a turn," she announced.

"May I join you?"

"That would be kind."

The path formed a large circle through the trees and brush. She guided him in the direction opposite that which Vergil had taken.

"Will you be leaving with the others tomorrow?" she asked.

"I think that I will stay a few more days."

"Charlotte says that you find the country boring."

"This visit has been anything but, thanks to your company. And you? Can Laclere Park occupy you during the months ahead?"

"I confess that I doubt it. Fortunately, Pen has spoken of a visit to London soon, so that Charlotte can begin choosing her wardrobe for the season."

"I will make it a point to be there when all of you come."

They strolled into a spot where the trees fell away and only tall grasses and bushes flanked the path. Down a low hill, a little clearing filled with flowers lay near the lake.

"Look, bluebells. Help me down so I can pick some."

Dante was only too happy to help her down the hill. She knelt amidst the fragrance and began plucking up the buds. With an encompassing glance that noted their isolation, he settled down beside her.

She peered toward the tall bushes hiding the path, looking for Vergil's dark hair. He should be passing this way soon.

"You are very lovely there, surrounded by those flowers, Miss Kenwood. They make your eyes even bluer."

"Call me Bianca, Dante."

He looked like a man pleased with a sudden good turn in fortune.

Still no Vergil.

"I am honored that you agreed to walk with me today. I was concerned that my behavior in the library had left you angry and afraid."

"Not angry. But a little afraid, I will confess."

"Such a reaction is what one would expect of an innocent girl. Kissing you like that was an inappropriate thing to do. I can only offer as an excuse that I was overcome by how lovely you looked in that subtle light."

"You do not need to apologize. I was not insulted, just surprised. If I reacted strongly, it was because of that."

"May I take that as encouragement that my addresses find some favor with you?"

It sounded like something Vergil would say. Only Vergil had said nothing of the kind before kissing her, and now this rake did. Men could be very confusing.

"That depends on your intentions."

"Completely honorable, Bianca, I promise you."

He hadn't touched her. He hadn't even moved closer. How much encouragement should a rake need? She glanced anxiously toward the path.

"Not too honorable, I hope."

He smiled in both surprise and delight, but he still didn't move. Where had this sudden inconvenient restraint come from?

"You cannot know how happy this makes me. Now, we should resume our walk and return to the others."

She couldn't believe her ears. "I do not want to return to the others just yet. I would rather stay here with you."

"I am flattered, Bianca, but—"

"I want you to ask to kiss me. You said that you would and that I would not refuse. I have thought about it and decided that you were right. I would not refuse."

He glanced around at their isolation, clearly torn. She did, too, and thought she saw dark hair finally moving between the bushes' branches.

"It would be best if we left now," he said.

What good was a rake if he got all proper just when you needed him to do something outrageous? When you had bluntly invited him to do so? In a few seconds Vergil would move to the top of the little hill and what would he see? Nothing.

Dark hair strolled closer. She stomped a mental foot in frustration. This chance might never come again.

Kiss me, you idiot.

Dante rose to his knees and offered his hand to help her up.

She lunged.

He fell back with her weight and his arms instinctively encircled her. "Miss Kenwood ... Bianca ..."

She pressed him to the ground and he grappled in confusion. In the flurry that followed, she rolled so he embraced her reclining body amidst the flowers.

The world righted itself and silence fell. She looked up at a face at first startled, then dangerously sensual.

"Well, sweet girl, if you insist." He lifted her toward a kiss.

Their lips never met. A rampaging animal crashed down the hill. A strong hand grabbed Dante by the neck of his garments and hauled him off her. Furious, savage blue eyes seared into one befuddled and astounded rake.

"I warned you," Vergil growled.

His fist sent Dante sprawling. Then that hand pulled her up, set her right, and brushed the grass off the back of her garment with swipes that stung her bottom.

She looked guiltily at Dante. She hadn't expected Vergil to react so violently.

She faced Vergil bravely. They stared at each other, her glaring a challenge and him barely controlling his fury.

Dante staggered to his feet. "Oh, hell," he muttered.

"Exactly," Vergil said.

That confused her. She looked quizzically from one to the other. Vergil shook his head in exasperation and stepped aside.

Her gaze followed Dante's.

Oh, dear.

Up on the crest of the little hill, Fleur, Pen, and Catalani watched from beneath their parasols.

"I tell you, she literally threw herself at me. One moment I'm offering her my hand and the next I'm sprawled on the ground with her on top of me."

Dante paced in front of the study's window, looking as agitated as Vergil felt.

Vergil stayed behind his desk, because if he got within ten feet of his brother he might thrash him. "Do you expect me to believe that Miss Kenwood jumped you, overpowered you, and then dragged you into an embrace? It is preposterous."

"*Listen* to me. I'm kneeling there, about to get up. She had just invited me to kiss her and I had demurred. Then suddenly she turns into a she lion and—"

"You were *on top of her.*"

"That part is a bit confusing. It all happened so fast. I have to tell you, her behavior has been astonishing. I am shocked, to be frank about it. I can't recall that I have ever experienced anything like it."

"You hardly looked as though you were fighting for your virtue."

"Well, she was so insistent. And I *am* human."

Far too human. He'd like to smash his fist into Dante's face again and then grab Bianca Kenwood and turn her over his knee.

"Nothing else for it, of course," Dante said. "What with the ladies seeing."

"If I discover that you decided to save time as you suggested that day in here, I will—"

"Don't know why you are so upset. It is what you wanted. I'm the one who has to marry a girl with very suspect morals."

"Suspect morals?"

"If she is so bold with me, one has to wonder."

Yes, one did. Especially if one knew for a fact that she had been kissing another man just two days ago. That explained partly why he was so angry. However, it was seeing them embracing that had caused the explosion in his head that still hurled sharp fragments.

She knew that such indiscreet behavior carried extreme consequences. He had spelled it out less than two days ago. How could she be so careless as to . . .

How, indeed?

He sank down in his chair and mulled that over. He had left first, followed by Bianca and Dante. The ladies must have begun their walk soon after. Pen and the others had caught up with him only because he had paused to think some things over. Things about Bianca, as it happened.

It all fell into place. She had planned it. She had intended him to find them together. To make him jealous?

She had definitely succeeded there, but he could not delude himself that it had been her intention. A woman's revenge for what had happened in the ruins? A declaration of indifference because she had noticed him watching her? He had tried to be very discreet about that, but he might have failed.

Damn.

"You were right about one thing, Verg. I will have to be very firm with her. No matter what is in the past, I will not have her taking lovers once we are married. She will have to understand that." The censorious line of Dante's mouth would put a bishop to shame.

"You think to dictate her behavior?"

"I'll not be made a fool."

"Dante, you have made a fool of half the House of Lords. Do you think that young woman will permit you to preach morality?"

"A husband has his rights, and I've a reputation to consider. Despite the likely blemishes on her virtue, no doubt the result of lax supervision, she is a sweet and accommodating creature."

Accommodating? "You amaze me."

"As to my own activities, I expect she will remain ignorant of that."

"No one in England is ignorant of that."

"It is obvious that she is in love with me, and she is, in her heart, still a wide-eyed child. I do not doubt that she will accept any arrangement that I present, and submit as appropriate to my supervision."

Wide-eyed child? Submit?

He shook his head incredulously. Dante had assumed the countenance of a *paterfamilias* who took for granted marital devotion and obedience from his wide-eyed, accommodating wife.

He doesn't stand a chance.

"If we ignore what this reveals about her character, one could say things have worked out very nicely. I will take the blame, of course, but she has played right into our hands."

She had certainly done that. He should be gloating in triumph, but the thought of what was to come only sickened him.

"Where is she?" Vergil asked.

"Up in her chamber. Pen has everyone in the library, trying to pretend nothing happened. The rest don't know, but it is bound to get out. I will speak with her at once and make my offer."

"We will speak with her together. She may need some persuading."

"Can't imagine that. Everyone knows the rules."

Yes, everyone knew the rules, but Bianca had not shown any inclination thus far to play by them.

chapter 9

For a warm September day, the study held quite a chill.

That probably had something to do with the icy blue eyes ostentatiously looking away while Dante knelt and proposed.

"Therefore, while I would have preferred to court you and then offer in the normal way, under the circumstances it would be best if we married immediately," he concluded, squeezing her hand and bestowing a reassuring smile.

Vergil lounged in his chair behind his desk, turned toward the window with a distracted, bland expression. He had sat there like a silent witness while his brother performed this most intimate of rituals.

She gave her attention back to the young man balanced on one knee. "Why would it be best if we married?"

"Why?"

"Yes, why?"

"Because, Miss Kenwood, the alternative is a scandal." Vergil's steely tone cut the air into shards. "You were seen with my brother, and as a gentleman, he will do the right thing."

She looked at the beautiful man kneeling by her side. Poor Dante. To have successfully raked all these years, only to get ensnared the one time he had tried to act very honorably.

She patted Dante's hand. "You are very kind to offer, but I must refuse."

"*Refuse?*"

"You will be relieved to learn that I do not exact such a high wage for such a small indiscretion." *As your brother well knows.*

He rose. He didn't look relieved at all. Incredulous and a bit insulted, but not relieved.

"Vergil . . ."

"I will manage this now, Dante."

Bianca shifted so she faced him squarely. "You will find that I am not inclined to be managed, least of all by you. It is unforgivable for you to force your brother, your own blood, into this for such a little thing."

"I assure you, Bianca darling, that I am not at all unhappy about it."

"A little thing? It was no mild flirtation that the ladies witnessed. You were lying on the ground together. Only if your garments had been in *dishabille* could it have been worse. What would have happened in Baltimore if you were found thus?"

"I imagine if my father were alive he would have shot Dante."

"Are you saying that you would prefer that I shoot my brother?"

"I am saying that I will not accept marriage under these circumstances. The punishment is far too permanent for such a small crime." *I have explained all this before. Remember?*

Vergil began to respond, but Dante cut him off with a quelling gesture. He lifted her hands in his own and gazed into her eyes. "My dear Bianca, I assure you I do not view this as a punishment. Rather, it is a dream come true. For your sake only do I wish the circumstances were different. You stole my heart immediately. I have spent these weeks praying for a sign of your affection. This only gives me my soul's desire sooner than I had dared hope."

Her heart sank into her stomach. He meant it. Not the parts about stealing his heart, but the rest. He didn't mind this development.

Out of the corner of her eye she observed Vergil. He appeared resolute and angry, but not one bit surprised.

Her heart sank further.

This had been the plan from the start. It was why Dante was here, and why Vergil wouldn't let her leave. Dante had been chosen for her. Her whole stay at Laclere Park had been a type of trap, and her own stupidity had sprung the clamps closed.

"So, let us hear no more talk of sparing me from punishment," Dante said, lifting her hands to his lips. "In a few days we will be wed, and I promise to make you very happy, darling. Doing so will be no punishment at all."

His soothing tone carried a note of seduction. Vergil's jaw clenched. Her stomach heaved.

She extricated her hand. "I am honored by your affection, but still I must decline."

A silence ensued, so tense that one expected invisible coils to snap. Bewilderment, then amazement, then annoyance flashed over Dante's face.

"Perhaps you should leave us, Dante. I would like to speak with my ward alone."

"Certainly," Dante said. "Bianca...Miss Kenwood." With a little bow he was gone.

She glared at Vergil, daring him to pursue this farce. He rose and paced to the window.

"With your mother long dead and your aunt unmarried, your education has been lacking. Forgive me if I must be blunter than men should be with women. You were seen prostrate under my brother in those flowers, engaged in lovemaking. When that is discovered, the only honorable course for the man and the only redemption for the woman is that they wed. You may not extract such a wage for indiscretion, Miss Kenwood, but society does."

"As I remember it, I was engaged in lovemaking with you and you accepted my refusal of your offer. I suppose that means you got to be honorable but I did not get to be redeemed. Fine. I will accept the same resolution with Dante."

"Do not...This is different. You were *seen*. The consequences cannot be avoided."

"So it is being seen that makes such behavior scandalous? How unfortunate for Dante. It is a good thing for him that I am not a slave to propriety."

"You did not hear me. When you lost control with my brother, you also lost control over the outcome should your behavior become known."

"What makes you think that I lost control with your brother? I don't remember it that way at all."

He turned abruptly with an expression of . . . what? Shock? Relief? "Are you saying he importuned you? Forced you?"

He almost appeared hopeful and, for a moment at least, not at all stern. Her chest filled with an astonishing yearning. He looked so . . . vulnerable. An odd thought, but that was what she saw for an instant. It made her wish that she could somehow abort this foolhardy plan. But what good would that do, especially now that she knew why he was so adamant about her staying with his family.

"I am saying nothing of the sort. Would it make a difference to society if I did?"

"No."

Nor would it make a difference to you. Not really, despite that look. Our passion was a blunder that almost botched things horribly. You planned for Dante to have me, after all.

She forced herself to act lighthearted despite the raw hurt ripping at her composure. "I did not think so. The thing is, you keep bringing up scandal and society, while I care about neither. You seem to forget that this is not *my* society."

"It is the one in which you now live."

"Only temporarily. You asked what would have occurred if we had been found thus in Baltimore. A duel or a marriage, such as families demand here, would be two possibilities. Or I might have been sent away. I suggest that we consider that last option now as well."

His expression lightened. Definitely relief this time.

"Ah, I see. Of course. I had wondered why you did it, but it is becoming clear now. Independence was your goal from the start and you still pursue it. But you have overplayed your hand."

And you are glad that I did. Glad that I sprang the trap so neatly. Glad that Dante will have me. Oh, Laclere...

"I assure you that I *did* it because I wanted to *do* it. Furthermore, I think that you will have to permit me to leave. I have no intention of rectifying things by marrying your brother. If the result is a scandal, so be it. I expect that it will be a very big one, but it will fall only on me if I leave soon. We will let everyone know that he tried to do the right thing, but that I refused him. Once I have left, it will all be forgotten."

He cocked his head. "Are you so determined that you would invite such scorn to achieve your ends?"

"I would invite even more if necessary. You really should let me go. Otherwise you may find your family the center of all kinds of outrageous behavior." She tossed her head in what she hoped was an imperious manner.

The silence crackled. She turned back to find him suddenly standing right beside her chair.

He did not look amused anymore. "You wouldn't dare."

"I have already dared. First with you and now your brother. It should be clear by now that I am not what you expected."

"What is that supposed to mean?"

"Open your eyes, Laclere. What kind of a woman would hop from one man to the next like that?"

"You tell me, Miss Kenwood." His quiet tone made her very uncomfortable.

"One too free-spirited to avoid scandal in your very proper society, I would say. Wouldn't you?"

"I haven't decided yet."

"What is to decide? You know that my behavior has been outrageous, and I don't even feel remorse. I refuse to be redeemed. The conclusion that you must be drawing is unattractive, but I don't even mind."

"What conclusion is that?"

The scoundrel was going to make her spell it out. She wobbled to her feet, trusting she would feel more brave if she felt less small.

"That I like men far too much for a decent woman. That I am too...experienced to remain part of English respectable society."

He cocked an eyebrow. *"Experienced?"*

"Dangerous, it is said in Baltimore."

"Dangerous now."

"Yes. *Dangerous.* In fact, there are those who say... I have even heard that some people think that I am... wicked."

"Are you saying that there have been other men?"

It had become difficult to act casual and flippant. He

was making her uncomfortable, but in a foolish, flustered way. Something of the expression at the ruins seemed to have deepened his gaze. Ridiculous, of course. He was probably just suitably appalled with her confession.

"Other men? You mean besides Dante and yourself?"

"I mean besides myself. My brother has told me how little actually occurred today."

That detail seemed to please him far too much. A flood of irritation emboldened her. She raised her chin at him. "Of course there have been other men. You don't think that the English air has suddenly made me lose my head, do you? Of all the atmospheres in the world, the stuffy one here would be the last to cause a woman to do so. There have been lots of other men."

He didn't like that. Good.

He hovered more, bending his face to hers. *"Lots?"*

"Many. Dozens."

"Dozens?"

"Hundreds."

They stood there toe to toe and nose to nose, glaring at each other.

A smile twitched. *"Hundreds?* You are a superb actress and would have been magnificent on the stage, but *hundreds?"*

"Yes, *hundreds."*

He laughed. "You should have stopped at *lots.* Or at least *dozens.* But *hundreds . . ."*

"You do not believe me?"

"Not at all."

He looked so handsome with the smile softening his

mouth and humor sparkling his eyes. Incredibly handsome. And reassured. Triumphant, if the truth be told. It vexed her to no end, and she suppressed the odd swell of emotion foolishly glowing in response to that smile.

She had gone to all this trouble, had risked being assaulted by a notorious rake, had created a scandal that for all her posturing would be hell to face, and he was refusing to see her disreputable character even when she threw it in his face. It infuriated her, even while her heart stupidly beamed with gratitude.

"You do not believe me because your male pride does not want to accept that you were merely one of hundreds, that is all."

"I am confident that I was not one of hundreds, or even dozens. I strongly suspect that I was not even one of lots, and quite possibly not so much as one of two. You will drop this ridiculous act at once."

Something dangerous burst inside her. Something rebellious and furious and even a little wicked.

She reached up with both hands and grabbed his head. She pulled him down and planted a very firm kiss on his lips.

She held him until his stunned shock began to pass, then released him and stepped away before he had completely recovered.

"Hundreds, Uncle Vergil. I am infamous for ruining saints."

She turned to exit upstage.

A firm hand closed on her arm.

With a gasping swirl she found herself turned and

pulled into arms, which encircled her waist and shoulders. The Vergil of the ruins looked down at her. Dangerously.

"You make me wish that were true," he said, lifting her until her toes scraped the floor, lowering his head.

She should push him away, but her arms would not obey her command. Her suddenly foggy mind scrambled for words to put him in his place, but her heart beat so loudly that she couldn't hear herself think. His warm lips touched hers and she didn't have a mind at all anymore.

He ravished her mouth with demanding lips and nipping teeth and exploring tongue. Disgraceful sensations cascaded through her and, heaven help her, she reveled in them, savoring his encompassing strength, losing herself in a warmth that obscured considerations of anything else.

He buried his face in the crook of her neck and kissed and bit a pulse there. It sent shocks to her breasts, her thighs, and all the way to her toes. He took her mouth again with a burning insistence. She welcomed him this time, parting her lips, inviting the arousing invasion.

His embrace moved into astonishing caresses, pressing to her hips and back and buttocks through her garments. The recently awakened, shameless Bianca thrilled at each possessive touch. His hand slid toward her breasts and her reckless passion lilted a plea for him to hurry and release the desire aching through her consciousness, building a breathless craving.

He stopped abruptly, like a slap had made him sane. His lips parted from hers. His head rose. He did not release her, but held her in a silent embrace, caressing her back with slow, soothing strokes.

The frenzy leaked away, leaving the Bianca Kenwood whom she knew too well in the arms of a man whom she should hate. But even this Bianca did not want to separate. She rested on his chest and floated in the friendly tenderness of that touch, because it kept the worst of her confusing emotions at bay.

Finally, she tilted her head. He gazed out the window with a sightless expression.

He looked down, touched her face, and set her away from him.

"I seem to have forgotten myself again."

He wanted them to retreat once more to their roles of dictatorial guardian and rebellious ward. Of course. What else would he want? Just as well. If he kissed her like this every day and held her with such gentleness afterward, she might decide that nothing else mattered in her life.

She saw no criticism in his face, but considering what she had just told him, she could imagine what he might be thinking. Even if he really had not believed her, she had undoubtedly just changed his mind.

Say something.

Of course he would not. But, oh, how her heart wished that he would speak whatever he thought right now, good or bad. She wanted with an inexplicable yearning to know this man, whoever he really was, sinning paragon or sordid fraud. She longed just once to enjoy the special intimacy of sharing his confidences along with his passion, even if the result was hearing condemnation for the woman she pretended to be.

The acknowledgment that he would never open to her in that way, that he responded to her with lust but nothing more, left that newly discovered corner of her heart anguished with regret.

"You really must permit me to go," she said softly. "You should be concerned with my influence on Charlotte, but perhaps you should worry for yourself as well, if I provoke you like this. It is abundantly clear that I must leave this family now."

He only glanced at her, that thoughtful expression still deepening his gaze.

"I will not marry your brother. If you do not let me leave, the scandal will encompass your whole family. You will be the talk of society for harboring such a female, and Charlotte will be tainted by my friendship. In your sister's interest, if not in mine and yours, allowing me to leave is the only decent choice for you."

Still he said nothing. Perhaps because there was nothing to say.

Somehow she turned away from him. Half-blind with tears, she found her way to the door.

He experienced no self-recrimination this time. No guilt or shock. No regret.

He was glad her brash kiss had destroyed the dam filled to bursting. Glad she had provoked him to release his tenuous hold on control. That was all her kiss had really been, an excuse that he had ruthlessly grabbed. He would not demean her by pretending it had been a deliberate invitation on her part.

How quickly the mind surrendered to what the passions wanted to do. His blood had roared and the next thing he knew she was in his arms.

She was not wicked or experienced, but she was definitely dangerous. To him at least.

She was right. She really had to leave. Within a day, everyone in this house would know about her and Dante. Within a month, the entire world would be whispering. She had not missed the implications of the lessons Pen had been giving her about the code of discretion in English society. She had deliberately arranged things to use the threat of scandal against him.

But that was only part of the reason why she should leave, and she knew that too. What a picture he must present to her. The saint lecturing her on behavior one moment and then ravishing her the next. A laughable figure at best, a depraved one at worst.

He lifted the little lead ball and sent it down its path on the toy. When it reached the bottom he did it again. The chinks and clanks beat out the pattern of his thoughts.

He should send her away and let her have what she wanted, but he could not do that. As long as possible, he needed to keep control of her, and not only because the relentless simmer had become an enlivening, welcome excitement.

He walked to his desk and fished a letter from amidst

the documents stacked there. He flicked it open and reread the information sent to him by Adam Kenwood's solicitor.

What a tangle.

He needed to keep her here because she might be in danger. He needed to keep her here on the chance that he still might bind her to this family.

He needed to keep her here because her absence would create a void in his life, but she had cornered him so he would have to let her go.

He smiled with regret and admiration. In overplaying her hand, she had managed to force his own.

The door opened and Penelope's dark head appeared.

"Vergil, may we speak with you?"

"Of course, Pen."

The other part of the "we" turned out to be Maria Catalani and Fleur. Fleur went to the window seat and the others settled themselves into chairs.

Penelope let forth a deep sigh. "This is a very unfortunate business. You cannot say that I did not warn you."

"That is true, Pen. I cannot say that."

"I expect that Dante offered to marry her when you had them both in here."

"I did not hold a pistol to his head, if that is what concerns you. He has great affection for Miss Kenwood, and had intended to propose, in any case."

"Did he? That is interesting, but that is not what concerns me. Or us, rather." She gestured toward Catalani and Fleur. "Bianca is too naive to protect herself from someone like Dante. We really should have warned her.

What is worse, I do not think that she has the same *tendre* for him that he does for her and it would be very unfortunate if Bianca is forced to marry him."

"Not *unfortunate*. Tragic." Catalani intoned. "I do not think that marriage to your brother was in her plans, Laclere."

"Plans sometimes change."

"That is a man's arrogant dismissal of a young woman's preferences. And this marriage—a man takes advantage of a girl's innocence, and the response of everyone is to marry them. Barbaric. It is worse in my country, but still it is barbaric."

"So you see, we do not think marriage is the solution," Pen said.

"Well, ladies, I suppose that I could defend her honor by killing Dante if you would find that more to your taste."

Catalani actually began to nod, but Pen looked aghast. "You misunderstand us. We have talked it over, and the point of their marrying is to blunt the scandal. We have come here to tell you that there can be no scandal."

"I would say there can be a very big scandal."

"Not at all. Maria and Fleur and I have realized—"

"That we did not see anything." Catalani finished triumphantly.

He settled into his chair and looked at them. "You did not see anything?"

"That is correct, Laclere. Nothing. So much for this talk of marriage. *Abbastanza.*"

"As I remember it, you saw quite a bit."

"Oh, no," Pen said. "Maria was explaining a new sleeve becoming fashionable in Milan and we were engrossed. Until the three of you came up that hill, we were not even aware that Bianca and Dante were there."

"You think to contain this among yourselves?"

"Yes, not that there is anything to contain. But if there were, we would never speak of it after leaving this room, even to one another. The fact that we saw nothing, that is."

He should resist this solution and hope that Bianca would change her mind, but the relief with which he heard Pen's scheme told him that he would have embraced this offer of silence even if Bianca had submitted to the marriage at once.

In that instant he knew that he did not want Dante to have her. Nor any other man. Except himself.

Which was impossible.

He turned to Fleur.

She noticed his attention. "I am the last woman in the world to force a girl into marriage, Laclere."

He considered this reprieve. She would not have to leave. She would be safe. He might yet rearrange those plans.

He would still see her.

"I have yet to hear of women keeping silent about such things, or men either. However, if you think you can do so, perhaps disaster can be averted."

"I can be a citadel of discretion when it is warranted," Catalani said with a meaningful arch in her eyebrows.

"Well, now that is settled, we must go dress for dinner,"

Pen said, rising. "It is very generous of you to be so under-standing about this, Vergil. I promise you, no one will ever know that you bent the rules just once."

"Very good, Pen. We certainly wouldn't want anyone to know that."

He found Dante alone in the library.

"It appears that you have been spared. The ladies insist that they saw absolutely nothing. Assuming Miss Kenwood does not start rumors about herself, which despite her bold-ness is unlikely, there need be no marriage."

Dante threw up his arms in exasperation. "Are you for-getting that we do not want me to be spared?"

"I made it very clear that I did not want the girl trapped against her will."

"I did not trap her, damn it, she trapped *me.*"

"It would be best if you left tomorrow with the others. Some time apart and she may welcome your attention again."

"You have more tenacity than I. The girl just refused me, in case you didn't hear it as clearly as I did."

"I heard a young woman refusing to be coerced by cir-cumstances."

"I do not care for the way she dismissed me. It was in-sulting, especially since the alternative was rather bleak. She all but implied that marrying me was a fate worse than death, and while I may not be some great prize . . . If it weren't for her inheritance, I would tell you to go to hell."

"Pen will be taking her and Charlotte up to London soon. I expect they will remain there at least a fortnight. I will accompany them and stay a few days, but it would be best if you took over when I left. Whether Miss Kenwood welcomes your interest or not, I do not like the idea of her alone in the city with just Pen watching out for her. She is too independent-minded, and may attempt to go about on her own."

"I daresay there will be men enough to watch over her once Pen starts taking her around."

"Exactly, Dante. If she does not marry you, I would prefer that she marry no one for some while yet. In particular, I do not want Nigel alone with her at any time. I want you there to see that she has no opportunity to get into any more trouble. With any luck, however, she will allow you to pick up the pursuit of your case."

He didn't really believe that, but if Dante continued to court her, it would mean someone was nearby who could be trusted. After what had just happened again in the study, it had become imperative for that someone to be other than himself whenever possible.

All the same, Dante's lack of enthusiasm heartened him, and relieved him of one potential opportunity for guilt. If Dante had fallen in love with her . . .

"It may be best if you made any new overtures very subtle," he added.

"I know how to handle women, Verg."

"Of course. My apologies."

"I will be subtle. Damned subtle. I don't fancy having the girl make me look like a fool again."

Vergil turned to go find Fleur. With any luck, Dante would be so subtle that Bianca wouldn't even notice him keeping watch.

Fleur was sitting on the bench in the garden where they met sometimes for conversation away from the hopeful eyes of her mother. She appeared, as always, utterly beautiful, like a figure molded in porcelain or painted by a great master. She turned at his footfall and her mouth pursed into a wry smile.

"I hope that we did not disrupt your plans too much."

He sat beside her. "Not really. Catalani's idea?"

"Pen's, although the solution had crossed my mind. On my own, however, I would have never proposed it. I did not know if you welcomed the development or not."

"The match would have been convenient, but the circumstances did not appeal to me."

They sat in the contented silence of friendship. He studied the serene, delicate profile that he had always admired with a peculiar objectivity. He had never felt any passion for this exquisite woman, even before he learned that she was incapable of feeling passion for him.

"My mother is letting her impatience show, isn't she? She has said things this visit."

"She has been more pointed sooner than I anticipated. I do not think there is cause for concern yet, but—"

She held up a hand to stop him, then let it fall helplessly to her lap. "Which means others are saying things to her. I know that it has been almost a year, but I had hoped to get another season out of it."

"As had I. That may not be possible."

"No. Oh, how I resent this, Laclere. Last season was the first one I enjoyed. No suitors bothering me with their silly petitions. No endless speculation about this match or that. No pressure from father, and best of all, a good friend with whom to enjoy the balls. A woman should be allowed to have such peace all the time if she chooses."

Her fervor would have surprised anyone else who knew her. However, he had seen her in tears, confessing the fears that led her to resist marriage, admitting that she could not contemplate the love of any man without freezing with terror. A deep friendship had emerged from that unexpected confidence, and a casual association had become a calculated deception. Such a ruse had a limited life, however.

"A woman with your beauty is bound to attract suitors, Fleur, especially if she has your fortune. If you looked more gently on them, perhaps one would—"

"Not you, too, Laclere. Please, do not. Forgive my outburst. You have been very kind, dancing attendance in a waltz you knew would end."

"Not kindness, Fleur. Remember that it also spared me the tribulations of the marriage mart. For my own reasons I would like to avoid pressure to take a wife right now as much as you would a husband."

"You never told me why. Not fair, to share confidences only one way. I was tempted several times to try and learn your secret. It is nothing sordid, I trust."

"That depends on what you call sordid."

"Nothing you would do, I'm sure." Her laugh turned into a sigh. "What a pair we are, Laclere. Do you think anyone has guessed our little arrangement?"

"No, but some have probably begun to wonder."

She turned thoughtful eyes to him and the frown returned. "I suppose so, especially if mother has grown so bold. It has been falling on you, hasn't it? The suspicion that you are behaving less than honorably toward me."

"Nothing has been said, Fleur, nor do I think that my reputation has been affected."

"But mother . . . yes, people are beginning to wonder. I will tell mother after we leave that you offered and I refused you. I will let it be known that it was my decision, as I always promised I would. Father will be furious, of course. He always is when I let a title slip away." She cocked her head. "Unless, of course, you have decided to accept the arrangement I proposed last spring."

He couldn't help but smile. "It had its appeal. A permanent solution for us both, and your inheritance as well. But I cannot marry right now, Fleur. If the day comes when I can, I will want children. A white marriage is not for me. No doubt you can find another man who will accept it."

"I will make that offer to no one else. I would trust no other man to honor the terms. Nor do I expect to find another whose company I enjoy enough to contemplate a lifetime with him. I think that once I break things off with you that I will go on a grand tour. A very long one.

By the time I get back I will be old enough to be on the shelf."

"There is no need to tell your mother immediately. Take your time if you want."

"I may put her off another month or so. Express some reservations first, that sort of thing."

He patted her hand. "There is no hurry, as I said."

Her soft palm turned up and grasped his with a child's desperation. "I do not fancy facing the loneliness again," she whispered. "Promise me that we will always be friends."

He wished he could spare her. He would obliterate her fears if he could, and send her off to find happiness with a good man.

He held her small hand tightly, to reinforce his words. "Of course, Fleur. I am always here for you."

The sabres clashed and rang under the watchful eye of the Chevalier Corbet. Vergil met the challenge of Cornell Witherby. On the other side of the large chamber in the Hampstead manor, Julian Hampton sparred with Adrian Burchard. Adrian's brother, Colin, and Dante formed a third pair.

"You have improved," Vergil said as he caught Witherby's sword making a new move.

"You have not."

No, he had not. It had been months since he had met the others here. What had been a regular sport before he became viscount had turned into a diversion that he had little time to enjoy anymore.

Not only his skill had suffered, but also the friendships that he shared with these men. Today he had made time for both them and the exercise.

The practice continued, with the old French chevalier snapping praise and criticism.

"Have your sisters come up to town with you?" Witherby asked as they paused and faced off again.

The light in Witherby's eyes revealed more than Vergil wanted to know. But then, he had seen how Pen's demeanor had changed since the house party. Her glowing happiness made it easier to accommodate himself to their escalating intimacy, but there was a husband who never would. Vergil trusted that if a love affair began, his friend would be carefully discreet, and not only because of their old friendship. No man wants to be named in court for criminal correspondence with an earl's wife.

"They have both come. It is time to prepare for Charlotte's first season."

Witherby rolled his eyes. "I have always considered it a gift from heaven that I had no sisters demanding such an expense."

"Well, we all find our way into debt, and a sister is as good a path as any."

"Speak for yourself. I am happily solvent."

No doubt he was offering reassurances to the brother of the woman he pursued, but Vergil found the admission interesting. It appeared that Witherby's printing establishment, which he liked to treat as no more than a gentleman's hobby, served the baser purpose of supplementing his income.

They engaged again, but the sounds beside them stopped. Hampton and Burchard strolled toward the entry to prepare to leave.

Vergil made a better show during the ensuing minutes. His lack of practice hampered him less with each move. He forced himself to concentrate on the task as well, and that made a significant difference. Instead of contemplating his unproductive investigation into Milton's death, or exploring improper thoughts about Bianca Kenwood, he honed his attention on the moves of his sabre.

The chevalier called a halt and treated them both to little lectures on how to improve. They joined Hampton and Burchard in the chamber used for dressing, while the chevalier turned his attention to Colin and Dante.

"I am glad that you could join us, Duclairc," Hampton said as he tied his cravat in the reflection of a small mirror tacked to the wall. "Will you be coming back to the club?"

"I need to escort my sisters this afternoon. Pen will be commissioning Charlotte's presentation gown."

"Say no more. Even with your oversight, the cost will be obscene. Left on their own, they will ruin you."

Adrian had already dressed, so he sidled over. "Will you be in town a few days now?"

"Two or three."

"I will call on you."

Vergil knew why Adrian planned to call, and what he intended to discuss. While Vergil wanted to know what Adrian had learned on his mission for Wellington, he had no desire to reveal his own investigations.

Hampton and Adrian left to claim their horses. Within a minute of their departure, the sounds of an altercation poured in the window of the dressing chamber. A carriage clamored up as a man's voice shouted curses.

Vergil grabbed his coat and headed out to the front drive with Witherby on his heels. They joined Hampton and Adrian just as a slender man with graying hair jumped out of the coach.

It was the Earl of Glasbury, Penelope's husband.

"Fiend," he snarled, striding to the men arrayed in front of the building's door, pointing with a walking stick. "You despicable scoundrel."

Witherby tensed. Vergil stepped closer to him, to form a human shield, and Adrian closed in from the side.

The earl advanced with the walking stick thrusting like a sword. His slack mouth formed a flaccid, scowling line and his face flushed redder with each step.

The tip of the stick did not seek its mark on Witherby. Instead, the earl thumped it against Julian Hampton's chest.

"I'll not be your prey," the earl said, poking the stick with each word. "Who do you think you are, daring to try and make a fool out of me?"

Hampton barely reacted. His hand grasped the stick's tip where it rested on his chest. He did not even remove it. He merely held it and walked forward, forcing the earl backward.

When he had him twenty yards away, he yanked the stick out of the earl's hands and thrust it aside.

A conversation took place that Vergil and the others could not hear. Vergil could not see Hampton's face, but he witnessed the earl's reactions. The man looked half-mad, and more than anger made him so. A frantic terror fired his eyes.

The earl turned on his heel and gave Vergil a pointed, disdainful glare as he climbed back into his coach. Insignia flashing in the morning sun, the coach pulled away.

"I'll be damned," Witherby muttered with annoyance. "Hampton? Who would have thought—"

"It had nothing to do with the countess," Adrian said.

Hampton's expression showed no reaction to the drama as he rejoined them. "A misunderstanding," he said blandly.

They all claimed their horses, to ride back to the city. As Vergil prepared to mount, he caught Adrian's eye. It was not hard to do, because Adrian was in the process of trying to catch his in return.

They soundlessly acknowledged their mutual conclusion regarding what had just occurred.

Someone was trying to blackmail the Earl of Glasbury, and the earl thought it was Julian Hampton.

Bianca shuffled through the fashion plates and plucked one out to set aside.

Very casually, Diane St. John removed it from the preferred plates and returned it to the original pile. "The waist is too high."

Across the elegant sitting room, Penelope and Charlotte bent their heads in consultation with Madame Tissot, debating designs for Charl's presentation gown. Diane had joined the party to offer her opinions. She and her husband frequently visited the house they owned in Paris, and she knew the latest developments even better than Madame Tissot.

Vergil patiently waited. Mostly he ignored the proceedings, while he gazed out the window or paced around the room.

"What is he doing here?" Bianca muttered to Diane. "Surely he could trust Pen's taste in these matters."

Diane cast Vergil a sidelong glance with her soulful eyes as she tilted her chestnut head toward an image of a morning dress. "Perhaps his attendance has nothing to do with taste in fashions."

"Well, he is underfoot all the time now. He left Laclere Park with the rest of you after the house party, but then inexplicably returned in time to travel with us up to London. Now every day he shows up at Pen's house, always in time to accompany us. These visits to the modistes must be boring him."

"His sister will represent the family when she is presented. However, perhaps he finds female company other than boring. Many men do." Diane spoke quietly and casually, but her little smile left Bianca wondering if Mrs. St. John referred to the company of one female in particular.

It horrified her that someone may have guessed about that, especially since Diane had probably heard about the episode with Dante by now.

Bianca was very sure that the viscount's presence had nothing to do with his desire for her company. Vergil was hovering about for some other reason, probably to keep an eye on the expense of Charlotte's new wardrobe. However, as a result, Bianca had not been able to slip away as she needed to. Worse, she had been forced to bear the discomforting presence of a man with whom she had twice now been shockingly out of control.

He did not appear at all discomforted. He acted so calmly one would think he had forgotten those embraces.

Except for the moments when she caught him regarding her with eyes that said he remembered all of it. Those looks served as little pokes at her composure. Scandalously exciting provocations.

A male hand reached around her shoulder and plucked a plate from the pile. "This one. Without the lace on the sleeves and in this rose color here."

With a fluid movement, Diane St. John rose and strolled across the room to where Madame Tissot was unfolding silken evening wraps.

"I rather thought this one," Bianca said, pulling out a flamboyant ball gown with an excess of frills. "In scarlet red."

"No wonder Madame Tissot has taken no orders from you. She has her standards."

"Then I will have to find another modiste to dress me as society expects. There will be no point in swathing myself in sedate rose if everyone sees scarlet anyway."

"You do not need to worry about that. It is clear that the episode with my brother remains unknown."

She looked up at him with surprise. She had assumed

that the force of his reputation had merely delayed the storm.

"It has been a fortnight, Miss Kenwood. If anyone in that house learned of it and intended to speak of it to others, they would have done so by now. You have been denied your scandal."

"Perhaps *I* will speak of it."

"I do not think so. Suffering shots from others' guns is one thing. Turning the pistol on oneself is quite another. It takes hopeless despair to do that. Stubbornness will not suffice."

He was right. She had steeled herself for the onslaught of scorn, in part by concentrating on her escape from it. It would take more determination than she possessed to deliberately provoke the gossip that might free her.

She suspected that he had found a way to thwart her. Just as well, then, that she had an alternate plan.

Madame Tissot unfolded a shawl with a flourish. Woven of the finest deep sapphire silk with violet undertones, it fluttered over Charlotte's lap like an eddy of water. The modiste cocked her head critically, then shook it with a sigh. "The hue is not right, mademoiselle. Since it is not a fashionable color this year, it must be just right for the woman who wears it."

Vergil walked over and lifted the exquisite shawl. It cascaded from his hand like a waterfall.

Madame Tissot noticed his appreciation. "However, with the right gown, a violet one perhaps . . ."

"It would suit my ward."

Madame Tissot turned to Bianca with new eyes. Within

moments the little French woman had draped the shawl over her back and arms.

"It is lovely on you," Diane St. John said. "You have an excellent eye, Laclere."

Charlotte clapped her hands. "It is beautiful, Bianca. You must have it. See what it does to her eyes, Pen."

"Yes, you must have it," Vergil repeated. "The violet gown too, Madame Tissot. Something modest and understated."

"Of course, Lord Laclere."

Madame Tissot escorted Bianca back to the inner sanctum, and a whirlwind of measuring and draping ensued. An hour later Bianca emerged into the front room again, to find only Penelope, Diane, and Charlotte waiting for her. The guardian who had just imperiously spent a sizable chunk of her income for her had disappeared.

Which meant only Penelope stood between her and a few hours of freedom.

"Let us walk back," she suggested while Roger, Pen's footman, carried the wrapped shawl to the carriage.

"Heavens, no," Charlotte said. "I am exhausted. Where do you get your vigor, Bianca?"

"It has been a curse all my life, and I really grow troublesome if I cannot walk it off."

Pen blanched at the word troublesome. "We are supposed to attend the theater tonight. Surely you would like to rest."

"I really feel the need for a good walk, Pen. A nice long one. Why don't you and Charlotte take Mrs. St. John in the carriage, and I will follow. I know the way."

Pen glanced around the street, as if hoping to see rein-forcements. Bianca had already determined that the general had left the field.

"If I was not expected by my husband, I would join you in this walk," Diane St. John said, giving Bianca a private wink. "One absorbs the life of the town when one strolls its streets. Why not permit it, Pen? Especially since it will avoid her becoming *troublesome,* as she says."

"If you insist. I must require that Roger stay with you, however. Please do not tarry, and be sure not to get lost."

"I can hardly get lost with Roger as an escort."

The other ladies left in the carriage. Bianca began walking away from the direction they had just ridden. Roger fell into step behind.

"May I ask where we are going, Miss Kenwood?" he ventured after a good half hour.

"To the City."

"The City? Nothing to see there and it is too far. Best if we turn back now. My lady said you should not tarry."

She began to respond but a passing carriage caught her eye. She turned and watched its progress down the street. Surely that had been Nigel by the window. And across from him, the shadowed figure of a woman.

Roger waited with strained forbearance. He appeared ripe for negotiation.

"No doubt this excursion keeps you from other duties, Roger. Perhaps it would be best if I found a coach. Show me where to hire one, and then you can return to the house."

He began shaking his head even before she finished.

Sighing with defeat, she turned and led him down the street. She would prefer to do this alone, but even if Roger spoke of it and word reached Vergil, she still would have accomplished her errand.

Like magic, his name summoned his memory and his memory summoned his presence. A curricle slowed into pace beside her. She glanced over to find Vergil holding the reins.

He had a whole city to ride in. He might have taken another street to wherever he was going.

He stepped out of the carriage and Roger rushed to hold the horse.

"I will take Miss Kenwood home, Roger. You are released of your charge."

The footman turned on his heel. Vergil gestured to the curricle.

"I am not returning to the house yet, Laclere, so I will continue walking."

"No, you will not. Whatever your destination, I will accompany you."

She let him hand her up. He settled beside her. "Where can I take you?"

"To the City. I wish to see Mr. Peterson."

He didn't turn a hair. "It is good that I happened by, then. Pen would have worried with your delayed return. It will not do for you to absent yourself for so long, even with a footman for protection."

A red arrow shot through her head. This man had the effrontery to scold her for not accommodating herself to the restrictions he created.

She welcomed the old vexation. Like a suit of steel for her heart, it blunted other reactions evoked by being alone with him again.

Embarrassing, confusing, dangerous reactions.

"I think that my cousin Nigel is in London," she said as they rejoined the other vehicles crowding the streets.

"He arrived a few days ago."

"It is odd that he has not called on Penelope."

"He called yesterday."

"It is odd that Pen did not mention he had left his card."

"She never saw his card. I procured it from the butler."

She turned in surprise toward his impassive profile. "Your sister will be insulted that you presumed to do so."

"I doubt that, since he did not call on Pen."

He said it with utter calm, as if the implications should not bother her at all.

"You discovered that my cousin called on me, and you removed his card so I would not know? How dare you?"

"Compose yourself. Anyone who sees us would think we were having a row."

"We *are* having a row. It is time that we had a right understanding on a few things, Uncle Vergil."

"Call me Laclere. It is disconcerting to have a woman whom I have kissed address me as Uncle Vergil."

She stared at him with astonishment. "You amaze me. You refer to that with equanimity even while you assume a posture of authority."

"I neither refer to it nor think of it with equanimity. I merely point out that Uncle Vergil has become a peculiar form of address. As for your cousin, I do not approve of his interest in you."

"Considering the man who did meet with your approval, your lack of it might be treated as the highest recommendation, and suspect in its motivations."

"I will not spar with you over this. I forbid you to ever see your cousin alone, and I must insist that you do nothing to encourage him. I do not take this course to further my brother's cause, but to protect you. I do not think Nigel Kenwood is what he appears to be."

He must have heard about Nigel's secret woman visitor.

"Not what he appears to be? Oh, my, dear me, goodness, goodness, what a shock." A storm of confusion, hurt, and resentment that had been gathering for three weeks broke and she let fury fly. "A fine observation coming from you. Excuse me if I am not undone by this stunning news, but I think that there is not a single man in your fastidious society who is what he appears to be. Aunt Edith warned me about the corrupt, immoral underbelly of the English aristocracy, and I begin to understand her. How dare you judge Nigel. If he is not what he appears to be, he is no more a fraud than you. Less of one, because he does not set himself up as some saint. Much less of one, because the last I heard, he did not make love to his ward *even* while he courts a fiancée *and* keeps a mistress up in Lancashire."

He almost didn't react. Almost. The slightest flicker of dismay lit his eyes, however. That instant of concern told her more eloquently than words that she had hit a mark with her last accusation.

Charlotte had been correct about his journeys north. He kept a woman there.

It sucked the fury right out of her. She sank back into the seat, overwhelmed with a sick desolation.

The depth of her disappointment staggered her. This detail irrevocably turned those kisses from impetuous passion into sordid follies.

"Fleur is not my fiancée," he finally said.

"A minor point, Laclere."

He drove slowly, as if some contemplation distracted him.

"Who told you that I keep a mistress?"

"Do not worry. No one at the house party made insinuations about it. The servants are not gossiping. Only those closest to you suspect. Your visits to her have been noticed. What attraction could draw you north so frequently? Charlotte suggested the explanation, but I would assume that Penelope and Dante have guessed."

She ached for him to deny it. She even wished he would lie. What could one more deception hurt?

He began navigating the City's narrow streets without a word, but a frown continued to crease his brow. Considering her own devastation, she was glad that she had given him something to worry about.

A public scandal about Dante would have been easier to bear than this private humiliation.

She entered Mr. Peterson's chambers with renewed resolve to shed herself of Vergil's presence in her life.

The solicitor smiled with relief when he saw that she was alone. Vergil had escorted her to the outer chamber and then gone off to conduct some business of his own.

She hurried through the usual pleasantries. "I do not want to appear abrupt, Mr. Peterson, but I expect the viscount to return for me quickly. When last you wrote, you indicated that you expected some news soon, and since I am in London I thought it easiest to come and hear it myself."

"As you requested, I have obtained the names of some of the men who have expressed interest in purchasing your business partnerships. Most were only tentative inquiries, but one was very firm."

He pawed through some documents. "Here it is. It is for the mill. That is the investment already yielding income. For one thing, the business has established itself. For another, you own forty-five percent of it. The mill's manager, a Mr. Clark, owns another forty-five percent. Your grandfather stood him to over half of the initial capital some six years ago when it was built."

"Who owns the rest?"

"Your grandfather was the majority owner. He left the remaining ten percent to his grandnephew, Nigel Kenwood. He intended the income to help maintain Woodleigh."

"Someone wants to buy the mill now?"

"Learning the details took a few pints of ale cajoled down the throat of a clerk to Adam Kenwood's solicitor. There has been a serious offer from a Mr. Johnston and Mr. Kennedy. Nigel Kenwood is eager to agree, but the manager has refused to entertain the offer. Mr. Johnston and Mr. Kennedy demand majority ownership and control of the business, so the new baronet's ten percent is worthless to them without the agreement of one of the principals."

She lined the details up and saw them paving a road back to Baltimore. "And I am the other principal. If I sell, and Nigel sells, the manager loses control of the mill."

"That is correct. He will still enjoy its success, assuming that the new owners pay out honestly, but there are many ways to see that minority investors do not reap the same benefits as those in control. It is easy to claim costs that do not exist, and divert funds accordingly. Not that I would cast any aspersions upon Mr. Johnston and Mr. Kennedy, but they *are* managers of mills. Unsavory types, for all the wealth they accrue."

He made it very clear such men were definitely beneath Mr. Peterson himself, who was hardly to the manor born.

"What has my guardian's reaction been to this offer?"

"The viscount is considering it and has asked for financial figures, which Mr. Clark has delayed in sending. No doubt the man plans to be an obstruction whenever possible. Still, the clerk with whom I imbibed indicated that the viscount seemed inclined to hold the investment. It does pay handsomely."

Which meant that it would pay handsomely again. Who was to know if part of the next payment got "diverted" now to the account Mr. Peterson had established for her? Not much, just enough to get her and Jane back to America.

If she promised the manager not to sell when she turned twenty-one, he would probably grab at her suggestion and see it as a mutually beneficial business arrangement.

"Mr. Peterson, I would like you to write out the information on this mill for me."

That night Bianca attended the theater with Vergil and Penelope. She wore the blue silk shawl for what she expected to be the first and last time. She intended to leave it behind when she sailed from England.

Its luscious fall reminded her of the life her inheritance offered, and that she would soon reject.

She did not want to return to Baltimore without visiting Milan. For all of her brave resolve with Vergil, she was not sure that she would find another way to affect her dream and plans. She pictured herself at Aunt Edith's age, always wondering what might have been.

Perhaps she did not need to repudiate the entire inheritance. Maybe, if she gave away half . . .

She mentally castigated herself. If she began making excuses for using some of Adam's ill-begotten fortune, she would probably end up seduced into the luxury the whole amount afforded. Baltimore it would be, and she would return as poor as she had left.

She noticed little about the performance on the stage down below. Not only her moral debate occupied her attention. So did the man sitting beside her. His mere presence made her warm. His smallest movement made her heart jump. Considering what she had learned about him today, her susceptibility infuriated her.

Yes, Baltimore it would be, and very soon too. When she was back home she would be able to forget this man who had her reacting like a fool, even though she knew he was a scoundrel and a fraud.

That night when she retired, she found a letter waiting for her in her chamber. It was one that Adam Kenwood had written to Milton.

In it he agreed to Milton's suggestion that he give to charity an amount that equaled what he had reaped when he sold his shipping business, to make reparations for the profit he had accrued through the slave trade.

Another note had been folded into the letter, this one from the current Viscount Laclere.

"I found this among my brother's papers and thought that you would like to see it. Today I visited Adam's solicitor to verify that the intentions expressed in this letter were carried out. They were, some three years ago. Therefore, the portion of his estate that you have inherited is not tainted. There is no guilt in accepting it. It appears that Adam came to see his son's rightness on this matter."

She stared at the letters as their implications sank in. Her heart beat rapidly with reborn joy and excitement. It would not be Baltimore, after all.

She pictured Vergil leaving her with Mr. Peterson and going to the solicitor to verify what had happened. It was not in his interest for her to know about this. The truth gave her back her dream—a dream that he did not approve of.

His generosity touched her profoundly. Her annoyance at his interference disappeared and her suspicions about his character became insignificant. Even the dream lost importance. Vergil's gesture of discovering the truth turned her heart inside out.

He might be a fraud, and he might be dangerous, but she would miss him badly when she was gone.

chapter II

Vergil poured two glasses of port and handed one to Dante. His brother had discarded his frock coat and now lounged contentedly in a chair in front of the study's low fire. He looked for all the world like a man whose various appetites had been sated. Vergil surmised that he had spent the evening with his current mistress.

"I expected you to join us at the theater tonight."

"I got distracted, and then the weather turned raw. It is bad enough that I have to start playing nursemaid to-morrow. No need for both of us there tonight."

No. No need. However, Dante's presence might have distracted Bianca, and pulled her out of the subdued mood into which she had retreated since their argument in the afternoon.

It had been an uncomfortable night. Bianca had cloaked her reactions in serene composure, but he had felt her thoughts, and even seen them on occasion in the lidded glances she gave him. By the time he escorted the ladies back into Pen's house, he had come close to pulling her aside and blurting out an explanation and begging her forgiveness.

Pointless. Hopeless. What could he say?

She had concluded he was the most dishonorable of men, not because of the mistress, but because of the implications regarding his behavior toward her. She had decided he was a predatory monster. Maybe she was right.

Certainly he felt a predatory desire with her continued proximity.

"Nigel Kenwood is in town. It is very important for you to stay in London until the ladies leave," he said to Dante. "It would be best if you resided here. I have instructed Morton to open your bedchamber."

"Laclere House is uncomfortable out of season, what with most of the house closed and most of the servants in the country. You may not mind living like a monk in a few rooms with only a valet, but I think that one of my clubs would be preferable."

"I want you near Pen's house, not in a club."

"You are acting like a fussy old aunt, Verg. What can Kenwood do? She cannot marry him without your permission, unless you fear them bolting to Scotland."

"That would not be beyond the imagination. However, I must confide in you that my concerns are more serious now." He went to the desk and retrieved the letter he had received at Laclere Park from Adam Kenwood's solicitor. "Read this."

Dante lazily flicked the paper open. "Seems common

enough to me. Miss Kenwood's inheritance is entailed. If she dies without children, it goes to her closest relative."

"Yes, common enough. Except for the clause that limits the relative to someone with Kenwood blood. I had barely noticed that when I read the testament, but the solicitor's letter makes it explicit. That rules out the great-aunt in Baltimore, and leaves only Nigel."

"So?"

"She is more valuable to him dead than as his wife."

"Barely, considering a husband's rights. Are you saying that you think that musician would harm her? Your imagination has gotten the better of you."

"Most likely. I may be doing Kenwood a disservice in my suspicions, but I would rather take a cautious stance. I have asked around, and he is thoroughly in dun territory both here and in France."

"Which is why he wants to marry her. Hardly a criminal offense. If I stood to inherit with her death, would you assume that I contemplated murder?"

"Of course not. Nor would I suspect it of him, if she had not come close to being killed twice in the last month."

That wiped the amusement off Dante's face.

"There were two very close accidents at Laclere Park. Unusual accidents, Dante, and I am not entirely convinced that they were accidents at all." He briefly described the incidents.

Dante pondered the tales. "Could have been nothing, of course. Just coincidences. Still, I can see where one might raise the caution, just to be safe."

"Exactly."

"Wouldn't it be best to warn her?"

"I can't impugn the man on such flimsy evidence, and I may be wrong. I suspect Miss Kenwood would attribute my warning to a desire to keep her and Nigel apart. If so, it could have the opposite effect."

Dante frowned at the fire for a spell. "Old Kenwood did you no favors in naming you her guardian, Verg. I am concluding that she is nothing but trouble. A firm hand doesn't begin to describe what is needed with her. I had thought that little episode in the lake was a charming misstep, but you tell me now that while at Laclere Park she slipped out alone in the early mornings for long rides and walks, unaccompanied. She is found rolling in the grass in my embrace and flouts all sense of decency by refusing to marry me. She has shown evidence of a very loose upbringing and unacceptable notions of independence, and in all likelihood she left her virtue behind long ago."

Vergil noted his brother's uncompromising, male expression. Did the Viscount Laclere look like that to her?

You do not know her. She is not trouble or indecent. She is a young woman with dreams, fighting for her life.

"I will tell you now that I am no longer amenable to marrying her, and to hell with her inheritance. However, I will see to it that she does not stir from Pen's house without a chaperon, and not only because she may be in danger. The fact is, Verg, I do not think that you have been strict enough with her. If we are not very careful, she might bring this family down."

Miss Kenwood's safety accounted for, they moved on to other things. But in the flames that he watched while they spoke, Vergil saw her body turned away while she watched the play tonight. She had worn the blue wrap, and its fluid silk cascaded in swooping curves along her back and over her arms, picking up the theater's low lights, bringing out the blond of her hair through a lovely contrast.

He had envied the way it caressed her, and was glad she had worn it. Madame Tissot's account would not be settled from Bianca's income, but she would never know it. He had taken enormous pleasure in seeing her wear his secret gift, even if her icy manner indicated that she would throw it in the fire if she knew he had paid for it.

Just as well that Dante had arrived. He had been enjoying her company too much, and contemplating her far too often. She had become a dangerous fascination. An impossible hunger.

He narrowed his eyes on the dancing flames. Time to be off again. To Lancashire. To his mistress.

"Then it is settled. You will host the reception next week." Mrs. Gaston made it sound as though she bestowed a great favor on Penelope.

Penelope lifted a beautiful little book off the table beside her chair. "I could hardly refuse, since Mr. Witherby saw fit to dedicate the volume to me. That honor should have been yours, as patron of the series."

"It would be vulgar for *all* of them to dedicate their

poems to me. I prefer less ostentatious acknowledgment anyway. Nor would we want anyone to infer that the genius of our poets was being bought like so much ham in a market."

Bianca watched Mrs. Gaston's face as she demurred her significance. Her high cheekbones appeared more prominent today, as if her skin strained against them. Bianca wondered if Mrs. Gaston had been nearly as delighted as she now professed, to find that her patronage had not been celebrated in Mr. Witherby's brief dedication.

Penelope, on the other hand, glowed with delight. Her gaze kept returning to the book's brown leather binding, and her fingertips drifted over the tooled decoration again and again.

"He would do better if you hosted the reception, I fear. There will be those who will not accept my invitation."

"Nonsense. I will see to it that the people who matter come. This will be an important event for you, my dear. A first step, as we relaunch you into the circles you deserve. Your situation has lasted long enough. Even transported prisoners eventually can come home."

Pen's wavering smile revealed skepticism, resignation, and hope. Bianca's heart twisted at the emotions flickering on the countess's face. Penelope always appeared accepting of her social fall, even glad for it, but it was obvious right now that she merely hid the pain.

Bianca looked to Mrs. Gaston with new eyes. She had not warmed to the woman before, but she did now. Mrs. Gaston had continued her friendship with Pen when many others did not. Now she was plotting Pen's rehabilitation.

Small wonder that Pen counted her as a dear friend despite her vain, overbearing manner.

"I will ask my brother if I can use Laclere House." Pen spoke with firm decision. "It will take a lot of preparation, of course, but perhaps he will agree."

"Make him agree," Mrs. Gaston said. "Explain what is at stake. More than a poet's success. Witherby is his friend, so Laclere should come around." She rose. "Now, I must go and make my other calls. I think that Mr. Witherby will arrive soon. He allowed me the honor of bringing you this first printing, but no doubt he wants to witness your pleasure in it."

She left Penelope gazing at the book, stroking its cover again.

Bianca went over to admire the little volume with Pen, and then sat nearby. She would have preferred broaching her request on a different day, when Pen was not so absorbed in the compliment of that dedication.

"Penelope, I would like to return to Laclere Park tomorrow."

That pulled Penelope's attention away from the book. "Are you saying that you are not happy here? I thought that you preferred the city."

"I do. However, I am very uncomfortable with Dante in attendance so much."

"Goodness, are you saying that he has—"

"His behavior is above reproach. I know that we are fortunate to have him escort us to the theater and such, and yesterday's excursion to the British Museum was very enjoyable. It is just . . ." She let her voice trail off.

Pen had never spoken of that day by the lake and what she had seen, but her expression indicated that she understood Bianca's reason for wanting to leave London.

"It wouldn't do to ask Dante to make himself scarce, Bianca. Charlotte rarely gets to spend time with him. As for departing the city, I have just promised to give Mr. Witherby the reception to honor his new book next week. I wish I could accommodate you, but until the reception is over, we are rather stuck here."

"I could return myself tomorrow with Jane, and you and Charlotte could follow as planned."

"I do not think that would be wise."

"Jane and I crossed an ocean. The ride down to Sussex is a minor thing, especially if we go in your coach. Once back at Laclere Park, we will be well cared for."

Pen began wavering.

"Please. The alternative is for me to take to my bed here and pretend an illness. With time I am sure that Dante's company will not embarrass me, but right now, so soon after . . . it is difficult to face him."

Pen patted her hand. "You are always so composed that I never realized how awkward it is for you."

"Very awkward."

"I think that I will permit it. Still, I will be giving my coachman strict instructions to take you directly to Laclere Park, and he will carry orders to the butler and housekeeper to see that you remain there. Vergil can hardly object with those precautions in place."

"Thank you, Pen. Will you make some excuse to Dante?"

"I will find something to say when he comes tomorrow. Eventually he will know that you have left, of course, but not right away." She bestowed a sympathetic smile. "He really is very gentle, Bianca, despite his naughty behavior. I hope that you will be at ease with him in the future. Vergil tells me that Dante holds the most honorable affection for you."

"Do you really think men are capable of that? I wonder if their affection is ever really honorable."

Pen shook her head with a little laugh. "I am the last woman to give advice on the topic." She caressed the book of poems with her fingertips. "Although, I find myself wondering if it might not be possible in a few rare cases."

The mail coach careened around a bend and its passengers braced to keep from crushing to the left. Bianca huddled inside Jane's light cloak, seeking some shelter from the damp chill that had reached her bones hours ago.

She had not expected this journey to be this miserable. The speed of the coach created a jaw-jarring ride despite the good roads.

There had been no alternative. Not only did she need to make this journey a fast one, but the money she had hoarded out of the twenty pounds extracted from Vergil would not pay for a private coach. She had permitted herself one break last night at an inn, and would do so on the way back, but she doubted that Jane could maintain the deception longer than three days.

She pulled the cloak snugger. Just her luck that the

only hooded outer garment that Jane had brought to London was lightweight wool.

The request for Pen's coachman to stop at a coaching inn near Laclere Park so that Jane could detour to visit an ill friend had not raised any suspicions. Nor had her own excuse to seek relief at the necessary. Back behind the building, she and Jane had exchanged cloaks and the wrong woman had returned to the carriage. Even the weather had cooperated, providing a light rain to explain the obscuring hoods pulled low over their faces.

Hopefully, when Jane arrived at Laclere Park, she had managed to retire abruptly with complaints of a chill. Snuggled in Bianca's bed for a few days, wrapped and capped and sleeping off an illness, she might just avert discovery of her true identity.

If not, Bianca expected to return before a full alarm could be raised.

The biggest inconvenience in the plan, besides her numb extremities, was the fact that she had not been able to bring any baggage with her. The only items of toiletries and clothing that she carried were stuffed in her reticule and inside her bodice.

The coach sped into the environs of Manchester, making a series of quick stops as the countryside gave way to sprawling villages that then bled into the edges of the city itself. An odd combination of raw newness and old squalor flanked the residential streets. Perhaps on sunny days, and if a visitor weren't bone-chilled and hungry, it would not appear such a dreary place. One knew without being told that this was a growing city. The congestion spoke of too many people cramped into too few domiciles.

Their pace slowed until the driver pulled to a halt. Two other passengers gathered their belongings. "If you want Manchester, this is it," one said. "Coach heads to Liverpool now, and the mail for the city will be picked up here by others."

Bianca stepped out into the drizzly mist. She entered the coaching inn and asked the man in charge where she could hire a gig and driver for a few hours.

Soon she was back in the damp again, this time squashed beside a portly driver snapping the gig through the city streets. She huddled inside her thin cloak with the hood pulled low against the mist.

"Is the Clark mill far away?"

"East a bit. Newer mill than somes the others, and a bit off on its own. Hard to believe it was almost open country there just ten years ago. City just keeps getting bigger, like a spider getting fat from eating those coming in from the land." He pointed to a young man standing against a building. "Like him. Can always spot them. They have that bewildered look. Then, if they find work in a good mill, they grow contented, and if they don't, they get mean."

"What is a good mill?"

"One with decent wages, such as they are. Where the machines are kept safe. Where families work the same times." He cast a sidelong look at her. "None of my business, but you sure you want to go to this mill today?

There's been a spot of trouble popping up here and there the last few months. Been gettin' worse, it's said."

"I must go today. I am sure that Mr. Clark has one of the good mills, so there should not be a problem."

He laughed. "When trouble spreads, there are no good mills."

It took almost an hour to make their way to the eastern environs and the long, low buildings of the Clark mill.

The driver hopped down and helped her descend. "He would be in there." He pointed to a two-storied stone square. "Manager's house. Not as fancy as some." He raised his head like a dog sniffing. "Seems quiet enough."

"Wait here, please. I will want to go back to the coaching inn for tonight."

She gathered her limp cloak around her and marched into the house. A young man sat at a desk in the building's first chamber.

"I have come to see Mr. Clark," she explained.

He gave her the once over and was not impressed by Jane's serviceable cloak. "He is in the works right now. Perhaps I can help you. I am Mr. Thomas, his secretary."

"Thank you, but it is Mr. Clark himself with whom I must speak."

He examined her critically again. "They don't usually send such young ones. Which reform group are you from?"

"I am not from a reform organization. I have business of a most critical nature with the manager."

"Tell me your name and I'll go see if he knows of this business."

"Mr. Thomas, I have no intention of giving you my name. I will wait on Mr. Clark's return. I promise you that he will not thank you for any interference."

His startled reaction hovered between a laugh and a frown. Amusement won. He showed her into the office.

A fire burned in its hearth. She stood close and savored the warmth that began burning away the damp.

She turned to give her back a little roast, and surveyed the office. The furniture was solid but plain. The desk's surface held only writing implements and a neat stack of documents. The whole room appeared rather blank. If it reflected the manager's personality, he was a colorless, uninteresting man. Hopefully that did not mean that he lacked imagination. She needed him to see that her proposal actually gave him what he wanted.

And gave her what she needed. The chance to get away.

She turned back to the fire. She pictured herself walking sunny streets and being gay and happy and singing for hours. Her life would be so bright and exciting that she would never think about this horrible interlude in damp, cloudy England, and how it had scrambled her emotions and turned part of her into someone she didn't recognize.

This would all become a brief memory, a stage stop on her journey to womanhood. Once she was gone, the ache that she carried inside her chest would disappear. A wonderful future waited. She would grab it bravely and not look back and—

A sound behind her broke into her hopeful reveries. A door opened and one footstep fell.

"Mr. Thomas said that you wished to see me, madame."

Images of Italy fractured like a hammer had smashed them. The fragments rained through her stunned mind.

Her mouth dropped open as she swung around and looked into the blue eyes of the Viscount Laclere.

chapter 12

H ell."

The low curse floated on his delayed exhale. They stared at each other for a dazed interval.

Slowly, her wits absorbed the implications of his presence.

Vergil and Mr. Clark were one and the same.

What a stunning discovery.

What an incredibly bad stroke of luck.

Then again . . .

He recovered first. "What in damnation are you doing here?"

Amazement left her speechless. Amazement, plus the fact that her explanation would hardly soften his expression. To say that he was less than pleased to see her was putting it rather too finely.

He looked subtly different. Still Vergil. Still tall and dark and stern. Still chiseled face and startling eyes. But his black frock coat was cut more austerely than usual and seemed of poorer quality. His collar points were less perfect somehow, and he wore a black cravat tied in a casual knot, something she had never seen him do before.

He was presentable enough in a dark, menacing way, but she couldn't shake the sense that he appeared a man new to fine garments, who didn't quite know how to put them together yet, and who lacked a good valet to show him. A wealthy man, but not born to it.

"I asked what you are doing here, Miss Kenwood?"

Despite her cursed outspokenness, she knew that there were times when silence was the best course. It would hardly do to blurt out that she had come to extort money from Mr. Clark so that she could escape her evil guardian.

"How did you get here?"

"The mail coach."

"That explains why you look half-dead. Is that your gig outside?"

She nodded.

"Where is your baggage? Did you leave it at your inn with Jane?"

Oh, dear. "No."

He frowned. "You came all this way with no baggage?"

Her lack of response did not delay the conclusion. He raked her with a very sharp look. "In fact, you came without Jane, too, didn't you? You made this journey alone."

She would have spun a story, an outright lie, if she could think of one. Her mind simply wouldn't cooperate.

"That was very, very reckless of you, Miss Kenwood."
He abruptly opened the door and left.

A few minutes later he returned.

"I expect that you are tired and cold, but I must delay
your comfort for a while longer. I have paid your coachman and sent the gig away. My carriage will be here
shortly. While we wait, I want you to tell me how you
arranged this journey, so that I can determine just how
large a calamity you may have created."

Feeling more like a naughty schoolgirl than she liked,
she explained the brilliant plan that had abruptly lost its
luster. "So, if Jane remains undetected, there may not be
any calamity at all," she concluded.

"And if your ruse was discovered, Penelope might already be raising the hue and cry all over England."

"She will know once she speaks with Jane that I was
not abducted. I expect she would wait a few days for my
return."

"Does Jane know where you went and why?"

"I did not confide the details to her. If you send me
back at once, no one will have reason to seek out Mr.
Clark. No one will know your secret."

"*You* will know. Until I decide what to do about that, I
have no intention of sending you back. However, we cannot discuss that here."

The sounds of the coach rattled outside. Vergil disappeared into a side room and returned with his great coat.
He draped the heavy garment around her shoulders and
escorted her through the front office to the door.

Morton held the reins in the coachman's seat of a

vehicle that bore no aristocratic insignia. The mouth buried between his beard and mustache opened in surprise when Vergil guided her out of the building.

"Well, now, my lord, this is an inconvenient complication."

"You have a gift for understatement, Morton."

"Rather bold of her, if I may say so."

"Yes."

"On the other hand . . ."

"Exactly."

What was that supposed to mean? The way she saw it, all of the "other hands" belonged to her.

Vergil settled across from her. He found a coach rug and tucked it around her legs. "Your shoes are damp. Silly, flimsy things to wear on a mail coach." He unstrapped both shoes and slipped them off, then swathed her feet in the fur rug.

He tucked and wrapped like she was some child. He pulled the coat snugly around her until her head stuck out of a huge bundle. It was very disarming of him to fuss like this, especially since the light in his eyes suggested that he thought she deserved it if she caught a fever from this escapade.

Morton guided the coach across a bridge and they headed south.

"Where are we going?"

"I have a manor nearby. We should reach it in less than an hour."

The manor. She wondered if the mistress was in residence. Since she already knew about that woman, she wondered if he would bother to keep her hidden for the few hours they might need to settle this "inconvenient complication."

He kept regarding her with intense speculation. It was the sort of calculating expression one sometimes catches on a person who thinks no one is looking. Having it directed at her for this extended length of silent time was very unsettling.

She felt no danger for her safety. Quite the opposite. But she couldn't shake the notion that the man sitting across from her had become very unpredictable all of a sudden, and that Mr. Clark might not play by the same rules as the Viscount Laclere.

"Unless you want me to conclude that you made this journey because you could not bear to be parted from me, you had better explain yourself."

The cool allusion to that other part of their relationship sent a peculiar alertness blotting through her.

"I came to see Mr. Clark."

"Why?"

"To have a little chat. To make his acquaintance."

"I am not in the mood to have my wits insulted. Since I am Mr. Clark and we made our acquaintance long ago, you will state your business now."

"Well, if Mr. Clark had been amenable, and I'm sorry to say that I do not think he will be, I intended to propose a mutually beneficial arrangement. Mr. Peterson told me about the offer to buy the mill and how Mr. Clark—that is, you—did not want to sell, and how if I sold and Nigel did, too, then . . . oh . . . *oh,* so that is why you tried to force me to marry your brother. To secure ownership of that mill. Really, Laclere, I am very disappointed in you."

"You have many reasons to be, but this is not one of them. I never tried to force you to marry my brother. You were supposed to be a meek, provincial orphan, who, like all women, would swoon with delight every time Dante smiled. You would fall in love, marry him, and that would be that. There was nothing dishonorable in the plan. As for what happened later, may I remind you that if you had not thrown yourself at Dante I would not have—"

"I hardly think *thrown* myself is a fair way to put it."

"—*thrown yourself* at Dante, I would not have found myself in the contradictory situation of trying to negotiate your way out of a marriage that could only benefit me."

"Why did you, then?"

The look he gave her knocked the breath right out of her. *You know why,* those eyes said.

"It has never been my intention to trap you into something that you did not want."

They were speeding past farms clouded in mist, leaving the city far behind. Potentially perilous did not begin to describe her situation. But this was Vergil Duclairc. A saint. Besides, he would hardly importune her when his mistress resided in the house.

"Morton obviously knows who Mr. Clark is. Does anyone else?" she asked.

"No."

"No one? Penelope or Dante?"

"No."

"Fleur?"

"Least of all Fleur."

"You will have to tell her. A man can hardly hide such a thing from a wife any more than he can from his valet."

"Fleur and I will not be getting married. She has no interest in it. Our courtship has been a feint to remove her from the marriage market for a while. I expect in a month all of society will know that she broke it off."

"I am sorry. I would never have expected her to deceive you."

"You misunderstand. I knew from the start. So you can acquit me of at least one crime. I did not make love to you even while I courted a fiancée."

She could do without him blithely repeating references to that. "It is odd no one ever found you out."

"The ease of the deception surprised me at first. But Mr. Clark keeps to himself mostly, and lives out of town. Refuse social invitations often enough and eventually they stop coming. I am not unknown in Manchester, especially among the other men of business, but I avoid gatherings where I will not know who will attend. Of course, the *haute ton* do not mix with mill owners, and the city has no representation in Parliament, so there were no members of the Commons about who would recognize me."

"Maintaining a double life must be very difficult and uncomfortable. I do not understand why you have done this. Why not be open about it?"

"Surely your perceptions are more astute than that. Gentlemen do not engage in trade, least of all this one.

We invest in certain ones, shipping and canals, but the mills are too sordid. And we never actively manage those businesses."

She remembered Mr. Peterson speaking of mill owners as beneath him, and Lord Calne calling their owners base. It would probably be very scandalous for a viscount to take his place among such men. Scandalous enough to ruin the social standing of his whole family.

Dusk was falling when the coach lumbered off the main road. They slowed as they passed some farms.

"Are these yours?"

"They are attached to the manor but are mortgaged to the hilt."

"Is Laclere Park mortgaged too?"

"The estate is entailed to prevent that, not that I would have ever done so anyway. A man does not gamble with his family's patrimony."

She kept her gaze out the window, looking for signs of a village. With an inn.

Morton took a turn and they trotted up a hill. An old Tudor manor stood at its top. In the waning light she made out a rambling collection of half-timbered beams crossing plastered walls that rose up from a stone first level.

Vergil hopped out as soon as they pulled up in front of the house. Not a single light shown through any window. The place possessed an eerie mood. It looked like the sort of manor one read about in the more fantastic stories. The sort where young innocents came to no good.

Vergil waited as if he knew that, whatever her misgivings,

she would conclude that she really did not have any choice except to go in.

She fought her way through the swaddling coat and rug only to remember that her shoes were off. He fished for them, slipped them on, and buckled them as if she were incapable of dressing herself properly.

An old man led the coach away and Morton hurried inside ahead of them.

"It looks deserted," she said as Vergil took her arm to support her under the weight of the clumsy coat.

"I do not keep staff here, except for old Lucas to tend the horses and serve as caretaker. When I am in residence, Morton does for me. He was army in his younger days, and is amazingly competent even in a kitchen."

No servants. She glanced askance at him. In the dusk his expression appeared dangerously alert.

The large, square entry hall held a hearth and chairs and settee. Old armor glimmered in the corners and an ancient tapestry hung on the wall leading up the stairs. Overhead one could see the beams that supported the second floor. Everything appeared in decent, if worn, condition. All this dark wood could use a good polishing, but Morton had managed to keep things clean.

Morton moved two chairs near the fire he had built. She swayed under the great coat while she walked around and peered through open doors into the rooms giving off from the hall. There was a library at one end and a proper drawing room at the other end beside a dining salon.

Vergil watched her inspection. "Are you looking for

my mistress? I keep her chained up in the attic. Morton, don't forget to bring my love slave her supper."

"That is not humorous, Laclere."

"She thinks that I am making jests, Morton. The thing is, that wench upstairs begins to bore me. Perhaps I will send her home and keep Miss Kenwood to take her place. What do you think, Morton?"

"A bit sharp-tongued, my lord, but a comely young woman."

"The luck of it is, no one will ever know. No doubt you will find it difficult to believe that any woman could be so foolish, Morton, but she snuck away from Pen and Dante and came north all on her own. Told no one where she was going. Left herself with no protection whatsoever. If she disappears, who is to say what happened? All sorts of accidents and mishaps could have occurred on this adventure. They won't even know where to begin looking for her."

"You astonish me, Laclere. This is very vulgar, and not at all like you," Bianca said.

"It is not the Viscount Laclere who contemplates your future. It is Mr. Clark. It is said that he is a strange man, not much given to society and friendships. Whoever would have expected an intelligent woman like yourself to put herself in the power of a man whom she knows nothing about? Yes, Morton, I think that she will do very well. She will need a bit of taming, of course."

"I hope that you are both enjoying yourselves. The potential danger in what I have done has been amply communicated. I am not amused by your insinuations, Laclere, nor the least bit frightened."

"Aren't you? You have more faith in my honor than I do, then."

He said the last in a thoughtful, musing tone. The rest had been a teasing scold, but that had not.

The silence of the manor suddenly pressed on her.

He stepped behind her. His hands settled on her shoulders and the skin from her neck to her waist prickled. His touch briefly lingered before he lifted the coat off her shoulders. "Go sit by the fire and get warm. Morton, would you prepare a hot bath for Miss Kenwood? It will be the only way to get the chill out of her. See about some other garments too. Her gown is holding the damp."

"No things here but yours and mine, my lord."

"Something of mine, then. Miss Kenwood is no stranger to breeches. And do whatever one does to prepare a chamber for a lady. It will have to be mine. None of the others are suitable."

His last order made her trip on her way to the hearth. He certainly did not expect her to remain here tonight, in his chamber.

She sat and unfastened the neck of her cloak.

He threw himself into another chair nearby. "You are warm enough? Morton will fix supper soon, but I could find something if you are hungry."

"I will wait." She pulled off her gloves and smoothed them together on her lap. "There is no mistress, is there? All of the journeys were because of the mill."

He just looked at her in that considering way he had

used in the coach. Finally he shook his head with an exasperated sigh. "What am I going to do with you?"

"The first thing you are going to do, is instruct Morton to drive me to an inn."

"I do not think so. Rain is falling, there is no moon, and the closest inn is miles away."

"I hardly need to remind *you* that it is unacceptable for me to remain in this house tonight. There are not even any servants here."

"Which means no one will ever know. Now, if you were some blushing innocent, I might be concerned for your delicate sensibilities. However, since you are so *experienced, wicked,* and, some in Baltimore even say, *dangerous,* we can dispense with inconvenient gallantry. I will not risk either Morton or my horses to cater to any concerns about propriety that you have suddenly discovered this evening. Besides, a woman who admits to having *hundreds* of lovers can hardly be reduced to the vapors by the notion of being alone with a man for a few days."

"A few *days*?"

"I cannot let you leave until we have come to some understanding."

"That should not take long at all. I promise to tell no one about your secret. See? All settled."

"Hardly all settled, as you and I both know."

His meaningful glance stunned her into silence. He was not only talking about his management of the mill.

The hall grew very quiet. His implications hung in the air, filling the gap between them with connections and memories, forcing the attraction to quiver more insistently than it ever had before.

The fire crackled, illuminating the two of them in a cozy glow. It created a little world of protection and warmth in the cold cavern of the hall. No, it was not the fire doing that. It was the presence of the man sitting a few feet away. She had always experienced an alluring security with him. Especially when he held her. He offered for a short while, just a little, that she could let someone else make the decisions and do the worrying. Not since she had been a young child had she been allowed that respite.

She nervously smoothed her gloves some more. She felt as though his silent contemplation was deliberately stripping away layers of camouflage, revealing something carefully hidden behind anger and resentment and clever sparring. It was leaving her terribly exposed to an intimacy that spread like the fire's warmth, circling their chairs, subjugating the adversarial postures they took with each other as surely as the hearth did the chill.

Did he sense it too? She snuck a look at him. He gazed into the fire with a face subtly expressive, its stern planes reflecting annoyance, but also something else. It was as if a transparent mask had been removed.

He turned to her. His eyes glimmered with anger and warmth and a flicker of vulnerability. Not a guardian's eyes. Not a saint's, either. Just a man's. The man who had kissed her at the ruins and held her in the study. Every piece of her remaining armor dropped and every ounce of defense disappeared under the honesty of that gaze.

"You might have been harmed. If that coach had gone into a river, I would have never known what happened, just that you disappeared one day," he said resentfully.

It was the first indication, the first admission, that he cared about her.

"Is that why you are so angry? I thought it was because I had discovered your secret."

"Give me some time and I will work up some ire over that too."

"I should have been more considerate of the worry I might have caused Pen and you. I am sorry. It's just..." To explain it would leave her even more vulnerable to the seductive familiarity she suddenly felt with him. In an indefinable way, she understood him much better than she had ever realized. In front of this hearth, with her protections peeled away and his mask shattered, she knew the important part of him as well as she knew herself.

"It's just that you saw a way around your interfering guardian and back to the pursuit of your dream," he finished.

"Yes. There was that."

"It's just that you saw a way to escape the hypocrite and fraud who forced his attentions on you when he was supposed to be protecting you." He voiced her thoughts in a frank way that suggested he intended to clear the air. "Perhaps that is why I am so angry. It is really directed at myself, and it is unfair to lash out at you instead. I cannot escape the conclusion that if anything had happened to you, it would have been my fault."

"Not entirely. Nor did you really force your attentions

on me. I have never lied to myself about that. But, as I said in the study, I decided it best if I left."

"As any sensible woman would have. Now you have discovered that your brave plan has only led you directly back to me. You must be dismayed."

"Not so dismayed. Better you than Mr. Clark, whom people say is a bit odd."

He laughed quietly at that. "So you came to Manchester to chat with Mr. Clark. Did you plan to threaten him?"

"Certainly not."

"Negotiate, then, if you prefer that term. Let me guess. You would promise not to sell the mill when you came of age if he gave you some money. The implication being that if he did not hand over the blunt, you would promptly throw in with Nigel once you turned twenty-one and sell out. Am I correct?"

"You do not have to make it sound like highway robbery. The money I wanted was mine anyway. Some of the profits, to be diverted to me and not sent to . . ."

"To your unreasonable guardian. Your solicitor did well by you, getting the information you needed. A brilliant plan, Miss Kenwood. You have my admiration."

"Would it have worked? I mean, if you hadn't been Mr. Clark, that is."

He smiled with stunning warmth. "It is charming of you to think that it makes a difference that I am he. You have me at a distinct disadvantage. I do not hurt myself by pointing it out, since it was only a matter of time before you realized it."

She had already realized it, as soon as she saw him in the office.

"Once you procured your funds from Mr. Clark, what then? Off to Italy, I expect. Immediately? With no baggage and no Jane?"

"I had intended to go back to Laclere Park, to fetch Jane."

"I suppose you would have had to leave without saying so. A letter propped on your writing table for Penelope is the best I could have hoped for." He pressed the fingertips of his hands to each other and studied her over the peak they made. "I am a little insulted at how this plan of yours did not take me into account at all."

"It certainly did not take into account that you might be Mr. Clark."

"I do not mean that. Perhaps I foresaw your scheme. Maybe I fed Mr. Peterson the information in order to lure you up here. Has it not yet occurred to you that the man whom you castigated in the coach that day might be that nefarious? Perhaps you do not think me clever enough to have plotted it."

It had occurred to her, poking into her mind with a momentary, silly caution. "Clever enough, but not nefarious enough."

Her judgment seemed to please him. "If this had played out as you intended, what did you expect me to do?"

"I expected you to be relieved, and to recognize it was for the best."

"Of course. The saint could return to his courtship of the lovely Fleur, and the fraud could return to debauchery with his mistress. A comfortable life again, with the troublesome, provoking Miss Kenwood out of the way."

"Something like that."

He angled toward her. "Shall I tell you that I anticipated some new attempt on your part to leave? I even warned Catalani of dire consequences if she should aid you. I have St. John checking the passenger lists at the shipping companies to see if you tried to arrange for berths."

"I planned to take the packet to France and travel overland, so you would not have been able to stop me that way."

"Then I would have followed."

"I see. You would not have wanted the mill's future depending upon someone you could not control, and you still had nine months to convince me to wed your brother."

He looked to the fire with renewed irritation. "Fetching you back would have had nothing to do with Dante, and very little to do with the mill. Furthermore, my legal rights as your guardian would have only provided the excuse."

His words and expression insinuated more than responsibilities and manipulations, although he appeared less than happy with the notion. The new Bianca flushed with delight at this evidence that she had been right about him and the old Bianca wrong.

A cough drew their attention to Morton on the landing halfway up the stairs, holding a candelabra.

"I have the chamber and bath prepared, my lord. If Miss Kenwood is ready, I will show her the way." He turned and retreated upward.

She rose and Vergil did too. She regretted having to relinquish the fresh honesty that had begun between them. They would probably resume to their old poses when she returned.

She mounted the stairs, sensing his attention on her. At the landing she glanced down to see him watching her.

"No."

She paused at the simple negative, even though it had not been a command for her to stop.

"No," he repeated. "To your question earlier. You were correct. There is no mistress. No mistress and no fiancée." He paused. "There is only you."

She thought that her legs would give way. The new Bianca wanted to climb over the banister and jump down into his arms.

"Since we are being honest, I should admit that you were correct too. There were not *hundreds,* or even *dozens.* Not even several, I'm bound to say. Only you."

He turned away with a wry smile. "Go to your bath, Miss Kenwood. Since I had intended to seduce you, I will need some time to decide if I am glad to hear that."

Vergil crossed his arms and stared out the dining-room window into the wet, black night.

If Bianca had any sense at all, she would never leave that chamber upstairs.

She was a virgin. Of course she was. He had known that almost for certain. However, the simmer had encouraged enough doubt so that he could ignore his better judgment and speculate on the possibilities that her arrival presented. Maybe she wasn't and then what he contemplated would be a bit less unconscionable. Perhaps, if he were to make love to her and do it well enough, then hopefully she . . .

Only you.

Two words had demolished all the "maybes" and "possiblys" and probably any "hopefullys."

He shook his head with a quiet laugh. Just his luck, and wonderfully ironic. He never thought he'd see the day when he regretted learning that the woman he had decided to marry was an innocent.

She would make a splendid wife. Bright and interesting and, in her exasperating way, unpredictable. The kind of wife one looked forward to spending time with and did not merely tolerate. The sort of woman who enlivened one's existence beyond the bed where you joined her for pleasure and procreation, although his determination to have her there played no small part in his attraction.

A perfect wife for him in other ways too. Not only because she would bring forty-five percent of the mill with her, although that would be convenient. The best part was that he would not have to hide his double life. She came from a country where men of business were not scorned. She already knew his secret and there would be no need to keep it from her.

That the woman whom he wanted should also be the only woman he could risk marrying struck him as a generous gift from Fate. It was during the coach ride that he had realized how her discovery had freed him to pursue her.

The Rossini aria that she had sung in the ruins began filling his head. He imagined the body that he knew better than he should, stretched out naked on that bed upstairs. She rested on her stomach, shoulders raised and weight propped on her forearms. The sheet hid her lower body to the middle of her bottom, the way the lake's water had. She watched his approach with teasing blue eyes that managed to combine worldliness with innocence.

His hand caressed down her soft skin and his mouth found her lips . . .

Only you. After playing out such a long and elaborate act of worldly experience, she *had* to go and admit that tonight.

"You are already grinning and you haven't even seen me yet," her voice said. "Did you catch my reflection in the window?"

He turned and choked down a laugh.

The frock coat dropped off her shoulders and its sleeves buried her hands. The trousers were so long that she had rolled up their bottoms into thick, clumsy cuffs. The whole ensemble immersed her in an ocean of cloth out of which her head bobbed and in which her body swam.

She stretched out her arms and flapped the coat's sleeves. "I feel like a little child dressed in my father's clothes. I must look bizarre."

He thought that she looked adorable. "The blue of the coat becomes you."

She held up her arm and tried to scrunch down the sleeve so her hand could emerge. "It may be impossible to eat supper, and I am very hungry."

"Then I will have to feed you." A delightful thought. "Or, we could build up the fire and you could remove the coat." That was an alluring notion as well.

"Would you? The fire, that is."

He got it to a high inferno just as Morton arrived with some soup.

"This should help warm you, Miss Kenwood, but I am sorry that the rest of the meal is a cold platter. We eat plainly here in the evenings. I will do better tomorrow night," Morton explained.

"I would not lay in stores, Morton. I expect to be on the road tomorrow night."

Morton shot him a look such as an officer would give a soldier who was shirking his duty.

"Why don't you bring the rest now, Morton. Miss Kenwood will forgive our informality."

"Certainly, sir."

Bianca shrugged off the frock coat and laid it on a chair. Her dark gray waistcoat also hung loosely, but its lines and fabric could not totally obscure her form. Vergil beckoned her to a place set at a right angle to his own at the end of the banquet table. Morton had made her place as close as possible without appearing too obvious. Certainly within easy reach.

She looked around at the mirrors and inset paintings and gold leaf that glimmered in the light of hearth and candles. "This is an odd room to find in such a manor."

"My maternal great-grandmother loathed this house for the primitive place it was, but her husband insisted on coming here. She decided that they would at least eat as civilized people, and she had this room done in the current fashion. He permitted it, but only for this chamber and her own."

She dug into her soup. Her full lips parted delicately to accept the warm broth, and the tip of her tongue swiped an errant drip. Her mouth mesmerized him, spoonful after spoonful.

This was going to be a very long night. A paragon's purgatory.

He guessed that she hadn't eaten a decent meal since leaving London. Rectifying the problem absorbed her attention for a while. When Morton brought the ham, she methodically tucked hers away. Vergil speared another slice and placed it on her plate.

She flushed a color that looked incredibly lovely in the candle glow. "I am being rude."

"You are being human. We should have fed you before you went upstairs."

She looked down at her garments and grinned. "Do I get port when we are done?"

"You do not drink strong spirits, and tonight is not the time to start."

"If I am dressed like this, I think that one glass of port is almost obligatory."

"If you insist, but only one very small glass. I do not want you accusing me of getting you inebriated."

She looked to her ham with a peculiar smile. "I am sure that you would never do that."

Oh, wouldn't he?

A small roll and a slice of ham later, she finally stalled. He practically saw her mind snap back to attention regarding the matter at hand.

"How did it happen? You and the mill?"

"It was another responsibility that I inherited from my brother. He, in turn, got involved in response to a dare."

"A dare?"

"From your grandfather. Adam Kenwood and Milton

formed a strong friendship, despite their disparate ages, backgrounds, and politics. Milton found him an interesting man with a mind as sharp as a honed sword. Very ambitious and very clever. You have a lot of him in you, by the way. Milton once said he found Adam a wonderful contrast to the philosophical abstractions that had filled his own life."

"So Milton left the manor to work in the factory?"

"Four years ago there was a demonstration in Manchester that turned bloody, one that has been dubbed Peterloo. The deaths of those people shook my brother badly. Milton was not so much of the tower that he could not see that the country was changing profoundly. Adam and he got into terrific rows about the moralities of what was happening in the new industries. Milton believed that the problem was the character of the men running them. Better men, less absorbed by greed, would mean better conditions and less unrest among the people. Adam challenged him to face the same risks and choices and see what he would do. He dared Milton to throw in with him on a new mill."

"It sounds like a very sly, and very expensive dare. However, I can almost picture the two of them, worlds apart, sparring over such things, and others as well. The influence went both ways, I think. Your brother convinced my grandfather of the error of his early trade, and Adam made your brother see how impractical some of his ideas were."

Her expression softened as she referred to her grandfather's slave trade. The way she looked in his eyes conveyed her gratitude for being informed that Adam had expiated that sin, and that her inheritance could be kept.

"It was foolhardy for my brother to agree to the dare. The family finances were already a disaster. Adam stood him to a large part of the financing, and offered to advise him, but it would be my brother's business. No doubt Milton saw it as a grand experiment, but also counted on Adam's business acumen to keep it from failing."

"Perhaps Milton thought it was not foolhardy, but a way to save the family."

"If so, he was correct. It turned out to be the only sensible decision about money that he ever made, and, with Adam's help, he made the mill profitable. He was the first Mr. Clark, you see. I think when he donned that identity, he literally became another man."

"Then when Milton died, Mr. Clark's brother, which was you, inherited his share. Did your double life begin then? Have you been managing that mill ever since?"

"With my brother's death, I began traveling north, relying heavily on your grandfather's advice while I learned what to do. Eventually the decisions became mine. It was essential that I manage it closely. The income from the mill had kept us from financial ruin."

It had also been useful to spend time in the north as Mr. Clark. Mr. Clark could go places and hear things that the Viscount Laclere never could. Mr. Clark could try to learn if the answer to Milton's suicide could be found somewhere in Manchester, where Milton also visited, and among the political radicals whose ideas Milton had supported.

He realized that he wanted to tell her about that, too, and regretted that he could not.

She inclined forward with her elbow propped on the table and her chin resting on her hand. He could see Adam Kenwood's shrewd mind working behind the thoughtful expression in her eyes.

"You said it scraped you through some bad years. Why don't you sell out now? The offer from Mr. Johnston and Mr. Kennedy is waiting. You could be free of this deception."

"Johnston and Kennedy run the worst mill in Leeds. Ours is paradise by comparison, even if it is still a hard life. If I sell the mill, I also sell any chance for a halfway decent future for the people who work there."

Morton had found some little cakes to present with the meal. She reached for one. Her small white teeth bit carefully, but some sugar topping smeared her lips anyway. Still thoughtful, she seemed unaware that her tongue snuck out to wipe up the sweet grains. She missed a few and they glistened against the pink swells, like an invitation for him to finish the job.

"You could sell to someone else. There must be other mill owners who are decent."

"That is true. I could probably do that."

"But you do not want to."

Perceptive woman. Delightfully so. Dangerously so.

"No."

She sat back and absorbed that. He wondered what the admission would cost him.

She smiled as if she had learned what she needed to know. "Can I have my port now?"

"I keep it in the library."

She walked beside him through the hall to the library. He noticed that she had cinched the trousers to her waist with a cord from the bedchamber's drapes. The white sleeves of his shirt floated around her arms and the collarless neckline showed a fair amount of skin despite the waistcoat.

He pictured her in nothing at all but that shirt hanging loosely from her shoulders and breasts, skimming her body with soft fabric, revealing naked thighs and legs.

Morton had built up the library fire. She sank into a corner of the settee and accepted the port he offered her.

He sat in the chair across from her, wondering when she would get around to negotiations. It was why she had come down for supper, after all.

Not yet, it seemed. She popped up and began perusing the volumes in the bookcases flanking the hearth. Her brow puckered. She reached for a candlestick on the mantel, lit it off the hearth flames, and held the light to the bindings.

"There are some volumes here by Edmund Duclairc. Was that your father?"

"Yes. The fat red one is his epic about Alexander's march to the Indus River. The brown one is an Anglo-Saxon view of the Battle of Hastings. Milton's literary efforts are in that blue folio on the bottom shelf. Unpublished, since he did not have the chance to finish them.

Not poems. He was writing a comparative analysis of your country's revolution and that of the French."

She had pulled out the brown volume. "It all sounds very erudite. Do you also pen great works?"

"My interests have been in other things, to my father's dismay."

"You were at odds with your father? Somehow I cannot picture you as less than dutiful."

"Like all youths I had my own ideas about my future. I wanted to join the army. Not the cavalry, which would be acceptable, but the engineers. Machines, buildings, earthworks, those things fascinated me. As a child I loitered around the carriages, not the horses. My request to have a commission was soundly rejected by my father. Off to Oxford for me, to study the poets and philosophers."

"Were you miserable?" Her face showed genuine concern.

"No young man is miserable at university. It is a free and privileged life. Those poets and philosophers had a thing or two to teach me. The experience influenced my thoughts, but not my natural inclinations. Your grandfather recognized that, I think. He and I became more familiar after my brother died. On occasion I went with him to see some of the new machines being built. I watched my first working steam engine with your grandfather by my side. When we left, he spoke his mind. 'Your world is dying,' he said. 'It will never be the same again.'"

"It sounds to me that he enjoyed your company." She slid the book back onto its shelf. "I think he was impressed by your interest in machines and how things work. It was unfair of your father to interfere with that."

Clever, clever girl. Subtly laying the foundations before she began constructing her argument.

She strolled back to the settee and perched herself carefully in the corner again. She appeared vulnerable and desirable in her baggy clothes and simply bound hair. The firelight broke her form into lovely glows and mysterious shadows.

He looked at her and she looked right back. Innocent wariness flickered despite her falsely carefree smile. Only a saint could ignore the anticipation pulsing through the air, and he was hardly that where she was concerned.

He found himself swimming against an incoming tide of indifference to notions of honor. The exhaustive effort began to seem increasingly futile.

Yes, she should have never left that chamber.

He kept looking at her. Directly. Intently. As if he waited for something. She suspected that he knew what his prolonged attention was doing to her and drew it out deliberately. Maybe he heard that physical hum drumming louder.

The silence became dangerous. Her skin flushed and her mouth dried. She kept expecting him to get up and come over and . . . but he just sat there. Waiting.

This would never do. Besides, they had business to settle. It was why she was here, wasn't it? She forced some semblance of composure.

"Well, Laclere, what are we going to do about this?"

He favored her with a small smile: "I would say that is up to you. What do you want to do about it?"

"I think that any understanding that we reach should be a mutual one."

"I am at a disadvantage here, and we both know it. Any resolution of the situation must be your initiative."

"The course is obvious, I think. It is unfair of you to demand that I spell it out."

"I suppose that it is, but I am incapable of stating a rational case for myself, because there isn't one. The only thing I want right now, the only obvious course that I can see, is to take you to bed and trust that a mutual understanding can be reached tomorrow."

Her heart skipped and then rose to her throat. "You misunder... That is not... We are speaking about the mill."

"No, we are not."

"*I* am."

"Are you? My apologies." He rose and paced to the hearth. She would have preferred he remain seated. He gazed into those flames for a while before turning. "Fine, let us discuss the mill and your discovery first."

First?

"My disadvantage in that matter is even more acute than in the other."

"I have already said that I will tell no one."

"I thank you for that. Now, what will it cost me?"

"Nothing that is not already mine. What is my income from the mill?"

"This year, at least four thousand pounds."

"Goodness. You must be a very good manager, Laclere."

"Thank you. However, since it grew to that amount two years ago, neither Adam nor Mr. Clark took it all out. We have been reinvesting in an expansion. If you demand the whole sum, I have no choice but to give it to you, however."

"How much did you reinvest?"

"Half."

"That still leaves quite a lot. More than enough."

"More than enough for what?"

"For me to live in Milan, of course."

"So the true cost of your silence is that I permit you to pursue this rash plan. If I refuse, you will announce to the world that I am Mr. Clark."

"I did not say that."

"No, you did not. Your blackmail was more clever than that. You will keep my secret, but if I do not agree to your terms, you will sell your interest when you are of age."

It would help her to concentrate if he didn't keep pacing around the settee. Circling, circling. It reminded her of that morning in the guardroom of the castle. So did his manner, and his eyes.

"The problem, as I see it, is that you cannot guarantee your side of the bargain," he said.

"Do you doubt my word?"

"I doubt your ability to foretell the future. If you marry, the decision whether to sell or hold that investment will cease to be yours."

"I will not be getting married."

He paused behind her. "You think not now."

"I know not, ever." She twisted and looked up at him. "You yourself pointed out that no decent man would want me if I performed. Besides, a woman cannot be a wife and mother and also an opera singer, no matter what society will permit. With babies, the career must end."

"You may change your mind someday about what is important to you."

Twisting to see him was uncomfortable, and he seemed disinclined to move. She turned and knelt on the settee. It brought her closer to him than she thought it would. "I told you once, this is essential to me. I must do it if I have the talent to even try. I will die if I do not. No husband will interfere with our bargain."

"I find that hard to accept."

"You doubt my resolve? You of all people have seen evidence of it."

"I do not doubt your resolve, but it has never been tested. Time has a way of turning life's blacks and whites into grays. The singularity you describe is a freedom that grows heavy and dull with the years. Trust me, I know. I think that the bargain that you offer in good faith tonight will one day become meaningless."

"You treat me like some silly child playing a game. It is as if you assume I am too ignorant to know my own mind. I realize that men think women are too stupid to think things through and weigh their decisions, but your attitude is very insult—"

Suddenly his hand pressed on her cheek, startling her

into silence. He looked down with an expression that suggested he had not heard one word.

"A mistake, Miss Kenwood. Letting your annoyance show. Innocence I am duty bound to respect. Worldliness I am adept at resisting. But the light in your eyes when you fly at me reveals a passionate spirit that provokes me until nothing else matters except possessing it." His thumb seductively brushed her lips. "Which brings us to the rest of what must be settled between us."

That thumb stroked and stroked, as if preparing her for him. She knelt dumbfounded, on wobbly knees, staring into a face darkly pleased by her mesmerization. Her lips tingled under the subtle caress. He coaxed a gap so he could skim the moist inner edges.

"Do you want me to kiss you?"

He had never asked before. She could not summon enough breath to respond. Her lips pulsed with swelling sensitivity at his luring touch. Her whole being trembled with anticipation, as if the expectant tension in the room had entered her body.

"Do you?"

"Yes." No sound came out, but her lips formed the word.

He did. Wonderfully. He cupped her face in his warm palms and his mouth replaced his thumb in those caresses. She grasped the back edge of the settee to keep from wilting right into him. The new Bianca soared with triumphant relief.

Gently, carefully, he obliterated thoughts of anything but him and the pleasure he created and implied. He tasted and savored with firm, acquisitive, titillating nips and slow, shallow, sweeping invasions. This was a different path to passion than the abrupt release in the ruins and the study, and she instinctively knew, a more dangerous one. His tender exploration of her consent aroused her emotions as well as her body. She wanted him to kiss her like this forever, even while that inner voice began its chant for more closeness, more pleasure, more giving.

The luring warmth hypnotized her. She could not move, even to embrace him. When he broke the kiss she could only look wordlessly into blue, deliberating eyes.

He caressed down her neck, his fingers splaying over flesh, pressing beating pulse, exploring trembling shoulders. He watched his hands' progress. That expression of hooded contemplation still veiled his eyes. It dully occurred to her that her mind might be blank to everything but this entrancement, but his was not.

Hands and gaze lowered to the valley between her breasts. She felt the top button on her waistcoat loosen. Then the next. She gripped the back of the settee harder.

The waistcoat fell open and he brushed the sides away. She glanced down. Hard nipples pushed against the shirt fabric like proud announcements of desire. He caressed around the sides and bottoms of her breasts, outlining their swells. Her eyes blurred as all of her body and mind and heart narrowed into one tiny, intense ache of waiting and want.

"Do you want me to make love to you?"

She almost didn't hear him. Her eyes met his and she struggled to recover the capacity to think and speak. He still stroked her breasts, distracting her, making her help-less. He studied her face as if he sought to read her mind.

"Do you know what it means if I do?"

She heard her voice speak. "I am not ignorant of such things."

Her words might have been sharp tools poking holes into their trance. Rationality leaked in. He smiled with amusement, and regret. "I was not talking about that."

He walked away. She sank around into the settee, flooded with confusion and a visceral disappointment.

He retrieved her candlestick from the mantel and brought it over. A strong hand beckoned her up. Her thoughts still were muddled, but her body practically shrieked with relief.

With disarming courtesy he led her to the door. Placing the candlestick in the hand he held, he closed her fingers around it.

"Go up now. Quickly."

She glowed at his thoughtfulness. Grasping her light, she scurried to the stairs. As she mounted them her thoughts unscrambled and the last minutes began making sense.

By the time she reached the landing she realized what had just happened. He had not sent her ahead to prepare for a bed that he would share.

He had no intention of following, now or later.

chapter 14

Bianca twisted restlessly. She punched the pillow, pulled another over to make a high mound, and flopped onto her back.

She certainly was fortunate that Laclere was such a decent man. Yes, indeed.

The nightshirt that Morton had laid out rucked up. Her exposed hips felt annoyingly titillating. Leveraging them, she pulled the fabric down.

A very decent man. Very honorable. A saint, by God.

Any other man would have ravished her right there on the settee. Any other man would have carried her up to this chamber and would be lying beside her right now....

And she would be facing the morning, knowing that she had made a mistake, probably worrying about all kinds of things.

Then again, any other man would be holding her in his arms, soothing her concerns with his embrace.

She could not get comfortable. She should be exhausted, but she was horribly awake. All of her. Awake and alert with a huge portion of her still waiting.

Half the night must have passed. Hours with her contemplating what he had meant by that last question. Endless minutes with her secretly wishing he had never found that decency.

Silence filled the whole manor. Somewhere Morton slept in his chamber. Somewhere else, in one of the rooms too unsuitable for her, Vergil did too. No doubt he snoozed the calm, deep slumber of the righteous. Even the ghosts dozed. She was the only soul wide-awake, twisting on this big bed, torn between gratitude and regret.

She flung back the bedclothes. Maybe if she read for a while it would distract her enough to aid her repose.

The nightshirt was warm enough in the bed, but a chill hit her once she stood. No one would see her, but she felt exposed in it too. She dragged a blanket from the bed and draped it like a cape. She grabbed the trousers and pulled them on.

She bent the candlestick to the coals in the hearth. She pushed her hair over her shoulders and carried the small spot of illumination while she clutched the blanket. Treading silently on bare feet, she descended the stairs.

The library's fire had almost died. Her little circle of candle glow barely penetrated the darkness. She skirted along the wall and made for the books beside the hearth. Holding the flame near the bindings, she searched for something dull.

A low noise crunched and a burst of light suddenly broke the shadows. She jumped in surprise and turned. Vergil crouched in front of the hearth, watching the flames climb from a new infusion of fuel. A dark counterpane lay rumpled on the settee where he must have been reclining.

He rose and her heart flipped. Coats and collar had been discarded. He stood in a shirt showing a lot of neck and a V of chest. Snug trousers delineated the lean strength of his hips and legs. She stared like an idiot at the magnificent image he presented. He examined the hearth with a casual stance while he waited to make sure the fire had taken.

Finally he turned to her. Flaring eyes raked her from head to toe and then met hers. He reached for a glass of port that he had set on the mantel.

"I thought that I would read for a while and ..." She stammered and flustered and held the candle toward the books, pretending to examine them.

He strolled over. "Poetry or prose?"

"Um, prose I think. Maybe your brother's."

He set down his glass and took the candle from her. "Allow me. You are in danger of setting your lovely hair on fire. You want the blue folio on the bottom."

He stood behind her, holding the candle to her search. She reached to pluck out the thin volume. Her hand shook beside his steady one.

"The treatise may not induce somnolence, if that is what you seek. My brother was brilliant."

She clutched the folio to her chest. She could not walk

away without turning, and she feared facing him. A power poured out of him, exciting parts of her spirit and unnerving others. "I thought you would have retired by now," she said, thinking it a good idea to clarify her presence.

He did not respond at first. He just stood there closely, as if he tested the attraction he could wield if he chose, even when he was invisible to her.

"I decided to wait, for you to return to me." Firm fingers fell on her right shoulder in a caressing hold. "For you to realize that sending you upstairs was my last bow to the gods of propriety where you are concerned."

The candle flickered away while he placed it on the mantel's corner. He reached around and removed the folio from her grasp and set it next to the glass of port on the book ledge. He stepped closer so that he entrapped her against the stacks.

Warm breath flurried through her hair. Two arms circled her shoulders. He gently pried her hands from her chest and spread them wide. Like a curtain the blanket opened, stretched, and fell. She found herself grasping at bookcase uprights to her right and left.

"I thought . . . I came for a book," she said a little desperately.

Hands on her waist held her to her vulnerable position. Kisses on her neck and ear lit shimmering lights in her body.

"No, you did not. You came here to give yourself to me."

It embarrassed her that he knew her heart better than she did. She *had* hoped he would not be gone. The dark room and dying hearth had provoked a spike of disappointment.

"No more facades, Bianca. No more pretending. That is one thing that this means."

It was the first time he had ever used her name. That, even more than his decisive handling, told her where he was leading her. He caressed up her back and around her neck and pried the top button of the nightshirt free. Its neckline slinked loose. He eased the fabric down her shoulder and kissed the exposed skin, finding spots of unexpected sensitivity.

So strange to feel protected and helpless at the same time. Her skin awoke with a thousand sparkles as the suppressed anticipation surged into a hunger crying for resolution. She dropped her hold of the bookcase and sank back into his surrounding embrace.

"What else does it mean?" Coming down the stairs had made negotiation irrelevant, but she should know what she agreed to.

His hands moved over her sides and midriff, learning the parts previously encased in her stays. "That you are only mine. I do not share. That you give yourself to me when I want, how I want. That . . ." He broke the explanation with a tingly nuzzle on her nape.

It was a lovers' pact that he sought. "Perhaps I will not like it."

"It is for me to make sure that you do."

He turned her. Holding her with one arm, he dipped his finger in the port. Like a painter working a delicate canvas, he smeared the rich liquid across her lips and down her neck. He lowered his head to taste.

It was a wonderful kiss, full of complex flavors and mysterious emotions. He licked the streak marking her neck, kindling tiny flames of giggly pleasure. The light glowed brighter in her breasts and thighs, a suffusing inner warmth anxious for more fuel.

His hand moved to the port again. She waited for the drips to heat her lips. Instead he drew the lines of his own mouth.

She had never kissed him before. She sensed that complying meant crossing an invisible line. Accepting was one thing and sharing was another.

The port glistened.

"I thought you said that I could not have more than one small glass," she said, trying to hide her fear that he lured her into deep water.

"A drop or two will hardly turn you into a Bacchic maenad."

"I'm not so sure."

"I will not ask anything else of you, but I want you to kiss me, Bianca."

And she wanted to. Very much so. That frightened her too.

She slid her hand behind his neck and pressed him down. She pursed her lips on his and then ventured to flick up the port. His mouth parted at the touch of her tongue and suddenly she was inside him. He pulled her into a tighter embrace and a quickly escalating response.

His reaction incited a different type of pleasure, and a reeling sense of power.

She watched her own fingers dip in the port and followed their path up to his neck. The liquid streaked down and meandered to the wedge of chest exposed by his shirt. With kisses and toothless bites she followed the daring stream. Her fingers pressed the taut skin beside her mouth while she lost herself in the sensations of touch and taste. Even her ears fed the sensuality, hearing the heartbeat and tight breaths that revealed what she was doing to him.

Yes, yes. Need me and want me like I do you. Fear me a little, like I do you. Lose part of yourself, as I have with you.

He took her hand and kissed her palm, her pulse, and the soft flesh of her inner arm. "I ask you again. Do you want me to make love to you?"

Tonight, in this manor, in this room, she wanted it desperately. An important part of her had never wanted anything more, not even success in her art. Admitting that startled her, but still she nodded.

"You are very sure? There will be no going back to innocence for you."

At this moment she had never been more sure of anything.

He backed away, leading her toward the hearth. "Here, then. The first time I saw you I thought of firelight and velvet counterpanes."

He pulled the coverlet to the floor and lowered her until she sat on his lap, encircled by the warmth of the hearth and the strength of his arms. It was bliss to melt into him and yield herself to his support. He looked at her in that considering way while he stroked her hair.

He tilted her to a long, ravishing kiss. Luscious sensations cascaded and her expectant senses whirled. The world constricted to the five feet of light and warmth in front of the hearth. The only solidity became the body of the man who cradled her on his crossed legs.

Yes, yes. So good. So delicious. Her heart reveled in the intimacy, and her stomach and loins tightened with that marvelous tension. *Ah, yes.* He kept his need in check, but she could feel it, a power coiling out of him and pulling her into its spiral. *Please.* His arm arched her back, raising her body to him. His kisses explored down the gap in the nightshirt, to the skin above her breasts.

She wanted his touch so badly that she let out a little cry when his hand enclosed her breast. He caressed softly and then teased at the nipple until she could not keep her body still.

"Do you think that you will like it?" He nuzzled at the other breast, warming her through the cloth with his breath.

"If it is all like this."

The gentle friction of his palm warmed her skin through the cloth. "It is better than this before the end."

Firm lips took hers in a gently exploring kiss. It was so good and right to be in his arms. She experienced utter peace with her decision.

"What do we do now?" she whispered.

"Now I give you the pleasure that you already know, and while I do, I undress you."

"Completely?" The notion of being totally naked for him both dismayed and excited her.

"Completely. Eventually. Right now I think that I will unfasten these buttons. You look very beguiling in my nightshirt, by the way."

"I feel a little wicked in it. It is modest enough, but knowing it was yours made putting it on more daring than if it had been the most shocking silken boudoir gown."

"I look forward to seeing you in one of those sometime, but I find this very charming tonight."

He released the second button and worked on the third. He took his time and his hand nestled tantalizingly between her breasts. The thin opening grew down the front of her body, revealing a line of skin and then the top of her trousers.

He laid her down, and brushed the halves of the shirt aside, exposing her body to her waist. The fabric hung off her shoulders and sagged along her sides. She doubted that being completely naked would prove more startling.

He caressed the soft skin of her breasts and circled and rubbed her nipples, unleashing a craving sensitivity that almost made her jump. Her back arched involuntarily, invitingly. *Yes, oh, yes . . . more . . .* She returned his kisses with increased vehemence, in an effort to assuage the pressure building and filling her. *Yes, yes . . .* Her hands and arms scrambled to find a hold on him that could not be broken. His shirt did not obscure his body the way the coats had, and the delight of feeling him only made her want more.

He took her breast in his mouth and sucked. The pleasure grew so excruciating that she wanted to weep. She clutched and his shirt became a frustrating impediment. Pulling it loose of his trousers, she dragged it up his body.

He released her to draw it off.

He really was quite magnificent to look at. She could not resist running her fingers along the ridges of the muscles defining his chest and shoulders.

He came down to her, sealing their bodies skin against skin. New astonishments spilled through her, of touch and scent and mingling breath and long caresses that learned and possessed. The intimacy left her helpless and tight.

He broke their fevered kisses and nuzzled her ear. "Now I give you the pleasure that you do not know yet."

"I do not think it can be any nicer than this."

"It is the difference between a drawing room melody and an aria." He untied the cord at her waist while he spoke. The trouser buttons loosened. Unspeakably wicked excitement charged through her while he pushed the garment down her hips and legs. Stomach and tuft of hair flashed through the nightshirt's low slit.

He pushed the hem up, covering her most intimate parts, but fully exposing her thighs. He stroked her legs like he molded their shape. A different demand fired, internal and hot and focused on the forbidden landscape he explored. *Yes, yes. Oh, goodness . . .* A trembling shook her that could only be relieved through movement. Her hips rocked silkenly, pressing into masterful caresses. *Yes . . . higher . . . so close. I want . . . I want . . .*

"You must trust me now." He peeled down her shoulders and lifted her into an embrace that made the sleeves fall from her arms. It became a rumpled white drapery around her loins. He slid it down.

Off. Gone. She looked at her naked body and realized that he did too. The exposure carried its own excitement. The heady eroticism of the moment intoxicated her. In a few moments he had kicked off the rest of his own clothes. She did not have the courage to examine him as he did her, but her furtive glances absorbed the strength of the body lined against her, skin to skin all the way to her toes.

A dreamy intimacy permeated her. Her body and soul waited within their harmony. Waited as they had all day and night. As they had for weeks. She wanted to hold him as closely as possible, so that she might possess a part of him no matter what happened beyond this fire glow and after the power of this precious night.

He gazed right into her eyes. She knew the next kiss would be different. He might have led her to this point with sweet seduction, but it would not end so restrained.

The passion of the ruins instantly swept her into a tempest. With fierce possession he kissed her senseless, his mouth and tongue conquering hers before joining his hands in their merciless stimulation of her body. Insistent need and an itching hunger joined her pleasure, converting it into something seeking a goal. Yearning pushed and ached with escalating intensity.

He boldly explored her nakedness, learning its secrets and feeling its tremors. Startled gasps leaked out amidst her ragged breaths, and that only seemed to coil his tension tighter. He took her breast in his mouth and sucked until she cried out. The pleasure turned toward a center, twining and twisting, wanting and waiting with a power that tormented.

Yes, please... She held on to him as if her sanity depended on it, grabbing frantically at his shoulders. *Oh, God, please...* He led her toward something dangerous and wonderful and she wanted both to rush forward and beat a retreat. *Give me...I want...* His caresses moved lower, to stomach and thighs. He firmly pushed her legs apart. *Oh, oh...yes, I want...please, higher, there, oh, I...I...*

He brushed his fingers through her lower hair, stroking down between her thighs. When his hand answered her plea, an acute spike of pleasure made her stretch away. He threw a leg over hers to hold her in place. His hard phallus pressed into her hip, startling her more.

"I am not taking you yet. You will enjoy this, I promise you." His finger slid down her cleft into slick moisture and hidden folds.

Oh. Touches. Strokes. The intensity of the sensations assaulted her in a relentless series of pleasurable shocks. The places he explored were scandalously sensitive. She lost sense of everything else but a groaning craving that left her begging.

Yes, yes, ah, yes. Desperate want vanquished virginal

fear. She spread her legs and moved into his touch, rocking closer. *Please...ah.* The pleasure only got stronger, sharper, worse. Building, building spinning out of control now, crying her single-minded thoughts, the flesh that he caressed, pulsing in time with her speeding heart. *I...I...oh, God...* Her awareness shattered into bright shards, blinding her senses. An unearthly pitch of shrieking pleasure exploded into an instant of suffusing bliss.

He moved on top of her and she clawed him to her. In her sated stupor he was the only reality besides her own physicality. The whole world existed in him.

He entered her carefully. A vague awareness of pain penetrated her concentration on his scent, his skin, and her relief. He lifted one of her legs up over his hip and that eased the tightness. *Yes, yes, so good...I want this. I want you.*

He pressed until he filled her. Controlled power poured out of him, tensing the shoulders above her and the arms flanking her. A sensual severity sculpted his face. She found his rhythm and rocked up to accept each filling penetration. *So good, so close. In me, with me. I want you. I love you.*

The end came too soon, but then morning would have been too soon. Holding her leg to his hip, he leveraged her up and thrust even deeper, ravishing her in a flurry of hard moves that incited a renewed wildness in her. A final savage kiss, a visceral tremor, and suddenly he was gone from her, leaving her arms full of him, but their joining over.

She drifted in a sweet cloud, dazed and stunned. Her

arms gripped him long after his own embrace had slackened. Newborn emotions saturated her and she did not understand them all.

Her mind slowly comprehended the end. He had withdrawn to protect her from pregnancy. His thoughtfulness touched her, but she also experienced a stab of inexplicable disappointment.

He brushed the hair away from her face and pressed a kiss to her cheek. "You never cease to astonish me, Bianca."

Slowly the sacred intimacy changed to something less holy and more solid. His possessive embrace broke and he shifted off of her. They lay together for a long while, and she sensed contentment luring him to sleep. She hopped up and scurried over to the bookshelves.

"What are you doing?" He watched her naked body in a way they both assumed was his right now. How quickly one became shameless about these things.

"Getting the port. I think that I should be allowed some more." She also snatched up the glass, and on second thought, lifted the blue folio as well. Back in their nest, she snuggled down and he tucked the coverlet around them until they were cocooned together.

He poured the port and shared it with her. He gestured to the folio that she had set aside. "You are in the mood to read? I can see that I will have to do better next time."

"If you should fall asleep I will need something to do, because I am very awake. I would like to read this someday, and see what your brother wrote about my country. Both you and Charlotte speak of him with pride."

"Pride to be sure, but Milton was not without his faults. He possessed an intellectual arrogance that managed to offend without intention. Also, he could be very impractical sometimes."

He might not have revered Milton, but she could hear his sadness, timeworn but still keen, when he spoke of him. She understood too well the quiet poignancy that grief assumes over time.

She moved the folio out of view, hoping the painful subject could be dropped as easily. To her surprise, he stretched for it and flipped it open. He ran his fingers down the large sheets, as if by doing so he could connect with the hand that had held the pen that wrote the words.

Her gaze followed his fingers, and she noticed the way the ink formed the letters beneath his touch.

"So, they were not from him," she said.

He looked at her curiously.

"There were some letters from Adam's desk at Woodleigh in the trunk in my chamber. I assumed they were from Milton and had intended to give them to you, but with the events of our last days at Laclere Park, I forgot. However, if this is your brother's hand, the letters were not from him after all."

"Did they bear his signature?"

"I did not check. I did not even read them."

"Why did you believe they were from Milton?"

Why had she? "The salutation on the top one, I

suppose. It was something like 'Dearest Friend,' and you had spoken of their fast friendship. It was stupid of me to assume they came from Milton. I expect that Adam had other friends."

He ran his fingertips over the page again. "Where are these letters now?"

"Still in my chamber at Laclere Park."

"I would like to see them, to be sure they were not from Milton."

She understood that. Didn't she clutch the little bits of her father's and mother's lives that she found in those papers? "It is always tragic when one so gifted dies young. Some claim that God takes the best the fastest. Everyone said that about my father, but I do not believe God to be so selfish."

Vergil looked to the hearth with a sightless frown. "God did not take Milton, Bianca. He died by his own hand."

"Oh, Vergil. I am sorry that I spoke of it at all."

"You could not have suspected."

"Do you know why?"

"I am trying to learn that. He could be melancholy, but I do not think that drove him to it." He paused in a way that caused her to think that he was picking his words carefully. "Like many men born to his station, my brother assumed the rules were necessary but intended for everyone but himself. He pursued his own interests quietly, secure that the world would leave him alone if he did not demand attention. He was correct, up to a point.

However, some of his ideas and behavior left him very vulnerable, and the day came when someone exploited that vulnerability."

"He was being blackmailed?"

"I am all but certain of it."

"You said that some of his political views were radical, but—or was it his involvement in the mill?"

"I had assumed it was the former, because Milton would never have found the latter so damning it demanded his death. There are those who advocate violence as the way to solve our current troubles, and there have been assassination attempts on government leaders. If my brother had any connection to the men who planned such things, any at all, and it became known— It was one reason why I took his place here. It was a way to gain entry to his life, and the radicals in this region. But I wonder sometimes if it was not politics that he was threatened with, but something much more ordinary."

"So the answer may not be here, you are saying, but somewhere closer to home."

His expression changed, as if she had startled him. "Yes. Closer to home."

She kissed his shoulder. "Is that why you became such a saint? To compensate for the scandal used to threaten your brother, should it still become known? I thought it was to deflect attention from your secret life."

He gave a slow smile. "Perhaps I became a saint because it is in my nature to be one."

She giggled and pointedly looked at their discarded

garments. Sneaking a hand around his waist, she tickled him and he jumped. "It does not appear to be in your nature at all, by my reckoning of things."

Maybe, just maybe, she enjoyed the next hours even more than she had the physical pleasure. In their little world of firelight, they told stories from their past and discussed people they knew. Bianca learned of his concerns for Charlotte's future and his hope that she would marry happily. She told him all about Aunt Edith, and how she once scolded John Adams at a formal dinner. They speculated on how Pen and Cornell Witherby had *tendres* for each other, and whether Dante would ever find happiness.

Finally, shortly before dawn, he bundled her in the blanket and carried her up to the lord's chamber. He unwrapped her and warmed her and made slow, soulful love, so beautifully that it wrung her heart.

When her emotions and body were sated, he showed her the final, most dangerous pleasure. That of falling asleep in the security of her lover's arms.

chapter 15

She appeared terribly vulnerable when she slept. With the clever mind silenced and the self-assurance in repose, she was all softness and innocence.

He had spent the last hour looking at her, delighting in the little twitches of her eyelids and lips, drinking in the sight of her, like some country boy enraptured by the first girl who had finally said yes.

Making love had only further confused the tangle. It might have helped if she had been less open and passionate. Less joyful. Whatever defenses he had retained against his feelings had been demolished by the pleasure.

Astounding pleasure. Incredibly intense. If he had ever experienced anything like it, he didn't remember. Even the few great infatuations of his younger days, of being mesmerized by Catalani and others, paled as superficial and immature in comparison. Certainly the efficient sensuality practiced in recent years had produced nothing remotely similar. A man did not permit true intimacy with professional women.

Was she even aware that she had gasped out audibly in her frenzy? Her melodic groans and urgings had filled his ears, making his hold on restraint tenuous at best. *Yes... I want this, I want you.* The echo had his mind reeling and an erection hardening. *I want you. I love you.* Did she realize that she had even thought that, let alone said it? He knew better than to put much stock in words spoken in the throes of passion.

Dante had been right. She would make a splendid mistress. He strongly suspected that she would agree to be his lover, for a while at least. Which was the problem that awaited him all too soon and tinted his preening contentment with misgivings.

He did not want her in a love affair smothered by discretion. He wanted her for a wife. He was not at all convinced that she would agree to that, in which case he had corrupted her last night, and possibly initiated her to the very life he had been warning her about.

Later. He would stretch what happiness he could out of this interlude first. There would be time enough to explain that she had to marry him now.

He laughed aloud. Leave it to Bianca to end his grand seduction with the tables completely turned. He was damn close to waking her and demanding that she do the right thing by him.

"What are you smiling about?" She stretched and blinked like a kitten awakening. Her sleepy smile turned up to accept his morning kiss.

"Just watching you and enjoying you beside me."

She nestled against his shoulder and peered around the bright chamber. "The rain has stopped. The sun . . . everything looks and feels so different."

"Not too different, I hope."

"Not too, but a little." She snuck a glance up at him. "Should I be embarrassed to find myself here with you?"

"That depends on whether you have regrets. Do you?"

She thought about that. "No, even though I am supposed to."

"I have always suspected that all of the 'supposed tos' were decided by people who lacked experience in the situations they pronounced upon."

"Aunt Edith says much the same thing, about different situations, of course. I think that you would like her. She does not much hanker to people trying to tell her what she is supposed to do or think. Mother may have been the same way, but since I was her child, she would not have voiced such ideas to me. Edith is too old to know restraint in her opinions, however."

He would like to meet the aunt, and regretted that he would never know the mother. He would enjoy seeing the city where Bianca had lived and the streets where she had walked as a child and a girl.

She tucked the coverlet up around her neck. Despite her brave front, she was not completely without embarrassment, and her vulnerability touched him.

"What do we do now?" She kept looking around the big chamber.

We get dressed, ride to York, procure a special license from the archbishop, and get married. "Whatever you like. I think that we can put off returning you to Pen for another day if you want, or I can order Morton to make the carriage ready at once."

She bit her lower lip. "Do you want me to stay?"

He realized that her embarrassment had to do with him. She wondered what morning-after judgments he was making. He should have considered that the new day might require some reassurances.

"I want you to stay as long as we can manage it, and heartily wish that nothing existed to put limits on our time alone together. If you want, we will take this day and make the most of it and decide about the waiting world tomorrow."

A beautiful smile lit her face. "I would like that. Is it very late? Have we slept most of the day away and wasted it?"

"Not so late. Not yet noon."

"Do we have time to go to Manchester? To see our mill?"

With any other woman, he would suspect that she flattered him by expressing interest in his life.

"If you do not want to, I understand, Laclere. After all, there is the risk that people would see me with you."

I would have the whole world see you with me. "I would very much like to show you our mill. We will go this afternoon. Is there anything else you would like to do?"

Mischievous lights flickered in her big blue eyes. She ran a finger along his collarbone and blushed prettily. "Well, it is still a little different and strange, what with the sun and day and all. Not too much, but a little. Maybe if you were to...if we were to...that is to say, it might be less so then. Different and strange feeling, that is."

He eased her head toward his kiss. "Except that I worried for you feeling overused, I would have, we would have, as soon as you opened your eyes. It pleases me that you want me, Bianca, and that you tell me so."

"Oh, yes," she whispered. "I do."

He inclined his shoulders up against some pillows on the headboard and showed her how to straddle his lap. Savoring her weight lying against his chest, adoring the face turned to his kisses, he embraced and caressed her like the precious gift she was. He slid the bed coverings away so he could gaze over her shoulder at the sinuous lines that dipped down her back before curving gracefully up her bottom and snaking back and forth along her bent legs. His hard phallus nestled between her thighs and he felt the wetness of arousal seep out of her.

He eased her upright so that he could see her body and her passion. A little different, what with the sun and the day and all. Not too much, but a little, and wonderfully so. He loved watching her ecstacy grow while he touched her.

He inclined her so that he could lick and suck her breasts. Her frenzy broke and those erotic affirmations began sighing out of her. Like flames, they set his blood on fire.

"Bring me inside yourself," he said, bracing himself

against the explosive urge to have her every way imaginable before accepting release.

She straightened with dazed confusion.

"Stay where you are and take me inside you. This is how I want you this time."

She looked down at his phallus nested between her thighs, its tip pressing visibly against her cleft. She had never touched him before. Her hesitation reminded him of the recent ignorance that her quick passion made easy to forget.

He was about to take over when she rose up and grasped him firmly, like a woman determined to meet a challenge. Then he was sliding into her tight velvet warmth while her eyes closed with contentment and a melodic groan of relief escaped her. He pulled her down and held her motionlessly in a firm embrace so he could merely revel in the feel of her for a spell.

She pushed up and squirmed until he was deeply imbedded. Her hands drifted down his chest in two slow inflaming paths. Cautiously, curiously, she rose up and lowered herself and blinked with astonishment.

She found a rhythm and he let it last until she began moving and frowning as if she searched for something out of reach. Her cries and gasps and hard absorptions singed his constricting consciousness. He slid his hand to her cleft and touched the spot that would bring her to climax. With increased wildness she rode him harder until she screamed a release that filled the chamber and drove him to his own completion.

He had to forcibly lift her in order to withdraw in

time. She collapsed on him, her head resting against his chest and her body wrapped in his arms. The sweat of her passion glistened all along her back.

Holding firmly to her warmth and heartbeat and slowing breaths, he dragged the coverlet over them both. He pressed his lips to her damp hair and allowed his soul to taste the rare, deep flavor of love.

Morton had disappeared. Like a busy ghost, he executed his duties but never showed his face. When they finally descended for a late breakfast, the meal was ready, as if he had divined the exact moment it would be needed. Hot water awaited their return to the bedchamber, and the carriage and its horses were prepared just in time for the trip to Manchester. Old Lucas sat at the reins because, as he explained to Vergil, the valet had some business to attend in the manor.

Bianca appreciated the total isolation that Morton's absence created. Not because of shame. She experienced none of that at all. The old manor had become theirs alone, a little world existing in dream time, and the solitude intensified their deepening intimacy.

It was Sunday, and Vergil escorted her around an abandoned works. He showed her where the raw cotton was received and cleaned, and the long, low buildings filled with steam-powered spinning machines. His commentary became animated and detailed when he described the improvements he had invented, and she delighted in the quiet pride he found in his achievement. Finally he took her to a new structure, larger than all the others.

"You should see this, since you will be investing in it," he explained.

The building held rows of large looms connected by vertical arms to iron bars overhead.

"They will be steam-powered, like the spinning. Only a few others have done this yet, and not on this scale. The engine is being built in the next room." He showed her the way and explained the huge metal cauldron and water pipes and valves that would make the metal arms move the looms' parts as required. "Most weaving is still done in homes. This will be much faster and more efficient. I have promised the jobs here to any home weavers who want to learn the new ways."

"Some will not want to."

"They will manage for a long while yet. The change will not happen overnight, but the craft will not exist for their sons. It is for them, much as your grandfather said it was for me and my kind. Their world is dying."

"It does not appear to me that your world is dying. I think that my grandfather was premature."

"Prophecies are always premature. As with the weavers, the change will not be overnight, and two hundred years from now Duclaircs and Calnes will still be lords with privileges. But we will be as quaint and picturesque as the medieval ruins in Laclere Park, I think. In my lifetime I expect our hold will be circumscribed as the cities like Manchester demand their say. My hope is that the change comes peaceably, and not with the violence that already tears at the country, reflecting the people's impatience."

He checked his office for any materials Mr. Thomas might have left for his attention. She peered over his shoulder as he sat at his desk and flipped through some letters.

"Mr. Thomas wrote these?" she asked, picking one up to examine it. "Well, that explains it, then."

"Explains what?"

"Those letters in my grandfather's desk. The ones I told you about last night, that I had thought were from Milton. This is the same handwriting. They must be letters regarding the mill, that Mr. Thomas wrote to Adam."

Vergil went very still. He no longer read the pages in front of him. She sensed a distraction that took him far away from her, to some place in his head where she did not intrude.

He turned a thoughtful gaze on her. "How did you say the salutation read? The one on the top letter that you saw?"

"My dearest friend."

"An odd way for an employee to address Adam Kenwood, don't you think?"

"They may have formed a fast friendship. Such things happen."

The frown turned into a scowl. "All the same, I want to know about those letters, and I don't intend to wait until I return to Laclere Park." He rose. "Mr. Thomas lives in the local village. If I am here, I may as well go speak with him about it now. It should not take long."

The village was a quarter-mile west, a single lane of cottages pressed shoulder to shoulder. The age of some of them indicated this spot had been inhabited for generations, and had been a farming community before the mill was built. Now many of the homes burst with people, and the lane this Sunday showed the community relaxing from the week's work.

"There are a lot of men here," Bianca said as she craned her neck to survey the commotion through the window. "It appears that some of these homes are crowded."

"We have been building new cottages, but give them to the families first. The men who come from elsewhere have to make do for now."

"I think that we will have to build faster, Laclere, if you intend to bring weavers in as well."

"If Adam Kenwood's granddaughter has decided to remain a partner, I'm sure that we can afford to build faster."

She smiled contentedly, in a way that reassured him. However, the points he had made last night, about her marriage to another man jeopardizing control of the mill, had not disappeared with their passion.

He really needed to settle their future together. Not now, however. Now he needed to have a conversation with his secretary, a young man who probably knew far more about the mill and the Duclaircs than previously suspected.

"I should speak with him alone," he said as the coach rolled to a stop in front of an old stone cottage that had seen recent improvements.

"I understand. We can hardly go calling together."

It wasn't that. He did not want her hearing this conversation. In fact, he could not even have it if she were present.

He walked to the door quickly. All the same, he was noticed. He sensed the lane go quiet, and felt eyes watch his progress.

Mr. Clark never visited this village, at least not in ways that its inhabitants noticed. His inspections had been as subtle and secret as the rest of his life in this region.

His secretary showed astonishment equal to the villagers. Taken aback at the call, he brought Vergil to a little sitting room and quickly took a chair near a table.

Vergil noted the man's guarded expression. "I have not come to criticize or chastise, Thomas, and certainly not to release you. This is a social call."

Harry Thomas was a large-framed, fair-skinned man, the sort whose face colored easily when he was angry or ill at ease. It was very ruddy now. His pose in the chair, with legs and arms crossed, made it appear that he braced himself for unpleasantness, or restrained himself physically from revealing his reactions.

He knew that, social call or not, the unexpected presence of his employer was not good news.

He was correct about that, but Vergil guessed that the

news would be worse for the employer than the secretary. Rather than delay the pain, he threw himself right on the blade after they had exchanged some banal talk about the fair day and the village's growth.

"You know who I am, don't you?" he said. "You knew who the last Mr. Clark was, too, I think."

The face got ruddier. The eyes glazed with caution. "He confided in me. I kept it to myself then, and I still do with you."

"I believe you." Did he? Was he looking at the answer to it all, right here in this chamber? Did Harry Thomas betray Milton's confidence and threaten to reveal the viscount's déclassé dabbling in industry?

It might have been Thomas, but the mill was not reason enough. Not for Milton. It was something far more damning.

The solution wanted to force itself into his mind, and his heart's rebellion barely kept it at bay.

Vergil strolled around the chamber, wondering how to proceed. His gaze lit on a low case of books, and one caught his eye. He slid the volume out of its spot. As he did, he heard a movement behind him, that of a man shifting in his place. He felt Harry Thomas's alarm.

"Homer's *Odyssey*. My brother loved this work." He cradled the book in his hands. He recognized the binding. This had been Milton's book, a part of his private library. It had been given to Milton by their father.

And now it belonged to Harry Thomas.

"He loaned it to me. I should have returned it. Take it now."

Vergil came close to accepting the explanation. He wanted to nod, take his leave, and stride back to the coach and Bianca.

Except this had been no loan. He just knew that. He suspected if he opened the cover he would find an inscription that made it a gift.

He kept the cover closed and looked at the other books, all of them new and with impressive bindings. Too impressive for a secretary of dubious fortune. He scanned the authors. Poets, philosophers, and historians. Milton had given Harry all of these, he was sure.

Had it been an exercise in education? An attempt to improve a naturally sharp mind with some culture? A Voltairian experiment?

The answer, he guessed, was inside the volume that he held. Milton would not have given away his own boyhood treasure to a mere student of literature.

"I have come to ask you some questions about my brother," he said, setting the book down on the table where they both could see it. Harry looked for all the world like a man who would like to snatch it and hide it under his coat.

"There are some letters from you to Milton. I am wondering about them."

"I wrote to him. Was my job, wasn't it? He came here less often than you do, and after Kenwood got ill, the mill was left to me to manage day to day. I had to keep him informed."

"I saw those letters. They were among his business papers, and sent to a London address, and addressed to

Mr. Clark. I speak now of different ones, probably sent to Laclere House in London, and to Laclere Park in Sussex. These were kept separate from the others, and saved together. In them you address my brother as 'Dearest Friend.' "

Harry's face turned so bland it might have been made of stone. "We formed a friendship. Here, at the mill, in the works, he was not such a grand man. Not the sort to think he was better than such as me."

No, he had not been that sort at all. Nor had he been the sort to worry that his friendship might be betrayed.

Vergil laid his hand on the volume. "I want you to think now. Were any of these letters indiscreet?"

"What are you insinuating? I'll not be—"

"*Do not* feign indignation with me. I was his *brother.* I may have ignored what I saw, but I saw it all the same. I need to know now if anyone who read those letters might surmise the depths of your friendship."

Harry's jaw tightened in anger, but his eyes were those of a man trapped and frightened.

"You are safe with me. I would never do anything to harm his name," Vergil said quietly.

Harry's stiff pose slackened, more in defeat than relief. "I suppose, it is possible, if they were read—but I thought they were destroyed."

"A sensible man would have burned them, but my brother could be foolish sometimes, and sentiment ruled him in this."

Beneath his dismay, the notion that his letters had been saved seemed to touch Harry. He nodded his head toward the bookshelves. "Had me reading philosophers and such. Wanted to open the world to me, he did." He smiled nostalgically. "Interesting stuff, but not much help when the workers got mad after he decided no children could work. They depended on the wages, those families did. I got him to agree to let the boys stay on for some hours, at least. Kenwood couldn't get through to him on some of his notions, but I could. Real life isn't so neat as in those books, I told him. Even good deeds can have bad results. You are more practical than he was. Kenwood said so too. Said this was in your blood more, and not only an experiment for you."

"It is good that you were here to help him. When he came north, did he visit you in this house?"

"None saw him. He was discreet. Didn't come up in a fancy coach as you just did."

In villages such as this, no discretion was great enough. "Did you and he ever visit Manchester together?"

"Sometimes. Nothing untoward was seen, if that is your question. It was natural for us to be together at meetings and such. We worked together."

That was true, but one wrong glance, one wrong laugh... "I regret that I must return to those letters. Did you ever write another sort of letter to Milton, asking for something of value from him?"

Harry's soft expression snapped away. "What are you saying?"

"Did you make any demands on him? His friendship with you made him vulnerable to anyone who knew of it, including you."

"Made me vulnerable as well. No point in my making demands."

"That is not true, and we both know it. He was a peer. Any scandal, let alone a trial, would affect him more. Men no longer hang for such things, but they can be destroyed. You could disappear if it came out, but he could not."

"Damn you. Damn all of you. Assuming that I'd be grasping, just because I'm not born to silver as you are. It wasn't like that, but I'd never expect the two of you to understand."

"What do you mean, the *two* of you?"

"You are not the first to come have this chat with me, *Mr. Clark.*"

"Another man has approached you about this friendship? Who?"

"Not a man. A lady came, all veiled and sneaky. Said she knew about the mill, and me, and worried for his reputation and that of his family."

"She knew who Mr. Clark really was?"

"To be certain. She said he was careless, and asked if there were letters to him as the viscount that should be destroyed. She was going to do it, you see. To protect him. Before she left she threatened me. Said if I ever told anyone, if I ever tried to use this for my own gain, she'd see me hang."

"Was this before or after my brother's death?"

"A good four months earlier. I didn't want him to know that she had figured it out. If he knew, he might . . ." He shrugged.

"She may have been veiled, but you must have known who she was if you spoke of anything at all with her."

Thomas sneered at him, as if he were an idiot. "I knew who she was, because she told me straight-out. It was your sister, the Countess of Glasbury."

The child peered at Bianca and Bianca peered back. The little girl had been scrubbed for Sunday, and her red hair blazed in the sun. Her big eyes examined Bianca's garments with astonishment, then she ran back to her mother who watched from the doorway.

Their cottage was small and tidy and new. A little row of them flanked the lane, facing the older homes that showed their age and indifference to care.

Vergil came out of Mr. Thomas's house and noticed her down the lane. He walked toward her with a troubled expression.

"Did you learn what you wanted?" she asked as he joined her.

"More than I wanted." He appeared tired and lost.

"The letters were from Mr. Thomas?"

"Yes."

"See, they were friends, as I said."

"They were not to Adam, but to my brother."

She shrugged. "A different friendship, then. Charlotte always speaks of Milton as being reclusive, so it must have been a joy to him to have some dear friends. It must make you feel better to know that he did, that he wasn't lonely in his life."

He gave her an odd look. "Yes, I suppose it makes me feel better knowing that. Now let us return to the house. Of the many lives I find myself living today, the one that includes you is the one I need right now."

As soon as they entered the coach, he took her hand and pulled her across the carriage to sit on his lap. "What did you think of your mill?"

"I think that perhaps I will let the manager continue for a few more years, at least. I am not sure that Nigel will be so sanguine, however. How have you managed to keep him ignorant of your role in it?"

"He was in France, and since his return Mr. Clark has dodged meeting him. We have a lively correspondence going. I am counting on him being content if his income surpasses what he could get in the funds, but if necessary, I will offer to purchase his share at a generous profit."

"Why not do so right away?"

"The offer from Mr. Johnston and Mr. Kennedy will give him fifty thousand pounds. I cannot raise that without mortgaging the mill itself."

"Fifty thousand...Why, that means that my share must be worth..."

"Over two hundred thousand. The value is in the equipment and the land and the accounts more than the annual profits. Are you sorry that you have promised not to sell?"

"I wouldn't know what to do with that much. You say the profits are better than the income from an equal amount in the funds, so I am better with the mill it seems."

"One bad decision by your manager and the mill's value diminishes."

She pecked his nose with a little kiss. "I think that I will take my chances. I trust my manager. Not because he is hungry for the gain, but because he has a passion for what he is doing and therefore will do it well."

One eyebrow arched rakishly. "Does passion lead to superb performance? I think that theory should be tested more."

A long kiss made his meaning clear. She emerged breathless. "Lucas..." she gasped while he untied the neck of her cloak.

"He won't hear a thing with all the noise the carriage makes."

It didn't seem to make much noise at all suddenly, but then his mouth was raising sensations that had blood pounding in her ears. "If we are stopped..."

"No one will do so except a highwayman, and these parts haven't seen one in a decade."

"We are almost home."

"At least twenty minutes away. But you are right, we wouldn't want to pull up at the wrong moment, and I am not inclined to make love to you quickly. Quite the opposite. I will have to pass the time with more leisurely pursuits."

"A game of cards?"

"I was thinking more in terms of discovering just how wild I can make you between here and the manor." His expression gave lie to his teasing words. The concern she had seen when he found her on the lane still veiled his eyes. "I am very grateful that you are here with me now, more than I can ever explain."

It turned out that he could make her very wild. Incredibly so. Sensations piled up and split and multiplied. Pleasure layered upon pleasure. She was not even undressed, but his hands found and touched with wicked precision through her bodice and under her skirt. The end never came and the frenzy doubled in on itself, pitching her up to a crazed peak of need. With observant deliberation he kept her balanced on a point of exquisite torture.

When they arrived at the manor he assisted her dazed body from the carriage. He guided her to the door with such nonchalance that Lucas could have assumed they had passed the time discussing roses.

The cool aristocrat disappeared as soon as the manor's door closed. In an instant she found herself pressed against the paneled wall of the hall, his mouth on her breast and his hands pulling up her skirt. In a blur of primitive need he opened his trousers and lifted her so that her legs encircled his hips.

Her arousal immediately centered on the glorious relief he gave. She felt him as she never had before and she wanted nothing else, no other touch, just this hot pressure, thrusting and filling. Desperate now, she urged on his feral power with bites and crazed kisses and clawing holds. *Yes. Love me. More. Harder, deeper. Yes.* Tremors awoke where they joined, and quaked and spread. A different end beckoned, almost terrible in its power. *Yes. Come with me.* His voice, not hers, against her breast, repeated again and again, the command emphasized by the rhythms of their violent passion. The spinning ecstacy frightened her and she grasped him like a mad woman. *I love you. I love you. Do not leave me this time. I love you.* She lost hold of the world and spiralled into a crescendo of pure sensation.

It took forever to find herself afterward. Neither of them moved for a long time. They remained entwined and pressed against the wall, with Vergil supporting her weight on his arms and hips. He was not inside her anymore, but she could not remember if he had obeyed her plea not to withdraw.

In her bliss she discarded any concern that she had just flirted with pregnancy. All she wanted now was for him to keep holding her, to never let her go, and to never stop filling all of her.

"I took the liberty of preparing the next chamber yesterday, my lord." Morton set down the breakfast tray on the bedchamber's table. Bianca still slept behind the bed's drawn curtains. "I thought that the lady would want some privacy on occasion. To wash and whatnot. I am preparing a bath for her in there now."

"You went to a lot of unnecessary trouble."

"It was my pleasure to arrange for her comfort. With your permission, I thought that I would go to the village and see if there is a suitable girl to come here and serve her."

"Also unnecessary. Miss Kenwood and I will be leaving today."

"York is a short enough journey. After procuring the special license, you may choose to return this evening."

"It is not at all clear that Miss Kenwood will agree to go to York, Morton."

The valet smiled indulgently. "Of course she will. What other course is there now?"

Obstinacy. It was past time to take matters in hand.

She hadn't once broached the subject herself as he had hoped, damn it. Nor had she picked up on his own allusions to continuing what they had begun. She appeared to accept that he would keep her here two days, take her virginity, make love to her repeatedly, and then blithely return her to London with no further ado. He would be insulted if he let himself contemplate her attitude very long.

He paced around the chamber, waiting for her to wake. The course was clear, obvious, inevitable. If she didn't see reason right away, he would have to be very firm with her.

Not that doing so had ever been effective before.

He heard her stirring behind the curtains and resisted going to her. He would not make love to her this morning. He did not want what might be the last memory to be one heavy with solemn emotions. If it came to an end, let last night's laughter and games and easy confidences be the closure.

She poked her head through the curtains, wiping her eyes with a charming gesture that made his heart ache. "You are up and dressed already," she said.

"There is breakfast here, and a bath waits in the next chamber for you after you have eaten."

The realization that the idyll was over dulled her eyes. She pushed the curtains aside and reached for the bedrobe of his that she had been using. "Of course. We need to be off early. You should have woken me."

"Come and eat something."

"I will just take some tea into the bath. I am not hungry." She marched over and poured. "Where is the tub?"

"This way." He opened the door that joined the two chambers.

He had not seen the mistress's bedchamber prepared for use in years. The white covers had been removed, the hearth cleaned, the gilt furniture polished, and the cloth beaten of its dust. The large room glimmered yellow and white and gold, its mirrors reflecting the clear morning light streaming in the washed windowpanes. Morton must have spent all of yesterday preparing this wedding bower.

"It is very grand. It looks like a queen's chamber." She advanced on the tub, plucking at the tie on the robe.

The midnight-blue silk flowed down her back much the way the water had done that day he saw her in the lake. He memorized every curve her body made while she bent and stepped into the bath. The possibility of losing possession of her beauty did not trouble him so much as giving up the easy familiarity that permitted her to undress with a total lack of self-consciousness.

She began to wash.

"We must talk now," he said.

"At the least, we need to get our story straight, don't we? Have you thought how you will explain finding me?"

"I would like to talk about other things." He began to move a chair closer.

The faintest rumble, like a small tremor in the manor's structure, stopped him. It grew in intensity until it became a commotion pouring down the corridor outside the chamber.

"Damn." He pivoted and strode to his bedchamber. He stepped through and closed the connecting door.

The commotion burst into audible voices muffled by the walls.

"I tell you, my lord is not receiving," Morton announced with furious desperation.

"He'll be receiving for *us*."

"Dante, we should let Morton wake him, and wait down below."

"I've spent the last fifteen hours in a hellish coach ride. I'll be damned if I'll await the lord's pleasure this morning."

The door flew open. Dante strode into the chamber, with Pen in his wake.

"Bianca bolted, Verg. God knows where the devil she's gone, or which scoundrel she is with."

chapter 16

Evidence of a female visitor dotted the room, but neither Pen nor Dante noticed.

"Bianca disappeared three days ago," Dante said. "I was keeping a close watch, but she talked Pen into letting her return to Laclere Park."

"She was distraught with Dante's continued presence, you see, and she requested . . . It seemed safe enough . . ."

"Face it, Pen, she is too sly for you. Anyway, on the way down she snuck off in Jane's cloak and then that maid hid in her chamber, pretending to be her. The housekeeper realized the ruse yesterday and word was immediately sent to us in London and we started out as soon as we heard."

"We thought it best to let you decide what to do," Pen concluded.

"As you should have," Vergil said.

Dante threw himself on the settee, right next to Bianca's

discarded chemise. He actually pushed it aside without realizing what he touched. "There is more, I'm afraid. Nigel has left London, too, and is not at Woodleigh. I think that we should ride with haste up to Gretna Green. If they thought themselves safe, they may not have pushed the journey and there is still the chance that they haven't married yet."

"Why don't you start for Scotland immediately while I go visit the shipping offices in Liverpool," Vergil suggested. "She may have decided to sail home."

"I don't think so," Pen said. "She took almost nothing with her, and she would never leave Jane behind."

"If she is with Kenwood, one hopes the man waited to—" Dante glanced at Pen and caught himself. "I apologize for not taking your concerns about Nigel more seriously, Verg. Presumably they have just eloped, but if it is the other thing . . ."

"I am confident that Miss Kenwood is safe for the time being, in that respect, Dante."

It had been at least fifteen years since Pen had visited the manor. She toured the chamber, distracted by her worry, absently fingering objects and touching furniture. Her aimless stroll took her near the table.

"We should decide our course at once," Dante said. "Who knows what has happened . . ."

Pen was vaguely admiring the silver service on the breakfast tray.

" . . . especially since there is no guarantee that Kenwood is even the man . . ."

A frown puckered Pen's forehead. One could practically

hear her counting the two plates and knives and forks. A blush rose up from her neck. "Why don't we go and discuss this down below," she interrupted, turning with a stricken expression.

"The way I see it, we don't have time to discuss anything," Dante said. He rose and paced to the window. The window directly above the bench still piled with the garments that two lovers had pulled off each other the night before.

"Dante, Vergil needs to finish dressing. You and I can plan the next step while he does so."

"He is impeccably dressed and shaved already. Probably has been since dawn. Now, Verg—"

"In any case, I think that I shall go below."

"Do as you wish, Pen. Now, Verg, the odds of Scotland are better than Liverpool, so it makes more sense for you to go north if anyone does—" His voice halted as his eyes fell to the garments at his knees. His head angled curiously.

"I'll be damned," he muttered, fingering the edge of a petticoat. "My apologies—" His voice stopped again as shock lit his eyes. He reached into the pile to touch a green sleeve. "Hell, this looks like one of..."

His exclamation halted Pen's retreat. She glanced back and saw the sleeve's color. Frowning deeply, she marched to the window, pulled out the garment, and held it up for inspection.

Of course they both recognized it. Bianca's wardrobe was not large and she had worn this many times in their presence.

Dante stared at him in astonishment. Pen appeared as if she might swoon. She turned with the gown displayed like the irrefutable evidence it was.

"Vergil," she began.

"Yes, Pen?"

She shook the gown at him accusingly. "Vergil, I think that you have been a very naughty boy."

Hell and damnation.

"Yes, Pen."

"Jesus." Dante paced with his arms crossed over his chest, the image of a man too staggered for words.

Pen had collected Bianca's garments and disappeared into the neighboring chamber.

"Hell."

"Is that all, Dante? If so, you must excuse me, as I need to speak with Bianca."

"Not yet, you don't, and do not presume to take that superior tone with me *ever again.*" He gestured erratically. "Have you gone insane? Lost your wits completely?"

"In a manner of speaking, I suppose that I have."

"Please tell me that she lost her way to wherever she was going and somehow landed on your doorstep this morning and has not been here all this time."

"I would not insult you with such a preposterous story, nor would you believe it."

"Damnation, Verg, this is the sort of thing *I'm* supposed to do, and even I would not be so bold. She is *your ward.*"

"You do not need to remind me of how dishonorable my behavior has been."

"Don't I? *Don't I?*" Dante peered at him furiously. "Badly done, very badly done. Clumsy and risky. If you intended to initiate an affair, why not do so in London or at Laclere Park? Having her sneak away to join you here..." Insight flashed in his eyes. "Yes, clumsy and risky. Too much for my careful, discreet brother. You did not plan this at all, did you? It was her idea. She followed you here and..." He drew himself into a posture of righteous outrage. *"Hell."*

Vergil did not like being upbraided by Dante of all people, but if he described how and why Bianca had really made this journey, it would scandalize his brother more than any affair.

"No wonder she turned me down. She had her eye on your title. To trap you like this, to take advantage of your fastidious honor...the mind reels that one so young could be so ruthless."

Upbraiding him was one thing. Insulting Bianca was quite another. "You will not say another word against her, Dante."

"Still has you addled, does she? Turns out you are only human, too, it seems. Wipe the fog of passion from your eyes, big brother, and look at the facts. Unless you intend to submit and make this lightskirt your viscountess, we had better put our minds together and find a way to thwart her."

To hell with protecting secret lives. "She did not come to this manor uninvited, nor was our time together planned by either of us. We met by accident when she came north in order to—"

"It is chivalrous of you to try to protect me, Laclere, but that will not be necessary," Bianca's voice interrupted.

She stood at the connecting threshold, in her green dress. Pen stood beside her.

Vergil went over and took her hand. She squeezed his gratefully, then released his hold.

"I have always been too impetuous. Penelope can attest to that," Bianca said to Dante. "As can you. But following your brother here was part of no plot. I am not that clever, nor do I seek to trap him into marriage. I came to demand my independence. The rest that occurred was not planned at all."

Not a word of it was a lie, but it obscured the details and protected his secret. Still, her story hardly absolved them.

"For your brother's sake, I ask that you both be discreet about what you have stumbled upon. I am sure that you do not want him ruined because I am too headstrong. Now, I think that I would like some time alone. I also expect that the three of you will want to make some decisions without me present."

She walked proudly out the door, but Vergil could see the humiliation below the surface of her bravery.

"Follow her, Pen, to see if she will accept your company. I will come down shortly," he said.

Pen was happy to escape. Vergil closed the door behind her and turned on his brother. "I may never forgive you that Bianca heard your damning words, Dante."

"Perhaps it is for the best that she witnessed that there will be some rational influence on you. I thank God that we got here before she bewitched you all the way to the altar."

"Do I look like a man bewitched and addled? You have got it backward. I brought her to this manor, and with the full intention of seducing her. Your arrival interrupted *my* attempts to cajole *her* into matrimony."

Dante's surprised reaction melted into amusement. "Why would you want to do that? She is pretty enough, but no great beauty. She is hardly suitable for you, and her free manner would only embarrass you and affect your position. Fleur will make a far superior wife, and you know it. If you found Bianca passionate and want to keep her for a while, it is obvious that you do not have to marry her for that."

"You are in grave danger of finding my fist in your face again, Dante."

Dante's lids lowered. "If so, it may end differently today, Vergil. After all, I will not be caught unawares because I am sprawled atop Miss Kenwood this time."

Vergil did almost hit him then. Biting back his fury, he walked to the door. "I am going to propose now. If by some gift of grace she accepts, and even if she does not, you will never again so much as raise one eyebrow where she is concerned. If you do, I am finished with you."

"For a man not bewitched and addled you are playing the fool. There are times to put honor aside, such as when you have been manipulated by a woman with her character."

"I have already put honor aside, and now it is time to take it up again. Are you so jaded that you cannot see the truth of what happened here? Her character was unblemished before she met me. She entered this manor an innocent and I deliberately seduced her even though I knew that."

He swung away from Dante's gape-mouthed shock and strode down to the hall. Pen sat in front of the hearth, looking tired and spent.

"Where is Bianca?"

"In the library." She held out a hand and he took it between his in a gesture of reassurance. "This had been a tremendous shock, Vergil. Even with Dante one would not expect . . . but *you*. I do not even begin to know what to do."

"Just promise to be a friend to her, no matter what happens. Will you give me that?"

"Of course." She looked up with a faltering smile. "Are you going to marry her?"

"Yes, if she will have me."

"Thank goodness. Of course you would do the right thing, especially after being discovered like this."

"It is the right thing, Pen, but not because honor dictates it, nor because you and Dante discovered us."

She paced the edges of the library, gazing at the chair where he had sat that first night. She could feel again the exciting anticipation that had pulsed between them, and then the bonds of intimacy that he had forged later on the floor. She blinked the heartrending memories away.

She had known when she woke that their dream world was dying. She had felt it in the empty space where Vergil's body should have been. Then she had seen him, dressed already, proud and tall and thoughtful. Nobility clothed him as surely as the frock coat and impeccably tied cravat. It imbued his casual stance with the magnetic self-confidence born of generations of privilege. *The Viscount Laclere,* her heart had whispered. Neither Mr. Clark nor Vergil her lover had smiled at her, but a peer of the realm.

She had looked at him and known that the freedom of their passion had ended with the night. He had said that they would decide what to do about the waiting world this morning. That waiting world was the viscount's world, and with the dawn he had left her side and dressed to meet it.

But the world had not waited after all. It had crashed in the door and robbed them of whatever soft moments were left. And the very honorable viscount had almost invited his family's censure in order to spare her a small fraction of the scorn, as if the circumstances that brought her to this manor and to his bed made any difference at all.

She could not remember ever feeling this wistful. Her heart ached, for reasons she could not name. It reminded her too much of grief's nostalgia over losing something important forever.

The door opened. It was not Dante or Pen, but Vergil.

She should be relieved, but instead that pang throbbed again.

"You look very lonely, Bianca. May I join you?" He offered his hand. "Will you come and sit with me, darling?"

She let him guide her to the settee, where he enclosed her in a gentle embrace. She rested her head against his chest and went boneless in the sweet security of his strength. For these precious moments she would pretend that he could make everything right and perfect and would carry her off to a secluded world where rules and shame never intruded. For this brief spell of quiet peace she would close her mind to everything but the reality of him, and his closeness and comfort and soft kisses pressed to her hair.

"I am very sorry that Penelope and Dante arrived as they did, Bianca. If I could undo the last hour I would, not because I want to hide what has occurred, but to spare you any embarrassment. I must be honest, however, and confess that I cannot find it in me to want to undo anything else about these last three days."

She had to grit her teeth to keep from weeping. He had spoken the only words that she wanted to hear. The slightest reference to regrets would have been horrible.

He looked so serious. Every crease of his concern was for her, not himself. Gratitude that he worried for her crashed headlong into panic over how he would try to save her.

"If they had to arrive today, I think when they did was much preferable to an hour earlier. I would rather have Pen discover me dripping wet in your robe than have Dante find me stark naked in your bed."

He smiled and caressed her cheek. "You are still astonishing. Your composure surpasses mine this morning. Most women would be in hysterics."

She did not move her head. Not even a fraction. She wanted and needed the warmth of his hand. She was desperate for any connection to him right now, because she was holding on to her much-lauded composure by a very thin thread of pride. Her heart cringed because she knew where this gentle conversation must inevitably lead.

He had come to offer more than apologies and warmth. He was an honorable man. This could only end one way now.

The wrong way, to her mind. For the wrong reasons.

"Are you disappointed that I am not in hysterics?"

"Well, I might find reason in your overwrought condition to thrash my brother, who certainly has it coming."

"I did not like hearing what he said, but considering what he discovered and how I behaved in the past, I cannot blame him."

"I have warned him to display only respect for you in the future. If he ever insults you, even subtly, you must tell me."

He dropped his hand down to hold hers. He thoughtfully watched his thumb caress the back of her palm. "I would not undo anything about these last days, but I would add a few things. Words that should have been said and offers that should have been made. Pen and Dante interrupted my efforts to say it when you woke. Now I wonder if you will believe that I am not coerced." He kissed the inside of her wrist. "I would like us to be wed at once. You believe that, don't you? That I speak with sincerity? Will you marry me?"

So there it was. Of course. What else could he do?

His words unleashed a battle in her heart. Pride and love clashed with confusion and fear. She hung her head, wishing the love did not fight with those other tumultuous emotions.

"Not entirely," she said.

"*Not entirely?* An odd answer. You do not entirely believe that I speak without coercion, or you will marry me, but not entirely?" He teased, but cautiously.

"The former. Although, if I could manage it, I should like the latter. That would settle things in an ideal manner."

"You think it would be ideal to find a way to be married to me, but not entirely so?"

"If you think about it, you would agree. We could go on as we have been here the last few days. We could both be free to live however we want, and still be faithful lovers with no scandal attached. We would be married and thus acceptable and proper, but not *married.*"

"I do not agree that would be ideal. I want to be *married.* Entirely so. In fact, I would like to be more married than most couples are." He sounded a bit like Laclere the autocrat. Two days of passion did not change a person completely, of course. Considering the declaration being announced, she found his tone more charming than exasperating.

The sweet happiness of love wanted to obscure her confusion. She yearned so much to submit, it pained her.

But her glowing heart also knew that this offer contained serious consequences. The shadows of what he gained and what she lost with this marriage crept around the edges of her love.

"I expect that maybe you would enjoy being very married. No matter how married we were, you could still do whatever you want and continue much as you do now. I am the one for whom everything changes. Which is why I wish Pen and Dante had not arrived today. If they had not, I think that you would have agreed to being not entirely married, or even not quite married."

One eyebrow rose suspiciously. "Not *quite* married, now."

"Two nights ago I specifically asked what making love meant, and you only demanded fidelity. If you had expected marriage, you could have said so then. That is why I do not entirely believe that you are not coerced by propriety now."

"I admit that the honest course would have been to state my intentions right then when you asked. However, I did not want to surprise you with the idea at that particular moment."

"I understand completely. You did not want to risk scaring me off and being left unsatisfied. I truly do understand, because, you see, at that moment, right then by the bookshelves, if you *had* said that making love meant marriage, I was in no condition to negotiate or walk away."

His lids lowered. "You would have agreed?"

"Undoubtedly. I had already lost my senses."

"And subsequently, if I had started making love and

then made continuing contingent upon an agreement of marriage—"

"I wouldn't have stood a chance. Which is why I do not really think that in your heart you want to marry me."

"Bianca, men do not trick women into marriage that way. We are almost physically incapable of doing so."

"Then how do you trick women into marriage? By intoxicating them with pleasure and trusting they will come back for more?"

He exhaled heavily and looked away in that exasperated way he had used with her from the beginning. "Bianca, this is me, the Viscount Laclere. If you have seen below the surface these last days, that does not mean the surface is entirely false. You must have realized that I would never have touched you while you were in this house if I did not intend to marry you. You cannot think me such a scoundrel as to seduce an innocent and then cast her aside. You must have understood what making love would mean, what that question meant, even if I did not spell it out."

Maybe she had understood. Possibly she had chosen to ignore the inconvenient truth in order to have him for a while. "Perhaps it would be best if you spelled it out now. What this marriage means, that is."

He did not respond at once. He knew what she was asking. "What it usually means, Bianca," he finally said.

"And my singing?"

"I do not want to keep you from what you love. You can train. We will bring the best voice tutor in Italy here for you. You can perform for our guests, and the ladies of the *ton* will often ask you to sing."

"But I will not perform in an opera house, in a full performance, with full accompaniment. I will not be known for my art, but only as your accomplished wife. I will not be respected by my equals in music, because they will not know me as a professional."

"You speak as though I am asking you to give up your soul. Would marrying me be nothing but sacrifice for you?"

"Hardly, darling. Marrying you has enormous appeal. I would have never permitted this intimacy if I did not feel that it was natural and inevitable to lie in your arms. So I face this choice with a heavy heart, because, no matter what I decide, it means giving up half of what I want, and, yes, half of my soul."

"You astonish me more than you ever have before, Bianca. You overjoy me by speaking of profound affection, and then dismay me by speaking of loss. You make me feel more of a scoundrel in offering marriage than if I had raped you and left you by the side of the road."

"You should not feel like a scoundrel at all. I wanted this. I came down to you that night. But I did not agree to marriage in doing so."

"So you ruthlessly used me for your pleasure, and now refuse to do the right thing by me." A wry smile played on his lips, but the lights in his eyes burned deeply.

"I have not refused you anything yet. I want you to understand why I do not fall into your arms at this offer. I do not want you to think that I played you false these last few days. My happiness was no act. If I marry you, I do not want to regret my decision, however, nor would you want the misery for us both if I did. I do not think that I should have to make this choice right now, with disaster raining down around us."

He did not like it. "And if I require that you do?"

"I would probably wonder about your motivations in forcing me to make a decision when I am at a disadvantage."

"My motivations?" An edge of ice sharpened his tone.

"Can you honestly say that my partnership in the mill does not enhance my appeal as a wife?"

He rose and paced to the hearth. "Have you concluded that this was all about the mill? Do you think me capable of such a cynical pretense of affection?"

"I have drawn no such conclusion. I do not really think—"

"You may have as long as you need to decide, of course." He spoke brusquely. "Since you will remain in England until your birthday, perhaps I can hope for a decision by then, if not before."

She did not think the mill had been his primary motivation, but it must have entered his head. His sternness now hid guilt as well as insult.

"I will speak with Pen and ask that you live with her. She will help you to procure a tutor in London until we invite a voice master to come from Milan. Staying in England until next June will not interfere with your plans, nor delay your development. I hope that you will forgive me this last exercise of my authority, Bianca. I will not let you leave until I must."

She went to him and slid her arms around his waist

until her palms rested on his abdomen and her head pressed against his back. "I had no intention of demanding to leave right away. I think that I would like to stay in England until June. Living with Pen will suit me fine, and make it easier for us."

He turned in her embrace and cupped her chin. "Do you think that I am making these arrangements because they will facilitate an affair with you? Pen will hardly countenance such a thing, no matter what my intentions toward you. Nor would I risk your reputation in that way."

"But I thought—"

"That your choice was between marriage or a love affair. *Not quite married,* as you put it before? It is out of the question, darling. You are not a woman of mature years and experience, but an unmarried girl. All of the discretion in the world would not save us if anyone guessed."

"Yesterday . . . last night you spoke as though . . ."

"I referred to the marriage that I have just offered you, Bianca, not a sordid affair."

"Sordid? Is that what you think this has been? What you think I have been?"

"Never. But the world will make it so, and we will both feel it. I will not live the way required to hide such a liaison, pretending indifference in public, slipping in your back door in the dead of night. It would debase what we have shared here, and ultimately smother it. Continuing what began here is no more practical for you outside of marriage than within it. I may well get you with child. For all we know, I already have, despite my efforts to protect you."

She had dreaded that he would take this stand. Her heart began tearing with a sharpness that left her physically pained. The tight burn of suppressed tears strangled her.

He pulled her into a comforting embrace. She buried her face in his chest. "Why did you protect me? If you wanted marriage, why did you always..."

Strong arms surrounded her and those firm, gentle hands stroked her back. She savored every detail, knowing it might be the last feel of him.

"I told you why. It was never my intention to trap you into something that you did not want, Bianca."

Vergil handed Bianca up into Pen's carriage. His sister smiled feebly from the other seat and then turned her confusion toward the girl who was proving oddly obstinate about having the right thing done by her.

Dante stood in the manor doorway with an expression of barely suppressed shock. Learning that his brother had seduced a virgin had undone him. That the virgin then refused to be redeemed by her seducer, who had the good fortune to be a landed lord of the realm... Dante was making it clear that the entire development struck him as madness at best and highly suspicious at worst.

Vergil leaned in the coach and pulled Bianca toward him for a long kiss that demonstrated to his two siblings that this sinner regretted his behavior not one whit.

He let it linger, absorbing her breath. Her spirit rose into it, a small reminder of the abandon of her passion, to add torture to the farewell. He tore himself away and closed the door. The wheels began to roll.

Vergil watched until the coach completely disappeared. That kiss might have to last him a very long time. Quite possibly the rest of his life.

Dante came down from the house to join him in staring at the empty drive. "None of this makes any sense, Verg."

It made perfect sense. He had interfered with Bianca's plans and proposed a different life than she expected. She understandably wanted to think before replying. Contrary to most girls, her dream had not been one of marriage and family. In fact, she had accepted that as impossible if she pursued her art. Even if she had swooned with happiness when he proposed, the excitement would not have lasted long before she debated the consequences.

What would she see when she stepped back from the passion and weighed his worth? She did not need his money, which was hardly plentiful, and his position meant nothing to her. She required no financial protection, and very little of any other kind. Her piece of the mill tainted the purity of his intentions.

He was in the position with her that Dante had once described for himself. He had nothing to offer the girl except pleasure.

It appeared that might not be enough.

The cool garden outside Daniel St. John's London house beckoned Vergil. So did Adrian Burchard.

He had been avoiding Adrian, but could no longer. Nor did he want to anymore. He needed to speak with someone about the things occupying his mind.

Not all the things. Not Bianca. If he ever confided to another man about that, it would not be Burchard. Daniel St. John, maybe. St. John's marriage had been preceded by an affair, Vergil was almost sure.

Vergil remembered how disapproving he had been when he suspected that. He had considered ending his friendship with St. John over the matter. It had seemed unforgivable for a man to seduce a young cousin who lived in his house and for whom he was responsible. That he now knew Diane was not really St. John's cousin did not change matters.

That the two of them were deliriously happy in

marriage did, however. So did the fact that the Viscount Laclere had behaved just as unforgivably himself, and heartily wished that he could continue doing so.

The weeks since leaving Lancashire had been slow torture where Bianca was concerned. He had gone to Laclere Park to find Thomas's letters and make some inquiries, and she had filled his head the whole time, creating a distraction he could not shake.

The days since his return had been much worse, however. Seeing her in Pen's house, watching her accept callers, listening to her train with her voice tutor in the drawing room—he kept hoping for evidence that she was miserable. Instead he saw a rising star of the artistic circles reveling in her independence.

He followed Adrian out the doors at the end of the dining room, leaving the rest of the Dueling Society to their port and cigars. St. John had invited them all to dinner, and it had been a joyful and raucous meal shared by men who had known one another for years and trusted one another completely.

"Have you discovered anything of interest?" Adrian asked.

"I have evidence that Milton had a relationship that would have been very damaging if others knew of it. A group of letters were found in Adam Kenwood's papers. They were letters to Milton from this other individual, and their contents would have caused trouble."

"How would Kenwood come by them?"

"Kenwood found my brother after his death. He came for a meeting, and entered the study looking for him. He was there first. I think that he quickly looked for anything that might have caused the suicide, found the letters, and took them, to protect Milton's name."

"But he never gave them to you."

"Most likely he wanted to protect my brother from my scorn as well. In any case, if such letters existed, and I now know that they did, someone could have obtained one and used it to blackmail my brother."

"The contents would be enough to do that?"

"Yes."

They stopped in the moonlight. In an upper window the form of a woman passed behind the curtain. It was St. John's wife, Diane, and she carried one of her children as she strolled back and forth.

The graceful, feminine image captivated Vergil. He watched, distracted, envying St. John his domestic contentment.

"Why didn't Kenwood destroy them?" Adrian asked, calling him back.

Vergil turned away from the window and continued their stroll. "I don't know. I believe, however, that he also saw a pattern of extortion and may have been looking into it. In his desk, along with the letters, was a paper with my brother's name and some others. Castlereagh's, for one. Also those of two other men who have sold large amounts of property in the last year."

"A pattern, or a list of his victims. That is what this discovery implies, isn't it?"

"I considered that Kenwood could have been the blackmailer, but I don't think he was. Lord Fairhall died after Kenwood, for one thing, and the Earl of Glasbury could not be his victim now, either."

They paced back up the garden, then turned and paced down again. Fallen leaves blew around their legs and the breeze moved ghostly clouds across the moon.

"I think that we are reaching the same conclusions, Laclere," Adrian said. "That episode with Glasbury in Hampstead was telling."

"I agree. I am just not sure what it told."

"It indicated that two of the people who have been blackmailed have connections to your family. That can't be ignored. It also suggested that the blackmailer is probably not from the north, nor from the known and predictable radicals."

"Someone closer to home, then," Vergil said, repeating the observation that Bianca, in her clear-sighted way, had made that night by the fire.

That one sentence had thrown light into the shadows of his search. Had he avoided seeing that conclusion? Had he ignored the evidence that said he had wasted his time looking for a radical such as those who had conspired to kill government officials in the past?

Had he secretly hoped that Milton's secret would be treason, rather than what it had been?

"It could be a coincidence that two of the victims are related to the Duclaircs, but let us assume not for now," Vergil said. "That means someone in our circles."

"Or someone who knows someone in your circles. Or we may be seeing a pattern where none exists. After all, if

Hampton could discover the Earl of Glasbury's secrets, anyone could."

Julian Hampton had already discovered those secrets, however. Also, Hampton had known Milton well, had been his solicitor, and could have easily examined more than ledgers while in Milton's study either in London or at Laclere Park.

The profile of the man in question could be seen through the door. Vergil disliked the sense of betrayal he experienced in calculating his friend's connection to the blackmailer's victims.

"Hampton knew Castlereagh as well. And Lord Fairhall." Adrian spoke offhandedly, but with an edge of determination, as if the subject could not be avoided.

"You also move in the right circles, Burchard. His ability to learn things is surpassed by yours. I know this man. I have since I was a boy. Furthermore, he would have no political motive, and in Milton's case, he knew there was no money."

"If you say he has no political motive, I believe you. I myself have no notion of where his beliefs are, or if he even has any."

Adrian made a good point. Hampton was a cipher in many ways, and Vergil's knowledge of him was more instinctive than based on any explicit discussions.

"I prefer Nigel Kenwood," Vergil said. "I have been asking about him in Sussex. He did not stay in France all those years. He visited Woodleigh at least a few times a year, and even accompanied Adam on visits to Laclere Park several times."

"It is far-fetched. He has no connection to Castlereagh, for example."

"We do not know that. Furthermore, there is something else." Vergil hesitated revealing this part. It could so easily be misunderstood. "I think that if Castlereagh was blackmailed, the information used to do so is also connected to my family. I think it came from Milton."

Adrian stopped walking. He just stood there, looking down the garden path, waiting.

"My brother and the Foreign Minister had a closer friendship than I realized. They had a rich correspondence," Vergil said. "I lied about this when I met with you and Wellington, because the letters I saw were political arguments, mostly. I have reread them, however, and if one was of a mind to, and if one had other evidence about my brother that encouraged a certain type of interpretation—it is possible that a letter existed that could be used badly."

"How badly?"

"On its own, I doubt it would have any special meaning. If Milton had already been disgraced, it might be enough to bring down another man."

Adrian did not move. Castlereagh had given him employment when Adrian was a young man whose father had cut him off without a pound. His loyalty to the late Foreign Minister was understandable and his stillness conveyed an icy anger.

"Let us speak frankly, Laclere. We are not talking about political embarrassments now, are we?"

"No."

"The letters to Milton that you found in Adam Kenwood's things were not from a radical, and do not indicate that Milton had gotten deeper into such things than we thought. The blackmail concerned private matters."

"Yes."

"And you are now suggesting that there may have been other letters, from Castlereagh to your brother, of a similar nature."

"No. I am saying that an expression of friendship between men that would mean nothing in most cases could be used to threaten a man in other cases. I am saying that the perception of something more could be read into some of these letters if one had reason to do so. It would be enough to make Castlereagh very worried if he was unstable to begin with."

Adrian crossed his arms and stared at the ground. "Damn."

"I am telling you this in privacy, of course."

"Hell, yes, you are. Do you have any idea whom we are looking for?"

"It may not be only one person doing this. I know now that a woman is involved."

He felt Adrian staring at him through the night. "That certainly makes young Kenwood a better possibility, if he has had help. Who is she?"

"I don't know yet, but I may have a way to find out." He had been avoiding that discovery for weeks now. He had tried to convince himself he need not pursue this evidence, that all could be resolved without learning this one piece of the puzzle. That appeared unlikely, however, and his gut twisted at the prospect of facing this part of the truth.

"Laclere, if what you suspect is true—if someone can damage the last Foreign Minister's name in this way, it must never come out, and not only for the sake of his memory and his family."

"That sounds like Wellington speaking."

"It *is* Wellington speaking. Castlereagh represented this country after Napoleon's defeat, and his reputation is tied to that of Britain in the capitals of Europe. Even his death does not sever that connection."

"Is that your mission, Adrian? To protect his name from this particular taint? If so, Wellington must have suspected how this might unravel."

Adrian hesitated, then spoke lowly. "When Castlereagh spoke with him before his death, he mentioned someone claiming to have a letter that could ruin him. He alluded to one such as you describe, one that could be misunderstood."

"We should not have avoided honest talk that day at Laclere Park. It would have saved us some time."

"No one can blame us for avoiding talk of it. Even now we do so, don't we?"

They aimed back to the house. Through the open door they heard St. John say something and Hampton respond. The whole table broke into laughter.

"What will we do when this blackmailer is discovered?" Vergil asked.

"I turn it back to you. What did you plan to do when you discovered his identity? Swear evidence against him?"

Vergil had faced that question long ago. Before Wellington had shown interest, and before he met Bianca. Whether the reasons for Milton's death were political or personal, he had decided there would be no trial of the blackmailer.

Milton's secrets would be buried in the sepulchre at Laclere Park, and the man who had all but killed him would be silenced.

chapter 18

If the St. Johns visit our box, can I tell them?"
Charlotte popped the question while Penelope inspected
Bianca's hair. Jane crimped some more curls.

"Absolutely not." Pen reached over and tweaked a
strand into place. "Not one word to anyone, Charlotte."

Charlotte slouched with a pout. "Being part of a big
secret is a lot less fun if you cannot tell anyone. Usually
you tell at least one other person, and this secret is the
best one I've ever had. That my friend is going to perform
onstage, in an opera . . . It is so deliciously daring."

"*You* only know about it because there was no way to
keep you in the dark."

Bianca pursed her lips. Pen was not making any effort
to pretend that tonight did not carry risks for their repu-
tations.

"Go and finish dressing, Charlotte," Pen instructed.

"Signore Bardi will be here soon, to escort us to the theater. Bianca must arrive early."

Bianca waited for Charlotte to leave and then dismissed Jane as well. There were some secrets too big for an innocent ingenue or a maid who might one day report to great Aunt Edith.

"Is he here?" Bianca asked.

"Signore Bardi? Not yet."

"I am not speaking about my music master and you know it. Is Laclere here?"

"My brother is in London, but I would be surprised if he shows tonight, Bianca. You know that he does not approve."

No, he did not approve. Signore Bardi, the *bel canto* tutor recommended by Catalani, had been impressed enough with her training to think that she was ready for some minor stage exposure. He had arranged her inclusion in the chorus of several performances. Vergil had reluctantly permitted it, but demanded that the exercise remain a secret.

She prayed that he would come anyway. She wished that he could take some joy in this night with her. It was the first time that she had ever sung in a real theater. It was an important night for her, even if she was only an anonymous member of the chorus in a minor comic opera.

"You repudiate his affection with this decision," Pen said. "He only permitted it because he is weak with you."

"I repudiate nothing, and it would appear that he is

not very weak at all, since he has no trouble staying away from me."

"Should he sit on my doorstep and pine? The two of you have gone too far for that, and displaying his interest would only raise dangerous speculations. But I saw how he kissed you when we left the manor, and I see how he looks at you now, and I tell you, Bianca, that nothing has changed."

It seemed to Bianca that in the last few weeks everything had changed. She saw Vergil when he was in London, but not often. He would visit Pen and Charl and sometimes join them at entertainments. In front of everyone, even his sisters, his behavior was so reserved toward her that no one would ever suspect that they had been lovers. Certainly the other young men who visited Pen's house never guessed. Even Charlotte and Nigel thought the two of them still at odds.

Only when they had brief moments alone did he let her see his feelings. The pending question burned in his eyes, and unfulfilled passion electrified his discreet touch. Whenever they parted he kissed her hand as gently as he had once kissed her breast. That brief contact had the same effect on her that his more intimate kisses once had, leaving her breathless and frustrated.

To make matters worse, she could not cry on the shoulder of the only person to whom she could confide. Pen continued to be a friend, but she had only supported this debut in the hopes that a few nights onstage would satisfy Bianca forever.

Would it? She almost hoped so. She had grown

miserable with how things stood. She missed Vergil terribly. A part of her spent their long periods apart merely waiting. It did not help her anguish that one word from her could end the waiting forever.

A footman announced Signore Bardi's arrival and Pen called for the coach. Bianca dawdled in finding her wrap, hoping that another announcement of another man would be made. It never came. Wobbly with excitement, she joined Pen and Charlotte and gray-haired Signore Bardi for the ride to the English Opera House.

They separated at the door of the opulent theater. Signore Bardi directed her toward the costume room so that she could be transformed into the village woman whom she would portray.

A half hour later she snuck onto the side of the stage and peered out at the gathering crowd. A curving wall of boxes towered to the ceiling, surrounding the orchestra and pit. The din of revelry echoed around her. The eerie glow of the gas lamps tinted the audience an unnatural hue. She squinted, trying to make out the faces in Penelope's box.

Her heart sank. Vergil still was not there.

She returned to the chorus room. Finding a corner for herself, she joined her voice to the others being tuned and warmed. She followed the exercises instinctively. Her enthusiasm felt dull and forced, as if she watched someone else prepare for this debut.

If only he had come to watch, maybe ... maybe what? Maybe it would be a sign that they could have some kind of life together? A life that need not sever her soul in two and then make her throw away one of the halves.

The bodies around her began rearranging. She joined the chorus filtering onto the stage and assumed her position in the rear. With the abstracting light and her costume and the crowd, it was unlikely that she would even be seen, let alone recognized.

Her melancholy thoughts instantly disappeared when the chorus joined in song. Thundering, joyful, exuberant voices surrounded and matched her own. Her spirit leapt with startled delight. Leapt and then soared.

She had never experienced such sound. It inundated her with a huge wave of sensibility. The curves of the stage and theater seemed to imbue the music with a complex resonance. She glanced around at her fellow singers and realized that they felt what she felt and that the density of their voices compounded the euphoria she had only known privately before. A few caught her eye and smiled at her awe.

Her blood pounded. The song took over. She had not felt this alive since... She looked to Pen's box. *Be there, please be there. Share it with me.* Nigel stood in the rear, speaking with Cornell Witherby. A tall dark figure hung in the shadows and her heart skipped. It moved into view and her disappointment was so intense that her voice faltered. It was not Vergil, but instead that Mr. Siddel who had insinuated himself into Pen's circle the last month.

The performance seemed to go on and on but still ended too soon. She loved everything about it. The singing, the waiting offstage, the comaraderie with the others, the glow of the gaslights, and the damp of the back rooms. The theater became a separate place, where life and emotions intensified, much like the manor had been during those days of intimacy. She savored every detail and ignored the cutting disappointment that Vergil had forsaken her tonight.

Finally, after the last curtain, she found herself crushed into one of the chorus rooms with the other women, changing into her own garments. Excitement turned everyone's exhaustion into giddiness, and most of the giggles had to do with the rumble of male voices out in the corridor.

"The boys are waiting and restless," a sloe-eyed soprano beside her said. "You are new, aren't you? A mother or sister waiting for you?"

"My tutor will be waiting."

"Just as well. Pretty thing like you . . . they don't know the difference, do they? Think we're all of a piece. Forget their manners sometimes."

She doubted that anyone would forget their manners with Signore Bardi around. His black eyes became satanic when he got angry.

Unfortunately, Signore Bardi was not outside the chamber when she emerged. At least twenty young men were, however. Students, clerks, and young solicitors milled in the corridor, waiting for their favorite songbirds to try and fly. Flowers, endearments, and blunt advances were pressed on her. They surrounded her two deep.

"You will allow the young lady to pass, gentlemen," a cool voice commanded from the periphery.

She looked through the confusion to see blue eyes

regarding her. He had come after all. She would have flown into his arms, but his expression pulled her up short. *See?* his eyes said. *This is what you will subject yourself to.*

Mumbles passed. "Laclere . . . viscount . . ." Some of the young men drifted away.

Disappointment stabbed her. His intention in permitting this performance had been to show her the indignities, not the joy. That saddened her so much that she succumbed to an impulse to strike back and deny him satisfaction.

She ignored Vergil's proffered hand and turned to a short red-haired student on her right. He held two yellow roses toward her. She decided that she might be flattered that, of all the female singers, he chose to give her this precious gift.

She took the roses with thanks. Encouraged, and shooting cautious glances back to where Vergil still hovered and watched, two other young men advanced to compliment her singing.

An older man inserted himself into the group. He pierced her with a demanding look and then cast Vergil a scathing glance. For all of his love of music, cousin Nigel was not amused to find her here.

"I thought that it was you, but could not believe it," he said, shouldering an anxious young admirer aside. "Really, Laclere, you must remove her."

"I am prepared to escort my ward home, but it would hardly do to pick her up and carry her away."

"I would not have expected you to react so strictly," she

teased Nigel. "You of all people know the importance of performing."

"Performing is one thing, doing so here is another. What were you thinking, Laclere? I trust that tonight will be the end of it."

His scold was interrupted by another man oozing forward. It was Mr. Siddel. He was of Vergil's age and similar in build and coloring. Perhaps he was even more handsome. He had made his interest in her known during the last month while he drifted around the edges of Pen's circle. Pen's warnings that he was dangerous had been unnecessary. He possessed a talent for making even subtle attentions invasive.

"I thought that I recognized you, Miss Kenwood." He took a position in front of her that left no room for anyone else. "I knew that you studied with Signore Bardi, but I had never heard that you performed." His tone conveyed speculative delight in the discovery.

Four steps away, Vergil's profile grew stern.

"See here, Siddel," Nigel blustered.

"It is an experiment, so that I can see how it feels to sing with a large chorus."

"Certainly. Why take lessons with Bardi unless one is very serious? Perhaps one day we will see you be the supreme performer in one of London's great houses."

He said nothing improper. Even his tone could not be faulted. But she heard a difference in the way he addressed her, and did not miss the insulting double entendre.

Suddenly Vergil was eye-to-eye with Mr. Siddel. "You

will have to excuse us. My sister is expecting Miss Kenwood."

"Of course, Laclere. I wondered, at first, whom you came back here to see. Not your style anymore, is it? I should have realized that only duty would be cause to make a saint's protection public."

He played with the words like he engaged in a game of wit, but almost every one held a double meaning. Vergil assumed a cool hauteur, to match Siddel's own.

"You go too far, Siddel," Nigel said, scrutinizing her with a sidelong, suspicious glance. "You come close to unpardonable insult, and if Laclere will not call you on it, I will."

"Siddel means no insult. His tongue merely runs more quickly than his brain. It has been the bane of his life since he was a boy, but the brain usually catches up in time to avoid a challenge." Vergil's lids lowered. "I am sure that his lack of judgment tonight can be attributed to imbibing too much port. Aren't I right, Siddel?"

"Undoubtedly. My apologies, Miss Kenwood. I would be wounded to learn that my poor attempt at humor in any way offended you, or alienated your affection." He bowed with a wry smile and sauntered away.

Nigel hustled after him. " . . . inexcusably rude . . ." she heard Nigel say.

"Open your eyes," Siddel replied with a laugh.

Vergil held out his hand again. "Are you quite done here?"

"Yes, I think that I am now."

He deftly extricated her from the crowd. His coach waited.

"Did you enjoy yourself?" he asked after he had handed her in. It disappointed her that he sat across from her. In the dark he became an insubstantial shadow barely articulated by the dim light that occasionally swept through the window while they rode.

"At first I was not nearly as excited as I expected, but once we were onstage, it was so thrilling I thought that I would burst."

"I was not speaking of the performance, Bianca."

No, he wasn't. His tight tone had told her that. "I do not think that those men even knew who I was, other than a singer who came out the door when they were nearby. Aside from Nigel and Mr. Siddel, I doubt that anyone noticed me in the back of that chorus."

"You were so exuberant that I expected you to take to flight. You may not have been recognized, but you were most definitely noticed."

"You saw?"

"I was in a friend's box."

"Was I . . ." she caught herself and laughed. "I was going to ask if I was any good, but of course there was no way to tell."

"You were magnificent, darling. It would seem that half of Oxford and Cambridge and most of London's articled clerks agree."

"You sound jealous, Laclere."

"I do not think that is the correct word for tonight, Bianca. Jealousy is what I feel when I see the attention that Pen's friends give you, and I know that I cannot stop it, short of a marriage that you will not accept. Jealousy is what I experience when I see your cousin openly court you. Tonight I was not jealous. Tonight I was raw with outrage when I saw the familiarity strangers felt free to show you outside a chorus room. Tonight I was furious when I heard the insinuations a drunken rake like Siddel made, and all because you dallied in that corridor in order to flaunt your independence in my face."

Tense anger poured across the coach, carrying the hard words. At first her heart sickened while she absorbed the onslaught, but then annoyance of her own began seething through her dismay. "I thought that you wanted me to dally. I thought that you wanted me to see it all, to face the reality of the life and taste the degradation of leering admirers."

"I never want to see men look at you the way those boys did."

"Then why didn't you stop them?"

"The bigger question is, why didn't you? I stood there expecting you to make a fool of me if I tried to pull you away. I found myself wondering if you were telling me through your behavior that you had made your choice—"

"No!"

"—and that I could publicly claim you as your protector or not have you at all."

Her eyes blurred. This was not Vergil. It was his phantom, demonstrating a man's reaction when his pride is wounded.

"I do not want to speak of this any longer," she

whispered, praying it could be stopped before they said the sort of words that can never be retrieved.

"I do. We have much to speak of, it seems to me."

The coach had stopped. She waited for the footman to set down the steps. "No, Laclere. I will not have a row with you. The evening has tired me. I bid you goodnight."

· She swept to the door. He followed two steps behind.

"You will not dismiss me like one of those spot-faced supplicants, Bianca."

"Pity." She led the way into the candlelit entry. The first floor had been closed up. Everyone else must have retired. "Since this is your sister's house, I cannot deny you admittance. However, I will not submit to your scolds and insinuations, Laclere. I am too tired to spar and too hurt to be clever. You have taken one of the most important nights of my life and reduced it to something shameful and sordid. It was glorious, and like a fool I thought that only your presence could make it better. Instead you ruined it. I may never forgive your cruelty."

Her accusations pulled him up short. A few of the storm clouds blew out of his eyes. "If I have been cruel, I apologize. Let us go into the library, Bianca. I want to speak with you."

"Pontificate and lecture to yourself, dear guardian. I am going to bed."

He grabbed at her as she mounted the stairs. "Come back down here, Bianca."

"Go away, Laclere. Do not make a scene or you will wake the household."

"I will wake the whole damn city if I want."

She shook her arm free. "Oh, stubble it, Vergil. Good-night."

Stubble it. Where the hell was she learning words like that?

He knew where. From the soulful, adoring, perfect-image-of-romantic-sensibility young bloods who gravitated to Pen's house like so many bees discovering a newly blooming garden. He spent most of his time swatting them away when he visited, but they always buzzed back.

He strode into the library. No fire or candles burned, but he found the port anyway. It didn't taste nearly as comforting as he thought it would, nor did it relieve his annoyance.

His mood was not only because of Bianca, he had to admit. Tomorrow he faced an unpleasant task in his search for the truth about Milton's death. The prospect of the waiting interview sickened him, and he had entered the opera house resentful and angry about that as much as Bianca's performance.

His world threatened to fall apart. Every friendship and love at its center seemed to have become as insecure, duplicitous, and masked as his own life.

Tonight had shown that Bianca was slipping from his life too. She lived here and practiced with Signore Bardi and made new friends and enjoyed her youth, and every new experience pulled her further away from him. He could feel the gulf widening. Sometimes he wondered if she remembered that she was supposed to be considering marriage to him.

He would have forbidden this debut if he could. He would have strangled Bardi, or at least bribed him, if he had surmised the tutor would propose such a thing.

She had loved it. Of course she had. Catalani had once told him that the magic created for the audience was felt ten times over by the performers themselves. What must it be like to stand surrounded by the sound booming off the ceiling? Like being submerged in an ocean of the senses. He had watched Bianca's amazement and known with certainty that in one night the odds had tilted against him in this competition for her life.

His mind recalled her excited smile when she saw him in the corridor, and then her retreat into cool poise when she noticed his anger. He had been so preoccupied with his resentments that he had not noticed at the time how beautiful that smile had been, nor that it had existed solely for him.

The worst of his bristling mood snapped and died. He set down the port, feeling subdued for reasons that had nothing to do with the spirits. He pictured that smile again and again, replaced by hurt.

His behavior had been inexcusable. Deliberately heartless, if he wanted to be honest with himself. He had reacted to tonight's events as if they had all been about him, when in fact he was merely a guest at another person's party. But for her happiness in his attendance, it really had not mattered if he were there at all. Maybe he had known that. Perhaps he had invited this argument to ensure that his supporting role would not be reduced to a walk-on.

The house throbbed with silence. He wished that one of the servants was about. He would send him to ask Bianca to come down for a short while. He did not want to leave tonight with things the way they were.

He strolled out to the corridor. Someone had locked the front door, a sure sign that no servant would appear. No more candles waited to light the way, but he knew this house as well as his own and could navigate it blind.

Silence pulsed. She might not be asleep yet. He would go and apologize, and then leave through the garden door.

She was not asleep. She had not even prepared for bed. She sat in an undressing gown in a chair by the hearth. When he entered she did not demonstrate the slightest surprise, just raised sad eyes. It was as if she had been waiting for him.

She acknowledged him, then looked down at her lap. Her hands lay twisted together there. "No more lectures, Laclere."

"No."

"What, then? It is dangerous for you to be here."

She looked so unhappy. He would take her in his arms, but he did not trust himself to touch her. "An apology. I did try to ruin tonight for you. Your pleasure in it... frightened me."

She rose and paced thoughtfully around the room's edges. "It frightened me too. All of this frightens me. It is a torture. Do not tell me that I can end it with one word. I know that." She cast an accusing glare at him. "You spoke of me tonight as if you did not know me at all. If I have become a stranger to you, do not blame me. I am not the one who stays away."

"I do not stay away."

"You do. I have rarely seen you the last few weeks. You sent no word that you would come tonight. I am left to wonder if you have forgotten me, and to be grateful for your small acknowledgments when you do visit."

"You knew that it would be like this, Bianca. I can hardly display my affection and announce to the world what has occurred. Since I cannot, I do not relish sitting in Pen's drawing room with other men who are permitted to openly court you while I must play the guardian."

"You could arrange—"

"No."

"You could at least kiss me when you leave. You could give me just a brief kiss to show that you have not grown indifferent."

"I am far from indifferent, which is why I could never give you *just* a brief kiss."

She still paced, like a restless spirit drove her and she found the chamber too small. She eyed him with a glint of defiance.

"I did it on purpose, you know. Encouraged those young men. Took the roses and spoke with them. I wanted to show you that they represented no danger to me or my virtue. That is how my mother treated the men who pursued her. Politely enough, but keeping a firm distance. Surely it could work for me as well."

"Undoubtedly it could, but the world's assumptions will carry more force than your actions. In any case, I cannot bear to watch it."

Her brow puckered. "You made that clear. Which is the other reason why I did it tonight, I think. To make you jealous."

"To make me jealous?"

"Yes, I think so. I really do."

"Bianca, I have been castigating myself for reacting badly. I have apologized for misjudging this evening and you have accepted that apology. Now you blithely add that perhaps I was correct all along?"

She shrugged. "I cannot honestly say that making you jealous had nothing to do with it, that is all."

"Other than our unhappiness, what could you hope to gain by that?"

She strolled so close that her perfume and silk robe clouded around him. "Well," she said, plucking at ribbons on the robe with slow, taunting pulls, "for one thing, it seems that I got you into my bedchamber, doesn't it?"

Her sly smile almost stopped his heart. The door stood five feet behind him, but suddenly it might have been miles away.

The bedrobe fell. She was not naked. Stays cinched her from midriff to hips. Chemise and pantaloons created a thin film of fabric over her breasts and thighs. White stockings remained gartered above her knees.

The world constricted to her and him and the space between them. The bold challenge in her eyes made desire scorch through his body.

"It is not wise to tempt a man who is hot with jealousy, darling."

Her lids lowered. "Just as long as you are hot, Laclere, I don't care why."

Damn. He walked over to her. "It appears that you are dangerous and a little wicked, after all."

"Only with you, Laclere."

"You just admitted otherwise."

"That was different, wasn't it? I wasn't really wicked with them. But I did use them to affect you, which was unfair."

They were as close as possible without touching. "Most unfair."

"Was it really very naughty of me?"

"*Very* naughty."

"I suppose that there is nothing for it, Laclere. You will just have to punish me."

With a pout of contrite resignation she climbed onto the bed. She pulled a mound of pillows over and settled herself with them under her stomach, raising her bottom in penitence.

She glanced back at him, and her expression aroused him more than her erotic position. The erection of a lifetime strained against his clothing. His blood pounded without mercy.

He caressed up her leg, grasped the edge of the pantaloons, and ripped. Gossamer shreds flew away from her buttocks and thighs. He flipped her and the pillows raised her hips so that she had to bend and spread her legs to stay balanced. Kneeling beside her, he kissed down the straps of her chemise until her naked breasts peaked high and hungry above the top edge of her stays. He licked and gently drew on each one.

He rose and undressed, never taking his eyes off the lovely body laid out with abandon for him. She watched the coats and collar drop, with eyes as hot as his. The musk of her arousal wafted to him. Just lying there, vulnerable and exposed, already had her hips subtly flexing with a sexual rhythm.

He removed his pocket watch from the waistcoat and checked the time, then placed it near the candle by the bed.

"Hurry," she whispered, reaching a hand in his direction.

"No." He discarded his shirt and stripped off his lower garments. He knelt between her knees. Lifting one ankle onto his shoulder, he began kissing along her leg's inner flesh. "This is not going to be hurried at all."

He rubbed his face against her back and kissed down the length of her spine. The tantalizing stays had been discarded sometime during the night as too warm. His kisses trailed over her bottom and down her thigh to the stocking still gartered on one leg.

She was not asleep, and she sighed in her contentment

and shifted her legs, reassuming the position on the pillow with which this had begun, welcoming him to repeat the new intimate kisses he had taught her tonight.

The fall of her arms around her head, the press of her cheek against the sheets, the arched offering of her body—to his amazement, the sensuality of her repose had him hardening yet again.

"It will be dawn soon. I must go." He rolled onto his back and pulled her into his arms. The beckoning day reminded him of the meeting he had arranged for this morning. He did not want to go to it, and not only because it meant leaving Bianca.

She sighed petulantly, as if the revolution of the earth were an inconvenience designed only to limit their time together. "Will you come back tonight?"

"No."

"No one will know. You stayed last night and—"

"And if we are lucky, all will be well. Repeating this will only tempt fate. Nothing has changed, Bianca."

She did not like hearing that. She kissed him sadly. "It seems to me it would be difficult to tempt fate more than you just have."

"I decided that if I was going to hang, it may as well be for a pound as a penny."

He gently lifted her away and swung from the bed. She watched him dress with a sleepy expression. He tried not to reveal his distaste for this part of it. The watched time, the secret departure, the strangling discretion—it reminded him too much of visits to the kind of women who never became wives, and of how she fluttered like a moth around the flame of a life that often led in that direction.

He stood beside the bed and looked down at her. Images of the night passed in their mutual gaze. He had taken liberties with her that many men never expect of their wives, further blurring how he should view this affair and his rights with her.

He brushed her cheek with the back of his fingers. She was so lovely. So joyful and innocent in her passion. He had met women who could degrade the sensuality of a simple kiss. Bianca's sense of wonder could turn the most exotic loveplay into a sacred ritual.

"Do you mean it? When we make love, you cry out that you love me. Every time you have done so. Do you even know that you say it?" It surprised him to hear himself voicing the question out loud.

"If I did not mean it, you would not be standing by my bed right now. I know what I risk. I would have never done any of this only for pleasure."

He supposed that he had known that. Still, it was nice to be sure. It gave him a bit more hope about how this would end, and love made a better rationale than lust if their behavior ended up destroying them both.

"Well, if you think that you love me, I expect that I can wait a little longer, darling."

Her eyes glittered with affection and concern. No one had ever seen him as clearly as she did. "Wait for what, Laclere? To decide to give up on me, or to decide to love me back?"

She could still astonish him. "Both, I suppose. It will probably have to be one or the other for me soon."

He stepped out into the dark corridor and silently closed her door behind him. Only the vaguest light penetrated from some lower windows. He found the banister and glided down the stairs, then crossed to the servants' stairway. Down again, this time to the kitchen.

He was less sure of his way in the lower chambers, and he felt his path along the walls. Near the spot where the door should be, he stumbled into another groping body.

"What the . . . Who the hell . . ."

"Damn! Watch where . . ."

They both froze.

"Witherby?"

"Laclere!"

"Arriving or departing, Witherby?"

"Oh, God. Laclere. This is most awkward."

"Leaving, I assume at this hour. The door is over here."

"Of course. Jesus." Cornell Witherby backed away a few steps and righted himself.

"Are you coming? I think we should discuss this outside."

With the cold air came Witherby's attempt at explanation. "I know how this must look."

"It looks as if you have initiated an affair with my sister, Penelope. It is Penelope, isn't it? Because if it is Charlotte I will have to kill you, and I'd hate to do that to an old friend."

"Charlotte! Zeus, man, what do you take me for? As for Pen, I assure you that she has my deepest affection and admiration. A goddess could not be adored more than I do her. She possesses such a sweet, gracious, lovely soul, and—"

"Yes, yes. The garden gate is over here, or do you know your way in the dark?"

"I assure you that I have never before—"

"I am sure that you understand that discretion is essential. If the earl discovered this affair, he would use it to remove her support, which is hardly substantial as it is."

Their boots kicked along the rocks, punctuating the silence.

"You are being very understanding about this, Laclere. I am, of course, overjoyed that you approve, but we thought you to be less sympathetic."

Vergil paused where the alley met the road. "I would have preferred not knowing enough to approve or disapprove. My sister has had too little happiness in her life, however. If she wants you, I will not interfere."

Ever so subtly, the night had grown less dark. He could make out Witherby's tall, slender form distinctly now, and even something of his expression. "This is not what we expected, Laclere. I daresay Pen will be as astounded as I."

Vergil turned to walk home. "Just make sure that I do not regret my liberal-mindedness."

"I will make her as happy as I am capable," Witherby said. "And since you are so generous, I will refrain from wondering why you were departing from that house at the same time and through the same door as I was."

The pistol cracked the autumn day. The ball *thwacked* into the tree trunk in the woods behind the Chevalier Corbet's fencing academy.

"You haven't been practicing enough," Vergil said.

Dante stood aside and began reloading. "It is only sport for some of us, Verg. I have no intention of killing a man in a duel."

Vergil sighted his aim. "And if some man intends to kill you?"

"I daresay if no husband has challenged me by now, none ever will."

Vergil fired his own pistol. It hit dead center on the paper tacked to the tree.

Dante whistled with appreciation. "You *have* been practicing, I can see."

"Anything worth doing, is worth doing well."

Dante laughed. "I agree. You and I just prefer to do different things."

He took his place again. Vergil watched his careless stance. It had only been by the grace of Providence that Dante had never needed this skill.

The pistol fired. Dante moved aside. "You haven't reloaded."

"No."

The word riveted Dante's attention. The hand holding the pistol fell to his side. "You have that look on your face. What is it this time? Did someone come to dun you for one of my debts again?"

"It is not that."

"Well, it is something, so out with it. You suggested we come and shoot, but I don't think two balls justifies a ride to Hampstead, do you?"

Vergil set his gun in the box. "I need to ask you about something. It is important that you answer me honestly."

Dante's head cocked back and his lids lowered. "Then ask."

"I have been trying to discover the truth about Milton's death. I have spent months doing so. I am convinced he was blackmailed."

"Blackmailed! What secrets could Milton have had? His politics were extreme, but he published his ideas in letters and such, and everyone knew he was really harmless."

"It was not politics. I think that I have discovered why and how he was blackmailed, but the details do not matter. There is a piece missing, however. I think that you can supply that piece."

"You think that I had a hand in this? That is a damnable thing to suggest. It would be a hell of a thing if the only time I challenged a man it was you, Vergil."

"I do not think that you had an intentional hand in it. Trust me, if I could avoid this conversation I would. I *have* avoided it, too long."

"Maybe you should continue doing so. You can't bring him back."

"It goes beyond him."

"Hell." Dante scowled and dropped his pistol into the box. "What do you need to know?"

"I have been asking the servants about things. I am told that a year ago you brought a visitor to Laclere House in London. A woman of good breeding. Who was it?"

"I do not discuss my women with other men, not even you."

"That is commendable, but this time you must. Did you ever have a woman in that house overnight?"

Dante's face assumed a mask of resentment. "If I did, you can be sure it was not an American virgin."

"This is not about our private failings, Dante. I want to know if someone besides a family member had access to Milton's chamber and study prior to his death. Were you in the London house with a woman while he was down at Laclere Park?"

"What are you implying? That she—"

"That someone, somehow, procured letters to Milton. Letters from a lover. A woman went to the lover, claiming she was Pen, to confirm what she already suspected, and then found a way to get her hands on the evidence. Then she blackmailed Milton."

"Letters from a lover? Milton? He lived like a monk where women were concerned. Really, Verg—"

"We are not boys anymore, Dante. Not children. Do not pretend that you are ignorant. Despite his care and discretion, I suspected. I think that you did too."

Dante glared at him. "If you are suggesting what I think—"

"You know what I am suggesting. It was our brother's

tragedy to live in a world where even his family had to deny the man he was. He had to hide this part of himself even from us, and so, as we grew older, he retreated from us as from so much else."

Dante turned away and stared at the paper tacked on the tree. "Damn it. *Enough.* I do not want to talk about this."

"No one does. We would prefer that men blow their brains out when their secret is discovered and exposure is threatened. It is a sinful waste, and the silence and shame killed him as surely as that gun. I'll hang before I will let the people who hounded him get away with it. Now, tell me, damn it. Who was she?"

Dante shook his head in dismay. Anger and astonishment fought a battle over his expression. "A lark, she called it. She said she was always curious about the old pile, and had never seen the inside of the house. Well, there hadn't been parties there for as long as I could remember. Asked if I would show her the interior."

"She stayed?"

Dante smirked with disgust. At himself. "Of course."

"All night?"

He nodded.

"While you slept, perhaps she did not."

"I don't believe it. I am sure that you are wrong."

"Are you? Truly?"

Dante crossed his arms and looked to the ground.

"Her name, Dante."

He sighed, and vaguely shook his head again. His jaw tightened and fury flared in his eyes. "If you are right, the bitch used me to destroy my own brother."

"You were unawares. Do not blame—"

"Don't," Dante snarled. He furiously raised a hand to halt the excuses, and also in warning. "Just, *don't*."

He dropped his hand, and his anger. Only pain remained in his expression.

"It was Mrs. Gaston, Vergil."

chapter 19

Nigel had said that he planned to go down to Woodleigh once again, so Bianca was surprised when he was announced several days after her secret debut.

He entered the drawing room, wearing a serious countenance. He chatted with Pen and Charlotte for a short while, but it was obvious that an important mission distracted him. Finally he asked Pen if he could speak with Bianca alone. Bianca could tell that Pen feared Nigel intended to declare himself. Reluctantly she collected Charlotte and left.

Nigel paced in front of Bianca. He looked more like a man set to scold than to propose. "I trust that you have not repeated your stage performance."

"Once more, the next night. No others are planned for some time."

"Siddel has been telling people. He frames it as a girl's

harmless caprice, but I fear that society will be shocked all the same."

"Do not concern yourself for my reputation, Nigel. I already have all of the Duclaircs doing that for me."

"It is precisely the Duclaircs' management of your reputation that concerns me." He faced her and took a deep breath. "What I am obliged to say cannot be discussed without some indelicacy. You are in the power of a man who is duplicitous and dangerous, and who has designs on you of the most dishonorable nature."

"I am? Of whom do you speak?"

"Laclere, of course. I had suspected that he intended you for the brother, and that was disturbing enough. Dante would have only brought you unhappiness. But it was a feint, I realize now, to obscure a much more disgraceful plan. I curse myself for not seeing their game earlier and for letting things get as far as they have."

"This family has shown me only friendship and affection."

"You are not one of them. Not of their blood or world. The honor that they give their women does not extend to you. You are a foreigner of lower social station, and that makes you vulnerable."

"The viscount has never behaved in any way that I consider dishonorable."

"He played the role of a singer's protector the other night. That he permitted you to be there and then called for you like his mistress—"

"It is his duty to protect me. I am his ward."

"Which makes his misuse of you all the more reprehensible." He resumed pacing. "I am your only relative here in England, Bianca. It falls to me to do what I can to prevent this. I had planned to wait until your birthday to ask, because I knew that Laclere would not approve. I think that it is essential for me to remove you from his influence at once, however. I think it best if we married now."

She was getting tired of men proposing like this. For the third time there had been some external coercion that required her reputation to be saved by hasty matrimony. Didn't Englishmen know how to do it the usual way? Was it necessary for events to wrench the offer out of them?

"Nigel, you are overwrought."

"Hear me out, Bianca. I am very fond of you, and I think that you care for me too. Furthermore, we have similar interests. I am sure that your grandfather saw the possibility for mutual sympathy and hoped that we would discover each other. It was the only reason to make Laclere your guardian instead of me. To leave the way free."

"You may be correct, Nigel, but we would be ill-advised to marry in order to fulfill a dead man's wish."

He heard the overture of rejection in her response. It provoked a sharp look as he halted his pacing. "I think that you should seriously consider my offer, cousin. It is in your best interests."

Something in the way he looked at her frightened her. A little flurry of warning fluttered up her spine. "I will consider it, and I am flattered, but I am obliged to say that it is unlikely that I will accept."

His mouth twisted into a sneer. "It is because of him, isn't it? You think you are in love with him, don't you?"

She wanted to deny that, but the lie died in her throat. His expression said that he would not believe her anyway.

"I saw you. When he met you behind the stage, I was in the corridor. I saw you when you realized that he was there." He stepped toward her and she instinctively tilted away. He cupped her chin and lifted her face so that he could inspect her. "I cannot permit it. He cannot have you as a lover. Or has he promised to marry you?"

"I do not intend to marry anyone right now. I will be continuing my training."

"It is as I thought. He has already corrupted you. Damn the man. We must get you out at once."

"I am going nowhere, Nigel."

Her firm tone caught him up short. He studied her from beneath lowered lids. A thin smile formed, which made him appear reptilian.

"I must insist. He will surely break your heart, Bianca. The best that you can hope for is that he keeps you like a caged bird who sings only for him. More likely he will coarsen you until you agree to sing for any with the right price or the right lies."

"You are the one being coarse, Nigel. I recognize gross insult when I hear it. I will not listen to you speak like this of him, or of me. I must ask you to leave now."

His agitation had transformed into a cool, sly swagger. "Do not get high-and-mighty with me, cousin. You are the great-grandchild of a man who began as a coster-monger, same as me. Your father was a third-rate Latin scholar, and your mother sang in as many taverns as she did churches. You do not belong with Laclere, and he knows it, if you do not. If he offered marriage, it was out of the sentiment of the moment." He flicked a bit of dust off his sleeve. "Now, as I see it, we should not go to Scotland. The Continent makes more sense. We can be married in France."

His proposal was preposterous, but the confidence with which he pursued it frightened her. He acted like a man holding more aces than the pack should contain. "I have no intention of marrying you in any country."

"You will not be bound by English law once you leave these shores. You are American, and Laclere's authority ends at the coast. After France, we will go down to Italy if you like."

"I will not be going to Italy with you."

"I am afraid that I am part of the package, dear girl."

"Then I will stay here."

"If you do, I will destroy him. I will tell the world about him."

He made the threat so calmly, so normally, that he might have been observing that the weather promised to be fair today. She faced him down, but her throat tight-ened. He looked so sure of himself. Too sure.

"No one will believe you. You are guessing and have no proof."

"Rumors are usually enough. People love to watch the self-righteous fall. You have never seen how this society can kill people with cuts and oblivion. Imagine little Charlotte suddenly without friends or decent marriage prospects. Pen snubbed even by her artists. Laclere himself a social outcast."

"If you destroy him with rumors, you also destroy me. A fine proof of your affection. I will deny everything. I will return to America before you can hurt him, if you begin spreading such damaging tales."

"A charming sacrifice, but unnecessary. Ultimately, seducing you is not the sin that will bring him down." He smiled smugly. "You see, I know about Manchester. I know about Mr. Clark. For that there is proof, and no forgiveness, especially on top of his dishonor toward an innocent."

He might have punched her, she felt so shaken.

"Manchester?"

"You do not know about it? I will have to explain on the way to France. Suffice to say that I have the means to ruin Laclere and his family completely and thoroughly. Do not doubt it, Bianca, and when you hear the truth of it, you will thank me. Your viscount is duplicitous in the literal meaning of the word. His interest in you is wholly about a mill up north. He wants to control you because of the share that you inherited. He needs to be able to dictate to you."

"And you, Nigel? My property and income play no role in your offer?"

"My primary concern is your safety and reputation. The property is obviously of interest, but at least with me you will be allowed to enjoy it. Once married to me, you can sing as you wish, and train properly, and perform with triumph."

She did not believe him. She doubted that she would enjoy her inheritance at all, or be allowed to use it to train in Italy. He wanted it. It was why he was here.

To blackmail her into marriage, and get at her inheritance.

Had he also blackmailed Milton? Was she looking at the man responsible for that? Had he seen or heard something during one of his visits to Woodleigh, and then used the information to try and bleed Milton? If Milton ever had an unsuitable lover visit, word could travel among the servants and tenants, just as she had learned about Nigel's own female visitor.

She saw him with new eyes, ones that perceived the danger beneath the fashionable persona. His life stood for nothing except his own indulgence. Yes, he could do it. He could dangle destruction with one hand while he held out the other for a bribe.

It was what he was doing right now.

He gazed down at her the way one would peruse an interesting new possession. "I think that you will agree that it is settled. There is little point in further discussion. You are going down to Laclere Park soon, are you not?"

She nodded numbly. She had been looking forward to several weeks in the country. Vergil had promised he would be there most of the time. In such a big house, with such extensive grounds, surely they could find some time alone together.

"We will leave from Woodleigh, then. I will send the

instructions to you." He bent and brushed his mouth on hers. Her lips stretched against her teeth in disgust. "Not a word about our plans, Bianca. Do not tell anyone, not even your maid, and definitely not the Viscount Laclere. Do not doubt that I will ruin him if he interferes, and enjoy doing it. I must leave you now, but I look forward to when we are together forever."

He left her limp with helplessness. She had no time to compose herself before Charlotte darted in and knelt beside her on the settee.

"Did he offer? He looked very handsome today. Pen was sure he came to offer, and was fussing that Vergil would like as kill him rather than permit it, but I don't think my brother is *that* strict and unreasonable. You are almost of age, after all. If you are determined, what can he really do. So, did he?"

Charlotte's face flushed so prettily when she was excited. Her eyes, brown and limpid like Dante's, glowed with deep lights. She exuded purity and sweet innocence and would not begin to know what to do if her world turned upside down.

Which it would, if Nigel held good to his threat. In a way, Vergil's secrecy had mostly been for Charlotte's sake.

"No, he did not offer," she lied. "He came to scold me for the chorus performances."

Charlotte's eyes sparkled with mischief. "It was very exciting knowing someone who dared something so naughty. A bit like getting to be naughty oneself without really having to be. I am still amazed that you got Vergil to agree to it. Perhaps he is growing to like you a bit more. Maybe someday you and he can even be friends."

Bianca laughed to hide her tears. Her mind raced, calculating the time left with the man who should not like her much. She prayed that he would visit, even while she dreaded his arrival.

Except for the dream days at the manor, the shadow of eventual parting always tinged her emotions when he was near. The drop of melancholy did not make the wine of love distasteful. It enriched and mellowed the flavor. But it would be different now. Nigel's blackmail made the separation imminent. The days remaining could be counted, and Vergil's surprise when she left could be imagined. How would she face him without his guessing?

She found out sooner than she wanted. He arrived the next afternoon. She remained in her chamber, attempting to muster enough composure to hide her distress. For the last twenty-four hours she had experienced the panic of a woman cornered by a predator. Every scheme for escape that she considered was hopelessly flawed.

Charlotte came looking for her. "My brother is here. He is wondering why you have not come to the drawing room."

"I am not feeling very well." That was the honest truth.

"He does not look as though he feels well either. He appears distracted and displeased. He asked Pen where Mrs. Gaston has gone, and then barely heard the explanation that Mrs. Gaston has left London to visit friends in the country. Now he has ordered me to come and call you to the library." Charlotte arched her eyebrows. "Have you done something else a little naughty, Bianca?"

She sorely wished that all she had to worry about was a little bad behavior.

He waited in the library, looking thoughtful and windblown and devastatingly handsome. A dark lock fell over his forehead, and she itched to caress it back into the thick tumble of his hair. His cravat's folds were not perfectly centered, and she almost reached out to straighten them. His burning eyes and straight mouth made her worry that he had heard about Nigel's blackmail and planned to berate her for not calling for his help.

He closed the library doors. "This will not do," he said.

"What will not do?"

"This." His arm gestured around the room, at the house in general and at her and him specifically. "You. Me. You fill my days, my nights, my thoughts, my heart. I cannot bear the torture of your presence, nor can I survive the hell of staying away. I cannot live like this. We must come to some resolution."

Laclere, no, please no. Leave it alone and give me the few days left. "You promised that I could have some time."

"You misunderstand me, darling. I did not come to press my advantage, but to admit that I have none. My feelings for you have rendered every other concern insignificant." He reached out to her. "You win. We will do it your way. Whatever arrangements you want. If you only want me for a lover, we will try to be discreet and hope for the best."

Devastation paralyzed her. She longed to grasp that

hand and press it to her heart. Love and gratitude spilled through her, but she could not demonstrate it.

She had hoped to run away and never see his reaction. To toy with him now would be inexcusable. He left her no choice but to throw his generosity back in his face.

He noticed her hesitation. His hand fell. "Of course, if you have decided that you do not want me at all, we can make arrangements regarding that too."

Not want him? Surely, no matter what she said this day, he would know that could not be true. He would realize that she did not follow her heart and that something else drove her.

Yes, if she was not very careful, he would indeed realize that. She could not allow it. She had to make him believe whatever story she gave.

She lovingly studied every angle of his face. Crystalline blue eyes regarded her carefully, curious about her reticence. She wanted to fly into his arms and tell him everything. But how could he get them out of this?

She turned away. "I have been thinking."

He became utterly still. He waited so silently that he might not have been in the chamber. She forced herself on.

"What has occurred between us... It is dangerous. Ruinous. We must have been mad. I have been thinking... you know that I have always believed that marriage was too permanent a punishment for so temporary a crime."

"The punishment would not be mine, so do not pretend that you spare me, Bianca."

His tone chilled her. She closed her eyes and grit her teeth. "No, I will not pretend that. It is my life that marriage will change, in ways that I do not want. Considering that, I do not think that any arrangement will suffice. If I want to pursue my music, I must go to Milan, we must part, and we only delay the sorrow by a few months this way."

The words barely made it out. Silence shuddered in their aftermath. She still did not face him, but she could feel him behind her, large and dark and burning. She discerned that he had moved, but whether he had retreated she could not tell.

He had not walked away. When he spoke, his breath touched her hair. "Since I initiated you in love, perhaps I should instruct you in this as well. It is cowardly to refuse to face me, and you are nothing if not brave."

"I am not brave. I am pitifully weak. If this is wounding you, I do not want to see it." She forced down the ripping anguish that provoked the outburst. "And if it is not wounding you, I do not want to see that, either. That is just how selfish I can be, Laclere."

His firm hand took her shoulder and turned her around. A crooked finger tilted up her chin.

Oh, how he looked at her. Not in anger. His eyes glittered with the memories of their intimacies. He looked at her so completely and openly that she knew it was the last honest look he ever planned to give her.

"It is always a lady's prerogative to end an affair, Bianca. A gentleman does not upbraid her for it or demand more explanations than she chooses to give."

How could he accept this so easily? It was as if he had never believed in his heart that they might stay together.

That was her own fault if true, but the thought produced a scathing disappointment. "You are being too kind and generous and making it too easy for me. I would prefer that you yell at me and accuse me of being wicked and flighty and bad."

"You are none of those things. I am sorry that you have made this choice, but I knew it was possible."

Unshed tears burned and knotted her throat and chest. *Do not look away. Do not listen to me. Take me in your arms. Make love to me here, now, on the floor. Refuse to accept this, please.*

He lifted her hand to his lips and held it there, closing his eyes. "My dear girl."

And then he was gone, walking away.

"Laclere." His name tore from her as the tears overflowed. "I was not false. I did not lie to you. It is just . . . it is just . . ."

He paused at the door. "I know that you were not false, Bianca."

Words choked her breath. "I did not lie to you. I do love you, I do . . . only . . ."

His expression revealed some anger now. Of course there would be some of that too. "I believe you. I think that you do love me. Only . . . not enough."

chapter 20

She did not sneak away this time.

She waited at Laclere Park until she received Nigel's letter, telling her when to come. Then she packed her valise, gave Jane a note for Pen, and the next morning at dawn called for the curricle to drive her to Woodleigh.

She had kept to herself the week since they had returned to Laclere Park. Pen knew that she had broken with Vergil. The awkwardness about that had made it easy to create a distance. Charlotte was so distracted by daydreams about her impending debut season that she did not notice Bianca's reserve.

Contrary to his initial plans, Vergil had not accompanied them to Sussex. Affairs suddenly demanded his continued presence in London, he had explained to his sisters.

Well, what had she expected? That he would absolve her inconstancy and rise above the insult?

The curricle rounded a bend and pulled onto the road that led to Woodleigh. Gray brush and dull fields fell away on either side of the road. Low clouds muted the light, leaching the color out of everything, blurring distant forms into one depressing mass. Woodleigh loomed ahead, its huge bulk barely alleviated by the elegant classicism of its design. A hired coach and four waited in the drive.

Nigel emerged from the house in time to meet the halt of her carriage. A footman removed her valise, while another helped her down. It appeared that Nigel had hired a staff of servants since her last visit.

"You simply rode away?" he asked as her carriage departed.

"You wrote that we would leave immediately upon my arrival. It seemed overly dramatic to lower myself from my window by the bedsheets and trudge through the forest. Pen will be told when she wakes that I came here, but I trust we will be long gone by then."

"Yes, long gone, and on our way to the packet at Dover."

"I should warn you that I have very little money with me. I left most of what I had with Jane. Since I am abandoning her, it seemed only right."

"Laclere will see that she gets back to Baltimore. Jane is no longer your concern. Nothing is. I will take care of you now."

He escorted her into the house. More new servants were carrying down trunks and tying them onto the coach.

"I will make a poor showing in France, cousin. I only have the garments in that valise," she said while she warmed herself near the drawing-room fire.

"You will look lovely in whatever you wear, and we will have a wardrobe made for you by the finest Parisian modistes."

He smiled and flattered as a fiancé should, as if he expected them to pretend that he had not coerced her into this.

The activity in the hall ceased. Nigel extended his hand. "We should be off, Bianca. We would like to avoid a race to the coast with your guardian in pursuit, if possible."

"He is not even at Laclere Park. But, yes, let us depart."

The coach was luxurious as hired vehicles went, newer than most, with four matched horses. Nigel was already making headway into her inheritance by way of credit on her expectations.

A footman opened the door and set down the stairs. Nigel handed her up. She halted halfway in.

A woman waited inside the coach.

Mrs. Gaston smiled a welcome.

"Please, darling, seat yourself. I will explain," Nigel said.

Bianca settled next to Mrs. Gaston. Nigel sat across from them.

"Mrs. Gaston has been kind enough to agree to accompany us and serve as your chaperon until we marry," Nigel said.

"How generous of her."

Mrs. Gaston patted her hand. "It is exciting, isn't it? Such a match this will be. Two musicians. Ever since I watched you both perform at the countess's party, I have thought this was fated."

"I did not realize you and Nigel were such good friends."

"We have had the pleasure of each other's company on occasion these last months, since meeting at Laclere Park. Your cousin is an accomplished musician, and I collect such stars in my circle."

"Mrs. Gaston has proposed a subscription series of concerts for me next spring," Nigel said with a broad, flattering smile at the great patroness.

"Goodness, Mrs. Gaston, your generosity to my cousin knows no bounds. Such an offer of patronage is extraordinary. Unfortunately, this elopement will ruin those plans. We will be in Milan in the spring. Isn't that so, Nigel?"

Nigel's smile turned a little crooked. "Of course."

Mrs. Gaston smiled benignly and patted Bianca's hand again.

Bianca bit her tongue.

She did not believe that the two of them had met at Laclere Park. She suspected that Mrs. Gaston was the woman who had secretly visited Woodleigh. There was no other explanation for her presence in this carriage and on this journey. Mrs. Gaston, patroness of the arts, would not interrupt her plans to serve as chaperon for two unknown, unestablished musicians.

Nigel appeared contented, as well he might. The

scoundrel was blackmailing her into marriage and would soon control her fortune, and he had not even bothered to get rid of his mistress for the elopement.

He misunderstood her expression. "All will be well, cousin. We are safe. Laclere will not interfere."

Laclere. She wished Nigel had not mentioned him. Pen would send word to him in London. He would know by tonight.

What would he think? That she had truly forsaken him for Nigel? If so, it would change the way he remembered everything.

The coach rocked with a rhythm that timed out her seething frustration. Across from her Nigel relaxed and closed his eyes. Blond hair wisped around his face. He might have been a child sleeping, he looked so untroubled.

She would allow him to enjoy his triumph. She would wait until they were in France before she let him know that she had laid a few plans of her own.

Vergil wanted to smash his fist into something. Pen's footman guessed as much and darted away so the something would not be his jaw.

The little bitch. That a grown man of his age, a respected member of the House of Lords, a confidante of the king's advisors, *a saint, damn it,* should have been made such a fool by a little colonial was bad enough. To now learn that her love had been a game, an elaborate jest, and that the whole time . . . his head split from the intensity of the outrage.

The footman tried to melt into the door.

"Damn it, go back to Sussex. I have no message for my sister."

The footman beat a retreat. Vergil slammed the door after him with enough force to shake the books on the library's shelves.

He stared down at Pen's note on the floor, and then at Bianca's letter, crushed in his fist. He uncrumbled the latter and pressed it out.

It was ostensibly written to Pen, but he could hear Bianca talking to him.

My dearest friend,

When you receive this, I should be on my way to France. I apologize for leaving this way, but I thought it unlikely that I would receive your approval if I announced my plans. I thank you for all of your kindness toward me, but it is time to do what I left Baltimore to accomplish, and there is no reason to wait any longer.

Nigel has graciously offered to accompany me. He anticipates marriage, but I do not see how such an alliance will benefit me. However, in the eventuality that he can persuade me otherwise, I have taken measures through Mr. Peterson to ensure that such a development does not create difficulties for any of my friends in England. For the next few months, I will no doubt have to live off my expectations unless Laclere agrees to forward me funds when I contact him. I daresay that Nigel will be an excellent tutor in delaying payment to tradesmen.

Please address my heartfelt thanks and love to your

family, Pen. I hope to see you again, if you have room in your circle for one more artist and room in your heart for one troublesome girl.

Please convince your brother that he must not follow me.

Your errant friend,
Bianca

He could hear her enunciating each word. He pictured her writing them. She did not sound or look smug or even excited. She appeared serious and determined and worried. She should be. She had no idea of the danger she may have put herself in by placing herself at Nigel's mercy.

What the hell was going on? Was she the most shameless of flirts, conducting an affair with one man while she rehearsed with another in the wings? This flight with Nigel suggested so, especially since she indicated that she might not bother to marry him, either.

He read that section again and experienced both delicious relief and dreadful misgivings. Shrewd, clever Bianca. She was absolutely right about the alliance benefiting her not at all. On the other hand, marriage to Bianca would settle things very nicely for Nigel.

Her cousin would be most displeased if she refused him. That displeasure, and the conclusions which it could suggest, kept presenting themselves to Vergil with merciless explicitness.

There had never been any proof that Nigel had tried to harm her. But over in France, if she blocked one path to her fortune... No one even knew her in that country. Who would voice suspicion if an accident should happen?

With a new, cold calm he read her letter once again. Its full implications unfolded. She made reference to arrangements having been made to prevent difficulties. His dread deepened. If that meant what he thought, she could be in grave danger when Nigel learned what she had done.

It also indicated that this had been planned while she was still in London, perhaps even before she had ended their affair. He tried not to put too much stock in the notion that Nigel had somehow forced this course on her, but a ridiculously heady beam of hope broke through the darkness that had filled his heart since that day in Pen's library.

Convince your brother that he must not follow me. The order read like a desperate warning.

He called for Morton. "Prepare for a journey of about a week. Also, send for Dante, will you? He is still in the city. I need to speak with him."

"Certainly. We will be going north again, I assume."

"No, we leave for France. I must go to the City now. See that Pen's footman is fed and rested before he heads back. Tell him to inform my sister that I will be following Miss Kenwood despite her instructions that I not do so."

"Mrs. Gaston is gone?" Bianca pulled her cloak tighter, to ward off the sea breeze blowing through the cottage garden. Nigel's great coat flapped around him.

"She has gone into Cherbourg to visit her friend."

"I should like to be in Cherbourg myself, Nigel, and not this rustic farmhouse. Actually, I would like to be in Paris. I do not think that we should have to stop here for days because Mrs. Gaston has a sick friend."

"It would be inappropriate for us to travel without her, Bianca. Unless you have changed your mind about marrying right away."

She broke the dried head off a spindly stalk of dead sunflowers. "Let us go for a walk, Nigel. Actually, I welcome her absence today, and the chance to have some private conversation with you."

He strolled beside her out the gate and through the orchard. They crossed the field of clover to the cliff walk. The wind whipped stronger here, icy from the water. It blew Nigel's hair into a tempest and ruddied his skin.

"I have changed my mind about marrying, Nigel."

"You are tired from the journey, Bianca. Once we are settled in Paris you will see things differently. More clearly."

"You mean that I will remember your threats about Laclere? I find myself thinking that the viscount can watch out for himself, dear cousin. And I am seeing things most clearly. Mrs. Gaston, for example. I see that she is more than an acquaintance to you. You must think me insufferably stupid if you believed I would not recognize the neat arrangement that you have made for yourself."

He exhaled a laugh of defeat. "I will admit that she is

an old friend. We met over a year ago when she visited Paris, and ... But it is in the past."

"After hearing the noise coming from her chamber last night, I am not inclined to believe that."

He had the decency to flush at least. Either her frankness or her worldliness had caught him off guard, which was exactly where she wanted him right now.

"Did you assume that I would be asleep, or that I would be too ignorant to understand? The two of you might have waited until I was not under the same roof."

"It was impetuous and indiscreet of us. I never thought that you ... I will explain to her that our friendship cannot go on."

"I would not be so fast to throw her over."

"Between her and you, there is no choice. It does sound as if you expect me to choose. It is very provincial of you, Bianca. Very American."

"You choose me so quickly? That must mean that she does not have a fortune and that her income is too small."

"Now you insult me. I understand if you are vexed because of last night, but my first concern is your safety and my second is my affection for you. Your income is the least of it."

"My income is hardly the least of it, although it surely comes after a few other things. The Manchester mill, for example. I know about the offer from Mr. Johnston and Mr. Kennedy. A very large sum of money just for your small share. With my forty-five percent under your control, not only could you sell them a majority ownership, but you could become very wealthy in the process. My yearly income is insignificant in comparison."

Nigel's expression darkened. Down below, the sea roared against the shore. Gulls glided overhead, and the snapping wind bore the scent of ocean salt.

"I will not deny that it would be convenient for me to sell my share of the mill, Bianca. I have some debts. Great-uncle chose to leave me virtually nothing besides the estate, and barely enough income to maintain it. I had expected more."

"You had expected everything, and lived in Paris as if it were already yours."

"I certainly did not expect him to renew a connection severed long ago and give so much to the daughter of——"

"Of his only son and the woman whom he loved," she interrupted. "That is not how you planned to say it, of course. You almost betrayed your true intentions for me, as well as your prejudices. That is the reason I will not marry you, aside from the fact that I can feel no love toward a man who is a blackmailer. You would never allow your wife to perform. If I were willing to be some man's caged bird, as you so aptly phrased it in London, I would have gladly chosen Laclere."

He faced her squarely, blocking her progress along the cliff path. "Your feelings for him are those of a child infatuated for the first time. They will pass. You will be happier with me. We have much more in common."

"How would you know what I have in common with him? Do you think that you know either one of us?"

"I must insist on the wedding, Bianca. It is not open

for negotiation. If you doubt my affection or find none of your own for me, we need not share a bed, but we will marry."

"You cannot insist on a wedding, Nigel. Even in France the woman must agree to it."

"You agreed to it by coming with me."

"I only came with you to get you out of England."

"Do you think it makes a difference where I am? I said that I would ruin him if you did not cooperate and I can do so from Paris as surely as in London."

"I do not think that you can. I think that his reputation will take more than one letter to an acquaintance to destroy. He is not his brother. He will not break so easily. You need to be there, stirring the pot, spreading the word."

"If so, I will return and spread it during high season. Do not play games with me, Bianca. I am not a man to cross."

Her resistance brought out the sullen aspects of his temperament. His expression had grown saturnine and his tone prickled with resentment and menace.

"I do not think that you will spread stories, Nigel. You see, I am prepared to pay you two thousand pounds a year to keep silent about what you know."

"As your husband, I would have much more."

"You will never be my husband, and if you ruin him, you will have nothing. If you demand one shilling more, I will give you nothing and let you do your worst."

He paced away in annoyance and cast her a hooded, inspecting sneer. "Who would have thought such a sweet face hid such a cunning mind, cousin? Mrs. Gaston said not to underestimate you, that you could not be all childish innocence if Laclere was interested in you, but I only saw those big blue eyes." He strode back and peered at her dangerously. She stood her ground. After all, when it came to hovering, Nigel could not begin to compete with Vergil.

"It should all be mine," he snarled. "Your father was dead to him, and I was all he had. If Milton had not stolen his affection he would have been kinder to me, but instead, all I heard about was that high-blooded Duclairc until I couldn't bear to visit the old man anymore. Then, with his death, he shackles me with Woodleigh, but makes sure that I don't have the money to enjoy it."

"Perhaps he challenged you with his bequest, to make something of the estate and thus of yourself. You could hire a good manager and learn. Laclere would help you."

"I do not want Laclere's help!"

"Then take the two thousand that I offer or be damned!"

He paced away and back again. Winter fields spread beside him on one side, and the cliff dropped to the sea on the other. This time he strode up so close to her that they almost touched.

She looked into his hard countenance and a tremor chilled her spine.

He had passed from annoyance to cold fury, and from resentment to bitterness. She glanced askance at her position on the cliff path. Very casually she tried to step away from him and into the field.

His arm swung up and blocked her. He swaddled her in the embrace of his great coat and studied her face as if he weighed a great judgment. Ten feet away, the ground disappeared where the cliff dropped to the sea.

"Unfortunately, Bianca, two thousand a year does not begin to solve my financial needs."

His apologetic tone made panic clutch her heart. The sea and ground appeared to swirl around her. His embrace tightened.

She clawed on his arm. "Stop this now. I am not worth murder, Nigel. The mill is gone."

He entwined one hand furiously in her hair. "What do you mean, the mill is gone?"

"I sold my share to Vergil before I left. For one hundred pounds. The papers were waiting for his signature at my solicitor's."

"You sold a partnership worth almost a quarter of a million pounds for one hundred? Are you a complete fool?" He yelled so furiously that her ears rang.

"Not a complete fool," she said. "Not *your* fool, for one thing. If you forced me into marriage, I had no intention of letting you sell that mill out from under Vergil. Nor would you enjoy the fruits of its sale. And if you chose to expose him out of spite, I made sure that he would at least be wealthy in his social oblivion."

"It is not legal. It cannot be."

"Why not? My trustee and guardian approved, I am sure. And if it is not, I am told that your courts work very slowly on such matters. We will all be dead before it is resolved."

"That is a very real possibility, sweet girl," Nigel snarled. "I was rather counting on selling that mill, you see. You have placed me in an impossible situation."

Her feet left the ground as he began carrying her. Frantic, she kicked and pummeled and bit. Grappling like a madman, he tried to haul her to the cliff.

Suddenly the fight left him. He set her down again and stared at her in shock. His gaze appeared inward, as if what stunned him was in his own soul.

"God, Bianca, I don't know what came over me. I would never—"

Something distracted him. His head turned, and a frown broke over his squinting eyes.

She caught her breath. Heart pounding, she followed his gaze down to the house.

A coach was stopping there. Mrs. Gaston had returned.

Bianca extricated herself from Nigel's hold and ran down the hill. She staggered out of the orchard just as Mrs. Gaston was handed out of the carriage.

The man who offered his help was not the coachman.

Bianca stopped a hundred yards from the house and tried to make sense of the sudden appearance of this visitor.

Nigel caught up. He came up beside her and his expression showed that he had not expected this development, either.

"What the hell is Witherby doing here?" he muttered.

chapter 21

Vergil's hired mount was tiring, but he urged him on. His impatience would not permit rest now. Too much time had been lost in Calais. It had taken him two days to track down the inn where Nigel and Bianca had stayed, and find the servant who had overheard their plans.

The discovery that Nigel and Bianca had not gone on to Paris, but instead had removed to an isolated cottage on the Normandy bluffs, only deepened his misgivings.

Two women were traveling with the man, the servant had said. The news hardly reassured him. The other woman was most likely Mrs. Gaston.

They were playing their old game, but the prize was very high this time. Too high. The value of Bianca's inheritance, hell, the value of the mill alone, exceeded anything they had gotten with their blackmail. If Bianca resisted once in France . . .

For all intents and purposes, they had killed before.

It had not been hard to follow them. Nigel had hired a superb coach for their journey, and such things were noted in villages. In the last one, some farmers had directed him to the cottage by the sea, which had been leased by the blond Englishman.

He angled toward the timbered and plastered farmhouse hugging the rugged rise. A sparsely planted garden cringed inside low stone walls. A screen of bare orchard blocked his view of the coast, but the roar of the sea droned louder as he approached.

No one emerged with his call. He dismounted and entered.

Three people sitting in the cottage expressed no surprise with his arrival. Bianca looked at him fearfully, Nigel only scowled, and Mrs. Gaston smiled with contentment.

Another person waited in the cottage too. Someone Vergil had not expected, and who grinned at the way Vergil reacted to the shock of seeing him.

"It took you long enough, Laclere," Cornell Witherby said.

Bianca jumped up and ran into Vergil's arms. "You should not have come," she said as she kissed him.

"He had to, Miss Kenwood," Witherby said. "Didn't you, Laclere? There was no way you would allow her to leave like that." He turned to Mrs. Gaston. "I told you that he would come."

Nigel rose and distanced himself from the other two. "I want you to know that I had no role in this, Laclere. I did not realize they sought to lure you here. I did not even know Witherby was this whore's cohort."

"To say you had no role is an exaggeration," Vergil said. "You may have been duped by Mrs. Gaston, and this may not be unfolding as you expected, but you did what was needed to get Bianca to accompany you."

"He said that he knew about us, and about you and the mill," Bianca said. "He threatened to ruin you."

He took her face in his hands and ignored the others for a precious moment. "You should have told him to do his worst, darling. If it meant having you with me, I would have gladly been ruined." He embraced her closely and looked at Witherby. "I know how Mrs. Gaston procured my brother's letters, but learning about the Earl of Glasbury— You are the worst scoundrel, Witherby. You befriended my sister and then betrayed her confidences. Only she could have told you about the earl."

"I really wish you had left it all alone, Laclere."

"You killed my brother. I could not leave that alone."

"I killed no one."

"You may as well have pulled the trigger."

"No one was supposed to die," Mrs. Gaston said. "We asked for a little money, that was all. Not even very much. A few thousand. Why the viscount and others felt the need to go and kill themselves—well, that isn't our fault they reacted so rashly."

She appeared annoyed by the bad behavior these men had shown, and the trouble it had caused.

"First Milton and Dante, then Pen. Finally me. You

two have used the Duclairc family again and again in this crime of yours."

Witherby got up and strolled over to the mantel of the hearth. A pistol rested on it. "Your family has been limping along for generations. The weakness begged to be exploited."

"It was not weakness that you took advantage of, but trust and affection. Why didn't you make it complete? You knew about Bianca and me, Witherby. Why didn't I get a blackmail note too? Why this elaborate game to bring me here?"

"It would have been just like you to take the fall, Laclere. Or worse, use it to find us out. I have known for months that you were looking for us. Your sister told me. Oh, she does not know the meaning of your absences, but I saw what you were up to when she described your frequent journeys and your deep interest in Milton's life. I knew it was just a matter of time. And that drama with the earl and Hampton—eventually you would remember that one other person knew Glasbury's secret. Your sister." He lifted the pistol off the mantel. "You really should have left it alone."

Vergil watched those fingers close on the weapon. "The accidents at Laclere Park. It was not Nigel trying to kill Bianca, but the two of you trying to kill me, wasn't it?"

Bianca's head snapped around. She looked at Witherby and Mrs. Gaston with shock. Vergil felt the chill of fear shake her.

Nigel's eyes widened. "You thought I was trying to kill my cousin?"

"Do not pretend that you do not have it in you," Bianca said softly.

For some reason, that checked Nigel's indignation. His face flushed and he averted his gaze from her.

"It entered my mind," Vergil said. "However, if Mrs. Gaston was visiting that day that Bianca and I went to see your uncle's effects, I think it is safe to say that the shots that missed us came from her."

Nigel turned in horror to Mrs. Gaston. "You said that you were in the park when I found you gone on my return. That you had slipped out so they wouldn't find you in the house."

"Laclere is guessing, Nigel. He is making accusations without basis."

"The rock fall, that was you, Witherby," Vergil said. "You had just arrived that morning. You saw me following Bianca, and followed me yourself."

"You were getting too close, Laclere. We learned that you had taken Milton's place in Manchester. Eventually you would learn about the visit to Mr. Thomas. I did not make the choice easily." He gestured with the pistol. "Nor do I make this choice easily, either. However, I see no alternative. I think we will all take a walk now. The sea is beautiful this time of day."

Bianca subtly cringed. Nigel went white. Vergil gazed at that pistol, and at the tight resolve on the face of a man he had trusted as a friend.

"Witherby, I did not come to France alone."

"You came *here* alone."

"I am ahead of the others by a half hour, no more. The

carriage must stay on the roads, while I rode cross-country. In minutes the others will be here. Even if they are delayed and you succeed in forcing us off that cliff and getting away, they know about Mrs. Gaston already, and will soon learn about you."

"You are bluffing. You would never risk having anyone else learn about your brother, or about you and your ward."

"I can trust the men I told."

Witherby gestured more distinctly toward the door with the pistol. "If what you say is true, I have nothing to lose. I will take my chances. Let us go. You, too, Nigel."

Mrs. Gaston began to rise.

"No," Witherby said. "You stay here."

Turning Bianca under his arm, Vergil followed Nigel out of the cottage. Witherby and the pistol hovered at their side.

"It was her idea, wasn't it?" Vergil asked, glancing back to where Mrs. Gaston sat on her chair.

"Not really. It was a game at first. When it worked with the first one, when this money just appeared so easily—it wasn't hard at all. The wonder is that it doesn't happen all the time. All those secrets that half the world already suspects but pretends they don't—hell, Lord Fairhall wasn't even very discreet about his taste for little girls."

"Are you her lover, along with Nigel?"

Witherby shook his head. "My interest in your sister was not a feint, Laclere. Mrs. Gaston and I are only friends, and business associates."

They approached the barren orchard. The tree branches made a web of snarled lines against the sky. Vergil looked at Bianca's face. She was being brave, but her eyes glistened with worry and fear.

He tightened his hold in reassurance, and stretched his hearing for the sounds of a carriage.

He heard nothing but the close roar of the surf.

"How did you know about my brother, Witherby?"

"His reclusiveness. His lack of marriage, despite being a viscount. It is a common pattern. No doubt many others suspected. As for Manchester, and Mr. Clark, that was an accident. I saw him entering a bookseller almost two years ago, and then leaving with a letter. I merely asked in the shop for the name of the man who had just left, and learned it was Mr. Clark. A pound procured the information that his letters came from Manchester. Well, it was a delicious mystery, and I had to look into it. Imagine my shock at learning how he had debased your family with that mill and that lover."

"And your friendship with me counted for nothing as you exploited that."

Witherby's face flushed. "I did you a favor. You got the title, after all."

"I did not want the title, least of all at such a cost."

Nigel, pacing ahead of them, suddenly halted in his steps and looked east.

"Thank God," he muttered.

Vergil and Bianca turned. The speck of a carriage rolled along the road, growing larger by the instant.

Witherby tensed beside them. For an instant his eyes went wild with panic. Then he sighed deeply and composed himself. The pistol fell, to hang limply from his arm by his side.

"Who is it?" he asked quietly in the voice of a man needing to know what he faced. It was the request of one friend to another, so that preparations could be made.

"Hampton and Burchard. St. John made one of his ships available to bring us over, so he may be with them." Vergil glanced to the cottage, where Mrs. Gaston remained. "I expect that my brother also insisted on riding along, although I suggested he remain in Calais."

"Almost the entire Dueling Society, then."

Not only the Dueling Society. As the carriage rolled up beside the cottage, it was clear that Dante sat up with the coachman because the carriage was full. After Hampton and Burchard and St. John stepped out, a man remained inside, his hook-nosed profile backlit by the far-open window.

The Dueling Society did not react much to seeing Witherby. Vergil could read them reaching the necessary conclusions, however, and saw the dismay in their eyes.

Adrian walked over and removed the pistol from Witherby's hand. "You will not be needing this just yet. If you choose pistols, you can have it back then."

Bianca stiffened under Vergil's embrace. She looked up into his eyes with a worried expression that made his heart clench.

Witherby shook his head. "I will only do it that way if you allow Mrs. Gaston to leave first. Otherwise there will be a trial and all of it will come out, Laclere. Your brother, the earl—all of it, I swear."

Dante overheard. He strode forward with flaming eyes. "She does not go free, Vergil."

Vergil released Bianca and took him aside. "If she goes back to England, if we swear the evidence we have against them—not only our brother's name will be ruined, but those of other men. Your name will come up too. I can't allow it, and if her freedom is the price of silence, I will pay it."

"What about what I am willing to pay? I don't see this as only your decision."

"If you think about it, it will be your decision as well."

Dante's expression turned hard. "Then let me stand to him. It is my place to do so."

"It is not yours any more than it is Pen's."

"I'll be damned if it isn't."

"Dante, you are not a good shot, and if he chooses sabres you will have no chance at all. He will kill you."

"He may kill *you*."

Vergil looked back at Witherby, whose face had gone impassive. "No, I don't think so."

Vergil nodded to Adrian, who entered the cottage. It took him a while to explain things to Mrs. Gaston, and Vergil wondered just what Burchard was saying to her. When they emerged, her face was flushed and Adrian's dark eyes glowed.

Wellington climbed out of the coach, and subjected Mrs. Gaston to a scornful examination. "I trust that I will not see you again in England, madame."

She turned even more red.

The Iron Duke gestured to the road. "I recommend

that you head west. If I catch up with you on the road later, I cannot promise to behave as a gentleman."

Composing herself and assuming a disdainful expression, Mrs. Gaston walked toward the stable where Nigel's hired coach waited. She did not look back.

Wellington turned his attention on Witherby and became the image of barely contained rage. "Tell him to choose his weapons."

Alarmed, Adrian strode over to him and gestured for Vergil to come as well.

"You must not," Vergil said. "If you do, what reason will you give? It will only feed the flames of rumor about the Foreign Minister."

"Damn it, man—what reason will *you* give?"

"My sister's honor."

"Hell, no one will believe that."

"I don't care."

"It must not be you, Your Grace," Adrian said forcefully. "Any of us, but not you."

"Not any of us, Adrian. *Me.*" Vergil said.

Wellington narrowed his eyes on Witherby in disgust. "If you fail, Laclere, he is mine."

St. John had been speaking to Witherby. He came toward them. "Sabres," he said. He reached into the carriage and retrieved two swords.

Vergil returned to Dante. "I want you to stay here with Bianca, so she is not alone. Will you do that for me?"

"Damn it, Verg—"

"I ask for my sake, Dante. Not yours."

He did not actually agree, but he did not refuse, either.

The others began walking toward the orchard. Nigel, looking shaken, humiliated, and relieved, sought the sanctuary of the cottage.

Wellington, Witherby, and the Dueling Society disappeared into the trees. Twenty paces away Bianca stood rod straight.

Forcing containment on the emotions trying to submerge his sense of justice and duty, Vergil opened his arms.

She ran to his embrace.

"Do not say anything," she whispered, stretching up to his kiss. "Nothing. I will not lose you today. My heart knows it."

Those big blue eyes could create a world that existed only for them. He savored the bliss that she could inspire in him. "I must speak. I must tell you how much I love you, Bianca."

"You have told me often before, Laclere, in ways more meaningful than words."

"I find myself thinking that if I die today, loving you will have been the best thing in my life. So it is important to me that you know that I love you, very clearly. I would never want you to wonder."

Her lids lowered and she flushed. "As you wondered?" she whispered.

He kissed each lid and her cheek, and held her face so his lips could taste hers. "A man's pride can be a stupid thing. My heart has always understood you. I just did not want to accept what it meant for me, that is all."

He held her to his body, trying to absorb her into his

essence. He had not had time to be grateful she was safe, and relief now washed through him, shaking his soul.

She looked at him with an expression of love and trust that obscured the danger waiting.

"Go inside with Dante, Bianca."

He walked away, but she did not go into the cottage. At the edge of the orchard he looked back and saw her still outside, watching him.

From the threshold to the cottage, Dante watched as well.

Vergil's gaze swept the cliff line and the gray void of the ocean beyond. There was something elemental about nature's forces on the coast. The violent abstractness of the sea, the bleakness of the cliffs and beaches—civilization ended where that water began, and man and his rules simply disappeared in a wave.

He joined the others. Witherby already held his sabre, and Hampton walked over to give Vergil the other one and take his coat.

"An appropriate setting," Hampton said quietly.

"Yes, as places for dying go, a seacoast is among the best."

Hampton gave one of his rare smiles. "I always thought so."

St. John came up alongside him. "We seem destined to assist each other in unpleasant matters, Laclere."

"It would appear so."

"The chevalier is not here, so it is left to me to remind

you of his first lesson. A clear head, and cold blood. The mind must rule, not the heart."

Vergil doubted his mind would rule entirely. The justice of this course did not make it easy, and the man waiting was not a stranger, nor completely evil.

Hampton and St. John stood aside. Under the watchful gaze of Wellington and the Dueling Society, Vergil walked over to Cornell Witherby.

"Hell of a thing," Witherby said. "To have practiced together all these years, and to now find ourselves doing it for real with each other."

Vergil suddenly saw all those years. His mind pictured Witherby at university, always ready with a joke and indifferent to his studies. He saw Witherby excited when his first poem was published, and bringing life and humor to the meetings of the Dueling Society.

More recent memories flashed through his head too— those of Penelope, happy for the first time in years because of this man.

"You can take comfort in knowing that even if I win, I also lose," Vergil said. "I will be the one who has to return to London and tell my sister that I killed the man she loves."

Witherby's expression fell. In the pure, diffused light of the overcast day, he looked very young and sad. "Let us be done with this, Laclere," he said softly. "There is nothing else for it."

They saluted with their sabres and the roar of the surf entered Vergil's head.

.   .   .

"You aren't going to obey him and wait here, are you?" Dante asked as he strolled toward her.

Bianca watched the spot where Vergil had disappeared into the orchard. "No, I am not going to obey him."

"Of course not. No reason for you to start now, is there? At least your willfulness spares me from playing nursemaid." Dante passed her and headed into the trees. "Come on, then."

They walked quickly through the orchard. Halfway down its path, Bianca thought she heard the faint sounds of metal on metal. She and Dante broke into a run at the same time.

They emerged onto the field of clover. Up on the rise, near the cliff's edge, the tiny dark spots of six men could be seen against the gray sky. Specks of light flickered off the slashing sabres.

Dante took her hand as they stumbled across the field. She could not take her eyes off those dark spots. Four of them stood like statues, stoic witnesses to the other two's dance of death.

"Laclere is very good at this, isn't he?" she said. "Please tell me he is an expert swordsman, Dante."

"He is better with pistols."

She had never seen Dante so serious. So concerned. He did not look like a man who assumed his brother would win this duel. His expression sapped her confidence and fear took its place.

She stared desperately at the distant drama and ran faster, not knowing what she rushed toward. She doubted her mere presence could stop it now.

Worse, it might even distract Vergil.

That thought made her halt abruptly in the middle of the field. She jerked her hand from Dante's. "You go. I will stay here. He does not want me there for a reason."

Dante nodded as he turned to continue. Suddenly he stopped too. His gaze locked on the figures moving against the sky. Vergil and Witherby's expressions could not be seen, but the progress of the duel was clear.

"He does not want me there, either," Dante said. "We will wait here together."

He backed up and stood beside her. Shoulder to shoulder, down in the field that had ceased to exist to the men on the cliff, they watched the silent, horrible contest.

Suddenly two forms became one. Bianca's heart stopped and her breath left her. She waited, numb with shock, for one man to drop to the ground.

Beside her Dante ceased breathing too. Their hands instinctively sought each other's, and their fingers entwined with all the strength of their shared fear.

Vergil and Witherby separated. One did not drop. Instead Witherby just stood there, as still as the sentries witnessing this ancient form of judgment.

Suddenly he was gone, and only five men stood on the cliff path.

"Jesus," Dante muttered.

It sounded more like a prayer of gratitude than a curse.

chapter 22

H e showed some honor in the end," Wellington said.

He was the first to speak after the silent group made their way back to the cottage.

Vergil held Bianca in his arms, not giving a damn who saw. None of that mattered now. He needed to feel her warmth and vitality and the world could go to hell if it objected.

None of the world surrounding them in the cottage did.

"I will send boats out from Cherbourg," St. John said. "If his body is found, there will be no wounds from weapons. We can say it was an accident, that he fell from the cliff. No one will know that there was a duel under way."

Vergil pressed his lips to Bianca's silken hair as he tightened his embrace. He closed his eyes and saw Witherby on the cliff.

The man had lowered his weapon and his defense deliberately, and exposed himself to death.

Vergil had not pressed the advantage. He had not lunged.

He doubted he would ever forget the look in his friend's eyes as they slowly met the gazes of the witnesses, and then Vergil's own. One last sad smile, and Witherby had stepped back, until his boot landed on nothing but air.

"One person will have to know," Vergil said, relaxing his embrace of Bianca, but not letting her go. "I must speak with Pen. I will not live with a lie between us."

"The countess is stronger than most people know, Laclere," Hampton said. "Although, sparing the earl from the fruits of his sins—well, of all the men who were blackmailed, I did not cry for him."

That was the worst of this business, and a miserable irony. Not only had today taken from Pen the man she loved, it had left her shackled to one she hated.

"I will explain it to her," Dante said firmly, darting Vergil a glance that dared him to object. "That way I will be sure that she learns the *whole* truth of it."

"It is getting late, and we should depart," Wellington said. "There is a small matter of transportation now. What with Miss Kenwood and her cousin here, there is not enough room in the coach."

"I will ride Vergil's horse, and Kenwood will take my place with the coachman," Dante said. "Vergil, you and Miss Kenwood will have to wait here until we can send a carriage for you."

Wellington's lids dropped to half-mast. He examined the embracing couple.

Everyone else assumed utterly bland expressions.

"Your Grace?" Adrian said, gesturing to the door.

"Quite." Wellington exited, and a line of men filed after him.

"Why not make a visit to Paris, as long as you are on the Continent?" St. John said as he passed. "My sister, Jeanette, would be happy to receive you."

"Perhaps we will do that," Vergil said.

The rest of the Dueling Society departed, leaving only Vergil, Bianca, and Dante.

"Going to Paris may be a good idea, Verg. Do not worry about Pen. I will take care of her. It is the least I can do."

"Thank you, Dante."

Dante stopped at the threshold. "It may be that the carriage cannot come until the morning," he said. "I trust that you will be a saint, Verg, and that Miss Kenwood is safe with you."

"Of course."

Laughing, Dante left. Vergil and Bianca followed him and watched the men climbing into the coach.

Nigel approached them. "I would like to know if you will be bringing witness against me, cousin. I should like to return to England, but obviously cannot do so if you choose to prohibit it."

"I will not bring evidence. When the choice came, you did the right thing," Bianca said. "The price, however, is that you not speak against Vergil, that you keep silent about what you discovered."

"I intended to do so anyway. I find that I do not have the taste for blackmail that some others do. It brings out parts in a man that are better left buried."

Bianca beamed with approval, but Vergil felt less sanguine. Nigel appeared sincere enough, but who knew what the morning would bring. Good sense and constancy were not this man's strongest virtues.

"Woodleigh is a good estate, Kenwood. With the right manager, it could be productive enough to keep you. Not like a duke, but well enough," Vergil said. "When I return to Sussex I will ask my estate manager to visit you. He may have some suggestions for a good man to see to things for you."

"I thank you for that. Perhaps it is time to put down roots back home. Maybe you were right, Bianca. Your grandfather may have had his reasons for arranging things as he did."

Nigel walked toward the coach and climbed up with the coachman.

"What did you mean when you said he did the right thing when the choice came?" Vergil asked.

"Let us just say that I think that the devil has been fighting for his soul, but did not win." She watched the carriage take him away. "Do you think that he will remain silent?"

"Probably. Not that it will matter, since Mrs. Gaston is certain to tell all to whoever will listen. Eventually her stories about me will get to London."

"Oh, darling, can't we find some way to stop her?"

He placed two fingers on her soft warm lips. "I do not care. I think that I will be glad for it. I am tired of the double life, Bianca. I am tired of denying part of who I am. Doing so left my brother vulnerable, and eventually killed him, and I will not live like that. I am proud of what I have done with the mill. It is important to me, essential to me, and I am not inclined to give it up, either."

"I think that I can understand that."

"Yes, you can. And I can understand you. I understand that embracing your dream and your art does not mean rejecting me, even if it does mean that you cannot stay with me."

She sank against him. It felt so good to hold her feminine warmth. However, her embrace acknowledged that it was time for decisions to be made. The beauty of her sadness made his heart shake.

"What do we do now?" she mumbled.

She was asking for help in seeing it through.

"We will visit Paris and then you will continue down to Italy. I brought a bank draft that you can take. It will see you clear until more formal arrangements can be made. We will send for Jane while we are in Paris and settling the plans for your journey south."

Her big blue eyes widened in her erotically innocent way. "That is not what I mean, Laclere. What do we do *now*?"

His blood fired immediately in response to her quiet invitation. He pulled her to him and kissed her with a ferocity born of relief and regret. "You are a most dangerous lady."

She backed into the farmhouse. "Only dangerous for you, my lord. You have my promise on that."

He followed where she led, over to a sheepskin rug by the fire. With eyes speaking of the passion to come, she dropped her cloak and began to undress him.

"I thought of you often while I walked by the sea." She slid his waistcoat off and plucked at his cravat. "The power of the waves, the rhythm and force of them, the glory of all that untamed nature—it can saturate a person the way love and passion can. Very moving. Like music, actually. Yes, a lot like music. I would watch the sea and want to make love to you and sing my heart out."

"Then we will." He grabbed up her cloak and threw it around her. "On the cliffs. We will make love there and you will sing for me, and we will join our passion to that of creation and remember this day forever."

Flying on desire, they made their way to the cliffs, huddled together against the wind, almost spilling their love in the orchard when he stopped to warm them both in an embrace. They climbed up the walk to the highest point, where the western sun still gave a little warmth and an ethereal pink light bathed an outcropping.

Bianca faced the sea, so close to the edge one expected her to take to flight. The wind whipped her cloak and gown and hair until she appeared like the center of a tiny tempest. She closed her eyes and just felt it, and he felt it through her. Her voice warbled up and down the scales as she announced herself to the elements.

"It is divine," she whispered.

He stepped close behind her. "Sing the Rossini," he said. "Sing as you did the day at the ruins."

"You favor that? Do you know what the words say?"

"The singer explains how she will not marry her evil guardian, but will find a way to be with her true love."

"Very apt that day in the ruins, except that the true love was in fact the evil guardian."

"In his heart the evil guardian wished for it." He embraced her. "Sing it for me."

At first he could barely hear her. The wind stole the sound out of her mouth and carried it to the clouds. But her breath and voice found its strength and the music flowed out of her, another wind blowing its passion, another force drenching his soul. He sensed her with him, pulling him into it, glorying in the elemental energy of her voice and womanhood.

He lowered her to the ground and took her while she sang. The joining left her breathless, unable to sound the notes, but the aria continued silently in his head, filling out the roar of wind and sea. Her soul sang it too. She expressed her ecstasy in her kisses and holds and cries until a completion erupted that merged them into the coast's sublime fury.

She clutched the hearth wall as pleasure of stunning intensity left her limp. Only her grip kept her upright on her knees as Laclere's tongue made her vulva throb with astonishing sensations.

He reached for her waist and brought her down until she straddled his hips on the sheepskin rug in front of the cottage's hearth. She laid against his chest and blinked her senses alert.

In that instant, with the solidity of his body beneath her and the heat of their passion burning, she saw her future. She knew how it must be. No regret tinged the joy that the decision gave her. In the years ahead she might experience some nostalgia for what she relinquished, but she would never grieve.

She felt him hard beneath her, his need intensified by the kisses he had just given her. She rose and sat back on his thighs and looked down at the man who had intruded on her plans, only to become the center of her life. "I want us to be lovers forever, Laclere."

"We will be, darling. I will come to Italy often and the separations will not be too long."

She caressed down his chest, wonderfully alert to the feel of his skin and body. "I want no distance. No separation. I cannot leave you, Laclere. My heart will not let me. I want to get married."

Her declaration surprised him. He gripped her hands to stop their caresses and looked in her eyes.

There was no triumph in his expression. She saw only relief and love and astonishment.

Then a deeper comprehension shadowed the brighter emotions.

"You said that denying your dream would mean giving up half your soul. I do not want that."

"I can sing anywhere, Laclere. In my chamber and

yours. In a ruined castle. I do not need to be in Italy for my soul to be whole. I do not need to train for performances in order to have my art."

Her capitulation appeared to trouble him. His fingertips skimmed her breast's swell while he thought, as if its shape aided his contemplations. "You must continue training, darling. When you surpass Signore Bardi's skill, we will bring another voice master from Italy, as I promised."

He pulled her down into an embrace. He pressed a long kiss to her as he smoothed slow caresses over her body. "You will train, and then you will perform when you are ready. If I do something so outrageous as manage a mill, having a wife who performs is almost insignificant."

It was her turn to be astonished. "It will not be so simple, Laclere. There will be a high cost if you permit this. I do not want your family hurt because of me."

"It will be some years before you go onstage. Charlotte will be married by then, so we will not harm her future. As to Pen and Dante, they are hardly paragons of propriety themselves. Maybe everyone will just think I have become eccentric, like my father and brother. If not, I do not care. Your happiness is worth any price, my love."

Her throat burned and her eyes misted. She loved him so much at that moment that holding the love inside her made her heart gloriously full. "Thank you for wanting to do this for me, but you are not being practical. By the time I am ready to perform, I will have children."

"Then we will have an army of nurses and tutors go

with them when you travel to your engagements. You will have your dream, Bianca. If you will stay with me, I will not allow our marriage to deny you any of it."

She kissed him. The warmth of his lips seemed to make the sweetest connection they had ever shared. She knew with a woman's certainty that this marriage would indeed deny her part of the dream, but she did not care about that. His desire to give it all to her was what she would always remember.

"I do not expect to travel very much. I do not have to perform on the Continent. I do not want to build a career for the fame, Laclere. However, it will be nice, sometimes, to have the opportunity to sing until hundreds of people weep."

He lifted her body and lowered her so that he filled her. Holding her to his heart he led her back into passion.

Afterward she lay drenched by his presence. The soft words of love that he had spoken at the end still played in her ears, and she slowly realized that he still repeated them. She forced her sated senses back in order.

And realized that for the first time he remained inside her.

She rose up on her forearms and looked at him.

Unconditional love looked back.

They shared a flawless unity in that honest gaze.

What a terribly wonderful thing love could be, she thought. One both found oneself and lost oneself within its quiet power. Love was more transporting than the ecstasies of music and nature. More thrilling than the edge of a sea cliff or the release of passion.

ABOUT THE AUTHOR

Madeline Hunter has worked as a grocery clerk, office employee, art dealer, and freelance writer. She holds a Ph.D. in art history, which she currently teaches at an eastern university. She lives in Pennsylvania with her husband, her two teenage sons, a chubby, adorable mutt, and a black cat with a major attitude. She can be contacted through her web site, www.MadelineHunter.com.

And look for two more
tantalizing tales from Madeline's
Seducer series . . .

Madeline Hunter's

THE SEDUCER
Daniel's story

and

THE CHARMER
Adrian's story

Read on for a preview . . .

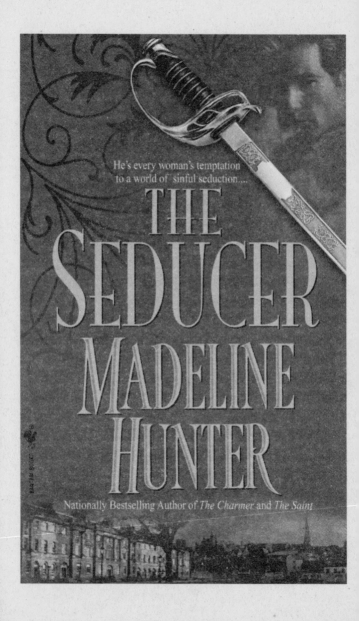

He's every woman's temptation
to a world of sinful seduction....

THE
SEDUCER

MADELINE
HUNTER

Nationally Bestselling Author of *The Charmer* and *The Saint*

THE SEDUCER

"... if she goes unpunished, I must insist that she leave. I cannot have the virtue of my girls corrupted. ..."

Madame Leblanc rambled on in severe tones. Distracted by thoughts of the unfinished business he had left in Paris, Daniel St. John only half-listened.

Something about a book. Of course the girl would have books. It was a school.

He forced his attention to the gray-haired, buxom schoolmistress and broke her incessant flow. "Your summons said that this was serious, madame. I assumed she had taken ill and lay on death's door."

Madame lowered her chin and glared at him. "This transgression requires more than bread and water for a few days, m'sieur, and you gave strict orders she was not to be punished with the rod without your permission."

"Did I? When was that?"

"Years ago. I told you that such leniency would lead to grief, and now it has."

Yes, he vaguely remembered the earnest expression on a gamine-faced child, asking him for justice. He could not recall giving instructions about it. If he had known it would prove this damned inconvenient he would not have been so generous.

He straightened in the chair, prepared to rescind the order. His gaze fell on the willow rod lying across the desk. The memory of tearful eyes and a choking voice accusing Madame Leblanc of unwarranted brutality came back to him again.

"You said something about a book. Let me see it."

"M'sieur, that is not necessary. I assure you that it is of a nature to be forbidden, to say the least."

"That could mean it is only a volume of poems by Ovid, or a religious tract by a dissenter. I would like to see it and judge for myself."

"I do not think—"

"The book, madame."

She strode to a cabinet. Using one of several keys on a cord around her neck, she unlocked it and retrieved a small, red volume. She thrust it at him and retreated to a window. She took up a position with her back to him, physically announcing her condemnation of the literature in his hands.

He flipped it open, and immediately saw why.

Not literature. In fact, no words at all. The thin volume contained only engravings that displayed carnal intercourse in all its inventiveness.

He paged through. Things started out simply enough, but got increasingly athletic. Toward the end there were a few representations that struck him as totally unwork-able.

"I see," he said, snapping the book closed.

"Indeed." Her tone said he had *seen* more than was nec-essary.

"Call for the child, madame."

Satisfaction lit her face. "I would like you to be here when it is done. She should know that you approve."

"Send for her."

Madame Oiseau escorted Diane in.

As expected, a visitor waited in the headmistress's study. The Devil Man lounged in Madame Leblanc's chair behind the fruitwood desk. Madame stood beside him rigidly, a bulwark of censure. Two items lay upon the spotless desk. A willow rod, and *the book*.

Typically, Daniel St. John barely glanced at her. He ap-peared a little annoyed and very bored. She half-expected him to yawn and pull out his snuffbox.

He did not really look like a devil. She had given him that name as a young girl because of his eyes. Dark and intense, they were framed by eyebrows that peaked in vague points toward the ends. Those eyes could burn right into you if he paid attention.

Since he never did, she did not find them so frighten-ing anymore.

His mouth was set in a straight, hard, full line, but then it always was. Even when he smiled, it only curved enough to suggest that whatever amused him was a pri-vate joke. Along with the eyes and chiseled face, it made him look cruel. Maybe he was. She wouldn't know. Still, she suspected that women thought him very handsome, and maybe even found his harshness attractive. She had seen Madame Oiseau flush and fluster in his presence.

He was not as old as she had once thought. He had grown more youthful as she had matured. She realized now that he could not be more than thirty. That struck her as peculiar. He had been an adult her whole life, and should be older.

It was easy to forget how hard he could appear. Every year the months hazed over her memory. Seeing him now, she knew that her plan had been stupid. He would never take on more inconvenience, and she would be left here to await Madame Oiseau's vengeance.

"M'sieur has learned of your disgraceful behavior," Madame Leblanc intoned. "He is shocked, as one would expect."

He quirked one of his sardonic smiles at the description of his reaction. He tapped the book. "Is there an explanation?"

Diane made her choice. The safe, cowardly choice. "No explanation, m'sieur."

He glanced up at her, suddenly attentive. It only lasted an instant. He sank back in the chair and gestured impatiently to Madame Leblanc.

The two women readied the chamber for punishment. A prie-dieu was dragged into the center of the room. A chair was pushed in front of it. The headmistress lifted the willow rod and motioned for the sinner to take the position.

The Devil Man just sat there, lost in his thoughts, gazing at the desk, ignoring the activity.

He was going to stay. Madame Leblanc had insisted that he witness it.

Diane had known remaining here would mean punishment. Madame Leblanc firmly believed that sins deserved whipping, and she did not reserve the rod for her students. Several months ago a serving woman of mature years was caught sneaking out to meet a man and the same justice had been meted out to her.

Burning with humiliation and praying that he remained in his daze, Diane approached the prie-dieu. Stepping up on the kneeler, she bent her hips over the raised, cushioned armrest and balanced herself by grasping the seat of the chair.

Madame Oiseau ceremoniously lifted the skirt of her sack dress. Madame Leblanc gave the usual exhortation for her to pray for forgiveness.

The rod fell on her exposed bottom. It fell again. She ground her teeth against the pain, knowing it was futile. They would whip her mercilessly until she begged heaven's pardon.

"Stop." His voice cut through the tension in the room.

Madame Leblanc got one last strike in.

"I said to stop."

"M'sieur, it must—"

"Stop. And leave."

Diane began to push herself up.

Madame Oiseau pressed her back down. "It appears her guardian is so outraged that he feels obliged to mete out the punishment himself, Madame Leblanc," she said in oily tones. "It is appropriate for such a sin, no?"

Madame Leblanc debated in a string of mumbles. Madame Oiseau walked around the prie-dieu. The two women left.

She heard him rise and walk toward her. She hoped that he would be quick about it. She would gladly accept any pain just to be done with the mortification that she felt, positioned there, half-naked.

The skirt fluttered down. A firm grasp took her arm. "Get up."

She righted herself and smoothed the sack gown. Biting back her humiliation, she faced him.

He sat behind the desk again. No longer bored. Definitely paying attention. She squirmed under his dark gaze.

He gestured to the book. "Where did you get it?"

"Does it matter?"

"I should say it does. I put you in a school that is almost cloistered. I find it curious that you came by such a thing."

Madame Oiseau's threat rang in her ears. She could do it. She could kill someone. And when it happened, the Devil Man would not care at all. He would be grateful to be spared the journey each year.

"I stole it."

"From a bookseller?"

"I stole it and Madame Leblanc found it among my belongings. That is all that matters. Madame says that excuses and explanations only make the sin worse."

"Does she? What nonsense. Do you understand why Madame was so shocked that you had this book?"

"The women are undressed, so I assume that it is about sins of the flesh."

That seemed to amuse him, as if he thought of a clever response but kept it to himself. "I believe that you stole this book, but I think it was from someone here. Madame Leblanc?"

She shook her head.

"I did not think so. It was the other one, wasn't it? The one more than happy to leave you alone with me." He speared her with those eyes. "Tell me now."

She hesitated. He really didn't care about her. This was the first time in years that he had even really looked at her.

He was definitely doing that. Sharply. Deeply. It made her uncomfortable.

He had helped her that time when she complained. Maybe if she told him, he would agree to keep silent and things could continue as before. Or perhaps if he complained, Madame Leblanc would believe him, and Madame Oiseau would be dismissed.

There was something in his expression that indicated he would have the truth, one way or another. Something determined, even ruthless, burned in those devil eyes.

She much preferred him bored and indifferent.

"It belongs to Madame Oiseau, as you guessed," she said. "There is a young girl, no more than fourteen, to whom she has been showing it. The girl told me how Madame Oiseau described the riches to be had for a woman who did such things. I went to Madame's chamber and took it. I was looking for a way to bring it down to the fire, but Madame Oiseau claimed a brooch had gone missing and all the girls' chambers were searched. The book was found in mine."

"And the brooch never was found, was it?"

"No."

His eyes narrowed thoughtfully while his gaze moved all over her, lingering on her face. He was trying to decide if she spoke the truth.

"How old are you now?"

The annual question, coming now, startled her. "Sixteen."

"You spoke of your friend who is fourteen as a young girl."

"She acts younger than that."

He scrutinized her. He had never looked at her so long or so thoroughly. No one ever had.

"I brought you here, what, ten years ago? Twelve? It was right after . . . You were a girl then, but not a little child." His gaze met hers squarely. "How old are you?"

Her foolish plan was unfolding in spite of her cowardice.

Only she did not want it now.

"Sixteen."

"I do not care for young women trying to make a fool of me. I think if we let down your hair from those childish braids, and see you in something besides that sack, that we will know the truth."

"The truth is that I am sixteen."

"Indeed? Indulge my curiosity, then." He gestured at her head. "The hair. Take it down."

Cursing herself for having attracted his attention, she pulled the ribbons off the ends of her braids. Unplaiting and combing with her fingers, she loosed her hair. It fell in waves around her face and down her body.

His sharp eyes warmed. That should have reassured her, but it had the opposite effect. Caution prickled her back.

"How old are you?" His voice was quieter this time, with no hard edge.

He had her very worried now. "Sixteen."

"I am sure not. I suspect that you concluded it was in your interest to lie. But let us be certain. The gown, mam'selle."

"The gown?"

"The gown. Remove it."

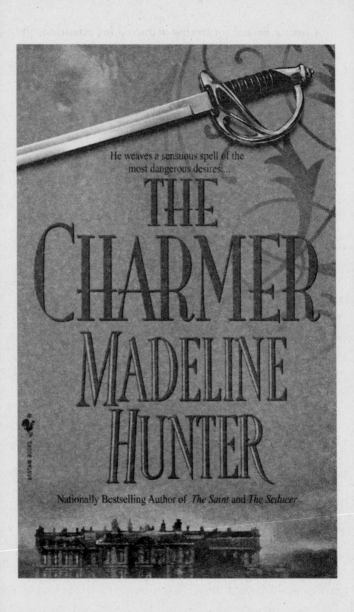

THE CHARMER

Adrian crossed the drawing room threshold and found himself in the middle of an Arabian harem.

Women swathed in colorful pantaloons and veils lounged beside men dressed in flowing robes. A fortune in silk billowed down from the high, frescoed ceiling, forming a massive tent. Two tiger skins stretched over the pastel tapestry rugs, and bejeweled pillows and throws buried settees and chairs. An exotic, heavy scent drifted under the fragrances of incense and perfume. Hashish. In the darkest corners some men kissed and fondled their ladies, but no outright orgy had ensued.

Yet.

A man on a mission with no interest in this type of diversion, Adrian walked slowly through the costumed bodies, looking for a female who fit the description of the Duchess of Everdon.

He noticed a canopied corner that appeared to be the place of honor. He aimed for it, ignoring the women who looked his way and smiled invitingly.

The canopy draped a small dais holding a chaise longue. A woman rested on it in a man's arms. Her eyes were closed, and the man was plying her with wine. Adrian's card had fallen ignobly to the floor from her lax fingers.

"I am grateful that you have finally received me, Duchess," he said, announcing his presence. Actually, she had not agreed to receive him at all. He had threatened and bluffed his way past the butler.

Her lids slit and she peered down her body at him. She wore a garment that swaddled her from breasts to bare feet, but that left her neck and arms uncovered, revealing pale, glowing skin. In the low light he could not judge her face well, but her hair was a mass of dark curls tamed by a gold band circling her head.

The duchess gave Adrian a frank assessment and he returned one of his own. The only daughter of the last Duke of Everdon had attained instant importance with her father's unexpected death. For the past two weeks everyone who was anyone in England had been speculating about Sophia Raughley, and wondering what she had been up to during her long absence from England.

Adrian did not relish reporting the answer to the men who had sent him here. From the looks of things, the new duchess had occupied herself these last eight years in Paris with becoming a shameless libertine.

She twisted out of her lover's hold and stretched to grope for the card, almost falling off the chaise longue.

She appeared childishly clumsy suddenly, and a bit help-less, and Adrian experienced a pang of pity. He picked up the card and placed it in her fingers. She squinted, and gestured to her partner to bring a candle close.

"Mister Adrian Burchard," she read.

"At your service, Your Grace. If we could speak pri-vately, please."

Gathering her drapery, she rose to her feet. With the breeding of centuries stiffening her posture, she faced him.

"I think that I know what service you offer, and you have wasted your journey. I am not going back with you."

Of course she was. "Again, I ask to speak with you pri-vately."

"Come back tomorrow."

"I have come the last two days, and now tonight. It is time for you to hear what I have to say. It is time for you to face reality."

Anger flashed in her eyes. She advanced toward him. For a moment she appeared quite formidable. Then her foot caught in the flowing silk. She tripped and hurtled forward, right into his arms.

He grappled with the feminine onslaught, gripping her soft back and bottom. She wore no stays or petticoats un-der that red silk. No wonder her blond Arab gleamed with expectation.

She looked up in dazed shock, her green eyes glinting. Her smile of embarrassment broadened until he expected her ears to move out of the way.

She was drunk. Completely foxed.

Wonderful.

He set her upright and held her arm until she attained some balance.

"I do not much care for reality. If that is what you offer, go away." She sounded like a rebellious, petulant child, provoking the temptation in him to treat her like one. She waved toward the drawing room. "This is real enough for me."

"Hardly real. Not even very accurate."

"My seraglio is most accurate. Stefan and I planned it for weeks. Delacroix himself designed the costumes."

"The costumes are correct, but you have created a European fantasy. A seraglio is nothing like this. In a true harem, except for the rare visitor, all the men are eunuchs."

She laughed and gave Stefan a playful poke. "Not so loud, Mister Burchard, or the men will run away. And the women? Did I get that right at least?"

"Not entirely. For one thing, an entire seraglio exists for the pleasure of one man, not many. For another . . ."

Stefan's expression distracted him. His smile revealed the conceit of a man who assumed that if only one sultan were to enjoy the pleasures of this particular harem, it went without dispute that it would be him.

Stefan was going to be a problem.

"For another, except for a few ornaments, the women in a harem are naked."

Suggestive laughter trickled to the dais from the onlookers. Bawdy shouts pierced the smoky shadows. As if his words had been a cue, a woman on the other side of the room rose up from her circle of admirers and unclasped a brooch. Her diaphanous drape fluttered to the floor amidst shouts and clapping.

Another woman rose and stripped. The situation deteriorated rapidly. Garments flew through the air. The shadows filled with the swells of breasts and buttocks. Embraces became much more intimate.

The duchess's eyes widened. She appeared dismayed at the turn things had taken. Ridiculous, of course. She had just explained that she had planned it herself.

Stefan reached for her. "Come, Sophia, *moi skarb.*"

The duchess staggered back with his pull and fell onto his lap. Adrian watched, a forgotten presence. Stefan began caressing her arm while he held the goblet to her mouth.

Adrian turned to go. This promised to be a distasteful task.

Still, it was essential for him to complete it. A lot was riding on this foolish, debauched woman. Quite possibly the future of England itself.

He glanced back to the chaise longue. Stefan had loosened her gown from one shoulder and now worked on the other. Her head lulled on his shoulder but her dull reaction did not deter Stefan in the least. She sat limply while the man undressed her.

Adrian stepped back onto the dais just as Stefan bared the duchess's pretty breasts.

"Perhaps in your amorous zeal you have not noticed, my friend, but the woman is no longer with you. She is out cold."

Stefan was pulling the canopy's drapes closed. "Mind your own affairs."

"Gentlemen rarely mind their own affairs when a lady is about to be raped. But then, you would not know how gentlemen react, would you?"

Adrian bent and slid his arms under the duchess. "I am taking the duchess to where she can recover. Interfere, and I will kill you."

Stefan was almost drunk enough to ignore the threat, but, to Adrian's disappointment, not quite. With a scowl he moved away.

Adrian carried the duchess off the dais. Movement caused the loose garment to shift so that a breast peeked out of the red silk. Noting once more that her breasts were quite lovely, he bore the duchess out of the seraglio with as much dignity as he could muster for the two of them.

The old butler lurked in the corridor. Adrian called for the man to accompany him.

"Your name."

"Charles, sir."

"Show me her chambers, Charles, and call for Jenny and two other women whom you trust. Then I will give you instructions for packing. The duchess will be leaving Paris. If you have any doubts regarding my authority to initiate these plans while she is indisposed, I should tell you that I have a letter from King William himself summoning her home."

Charles pointed him down a corridor and they stopped at large double doors. Charles turned the doors' handles.

Adrian entered and stopped in his tracks. Dozens of inhuman eyes peered at him from around the chamber.

He had escaped a harem only to find himself in a menagerie.